Praise for *When the Elephants Dance*

"A formidable first novel, worthy of a Verdi opera."
—*The New York Times*

"Holthe's novel is unblinkingly intense and at times gut wrenchingly horrific. But it is important to note that while it demands a good dose of fortitude on the part of the reader, it ultimately honors that commitment by renewing the reader's sense of humanity and compassion, not diminishing it."
—*The Seattle Times*

"This marvelous book provides a truly transcendent experience."
—*Rocky Mountain News*

"Reading Holthe's *When the Elephants Dance* . . . is like leafing through the pages of an Amy Tan-Gabriel García Márquez-Toni Morrison novel rolled into one."
—*Filipinas*

"A well-orchestrated chorus of voices that should strike a chord with many."
—*Kirkus Reviews* (starred)

PENGUIN BOOKS

WHEN THE ELEPHANTS DANCE

Tess Uriza Holthe lives in northern California with her husband. She grew up in a Filipino-American family in San Francisco. *When the Elephants Dance* is inspired, in part, by the experiences of her father, who was a young boy in the Philippines during World War II.

To request Great Books Foundation Discussion Guides by mail (while supplies last), please call (800) 778-6425 or E-mail reading@us.penguingroup.com. To access Great Books Foundation Discussion Guides online, visit our Web site at www.penguin.com or the foundation Web site at www.greatbooks.org.

WHEN
THE
ELEPHANTS
DANCE

A NOVEL

Tess Uriza Holthe

PENGUIN BOOKS

PENGUIN BOOKS

Published by the Penguin Group
Penguin Group (USA) Inc., 375 Hudson Street,
New York, New York 10014, U.S.A.
Penguin Books Ltd, 80 Strand, London WC2R 0RL, England
Penguin Books Australia Ltd, 250 Camberwell Road,
Camberwell, Victoria 3124, Australia
Penguin Books Canada Ltd, 10 Alcorn Avenue,
Toronto, Ontario, Canada M4V 3B2
Penguin Books India (P) Ltd, 11 Community Centre,
Panchsheel Park, New Delhi – 110 017, India
Penguin Books (N.Z.) Ltd, Cnr Rosedale and Airborne Roads,
Albany, Auckland, New Zealand
Penguin Books (South Africa) (Pty) Ltd, 24 Sturdee Avenue,
Rosebank, Johannesburg 2196, South Africa

Penguin Books Ltd, Registered Offices:
80 Strand, London WC2R 0RL, England

First published in the United States of America by Crown Publishers,
an imprint of Random House, Inc. 2002
Published in Penguin Books 2003

10 9 8 7 6 5 4 3 2 1

PUBLISHER'S NOTE
This is a work of fiction. Names, characters, places, and incidents either are the product
of the author's imagination or are used fictitiously, and any resemblance to actual persons,
living or dead, business establishments, events, or locales is entirely coincidental.

ISBN 0-609-60952-1 (hc.)
ISBN 0 14 20.0288 7 (pbk.)
CIP data available

Printed in the United States of America
Designed by Lauren Dong

~ FOR MY HUSBAND, JASON

ACKNOWLEDGMENTS

I WOULD LIKE TO THANK:

My *lola*, Pelicula Fulgencio, and my parents, Salvador and Gloria Uriza, for filling my life with their love of stories. My best friend and husband, Jason Holthe, for his tough criticism and never-ending encouragement. The Uriza, Holthe, and Sirate families for their love and raucous laughter. My nephews and nieces: Paul and Bernadette Sirate, Anthony Mandap, and Gene, Sarina, Roman, Karl, and Chelsea Uriza for keeping me smiling. Nellie and Earl for keeping me on my toes.

My wonderful and wise agent and friend, Mary Ann Naples. Thank you for believing in this book and sending it down that yellow brick road. My editor, the talented Kristin Kiser, for helping me to give Domingo a heart and leading me through Oz. The Maui Writers Conference for allowing me to meet these two exceptional women in paradise. To everyone at Crown, Chip Gibson, Steve Ross, Andrew Martin, Katherine Beitner, Claudia Gabel, Lauren Dong, Jennifer O'Connor, Trisha Howell, Leta Evanthes, and the entire group, thank you for welcoming me into your family and embracing this book. The Book Passage of Corte Madera, for providing me with good coffee, great books, fine authors to meet, and a safe place to dream.

Robert Lapham, author of *Lapham's Raiders,* University Press of Kentucky, where I found and was inspired by the quote "When the elephants dance it is unsafe for the chickens." My dear friends and fellow writers Ellie Wood, John Fetto, Katrina Davidson, Desda Zuckerman, and Julie Tayco. Your friendship has been a blessing. Linda Watanabe McFerrin for your exercise A Myth in the Family. Christine Hom for encouraging me to "keep reaching." Fellow writer Don Christians of KWMR 90.5 West Marin for trusting your radio program with my stories. The following friends who did not change the subject when I told them I was writing a book: Kristi Taylor, Rosalva Depillo, Paula Kravitz, Michelle Marks, Claudia Ruggles, Susan Cubinar, and Paul and Sandy Schaum-leffel. God, for always lighting my way.

My parents, Salvador and Gloria Uriza,
in 1951.

AUTHOR'S NOTE

EVER SINCE I CAN REMEMBER, my father and *lola* (grandmother), who were both Filipino, entertained my family with tales of the supernatural, stories of ghosts and witches, always told with delicious darkness and magic. My brothers and sisters and I would sit, riveted, holding our breath. Their storytelling would cast a spell on me each time. I relished every word.

In addition to these tales, they spoke of their firsthand experiences during the Japanese invasion of their homeland, the Philippines, during World War II. These stories were told with the grave respect and pride that comes only from having survived such a tremendous experience. It is not surprising that many years later I have written a novel that interweaves both the devastation of the war and the kind of mythological tales I was told.

Both of my parents and their families experienced so much during the war. My mother Gloria was only eight years old. Though her family was further out in the Visayan countryside and not near the heavy fighting, they were not immune to the war. Her father, my *lolo* (grandfather), was serving in the United States Navy on the *U.S. Blackhawk* in the nearby Mariana Islands. His ship was sunk by Japanese aircraft during the Battle of Midway. He survived by holding onto pieces of the ship.

My father was thirteen years old when he and a group of other civilians were caught by the Japanese while chopping wood in an undesignated area, near the American army base in Luzon, Philippines, known as Fort McKinley. Their group was led into one of the nearby buildings and tortured. The opening scene of my novel is fictional, but based on his experience. My father's family lived in Paco near the center of the American-Japanese battle for Manila. He remembers running for shelter carrying one of his sisters on his back as explosion after explosion ripped by them. "I shall never forget that time," he used to say to us. Thirty-four years later, neither have I.

Researching this time period for the backdrop of my novel was like opening a treasure trove of memories. The images and voices of the people in the accounts and personal interviews that I have read paralleled many of the stories

I heard growing up. At times I felt like I was not alone in the room, that my *lolo* and *lola* were nearby, their spirits urging me on to write about our people. Growing up I longed to find the kind of fictional stories of the Philippines that I was told by my father and *lola,* but the shelves in the libraries held only travel guides. This book is my humble contribution to the empty shelf that I always longed to fill.

Many readers may wonder at the Spanish surnames given throughout my book. Few may know that the Philippine Islands were a Spanish colony for three hundred years. In fact, the archipelago of 7,107 islands was named after the Spanish king Philip II. In 1510 the Portuguese explorer Ferdinand Magellan was granted an expedition by the Spanish king Charles V, and in 1521 he "discovered" the Philippine Islands, though in fact Chinese, Japanese, Indian, and Arab traders had been visiting and trading with the islands long before Magellan arrived.

Following is a brief historical note on the Philippine struggle for independence:

In February 1898, the U.S. Congress declared war against Spain. In the ensuing battle the United States defeated Spain. Spain then ceded the Philippines, after three hundred years of Spanish rule, to the United States under the Treaty of Paris.

Public schools were opened with American, Spanish, and Filipino teachers. The Spanish language was kept as a means of communication, but the Spanish legal system was exchanged for the American system. American troops were then installed on the islands and a military government was established by the United States. But the Filipinos had had enough—they wanted to rule themselves. What followed from 1899 to 1902 was the Philippine-American War for Philippine Independence. The war ended with the defeat of the Philippines, but the nationalist movement continued to receive popular support.

Before the Philippines could gain independence from the United States, World War II broke out in the Pacific theater. Pearl Harbor was attacked by Japan on December 7, 1941. The following morning the Philippines were bombed by Japanese warplanes. The Allied troops, led by General Douglas MacArthur, a resident of the islands and military advisor to the Philippines, retreated to the Bataan Peninsula and the fortified island of Corregidor. Before his departure, MacArthur declared Manila an open city to spare it from Japanese bombings. The Japanese did not respect this edict and continued to bomb the city.

What followed for 70,000 American and Filipino troops was the horrible Bataan Death March. The troops, brutally treated by the Japanese, were forced to march from the Bataan Peninsula to Camp O'Donnell in Tarlac where they were interned in P.O.W. camps. The Japanese continued to bomb the islands. Ill-prepared for such an attack, General Jonathan Wainwright, MacArthur's successor, surrendered Corregidor on May 6, 1942. General Douglas MacArthur had retreated to Australia, where he would later help to organize a guerrilla island force in the Philippines via radio communications. The Philippine people were left to fend for themselves against the Japanese Imperial Army. The Japanese came under the guise of "Asia for the Asians" and with propaganda for stamping out Western imperialism. American schoolbooks were destroyed and schools later shut down. Any American troops and their families who had been left behind were interned as prisoners of war.

Houses were commandeered by the Imperial Army. Food became dangerously scarce and the civilians starved. The barter system came into play as people foraged for food to save their families. Families hid in cellars to avoid any suspicion of being guerrilla fighters and later to survive the battles and the bombings. For the next three years both Filipino and American guerrilla groups would start to form in the jungles, in the Zambales Mountains, and on the islands of Luzon and Mindanao, waiting for General Douglas MacArthur to keep his famous promise, "I shall return." In October 1944 MacArthur did return and battled through to Manila with four Allied divisions. Finally, in 1945 the Japanese commanding officer general Tomoyuki Yamashita surrendered the Philippines to MacArthur.

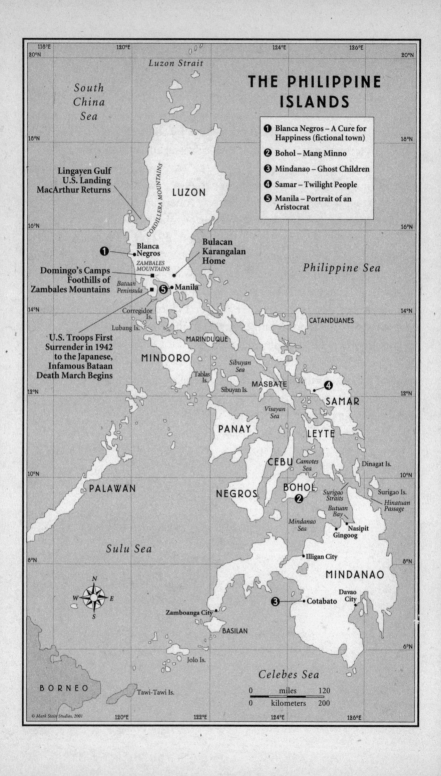

THE PHILIPPINE ISLANDS

1 Blanca Negros – A Cure for Happiness (fictional town)

2 Bohol – Mang Minno

3 Mindanao – Ghost Children

4 Samar – Twilight People

5 Manila – Portrait of an Aristocrat

Luzon Strait

South China Sea

CORDILLERA MOUNTAINS

LUZON

Lingayen Gulf
U.S. Landing
MacArthur Returns

Philippine Sea

1 Blanca Negros

ZAMBALES MOUNTAINS

Bulacan
Karangalan
Home

Domingo's Camps
Foothills of
Zambales Mountains

Bataan Peninsula

5 Manila

Corregidor Is.

CATANDUANES

Lubang Is.

U.S. Troops First
Surrender in 1942
to the Japanese,
Infamous Bataan
Death March Begins

MARINDUQUE

MINDORO

Sibuyan Sea

Tablas Is.

MASBATE

4

SAMAR

Sibuyan Is.

Visayan Sea

LEYTE

PANAY

Dinagat Is.

CEBU

Camotes Sea

PALAWAN

NEGROS

BOHOL

2

Surigao Straits

Surigao Is.

Hinatuan Passage

Butuan Bay

Mindanao Sea

Nasipit
Gingoog

Sulu Sea

Illigan City

MINDANAO

N
W · E
S

Davao City

Zamboanga City

3 · Cotabato

BASILAN

Celebes Sea

Jolo Is.

B O R N E O

0 — miles — 120

0 — kilometers — 200

Tawi-Tawi Is.

© Mark Stein Studios, 2001

WHEN
THE
ELEPHANTS
DANCE

part 1

ALEJANDRO
KARANGALAN

FEBRUARY 1945

~ **PAPA EXPLAINS THE WAR LIKE THIS:** "When the elephants dance, the chickens must be careful." The great beasts, as they circle one another, shaking the trees and trumpeting loudly, are the Amerikanos and the Japanese as they fight. And our Philippine Islands? We are the small chickens. I think of baby chicks I can hold in the palm of my hand, flapping wings that are not yet grown, and I am frightened.

Papa is sick. His malaria has returned double strong, and his face is the color of dishwater. He sweats in his sleep but shakes beneath the woven blankets. When he talks there is phlegm and a quaking in his voice that is hard to listen to. As eldest son, I have been given the duty of food trader for the day. I go in search of rice, beans, camotes, papaya, pineapple, canned tomatoes, Carnation milk, quinine for the malaria, anything I can find. Even the foul-smelling durian fruit with its spiked shell would be a blessing. Pork would be a miracle. We are all very thin like skeletons.

Since the Japanese chased the Amerikanos away three years ago, a kilo of rice now costs fifty centavos, more than four times the original price. The Japanese have created new money, but it is no good. We call it Mickey Mouse money. We trade for everything these days, work, food, medicine.

I carry my basket of cigarettes to barter with. I worked twelve evenings in Manila to earn these, serving coffee and whiskey to the families on Dewey Boulevard who have been allowed to remain in their mansions and villas. These families were the ones who stood in the streets and waved white flags for the Japanese Imperial Army when they first arrived. I would walk twenty kilometers south each day from our hometown of Santa Maria in Bulacan province to work these houses in Manila. I kept watch as the men smoked and played mah-jongg on the stone-and-marble verandas. Their tables faced Manila Bay, her violet sunsets, and the streets lined with coconut palms.

At the end of each evening, I would go to see the hostess, Doña Alfonsa, her face white like a geisha's from too much talcum. She sat in her spacious parlor beneath a row of matching ceiling fans. The blades were made of straw and shaped like spades. Each night she lifted opal-ringed fingers and counted three packs of Lucky Strikes. One for every four hours that I worked. She paid me in cigarettes, and I made certain the cups were always full.

My brother, Roderick, accompanies me in my search for food. He is two years younger, and today is his tenth birthday. We must be careful not to step on the dead, and the Japanese soldiers must be avoided at all costs. The first is Mama's request, the second, Papa's order.

"Pay attention." I grab Roderick by his shirt and point to a man lying face-down.

He frowns. "It is impossible. They are everywhere."

The stench is terrible in this heat. It rises like steam from a bowl of bad stew. I try to breathe through my mouth. Mrs. Del Rosario has been staring at the sky for three days. Her skin has rotted, and the animals have taken their share. Her robe is thrown open, and her right leg is pointed in a strange direction. I try not to look when we pass. Roderick becomes stuck to his spot. He was a favorite of hers.

"Don't look. We must go." I nudge him.

He turns to me. His eyes are angry and red. He looks away.

The blue flies cover the bodies like death veils. They land on our faces, bringing kisses from the dead. We swat them away quickly.

Early this morning, before light, we heard the rumble of tanks and saw many Amerikano soldiers in green uniforms and heavy boots marching in the dark. Papa said that their destination would be the Paco railroad station, an area well guarded by the enemy.

Ever since General MacArthur's voice was heard on the radio saying that he has returned, all citizens have taken to hiding in their cellars. No one leaves their homes unless it is an emergency. It is best to stay hidden from the Japanese soldiers. Their tempers are short now that the Amerikanos have reappeared. They are quick to slap us on the face or grab a fistful of our hair. Everyone is under the suspicion of being for MacArthur.

There are barricades and checkpoints every two kilometers. At these spots the Japanese stand with bayonets and their special police, the Kempeitai. There are Filipinos who stand with them called Makapilis. It is short for *Makabayang Pilipino*, which means "our fellow countrymen." The Makapili are Japanese sympathizers. They are pro-Asian and do not want the Amerikanos to come back. The Makapilis help the Kempeitai hunt for guerrillas. Papa calls the Makapili cowards because they hide behind cloth masks. One finger from them and a Filipino can be sentenced to death. They will turn in their countrymen without hesitation. The Japanese have poisoned our minds against one another.

Amerikano bombers fly in a V shape above. We watch their silver under-bellies, ripe with strength.

"This way," I tell my brother.

"V for victory. Go, Joe!" Roderick shouts with fist raised.

"Quiet," I tell him. We hurry, crouching low to the ground, ready to dive. The ground shakes and the sky rumbles from their passing. My head spins from our quick movements. I steady myself against a tree. Roderick is the same way. We have grown much weaker in the last month from lack of food. There is no food to be found. Any supply trucks are ambushed by the guerrillas. It was better when we had the cow; at least we had milk. Papa worked so hard not to slaughter her, only to have someone steal her when we slept.

"We must not move so fast. Stay close," I tell Roderick.

"Papa said to stay away from the city," he protests.

"I know." I keep moving, and he follows as always.

We walk south toward Manila.

"Papa told us not to go toward the city." Roderick catches up to me. He pulls my arm in frustration.

"It is okay," I tell him.

From behind comes the sound of tanks approaching. We stop arguing and jump into a banana grove. Five Amerikano tanks, followed by fifty soldiers on foot. We come out of our hiding place. A few of the soldiers look our way.

"Tommy guns," I breathe.

"And carbines," Roderick adds, shooting the trees with imaginary bullets. "But where are the big guns that have been shaking our house?"

"Already in Manila. Come. We will follow behind."

Roderick stares at me.

My stomach twists from hunger. Already my brow is dripping with sweat from the heat, and the dust is caught in my throat. I take my palm and swipe it across my eyes. "We have to find food. Papa's sickness is getting worse. Do you want to go back? Why don't you go back." I leave him standing with his arms crossed.

He follows. "Why do they not bury her?"

"Who?" I ask, looking at the scattered bodies. It is difficult to see whom the faces once belonged to.

"Mrs. Del Rosario."

"For what? She is gone."

"I hope someone buries me," Roderick says.

I look at my brother. "Do not say that. Make the sign of the cross." He does so. His blue shirt is too large. The collar falls over his shoulder, and I can see his skin stretched over the bones.

"Alejandro?" He holds my gaze.

"Yes?"

"Will that happen to us?"

AFTER SIX HOURS we have covered twenty kilometers and reach the outer part of Manila. The tanks and soldiers have long ago moved on ahead of us. We stay to the east side of the city. The scattered sounds of rifle fire in the distance greet us. Another kilometer and we pass Nichols Field and Fort McKinley. There is smoke everywhere. Our eyes sting, and we pull our shirt collars over our mouths. There is a barricade before us. A group of Japanese soldiers stand with bayonets.

"I told you." Roderick grunts and brushes an angry hand through his hair. He kicks the dirt.

My stomach rumbles and twists. I look behind us. "We shall go around. The other way. Past Herran Street." But even as I say this, the soldiers motion for us to come forward.

We bow low from the waist and walk toward them. I feel the knocking of my heart. We are ten meters from them. There is not even time to hide the basket of cigarettes. I glance quickly at Roderick. His eyes are as big as plums. He grips one hand in the other, cracking his knuckles.

"Let me talk," I instruct.

"I can speak for myself."

"They will try to anger you, trick you into saying something. Do not mention that Domingo has been to our house."

"Why would I do that? I'm not stupid." Roderick glares at me.

"Roderick," I say. I look toward the soldiers. My feet refuse to go farther.

"Come, come." A Japanese soldier waves to us. His palm faces downward, as if he were swatting a fly.

I nudge Roderick forward and he shoves back at me.

"Nem," the man barks at Roderick.

"Roderick Karangalan," my brother answers.

"You." The man points at me.

I stare for a moment at the accusing finger. "Alejandro Karangalan."

"Where go? You have guerrilla friends?"

I shake my head.

"You deliver something? That. What that?" He motions to our basket. I place the cigarettes on a folding table.

The soldier stabs a pack with his bayonet and opens it. "You send message in here?" He squints at Roderick. "Ha?"

"No," Roderick answers. His eyes are fixed on the man's shirt.

"You, where is message?"

"No message," I answer.

The soldier slaps me on the head. I grit my teeth and stand still. My eyes water, and it angers me. From behind the soldier a Filipino approaches, a Makapili. He does not wear a mask, as the others. He is thin, with long hair that smells of old pomade. He stands before us, folds his arms, and smiles. He pushes the boxes aside, inspecting the different brands that I have collected. The Makapili picks one, opens the package, and places a cigarette in his mouth. I count two ruined boxes.

Roderick lifts his head sharply and stares at the man. I can see the small muscles of his jaw.

"*Ikáw,*" the man says to Roderick. You. "Who do you think you are, staring at me like that? Come with me."

He reaches for Rod, but I put a hand on my brother's shoulder. "I am the eldest."

The man snorts and lights a match, watching me. "You know the name Domingo Matapang?"

"No," I answer.

"He is a guerrilla leader. You know him." The man nods.

I shake my head. "I do not know that name."

"He is this tall. Is he not?" The man raises his hand higher than his own head. "What does he look like? Tell me, and I will instruct them to let you go."

"I do not know this man. How can I tell you what he looks like?"

"He lives north of here, in Bulacan." The Makapili points downward insistently. "You are from Bulacan."

"Quiapo," I lie, holding his gaze.

The Makapili blows a stream of smoke into my eyes. "How could you not know him? Suddenly everyone here is a stranger? No one knows anyone? Where does he hide?" The Makapili blows smoke upward and glances at Roderick, then back to me.

"I do not know this man." My throat tightens and my voice sounds weak.

"Liar." He puts his face close to mine. His teeth are yellow. "Liar," he says again, and slaps me harder than the Japanese did.

I taste blood inside my mouth. It streams down to my shirt. I bring my fingers to my lips and hold my hand there.

"*Puta ang iná mo!*" Roderick yells—Your mother is a whore!—and shoves at the man's stomach with all his might.

"Rod!" I shout.

It is silent. The Makapili tries to smooth his face. In his eyes is a look of furious disbelief. The Japanese study my brother. I stare at the sharp bayonets, unable to breathe. My chest folds inward and I glance quickly at all the faces. A soldier begins to laugh, and the others join him. They throw their heads back and laugh from the belly.

The Makapili moves toward Roderick, who has his fists up. I step forward, but the Japanese soldier puts out a hand and waves us on. "Go."

Roderick's tears are streaming. He reaches for the cigarettes, but the Makapili blocks him with a rifle. "I will keep these."

"Our father is sick. I need the cigarillos to trade for quinine," I tell him. I memorize the Makapili's face.

"What? What?" The Japanese slants his head.

"Quinine. I need these to trade. My father is sick," I repeat, trying to keep the anger from my voice.

"Leave here," the Japanese tells me. He turns and barks something to one of the soldiers. The soldier returns with a glass container the size of my little finger. "Take medicine. Go. You take."

I look at them suspiciously. They nudge one another. I give the basket of cigarettes one last look, then urge Roderick away.

They watch as we go. When we are down the road, Rod raises his arm and wipes his eyes. "They do not even know what Domingo looks like."

"Shh. Do not speak his name, even at this distance."

"Is that any good, you think?" He nods toward my fist.

"I don't know," I answer. I throw the container far into a ditch. It makes no sound as it lands. A hundred flies lift in the shape of a fishing net and settle again.

We hurry back, cutting closer into the heart of the city, ducking from building to building. The sounds of gunfire rattle like a drumbeat. We keep our eyes up for snipers. We are almost at the end of the street when we hear running footsteps, and suddenly my chest is hit by a force. A body has collided with us, and we tumble. My head hits the stone floor, and I feel it swell immediately. Roderick moans nearby, and I call out his name.

"*Kuya?*" he says groggily. Big brother?

I look around in confusion. There is a boy crumpled next to us. His face is dripping with sweat. There is blood on his cheeks, and his neck is covered in red. His shirt is soaked and sticks to his body. I recognize his eyes, and then the face becomes familiar. It is Necessito Aguinaldo, an older classmate.

"Nesto, you have been hit." I point to where the blood is darkest, near his belly.

He looks down at his shirt in surprise, then shakes violently. "No. Give me your shirt."

"What?" I ask.

"You have two," he says, breathing hard.

"He hit his head too hard." Roderick watches Necessito.

Nesto shakes his head. "Alejandro, give me your shirt. They are coming for me. I am not bleeding. It is not my blood. He has hurt my family for the last time."

"Who has hurt you?" I ask.

"Give me your shirt." He tugs at my sleeve.

I am wearing two shirts, one short-sleeved over one with longer sleeves. "Hurry, Alejandro." He stomps his foot and pulls off his bloody shirt. There are tears in his voice.

I give him a shirt, and he pulls it quickly over his head. He looks around fearfully. His eyes fill with tears.

"Here they come. Here they come. Oh, my God! Run!" Nesto shouts. The sound of many feet pound the cobblestone. Nesto turns and runs in the opposite direction.

We watch him flee. My body shakes for him. He does not get far. There is another barricade at the end of the street. The Japanese soldiers hold up their hands, gesturing for him to halt.

I urge my brother away. "There is nothing more we can do." I watch as Nesto walks toward them. He drags his feet. *Run. Run,* my mind calls out to him. Nesto becomes like an old dog, obedient and timid. He nods at something that the soldiers have said and bows his head.

"What will they do?" Roderick asks.

"Let us not wait to find out. We must tell his mother."

"You know where to find her?"

He is right. I would not know where to look. All the houses now belong to the Japanese.

We turn to go, but more soldiers approach. They come in groups of three and four, pressing near, with angry faces, pushing other captives forward. Filipino men and boys are herded into a circle. A soldier motions for my brother and me to join.

I shake my head. "We have done nothing. We are on our way home."

"No speak. Join others." The soldier points.

Roderick looks at me. I gesture with my chin. We move into their circle.

A soldier announces in a loud voice, "Say who has committed crime, and all can go."

Roderick stares at my shirt with horror.

"What?" I follow his gaze, and the breath is stolen from my chest. My hands and the edges of my shirt are stained with blood from my contact with Nesto. My body begins to tremble. I stuff my hands into my pockets and press myself close to the others.

We are gathered and then separated into three large trucks used to transport the farm animals. These trucks, like most of the houses, have been commandeered from the citizens. Each bed carries ten people standing. There are tall wooden boards on each side and a short gate at the rear. Nesto is placed in a different one from ours. When our convoy starts, everyone speaks. I spit on my hands to clean the blood from my body. Roderick spits directly on my neck and rubs as hard as he can. We are like pigs headed for the market.

"What is it? What is happening?" someone demands.

"A murder, one of their officers," a voice answers without emotion. "As always, they are looking for someone to blame. Hundreds of us dying at their hands. One of theirs is slain . . ." The voice laughs bitterly. "And suddenly it is murder."

I know that voice. I squint my eyes at the sound of it. Roderick cranes his neck. I curl my lip in warning, and he stares immediately at the ground. The wagon finds a hole and plunges to the left. We fly to one side, pressed against one another like canned fish. I look in the direction of the voice and catch a glimpse of Domingo Matapang.

I have not seen him since he left our house four days ago. His wife, Ate Lorna, stayed behind with us. She has not been able to sleep. She calls out for him in her dreams at night. Domingo looks at me. There are purple rings under his eyes. He lifts his chin in greeting. The wagon rights itself, and his face disappears in the sea of filthy clothes and frightened faces. The wagon reeks of sweat and unwashed bodies. Already the day has warmed considerably. Roderick bares his teeth and crosses his eyes. His nose is pressed directly into a man's armpit. I laugh so hard from fear that my teeth chatter.

We are driven farther south to Fort McKinley, to the rear of the barracks where there is a field surrounded by trees. The heat is suffocating and the sky threatens rain. Gray cottonball clouds press together against the blue. The sounds of shelling explode like distant thunder. The gates of the wagons are thrown open, and the soldiers wait at the end with rifles. They pull us down roughly. We look around in confusion.

They place Domingo directly to my right, but he does not acknowledge me. We are made to stand side by side in three rows. There are fewer than thirty of us. Nesto is shoved in front of me. He glances at me, and in that short meeting his eyes are pleading. I look to see if Roderick has noticed Nesto. I look to my left, then forward to the other two rows. I count the bodies lined next to me. My heart begins to dance. I do not see my brother.

"Stop that," Domingo says from the corner of his mouth.

I take a deep breath and force myself to look straight ahead.

He speaks softly, so softly that I almost do not hear it. His voice rides like a feather caught in the wind. "Say nothing."

My mind races. *When did I lose sight of Roderick? When did we last speak? Was he in the truck that last moment before we stopped? Is he in those groupings of trees? Did a soldier pull him away? Was he taken to one of the concrete buildings? What will I tell Father? Maybe he has escaped. Think. Think. Maybe he is dead.*

The first two lines have been separated. I watch as they walk Nesto's row away. He follows with head bowed.

At the far end of the field is a thick wooden fence. It stands twelve feet tall, with each cylindrical post at least eight inches in diameter and ending in spear-shaped points. There are two heavy beams that cross horizontally near the top and at the bottom. The first captive is led to the fence. His eyes are large. I feel his terror. I cannot catch my breath.

"Please, sir. I did nothing wrong. What have I done?" His eyes swell with tears.

"Silence."

They make the captive stand with his back to the fence. They take his arms and spread them wide. Each soldier holds a length of rusted wire that they wrap around the captive's thumbs. We watch, curious of what comes next. The soldiers stand on tiptoes and tie the other end of the wires to the top beam, forcing the captive to stand on his toes as well. He shouts in pain, and the legs of his trousers leak. The soldiers jump away in anger. They stare at him with disgust. They take the next man and do the same. I feel a weight on my chest.

Are we to be set on fire? A firing squad? I will not cry. My breathing comes fast, though I try to slow it. They lead Domingo to the fence, and I am left to stand alone. My legs grow weak. I feel dizzy, and the sky becomes the ground.

The soldiers approach. I hold my chin up, though my head is shaking. A soldier points to the blood on my shirt. Soon there are six soldiers gathered around me.

One of the soldiers speaks good English. He is called Tanaka.

"Where did you get blood?" Tanaka asks.

"I was hit," I answer. "At the checkpoint."

"You were not hit," he responds, watching my eyes. He calls out in Japanese and a soldier runs forward, carrying a great samurai sword in a beautiful gold-and-emerald scabbard. There are two attachments on the scabbard for carrying and a small length of leather tied on the handle. He pulls the blade from its sheath, and the sound rings in my ears and hums in my chest. I stare at the sword with fearful admiration. It has a wide curve with written carvings and a fiery dragon on the blade and a golden hilt. Tanaka holds the butt of the sword to me. I look up at him.

"Take it," he orders, watching me carefully.

I take the large handle with both hands. It is too heavy. The blade immediately drops to the dirt. The soldiers shout at me for my clumsiness.

"Show me how you killed my comrade."

"Wh-what?" I stammer. My stomach cramps at his words.

"Show me how you sliced neck!" Tanaka shouts in my ear.

I drop the sword and hold my belly.

"There is two of you. Where is other?"

I shake my head.

"Send for Yoshido," Tanaka instructs.

A soldier approaches and they make way for him. It is the soldier from the checkpoint, the one who stabbed our cigarettes with his blade. He looks at me with boredom. He grabs my face with one hand and turns it from side to side. He studies the blood on my shirt. He squints his eyes.

"I hit him. He not give where of Domingo, the guerrilla," Yoshido explains.

Tanaka is not convinced. He looks at me in a suspicious way.

"Tie him," he orders. He watches as I am strung with the wires. There are sharp edges in various parts; they slice through my skin and make me gasp, then scream. I feel the spit rise in my throat. A rifle is shoved into my belly and the air closes up. When I catch my breath, the bile surges up my throat and I vomit. It is left to dry on my chin and chest. I am so ashamed. I cannot stop my tears.

They have tied us so that we stand on the tips of our toes. I am too short, so they have placed wooden logs under my feet. My toes scramble to find balance on the logs. If I stand still, the wires do not cut deeper. I struggle to find a comfortable position, but there is none. The Japanese stand back to inspect their work.

I can feel my heart beat in my thumbs. I try not to move. *Please, God, set us free.* My body shakes.

The soldiers retreat into the shade of the trees to watch us. They sit with their backs to the trunks, legs spread open, bent at the knees. I do not understand why they still wear the long boots in this heat. They pass a container of water among them and wipe their mouths on their sleeves. I try not to look, but I cannot help watching the container as it is passed from hand to hand.

It is the dry season for the Philippines. Each time I swallow, my throat feels as if I am swallowing one of the pointed sticks Papa threads the chicken meat with. The leather necklace of the Virgin Mary Mama has tied around my neck is broken and dangling. The small cloth picture of the Virgin, with its felt green edges, is stuck to my skin from sweat. My body moves, though I try to keep still. It is difficult to breathe.

After an hour I moan, "Let me down." My rubber slippers have fallen off and lie on the ground. I take a deep breath and push on the tips of my toes to take the weight off my shoulders and arms. I do this until my legs shake beneath me and I see small stars dance around my eyes. The movement causes the logs beneath me to fall away and I lose my balance. I jerk painfully, and the wires slice through my skin. I hang only by my thumbs. The pain is so blinding, I cannot shout at first.

"My hands. Please. It hurts," I call out, but my tongue is thick and swollen. It crowds and pushes against my teeth. They watch me with stone faces. Soon, all that can be heard is my blubbering. Finally, a soldier bends and replaces the logs beneath my feet. I cry for a long time.

Tanaka studies us. He walks with chin raised. "A great tragedy was committed today. My comrade, Lieutenant Colonel Ono Higoshi, was stabbed by his own sword. I do not believe that all here committed crime. Two, maybe three of you." He holds up two fingers and eyes me strongly. "Your choice. Die honorably, accept guilt, or all suffer and die with you." He looks at me again.

The other captives begin to crane their necks at me. *Die honorably.*

Tanaka waits with his hands on his hips. He moves his weight from one foot to the other. He shakes his head. "Bring other boy."

I struggle to see whom they bring. They drag Nesto forward. He is wearing my shirt, and though there is no blood on it, his hands and neck are red.

Tanaka has been watching me. "One man could kill with the sword. Or maybe two boys, ha?" His eyes are sharp. "Do you accept responsibility, or let others die?"

I remain quiet.

Tanaka shakes his head in anger and points to Nesto. "Put this one next to him. Maybe they talk, accept guilt."

Nesto is silent when they raise him beside me. He wears a look of defeat.

"Boy," a captive calls to me. "Boy." His voice is insistent, angry.

I look over at him.

"I have a wife. I have a daughter. Please, accept your actions. Take the blame for what you have done. Perhaps they will be lenient with you."

I turn away from him. Nesto hangs with his head bowed. I pity him and I hate him for not speaking.

"Look at me!" the captive shouts again. "Boy, we will not pay for your crimes. Do you understand? We will not."

Another captive joins him. "You have killed an innocent man. Why make us pay for your crimes?" He calls out to the soldiers. "They are the ones who have murdered. Why not let us go? We are innocent."

"Speak, you must speak," the others echo.

The sweat rolls down my face and burns my eyes. I feel alone. I hang my head and let the tears fall. It was not always this way. Long ago, before the Japanese invasion, neighbors protected one another. One child was everyone's child. I think of my father. Papa would take the blame to save the others.

"Look at yourselves," Domingo hisses in Tagalog, and all becomes quiet. "How can you believe their accusations? This is why their nation can come and put their flag above us. We are always divided. We are grown men. This is just a boy. I would give my own life before I let them hurt him. If we ever hope to take our country back, we must stand together and fight. Do not let them divide us further. You must risk your lives. There is no other way."

I look to Domingo. I cannot even speak words of thanks.

"Do not admit anything. Do not let them see you cry," he whispers.

The whites of his eyes are yellow, with red lines. The strength of his stare scares me just as much as the soldiers do. I want to be as strong as he is, but I cannot control my fear.

The Japanese watch us with curious faces. We have become a show for them.

Nesto is quiet beside me. I become angry. How can he rest? I wish to throw my leg out and kick him. I remember his master, the Japanese who took over his family's home. The man threw out Nesto's grandmother, then his father. His mother and sister were kept a long time. There was much talk about this. The man was very bad to Nesto; often he would come to school with bruises on his face and dark welts on his cheeks in the shape of a palm.

I turn to Domingo. "Will they kill us?"

Domingo looks at me and frowns. "Be strong, Jando."

He has called me by my pet name and not Alejandro, my proper name. This makes me think of Papa, and I become more sad. Papa said the Japanese no longer support the idea of pro-Asia. They have dropped their costumed promises, and their campaign now is only pro-Japan. Mama warned him not to speak that way.

We face northeast, toward the long snake that is the Pasig River. Farther north is Lingayen Gulf, where the American troops landed after Leyte last month, just as General MacArthur promised. First there was scattered fighting, but in the last week the battle has grown like a hurricane. To the west is Nielson Field, and farther west is the blue stretch of Manila Bay, the old *luneta,* and the cobbled streets of Intramuros. The old Spanish city, where Roderick and I used to play.

Tanaka swings the samurai sword. He cuts the air, *whoosh,* the sound of the wind being sliced. The silver of the blade is thick and sharp. He walks to one end and points the blade at the throat of the first captive, the one who insisted I confess. Tanaka pulls away, then turns and pretends to chop at the man's stomach.

"Aggh!" the man shouts in fear.

Tanaka roars, "Stop that. Your people have no pride. No sense of *ah-noh.* You bow before everyone. First Spaniards, then Americans, now the Japanese."

The captive begins to cry again. My father would never cry. He would be strong like Domingo.

"Stop it." Tanaka slaps the Filipino.

The Filipino sobs. "Please, please, sir."

"What is the name of your guerrilla leader? Answer and you will be pardoned."

We hold our breath. I do not dare look at Domingo.

"I repeat. Give name of guerrilla lee-dah." Tanaka brings the point of his sword to the man's neck. He presses until he breaks the skin and a thin red stream appears.

"Domingo Matapang," the man chokes.

"Good. You are learning, little dog. The name, I already know. Where does he hide?"

I look away. I cannot bear to watch. I wait, grinding my teeth. There is no answer, and my eyes are pulled again toward the weeping man. Perhaps he is more afraid of Domingo.

"I do not know. Please, sir," the Filipino begs.

Tanaka nods; he lifts the man's chin with the point of his sword. "I believe you."

Relief crosses the man's face.

"But you disgust me." Tanaka spins around and, *swoosh,* the heavy blade cuts through the air, downward in a terrible arc. It slashes into the man's neck, and his head falls forward. There is a gurgling sound, then only the silence.

I shout. I shout as loud as I can. The sight makes us crazy. We pull and shake at our ties. I cut my fingers from pulling on the dirty wires.

"Be still," Domingo warns me. "You will cut deeper into your thumbs."

I take a breath and my whole chest shudders.

Tanaka is walking back and forth with his hands behind him. He stops in front of me, and I feel sick in my stomach. I shake so strongly that my teeth click together. One glare from him and I wet my pants. I am so ashamed.

I force myself to study Tanaka's uniform. I stare at the medals on his jacket. He does not wear the knee-high leather boots with his trousers stuffed inside. He is wearing rubber split-toed shoes. His pants are too short, and they show his socks, which have fallen around his ankles. He walks with his feet pointing outward, as if each wishes to go its own way. "Do you speak now?" he asks me with a false smile.

THE JAPANESE HAVE been here for three years. They were happy at first, and I thought it was to be a long celebration. They made it appear that way. We were told to make Nippon flags when they arrived, to put outside of our houses to welcome them. My brother, Roderick, and I made a flag to display at our home. Papa said that it would keep our house safe. Some of the children were given white armbands that said "Collaborator." Roderick told Mama that he wanted a special band.

"Better to wear the red band," Mama muttered to herself, "than be labeled a traitor to your own people." The red bands are for enemies of the Japanese. An Amerikano would wear a red band. The Amerikano families that have been left behind wear these bands if they are out on "leave" from the prisons, like when an Amerikano woman is let out from Santo Tomas prison to visit with friends. Some guerrilla fighters wear the red bands out of defiance, Mama says.

When MacArthur first returned, we heard his voice on the radio. We were all amazed and thought it was a trick or a joke. Everyone knows the Japanese are the only ones allowed to speak on the radio. But it was MacArthur, and I remember exactly what he said, because Roderick and I repeated it over and over. He said, "People of the Philippines, I have returned. By the grace of Almighty God, our forces stand again on Philippine soil. Rally to me."

We were so surprised, even though papers had been appearing that said such things as "The Americans are coming." Children too young to talk were given chocolate bars wrapped in paper that said, "I have returned."

A HIGHER-RANKING OFFICER approaches in dress uniform. He has more medals than Tanaka. His hair is gray and very white near the ears. He stands straight and appears taller than Tanaka, but he is not. The soldiers get up from under the shade and stand to attention. They line up before him and bow.

The commander studies me, then Nesto.

"How old?" the Japanese commander asks in thick English. When the Japanese first invaded our islands, they threw out all our Amerikano textbooks and insisted we use only our national language, Tagalog, to keep our Asian-ness and stamp out the Western imperialist influence. Yet the commander himself has not learned to speak our language and instead relies on English to communicate with us.

I look around in fear. *What am I supposed to tell him?* Domingo and the others look straight ahead. *Am I not supposed to speak at all?* I feel the spit rise in my throat.

"How old?" the commander repeats, much louder.

"*Labing-tatlo,*" I croak. "Thirteen."

"Name," he says. Only, I hear "Nem."

I squint my eyes, trying to understand his words.

"Nem! Nem!"

"Alejandro Karangalan," I gasp. I cannot catch my breath. He says something to Tanaka, and Tanaka comes forward.

Tanaka takes out his sword and brings it to my chin. "We make bargain. Tell where is Domingo Matapang, guerrilla leader. I let you go. No murder happen. I say you not kill comrade."

"I did not kill anyone. And I do not know this Domingo you speak of."

"How you not kill? Blood on hands." He slaps my raised hands with the flat side of his sword. "Blood on shirt." He pulls my shirt up to my eyes. It causes me to swing forward, and I feel a hundred blades slice at my thumbs. "But not your blood." He stabs a finger at me. "Now, now is your blood." He lifts his sword. I shut my eyes and scream.

At the same time, Domingo shouts, "Leave him alone!"

All eyes turn to Domingo. There has been talk about Domingo in our town of Bulacan. People say that it is he who has been passing around papers that say, "Down with the Japanese. The MacArthur will return soon." Domingo is rumored to be a guerrilla commander, but I know for certain that he is. I have carried messages for him as far west as the Sierra Madres, without telling Papa.

The Japanese commander walks to Domingo. "Silence!" he shouts. Another soldier pokes Domingo harshly in the stomach with a shiny black walking stick. Domingo spits at the soldier, then raises one leg and kicks the commander. The commander topples to the ground like rotten wood. He falls on his side, blinking, with his arm still held up to protect himself.

There is much shouting. The captives call out, "Apologize, you fool."

"Cut him down," the commander roars as he struggles to get up. His soldiers run to help him, but he pushes them away.

They take Domingo down and walk him toward the woods. He holds his head high, though his feet stumble before him.

A soldier prods him with a rifle as they march. Domingo grabs the man's arm. The two struggle quietly until another soldier clutches Domingo and they pull him forward. Domingo continues to fight. I hear his voice, harsh and guttural: *"Isinu sumpain kitá."* I curse you.

The three of them clash, like one body. They are horrible to look upon, like a fish out of water, its body twisting and turning, wrestling for air. I begin to pull and strain. I want to run and push them away from him. My neck and face grow hot with anger. I watch until the trees swallow them.

We are silent now. The faces change. Nesto's eyes are red. One shot echoes through the trees. After a few minutes the soldiers return without Domingo. I swallow the air as if I am drowning. Tears burn my eyes. The commander nods with satisfaction. He wipes the dust from his face.

"You are ready to speak?" Tanaka asks, pressing me with his stale breath.

I look in the direction of where they took Domingo. I cannot take my eyes from those trees. I feel a laugh come out of my mouth. It is a frightful laugh, a hopeless one. *Tell them, save yourself!* my mind screams. *Do not tell them anything:* I remember Domingo's words. And all the while, I cannot stop the laughter.

"Stop that." Tanaka presses his sword to my neck.

Tears leak from the corners of my eyes. I am confused. I do not remember the question. *Or have I already answered it? Do they ask about Domingo the guerrilla, or Nesto the murderer?* My face stings from the loud smacking of

Tanaka's open palm. *Should I tell them? What would be the harm in it? Why am I still keeping it a secret?*

Tanaka slaps me with his left hand. *Pack,* then with his right, *pack, pack.* I am so frightened, I cannot control my laughter. I can hear myself shouting, calling for my mother. I am a disgrace.

Tanaka studies Nesto for a long time. Nesto stares back without expression.

Tanaka looks at me and smiles as if he is going to tell a funny story. "Tell me who kill Lieutenant Colonel Higoshi, and you shall be exonerated."

"I do not know," I answer.

The inside of my mouth is cut and swollen. I taste the blood even before I realize Tanaka has hit me with his fist. He stands back.

"Who is murderer? Last chance."

"I have told you," I sob.

"Stupid." Tanaka's eyes bulge. His entire face is bright pink. I think for a moment his face will explode. He hits me in the stomach, and I grit my teeth. I feel my anger grow like a fire in my chest. I spit blood.

"Tell him, Alejandro. Tell him who did it." Nesto's voice is sad.

Tanaka's eyes brighten. "You see? You see?" He looks to his commander.

"I do not know who killed Higoshi," I answer, feeling very tired. I feel the weight of my face. My eyes wish to close. I fight to keep them open. Tanaka raises his sword.

Nesto begins to shout. "I did it. I killed Higoshi. I killed that whore's son. I killed him. I did it. Me. Necessito Aguinaldo. Necessito Aguinaldo!" Nesto is unstoppable. He yanks at his ties, and I flinch. His thumbs drip dark blood, thick, like the sap from the trees. "Alejandro had nothing to do with it. I tumbled on him. We fell." Nesto's voice loses its fire. "We fell. It was an accident," he whispers.

Tanaka leans back and folds his arms. He looks at his commander. The commander claps him on the back in congratulation. Two soldiers come to take Nesto down.

"No, don't hurt him. Stop it. Please, Nesto!" I shout. Nesto walks limply beside them in the same direction they took Domingo. He looks so frail. The shirt I have given him is one size too big. He used to weigh much more than me.

The commander strolls in front of me. I cannot catch my breath.

"Untie him." He points at me.

I taste my tears, salty, as they roll over my shaking mouth and mix with the sweat. I look at the other captives, daring them to speak. *The soldiers will take me deep into the forest.* They cut the wires and place me on the ground. My legs do not hold my weight. I fall forward on hands and knees, trying to blink the stars away. *Quick, think clearly.* The soldiers lift my arms and stand me slowly.

The commander points a callused finger at me. "This one has honor. He not like rest. He rather die than give his friend. This is rare in their country." The commander takes a step and pushes me. I stumble backward. "Go—" He points. My eyes follow the direction of his fingers, then back at the other captives. They shout all at once, as in the cockfights. I do not try to hear. I look at the commander. He nods again. "Go."

I look at the prisoners one last time, then run toward home.

IT IS DARK now, with just the top quarter of a moon. There are clouds around the moon, and it stares down like a watchful eye. I trip through the trees, dizzy and sobbing like a girl. When I see a shadow crouched at the edge of the woods, my heart stops. I realize it is only my brother, Roderick. He stands, and I run and hit him in the head with my palm.

"*Saán ka galing?*" I ask hoarsely. Where have you been? I thought he had died.

"*Tumakbó akó,*" he answers, rubbing his head sorely. I ran.

I grab his wrist, and we hurry north toward home. A loud siren cuts through the stillness of the night like a wailing dragon. This signals the beginning of curfew, and we run even faster. We dive into the Pasig and swim until we feel like drowning. When we reach the other shore, we break into a run again. After several hours we stop to rest at the edge of Bulacan. Our village seems strange to me. The candles are blown out in every house. The blackout curtains are drawn in each window. We rush past the cemetery, where we used to play hide-and-seek. The forest is charred in many places from the big guns. Gone are the echoing taunts of the mynah birds. There are no spider monkeys swinging on branches, not one monitor lizard running into the brushes, only bats squealing and taking flight at the sound of our footsteps.

The red-and-white banners that our village made to welcome the Japanese three years ago hang tattered and faded. They snap in the night like snake tongues. When we near our home, we see Japanese guards walking. I thrust out a hand and motion for Roderick to stop. We wait until their voices grow dim, I grab Roderick's wrist and we cross the last bit to our house. A few feet ahead of us I see a small form lying still. I run and kneel beside it.

"Baron," Roderick says to our dog, "get up." He shakes him. "Jando, is he all right?"

I do not point to the red wound near Baron's neck or the dried blood and thin pieces of shrapnel around his chest. I press my eyes to force back the tears. Baron was my dog. He followed me home from the market one evening, always careful to stay a few meters behind. If I stopped, he would retreat a few steps and hunch his head. I reach out a hand and pet his nose. It is still moist. "He sleeps now. Let him sleep."

"Yes, he sleeps now." Roderick's voice is raw. He walks quickly ahead of me. His shoulders shake soundlessly.

Our house when we enter is dark and abandoned. The crickets call out to us. Roderick clutches at my arm. We crouch low, our knees and hands touching the floor. We scoot forward, feeling with our palms until I find the metal latch. When I try to close my fingers around the handle, pain shoots through them like a thousand needles ripping into my hand. I grit my teeth at the sharpness and pull up quickly. The sound of the wood and the metal makes a loud disturbance. We peer down into the cellar.

"Alejandro," I hear my mother gasp as I put one foot down the ladder, searching for a step. "Alejandro, we thought something had happened to you." Mama is weeping. She covers her face with trembling hands. My father pulls me off the ladder and holds me to him.

"They took the cigarettes. The soldiers," I try to tell them. I cannot face the others. I bury my face in Papa's chest. Roderick shifts his feet.

"Shh . . ." Father grips my shoulders. He reaches out an arm and holds Roderick. "You have come home safely. That is all that matters. I should not have let you go. The fault is mine." Father's eyes are red. I cannot look at him.

I feel embarrassed as the others watch. I have failed. They cannot hide their disappointment. Most of them look away as Roderick explains how we lost the cigarettes. "Jando was caught by the Japanese soldiers. They tied him by the thumbs." Roderick points both thumbs in the air.

"You frightened your mother," my mother's friend Aling Ana says, but she bows her head and looks away quickly before I can respond.

Our neighbor Mrs. Yoshi pats my hair gently. "You boys must not go out again. It is too dangerous," she says. "One of the grown-ups should go next. Me, I will go next time." A few of the men protest the idea of sending a woman out. She ignores them and comes to me with a damp rag and pats my neck gingerly to clean the blood. "You are a brave boy." She holds my face. Before the war she used to wear a special powder on her face that made her skin appear paler. I remember the sweet chalky scent of it as she stands near. "He will be fine, Louisa," she tells my mother. She puts her arm around Mama and holds her close for a moment.

Mama places a hand to her chest as she reaches out to touch me. Papa takes my hands and looks at my thumbs. He breathes heavily and stares at them quietly. He says nothing for a long time. He swallows with difficulty and avoids our eyes. Then finally he says, "*Salamat sa Dios.*" Thank God. "You are home safe."

"I cannot move my thumbs," I tell Papa.

Mama falls to her knees and kisses my hands. She holds them to her face and sobs into them. The others watch quietly.

Papa rests his palm on my back. "I will clean and wrap them. Then we will pray for God to heal your hands."

"They killed Nesto Aguinaldo," I tell them. They nod solemnly without asking how. "They almost killed me." My legs shake beneath me and I sit.

"But you are here now, with us," Papa says. "That is all that matters."

"Your sister has not yet come home," Mama tells me.

My sister, Isabelle, is seventeen and my mother's pride. She was to study medicine at Santo Tomas University before the war broke out and the university was made into a prison for the Amerikanos. My mother and Isabelle fight a lot.

"*Ate* is not home yet?" I ask, using the term for "big sister." I look to my father. "Should we not send someone to find her?"

Everyone looks around nervously when I say this. I tell Papa of the tanks we saw earlier this morning, and he nods quietly. I remind him how Domingo told us we must help the Amerikanos when they arrive.

"Domingo is a reckless fool," Mang Selso, my father's friend, chides. "He cares nothing of his own life. We would all be killed. How can we fight without guns?"

"I will take my chances in this cellar," Aling Ana declares. "Why look for trouble? As long as we stay out of the Japanese's way. They will have no reason to harm us."

"We cannot hide forever. We must find food," Papa tells them. "Domingo is right. We must band together and help the Amerikanos. It is our only hope."

"If only we could be assured the Amerikanos will win this one. But how can we have faith when they did not win the first time?" Aling Ana asks. "They failed in their defense of our islands. They let those savages in."

Our basement is filled with our neighbors. This is the way it has become. The Japanese have commandeered the nicer houses for themselves. It is common to have four to five families crowded into one house. Our house has four families, and a few without families, thirteen people and two small children. We have been together now for two years. It was not so bad when we slept upstairs in the house. But the bombings and Japanese accusations against the citizens have driven us down to the cellar to hide. Most of the houses in our area are too small and unwanted by the Japanese. Half are deserted. We make ours look abandoned. In the beginning of the Japanese occupation, many people fled to the countryside, but we had no second home to run to. And now we are too weak to move very far. Tempers are hot here in our basement.

We are all shoulder to shoulder in our small cellar, and the air is thick and stale. If someone lets out a bad smell, it soaks into your clothing for a long time. I wish we could go upstairs so that I could lie in my cool room with the thin mosquito nets. The cellar is small. It would fit six coffins. When we sit we try to pull our knees close, so we do not kick one another. The floor of our cellar is dirt. We have sticks and stones where we build a small fire to cook. We open the top latch to let out the air when we do this. When it is time to sleep, some of the others go back into the house. Since the gunfire and Amerikano tanks rumbled the ground twenty days ago, more people have been sleeping in the cellar with us.

We sleep side by side, and often in the night someone rolls off to the side and takes my blanket by mistake. Roderick likes having all the people here. He used to go from person to person to see if they would play cards. He stopped doing that after Tay Fredrico, the old Spaniard, shouted at him and shook him until Papa came and pulled Roderick away.

Domingo's wife, Lorna, looks at me. She clutches their infant daughter, Alma, and their six-year-old son, Taba. "Alejandro," she says, and I can hear the shaking in her voice, "did you see Domingo?"

I nod at her.

She will not let me look away. "What did he say?"

"He said that we must all stand together and fight the Japanese. We must not let them divide us against one another."

"Easy for him to say," Mang Selso grumbles. "He is a guerrilla commander. He can perform his hit-and-run missions while we civilians must bear the retaliation from the Japanese. We have no place to hide."

Mang Selso is my father's best friend; they worked together before the war, making rattan chairs. His wife and father, Tay Fredrico, are here with him. His father is very old and rarely speaks.

Ate Lorna ignores Mang Selso's comments. "Is he on his way home?"

I cannot answer her.

Aling Ana brings a wrinkled hand to her brow. Her gold rings catch my eye. "Please, Lorna, do not invite him back here. Your husband will bring danger to this household. If they find we are harboring a guerrilla, they will chop our heads."

Mang Selso nods at this. "Yes, Lorna. You must warn him not to return here."

Ate Lorna ignores him. "Alejandro, is Domingo on his way back?"

"Shh, all of you." Papa reaches for a bowl with a small portion of rice and fish. "Let Alejandro eat. There will be time for questions later." He hands the bowl to me. "*Jando, itó anák, kain na.*" Here, son, he says in Tagalog, eat now.

"Here, Alejandro, Roderick. You boys add this to your bowls." Mrs. Yoshi breaks her fish into two portions and gives each of us a piece. "I am full. Go on. You boys need it for your strength. Eat."

I sit down slowly. My body is so tired, so sore. I cannot even lift the bowl.

My father takes my hands; again he is silenced by the sight of them.

"*Manga hayop,*" he curses. Animals.

There are tears in his voice. I pull my hands away instantly. The cuts are deep, I can see my bone in several places, and my skin hangs off my right thumb. The moment Papa touches the skin to pull it back over the bone, I shout.

He prepares a heated cloth and splashes alcohol onto the rag. I begin to sweat and I want to run from the room. He splashes rubbing alcohol on one hand and I grit my teeth, then shout. He wraps the wounds with clean strips of cloth. He takes my other hand and I pull away. I cannot stop crying. His face is the last thing I remember.

WHEN I WAKE a few hours later, there is a loud roaring outside. We crowd together.

"Oh no," Ate Lorna says.

"Airplanes." Roman, the newspaperman, comes down the ladder with an excited face. "The Americans will finish them off." He talks like an Amerikano, this Filipino newspaperman. He says the letter *g* when he is amazed at something and "shoot" when something does not go right. He has studied abroad, in the United States. He said if I studied hard enough, he would help me go to the United States. He did not say if he would help me pay for it. He is another of our neighbors. My father took him in when the Japanese confiscated his family home.

"We have almost used our entire supply of rice," my mother whispers to Papa as she spoons a second small serving into my bowl.

My father's friend Mang Selso hears this and looks to Aling Ana. "Aling

Ana, everyone has contributed. It is time we trade your jewelry, the ones your sister left you. We must sell those."

"Those are not for selling," Aling Ana snaps, pulling her velvet blanket close.

"Of course." Mang Selso looks away with disgust. "What did I expect?"

Mang Selso likes to tease all the time. Before the Japanese arrived, he was a heavy man and shaped like a pear. Now he has a skinny neck and a saggy belly. My mother calls him "Gung-gong," which is like when the Amerikanos say "Dumb-dumb." He likes to pull candy from behind our ears or tie strings to paper money. When you go to pick it up, the money runs away from you. Roderick always falls for that trick.

Mama has promised to ask Aling Ana to trade a few of her belongings for rice. She says that Aling Ana just likes to do things in her own time. Papa said that if Aling Ana does not share, he will put her out on her backside "in her own time."

Aling Ana is a very rich woman who owns the biggest house on the hill. Of course, the Japanese took that house first. Most of the neighbors will not speak to her. They call her cheap and stingy. She always speaks loudly, as if she is angry with you. She never says hello in church, and she gives only one or two coins for prayer indulgence. She gives less than the peasants.

My father once joked that Aling Ana would need all of her money to make it into heaven, and Mama became very angry with him. She does not like jokes that sound as if they are making fun of God or any of the saints. Mama pities Aling Ana. She believes that Aling Ana has great hurts inside. She thinks Aling Ana is like a wounded animal that growls so that no one will hurt her. I do not like her. One time, when Mama and I visited her house, I broke a small music box and she pinched me so hard that I bled. She is here only because of Mama. Aling Ana came with two suitcases of clothing, two large bags of sugar, and a blue canister of tea. We had to leave it all upstairs because her belongings took the space of two people, and the others began to complain.

Papa tells us that the guerrillas have been attacking the food supplies again on the way to Manila. He says that many of the Amerikano internees at Santo Tomas and Bilibid prisons have died from hunger. My cousin Esteban claims that the Amerikanos rescued the internees yesterday, with great big tanks. One tank, he claims, had the words *Georgia Peach* written on the front, and *Battlin' Betty*. Esteban says the tanks crashed through the walls, but he likes to tell big stories. Papa says he will wait for a more trustworthy person to tell us the story before he believes it.

Esteban keeps looking up toward the ladder.

"You shall stay here tonight," my father tells him.

"But Tito . . . ," Esteban protests to my father, his uncle.

"Esteban, hah, it is too dangerous to be alone. They could mark you as a guerrilla. You have already seen what happened to Jando."

I watch Esteban. He sits twisting the clasp of his sandals. He has to run out to use the bathroom many times. Esteban has dysentery. He has been eating grass again. Papa says that Esteban's rear end now runs as much as his mouth.

My father tries to hide his coughing. Mama is very worried that he also has typhus fever, which is very common, because of his red rashes and bad headaches. The flies and mosquitoes carry the diseases.

"*Tay ka muna,*" Father says thoughtfully. Wait a minute. "Tomorrow I shall go to see that warehouse I heard the others talking about a few days ago. The Japanese are giving away two bags of rice to each family, for an hour's worth of work."

"It may be a trick," Mama protests. There have been rumors that people do not return from these places.

"Let me go instead," I offer. Papa does not look well enough yet.

"No, the head of the family should go. Are you the head of the family now, Jando?" Papa teases.

"No." I grin.

"I thank you for your help, *anák,* but you must rest."

Mang Selso and his wife are angry at Aling Ana because she will not share her belongings to trade for food; they keep making snorting noises and mumbling to each other about her.

"Oh, see? Now Carlito is going to find rice, and he is sick," Mang Selso sputters.

Aling Ana glares at Mang Selso. "Why don't you go? You are not sick."

"*Huy, huy.*" Mang Selso's wife rolls her sleeves and points to Aling Ana. "He remains to protect us."

"He remains so that we can protect him," Aling Ana snaps. "Coward."

Mang Selso stands at her words. His face is tight, and redness pours through his cheeks. "If you were a man, I would hit you," he hisses.

"Hunh!" Aling Ana's lip curls. "And if you were a man, I would hit you back."

"*Tigil na. Tamà na,*" Mama says softly. Stop it. Enough now. The sadness in her voice has the effect of a loud explosion.

"*Duwág. Tamád.*" Aling Ana sneaks in a couple of words as she fluffs her red blanket around her, calling Mang Selso a coward and a lazy man.

"I can go in the morning," Roman, the journalist, tells my father. "I should have gone today instead of the boys, but I wanted to see if I could hear more on the radio."

I like Roman. Yesterday he went out alone and found a small pheasant for us to cook and an old bag of rice. The rice had maggots and larva, and we began to pick them out, but Roman said that it was a good source of vitamins, so we cooked them in the rice and ate them. They were salty at first, but if you pretended they were pieces of steak tapa, it was not so bad. They helped to ease the hunger pains.

"Oh, okay. We shall go." Father is happy for the offer and claps Roman on the back. "See? I have someone to assist me. Rest now, everyone. There is no need to fight. We are all friends here."

Roman's full name is Roman Flores; he is twenty-three years old and already taller than my father. I asked him how tall he is, and he said six feet. I have trouble making kilometers into feet. I picture six shoes, lined up one on top of the other, and this does not seem very tall. His job is to write stories for the *Manila Herald*. My mother wonders why he works because he comes from a rich family.

Roman showed me how to work his radios. He calls one a short-wave. It speaks in codes and helps him to find places where things are happening. Of course, he has no job at the present, only his radios. The box is very big, with different knobs. He also has a smaller radio where sometimes we hear the Japanese speak and sometimes the Amerikanos. Most of the time we hear loud crunching that Roman calls static.

"I will go, too," Mang Pedro announces. He studies the ground when he says this.

"Good, Ped. That will be good." Father nods, pleased.

Mang Pedro is a quiet man. He worked in the same factory with Father and Mang Selso. He wears small glasses, and he rarely speaks. Sometimes he claims to have visions that Papa calls premonitions. Like when he dreamed two days in a row that my sister, Isabelle, had disappeared. He even warned her not to leave the other day, but she did not listen, claiming that she was going to be a doctor and that doctors do not believe in superstitions. As always, Mama was angry at her. When she did not come home, Mang Pedro was upset. He told Papa to look for a white deer and he would find her, but even I must admit that sounded silly. Deers are not white!

Papa said Mang Pedro once owned the factory himself, but he gave it up; now he spends all his time helping with the church, although he refuses to enter. He meets the priests on the church steps to give his donation money. Once, when Mama insisted he come in for mass, Mang Pedro joked that lightning would strike the church if he entered. Sometimes he can touch a personal belonging and gain an image. So when Roderick has done something bad, he stays away from Mang Ped's touch.

Mrs. Yoshi and her daughter watch from their corner. Mrs. Yoshi and her daughter are Japanese, but Filipino citizens. The daughter, Mica, is Isabelle's best friend. Mica was born in the Philippines and can speak full Tagalog. It is the most common language of Luzon, our main island, and our official national language among the eighty-seven different dialects. She knows it better than her native Japanese, which she can understand but not speak.

Mr. Yoshi was taken away to an internment camp by the Amerikanos when the Japanese bombed Pearl Harbor. Then, when the Japanese arrived and his camp was liberated, he was killed in the crossfire.

"*Ate,* take this brooch." Mrs. Yoshi holds out a pin to my mother, calling her "big sister." It is a gift her husband gave her a long time ago. This is the second time she has offered. "I have no use for it. I cannot keep it while we are hungry."

"Mama," Mica protests, and buries her face against Mrs. Yoshi's shoulder.

My mother shakes her head. "Yukino, put that away. That is all Mica has left of her father. We have other things we can sell before that."

Mang Selso makes a face. I can see he is getting ready to throw another tantrum. "That is what I am saying. Aling Ana, you must sell something. This blanket here. You are obligated to this family. They have given you shelter. You must give back something in return. We have all contributed. We are all starving." He makes a grab for Aling Ana's blanket, and she kicks his hand away.

"Why don't we send Yukino out? She is Japanese, they will not hurt her. Perhaps she can find us something to eat," Mang Selso's wife insists. "Yukino is the one who is obligated to us all. She must atone for her country's wrongs."

From the start, Mang Selso's wife has not liked the idea of sharing our house with Mrs. Yoshi because she is Japanese.

"What a thing to say!" Ate Lorna frowns angrily at Mang Selso's wife, forcing her to be silent. "Yukino has a right to be here."

"Yes, you should be ashamed." My mother clucks her tongue at Mang Selso's wife. "Sending a woman out alone. I should not have let my Isabelle leave. Now look." Mama's voice cracks. "Maybe they will torture her, as they have done to my Jando. Look at his hands."

I study my broken hands. I hold them out before me, wrapped in thick bandages. I try to bend my thumbs, but the pain shoots through me. Papa sees me and urges me to come close. He takes my hands and places them on my lap and holds them there. My nose begins to run. I think of old Mang Leo, whose toes rotted, forcing the doctors to cut them off.

"Will they cut my fingers like old Mang Leo's toes?"

"No one will cut your fingers," Mama says.

"No one," Papa repeats. "Old Mang Leo had diabetes. Stop your worrying. And enough fighting, everyone. You wish to speak of obligations? I will tell you all a story about obligations: those that are thrust upon us, and those we tie around our own necks. It has to do with a church."

"Ah, yes. And not just any church, the most beautiful of churches. The church of Santa Esmeralda in Blanca Negros. Magnificent, was it not, Carlito?" Mang Selso asks. "But that was before it sank into the ground."

"A church sank into the ground whole? But how did that happen? Was the ground hungry?" Roderick jokes.

"What? Hungry? No." Mang Selso puffs out his chest and dismisses my brother with a wave of his hand.

"I remember that church," Aling Ana says quietly. She is drawing circles in the dirt with a small branch. "That was the church in which the angel came in the form of the dog to test the humility of the parishioners. One day, a young couple was getting married, and in the middle of the ceremony a large she-dog walked in. They all pointed and laughed at her. God had sent the dog to see how high and mighty these people were. When they laughed at her, the dog began to speak, and she stunned all the congregation. She said, 'I wash my hands of you and your vanity,' and the minute she left, the church began to crumble and sink into the ground. Isn't that the story?"

Papa's eyes are dreamy. He is a child again, standing before the church.

"Perhaps that particular story belongs to another church, in another town. Maybe not, maybe all of it is true. But if I am to tell the true story, you must know from the start that the church was merely incidental. A symptom, shall we say, of deeper troubles. Few know what really happened. Most have forgotten and moved on with their lives. The church was never the crux of the story. There is an imbalance here, you see? More focus on the church when, really, the heart of the story lies with Esmeralda Cortez and with her mysterious disappearance. The catalyst of her strange departure was a mere boy of seven, and that boy was me."

~ a cure for happiness

IF I AM TO TELL THE STORY of the church that sank into the ground, we must first begin with the village of Blanca Negros, west of the Chico River Valley, Mountain province. There were secrets in that town, so much anger building underneath the perfect exteriors, the perfect faces, like streams of water criss-crossing in the ground beneath smooth, polished floors and sowing discord in the houses above. So much restlessness hidden by the white virgin beaches, the rich soil and rows of sugar cane. We lived in the most beautiful place on earth, yet it was just a facade. The people were not happy. That was the town I grew up in.

I lived with my father, in the upper room of a decaying house held together by chicken wire in some places, bamboo and rattan in others. It belonged to my aunt, a strange woman who in many ways resembled the house itself. Our room was nothing more than a small crawl space to keep one's old boxes and throwaway items. That was what we were, Father and me, throwaway items.

We lived in that room under a great obligation to my aunt, Father's younger sister, and she reminded us of this at every opportunity. Below us, my aunt and uncle occupied one room with their teenage daughter, Rosalie. In the other room my aunt's in-laws occupied a corner, with Rosalie's brothers, Julio and Eduardo.

I never met my mother and sister; they both died of dengue fever the year I was born. That same year, Father was diagnosed with tuberculosis and I with polio.

My earliest memory is of my hands, raw from working endless days in the bright sun, whether it be in the cane fields, in the fishing boats, or from scrub-bing floors in the wealthier homes. I was never a child.

My only escape was to watch Esmeralda Cortez. She was a great beauty by any standards, and not just that of our little town of Blanca Negros. I once heard a man from Cavite say she was like a ripe plum waiting to be picked. He said that her coloring was at the peak of perfection and that to wait would be a sin because she would begin to fade. Her skin was taut, not too soft, not too tough, he explained. To select her any earlier would have been a disgrace. Any later, and one would miss such an opportune moment. She was ready, he said.

I remember studying her after this man's words. But I could never find anything about her resembling a plum. She had dark hair that fell like a waterfall. Her cheekbones were high and wide, so that when she smiled, her chocolate eyes tilted upward at the ends. She smiled often.

She lived in the house beside ours, and each evening in the violet-and-orange sunset, I could see her clearly from my bedroom window. Our windows were so close together that if we were to sit facing each other, we could place a small wooden plank across our windowsills and pretend to have tea at the same table. But her room was larger than ours. Five steps down placed her into a bigger work area, where she greeted her customers. She always wore a long silk robe of emerald green, cinched at her waist by a matching sash embroidered with fruit trees.

I was only seven then, an ugly boy with unruly curls and fat lips. Often I hurried home as fast as my polio leg would allow. I would leave Bonita beach with its tall thin palm trees and climb upward toward the mountains of abundant green rising hundreds of kilometers high, the airy ferns brushing against my legs, just to watch Esmeralda. I would arrive home, my chest heaving, and pull off my shirt to wipe the white sand and ocean water from my feet.

I would go to Father and quickly give him his cough medicine, then hurry back to my mat, where I could watch her. Her room alone could hold me entranced. She had an oval-shaped table with two chairs where she met with her customers. Behind this, there was a wooden armoire with the two doors thrown open. There were four deep shelves ladened with wonderful bottles. The bottles were labeled with a strip of white paper handwritten in her bold script. There were tall burgundy wine bottles and small, stout cloudy bottles, all capped with cork. The labels all began with the words *Gamót sa,* meaning "Medicine for." There was *Gamót sa regla,* for when a woman is menstruating; *Gamót sa pagod,* herbs to cure exhaustion; *Gamót sa galit,* a potion to fix anger; and *Gamót sa selos,* to cure jealousy, to name a few.

On the bottom shelf, she had copper and silver flasks that were labeled *Kontra para sa,* meaning "To counter."

My favorite was a copper flask with engravings along the rim, though the label confused me: "To counter happiness." Have you heard of such a thing? A cure for happiness. A mixture to make someone sad. I only saw her use this once.

Each evening, I would take out my mat and sit cross-legged as she walked into her room. She pretended never to see me, though she wore the faintest hint of a smile on her lips. Sometimes I swore she actually waited for me. The evenings in our cordillera village were always deliciously hot, with the scent of the white *sampaguita* flowers that grew like flakes of snow around our house.

The heat remained trapped in our valley by the lush jungle-covered mountains of green on either side and the rice terraces like giant steps of velvet jade on the northern end.

I sat enthralled each time she began. First she combed out her long black hair with an ivory comb that reminded me of a fishbone. Twenty strokes on one side, then twenty more on the other. I would pin a scarf to my head and let it fall on both sides of my face and pretend to comb as she did. My cousin Eduardo played his guitar below us during this time. It was as if he quietly serenaded her. If she hummed "Dahil sa Iyo," "Because of You," or "Dandansoy," Eduardo quickly played it. The little birds chirping in the banyan trees joined in every time.

She always lighted three candles as the sky blushed good night to the sun. Then she would take out her scented sticks, traded from a Chinese client. Our rooms would fill with the scents of jasmine, cinnamon, coconut. She kept a gossamer sheet pinned to her window; it was much finer than the coarse ones we had to keep the mosquitoes out. The sheet rippled in the breeze and made her seem all the more a dream to me.

I remember the last week before her disappearance so clearly. I can remember indelibly every customer she prescribed a potion for and every word that was said. That Monday, her week started out so promising. Her first customer made my eyes pop, for it was not often I saw a senator's wife come to our part of town.

The senator's wife was named Aling Sofie; she had two perfect children and a house on the ocean with a private dock for their many boats. I could not imagine what ailment she would have. A sick child, I decided.

I must tell you now, the things I saw and heard were not always for a child to witness. But back then, I never considered myself a child. Someone who has to lie and steal time in order to go to the beach and play with friends is no longer a child.

Aling Sofie seemed embarrassed. Her body was closed in. The tight bun of her hair pulled the corners of her eyes back, giving her skin a painful pretense of youth. Her arms were folded tightly against her chest as she paced the floor. Esmeralda sat with her hands folded on the oval table, next to a turquoise-colored vase filled with pink lotus blossoms. She waited serenely for Aling Sofie to be seated.

"Perhaps this is a mistake." Aling Sofie's brow wrinkled. "I just had nowhere to go. I have heard you are very confidential. I thought—" She lifted her hand and let it fall. All this time she spoke as if to the floor, her eyes not meeting Esmeralda's.

Esmeralda lit a short candle the color of ginger, then poured a cup of tea. "Please, you have come a long way. Have a cup before you go." She extended her slender fingers to the empty chair.

Aling Sofie sat down with a big sigh that rolled onto the table. I think the sound of it surprised even her. "My husband wishes to do things in bed that I cannot—Improper things. I am too old for such things." She laughed nervously and glanced up at Esmeralda. "And for a senator's wife to comply . . . The mother of his children. Preposterous. I have an image to uphold in the community. It is expected of me. He clings to the past, to when we were younger."

Esmeralda stood and took down a small glass container with tiny pieces of tree bark and violet petals floating inside. "Give me your hands."

"Such a pretty concoction," Aling Sofie said, intrigued. She held out her hands.

When the bottle was uncorked, the scent of sunlight and the ocean filled the room. Esmeralda rubbed the lotion onto Aling Sofie's hands and dropped a few petals onto the opened palms. "Mm, I see . . ." Esmeralda nodded thoughtfully, then closed her eyes.

"What, what is it?" Aling Sofie searched her own hand as if these things would reveal themselves to her.

"I see you with your hair long and flowing. You wore your hair this way when you were younger?"

"Yes, yes." Aling Sofie became excited.

Esmeralda frowned. "No, no. Perhaps I have called the wrong image. That girl could not be you."

"Oh, but it is. Look, see?" Aling Sofie's fingers fluttered quickly behind her head, and her dark hair fell about her like a cloud. The face relaxed.

"Ahh, of course. It was you, after all. Here." Esmeralda plucked a lavender orchid from one of her bowls on the table. "Let us complete the picture, so that I have a better vision." She placed the orchid behind Aling Sofie's ear, then leaned back with a look of surprise. "Why, it is as if ten years have dropped from your shoulders. Why is it you no longer wear your hair this way?"

"Well, it is so . . ."

"Lovely," Esmeralda finished. "See?" She placed a small wooden mirror in Aling Sofie's hands. The frame was painted blue with clouds on the top and vines around the edges. I had seen that mirror many times. I called it the dream mirror.

Aling Sofie's eyes grew wistful, and a small smile teased the corners of her lips. She brought one of her wrists to her nose. "Such a sweet fragrance."

"These things your husband wishes you to do?" Esmeralda prompted.

Aling Sofie's face puckered immediately, as if she had tasted a dried prune. "I feel silly. I cannot . . ." She paused. "He wishes me to dance, to undress myself, to wear feathers. To tickle him with *puca* shells."

"Ah, things you've never done before. So he suddenly changed, wanted these extravagant things? Things only a beautiful wild temptress would think of. Where did he get such ideas?"

"Well . . ." Aling Sofie's face grew red. Her eyes looked mischievously into the candle flickering on the table. "Still, it would not be proper. A woman of my standing in the community. It is not acceptable."

"I see, you have a great dilemma. But one easily cured."

"Yes?" Aling Sofie asked.

Esmeralda stood and took down a very dusty bottle. The bottle had a brass stopper with two snakes rising up intertwined. She eyed Aling Sofie, then blew off the dust. "I must have your word. You must not let it be known that I have this. It will ruin everything. Too many women would want it. Ahh, perhaps I am being reckless, let us try something else." Esmeralda put the bottle back on the shelf.

"No. How much?" Aling Sofie stood, her chair falling back at the force of her desire.

"A small donation, but only after your first use of it. I am not allowed to keep the money if it does not work. And I have not used this since . . . well. Since the first woman died."

Aling Sofie pulled back the money she held in her outstretched hand. "A woman died from this?"

Esmeralda threw back her luxurious hair and laughed. "Oh no, no. Quite the opposite. A woman *lived* because of this. Oh, how she lived. This potion belonged to Lualhatte and only to her. While she lived I could not allow another woman to use it. It is that way with these things; only one person can use it."

"Lualhatte Cordoba? The descendant of the great Chief Kabo? They say she could seduce any man, even up to her death at the age of one hundred and two last year."

Esmeralda's lids lowered knowingly.

"No." Aling Sofie's eyes watched the bottle hungrily. "At that age she was still . . ." She paused. "Active?"

"Candle wax and rambutan were her bedroom tools," Esmeralda whispered, winking at the name of the egg-shaped fruit with reddish hairy skin.

"Oh my." Aling Sofie giggled.

"Your feathers and *puca* shells no longer sound so bad, hah?"

"Does this potion have any adverse effects?" Aling Sofie asked, but I could see that this was merely a formality. Her eyes had already bought the potion.

"Its only drawback is if used too much, it can make the woman a little bit, well, overly . . . sexed," Esmeralda whispered.

Aling Sofie shook her head to throw back her hair, in imitation of Esmeralda. She giggled. Already her voice was deeper in tone, her eyes half-closed.

"This bottle was found buried in a cave, the final resting place of a queen, whose name I am not allowed to speak. This queen, she was a legendary temptress.

"This potion allows the user to change her identity in private, to draw on the charms of this queen. But, as I said, one word to anyone that you have this in your possession and I will no longer be allowed to give it to you. I have your word of silence?" At Aling Sofie's nod, Esmeralda took a few drops from the bottle into a very tiny vial and gave it to her.

Aling Sofie took out a few pesos. "I know you said pay later, but this is just for your time. Take it." She winked at Esmeralda and then left the house. I watched as Aling Sofie descended the steps with light feet. She stopped at the bottom of the stairs and pulled her hair up into a loose bun. A secret smile grew on her lips, her hips swayed, and her hands swung freely at her side.

Esmeralda waited until Aling Sofie disappeared around a corner, then she took the snake bottle, added a few more purple petals and plain water from a pitcher. She dipped her hand in a tin filled with powder, sprinkled it on the bottle to give it a dusty effect, then replaced it at the back of her shelf.

After Aling Sofie, a gambling man arrived. I had seen him before, always dressed in such fine woman-catching attire. He wore wide-brimmed straw hats and polished black Western shoes. He pulled out the chair and sat down before being asked. He lit a big cigar that smoked up the room and caused my eyes to water even at my hidden distance.

"I want a cure for my wife's petty jealousies. They cause her to commit crimes against my mistresses." He puffed big circles of smoke as he talked.

"Go on," Esmeralda answered, poised as ever.

"She cannot control herself. Perhaps something to calm the nerves, eh? Surely you have something of this kind in one of your lovely bottles, eh, *maganda?*" The man asked, calling her beautiful. "My wife is very good with dramatics. She should have joined the theater, or the circus." The man slapped the table, causing Esmeralda's candle to flicker and the flower bowl to tip. He caught the bowl, frowning at it. "But truthfully, I am worried about her. I am not without heart. I cannot look aside as my poor wife is in such apparent misery. Oh, you should see her. She pulls out her hair. She carries on so. Each time we pass these women in the streets she wants to scratch their eyes out and boil them for my dinner. She has told me this! Can you imagine the embarrassment these scenes cost me? One of my mistresses has already threatened to stop seeing me."

Esmeralda received many customers like this man, always thinking the cure lay in the curing of others, never themselves. She gave him a bottle of soothing oils, then instructed him to send his wife over. The woman came in bent over like a fragile tree broken from a strong northern wind. Do you know, that woman's spine began to grow after each visit? Within days she stood straight and tall like a bamboo pole.

The man returned three days later demanding his money back. He claimed the sessions had not cured her at all; instead they had made his wife crazy. She defied his every command, until finally he'd come home to a note one day that said simply, "You are not worth one more grain of my strength, not one more tear from my eye. I am leaving you."

There were many others. A Swedish surgeon with clumsy hands and a fear of the dark. A young girl who had not spoken since her mother had confessed to being in love with the neighbor's wife. A woman who wanted her daughter to become an opera singer, where obviously the girl had no talent, but the mother, ahh, what a voice. They all came secretly disguised in hooded coats or high collars with big hats.

It was around closing time one evening when one of the nuns visited Esmeralda. It was Sister Mildred, the one who had discovered her as an infant in the church garden. In fact, it was just about the time the opera hopeful and her mother had departed. Sister Mildred moved aside to let the two women pass, then gave Esmeralda a daunting look.

"Ah, Esmeralda, you play with their hopes and fears. Things they should be confessing only to Padre Ramirez. He is the only one with a direct line to God." She made the sign of the cross when she said this. "This is a dangerous thing you do."

"I merely give them freedom to be themselves. I encourage them to speak their deepest desires." Esmeralda shrugged as she put away her jars.

"Are you listening to yourself? You speak as if you were chosen by the Almighty Himself. A kind of saint, is that what you are?" Sister Mildred picked off a piece of lint from her dark robe and smoothed the fabric before placing her pale hands on the table. "Well, let me tell you now, you are not. Would a saint be left on the church doorsteps unwanted? A product of the deepest of sins, I am certain.

"Haven't I told you to pray for forgiveness? For yourself, and especially for your parents, who I am sure tried to do right by you. You have a responsibility to correct their wrong. It was not a mistake that they left you on the church doorstep. Their intent was obvious; they wanted you to live a life of holiness. Nor is it a mistake that I found you. I am to be your teacher in this life. Your life was entrusted to me. Therefore, as I have told you countless times, you have an obligation to redeem yourself and your parents' souls by giving your life to the church. Now then, have you said your rosary for the evening?"

"No, sister." Esmeralda bowed her head.

"Sin clings strongly to you. Lend me some of your lotion. My hands grow dry from this weather. Not that one, the other. The one that smells of flowers. Now let us pray."

I fell asleep listening to their "Hail Mary, full of grace . . ." and the responding "Holy Mary, mother of God" echoed in my dreams.

AND NOW I must tell you about Sister Mildred, for as I said, it was she who found Esmeralda as an infant in the church garden. The church took the baby in, of course. It was a gift from God. And not one person questioned who the mother could be. They decided that it must have been a passing traveler. They never questioned the extra weight that Sister Mildred lost soon after Esmeralda was found. And who would notice any weight at all? Those hideous gowns covered so much of their bodies, and the long wooden crucifixes swung menacingly before them, to chase the curious eyes away. Not one person grasped the reason for Sister Mildred's brooding moods, how she would live between moments of serene reverence and hellish despair. The infant Esmeralda eclipsed all that surrounded them.

THAT EVENING AFTER all her customers had come and gone, I woke in time to see her last visitor. Her lover arrived. He was tall for a Filipino. His Spanish blood came through in his aquiline nose and languid strides. He was the Golden Gloves boxing champion of Blanca Negros, and his name was Tirso Batungbakal. I had seen him fight in the local boxing rings many times. He fought like a mountain lion, swift and ruthless. He was always immaculately dressed. Linen pants and loose cotton shirts with the sleeves rolled up were his usual attire. He never came without a gift, and they were always wrapped with ribbons. I once saw her open a delicate box that opened to reveal a smaller box, and on until she found a small white gold ring engraved with vines and one beautiful pearl. Another time he brought a gilded cage with two yellow birds that nestled close to each other.

That night they talked of the house they would live in with their children. "And how many children shall we have?" Esmeralda asked, combing her slender fingers through his hair.

"As many as you want. A dozen," he proclaimed.

"A dozen? Tirso, have pity. Do you know what I would look like after that many babies?" She laughed.

"Beautiful. Always beautiful," he replied. "We could live in Bohol, where you could gaze all day at the chocolate hills. Or Guimaras, where you can watch them repeat the crucifixion of our Lord. In Guimaras, there is the fragrant scent of the mango trees you adore so much. What about Cavite? We can live beneath the craters of the Taal volcano. What do you think?"

"I think I would follow you anywhere," she answered, slicing a large guava. She always fed her lover such fruits, holding her hands delicately as if in dance. He caught her hands and kissed the insides of her wrists as she laughed. I blushed. He got up and drew the shades. And the guitar continued to play long into the night.

But what of the church? Well, I am getting to that, but do not be led astray. It was only a product of what I am about to tell you. The church was unlike any you would ever imagine. It was not the typical Spanish design, or even of Filipino design. It was as if a cave had risen from the ground. The church was called Santa Esmeralda, her namesake, and like Esmeralda, it was beautiful and wholly wild and unexplainable. It was said to have been made during a volcanic eruption, though from which of our thirty-seven volcanoes, I could not tell you. I know only that it was charred black on the outside. It stood thirty feet high, with stone carvings inside that depicted the Resurrection and the Holy Trinity.

It went fifteen feet into the ground, and along through the sides was the constant sound of running water from an underground spring. Three large holes were bored into it during the Spanish time between the 1500s and the 1890s, and later these holes were set with stained glass the color of jewels. I remember the deep amber and green of one of the glasses, for it was broken in the corner during one of our monsoons. The parishioners of Blanca Negros were very proud of this church. They strutted and talked to foreigners as if they had built the church themselves. "Yes, isn't it lovely? There is no other like it."

~

THE LAST TUESDAY before her disappearance, I was serving as altar boy. This was, of course, at my father's urgings. I had to wear the brown Franciscan robes, with the hooded cowl necks and the white ropes tied around my waist. Padre Ramirez insisted on an extra night of mass before Sundays so that the parishioners would not become lost in sin before the Sabbath.

I cannot tell you how humiliating it was for a young boy to be seen wearing a dress, and an ugly one at that. My aunt and uncle would sit in the front pews. My cousins would point and snicker at me. Before mass, I would pick one of the statues of the saints to pray to, Santa Teresa or Santa Lucia, and drop a coin in one of the jars as an offering to pray for the souls of my mother and sister. Esmeralda became to me like part of the altar, and the statues of the saints, and the image of the Virgin Mary.

The senator's wife was present that evening, wearing a smug smile on her lips. The senator was in extremely jovial spirits. In fact, half the church consisted of Esmeralda's customers. You would think, then, wouldn't you, that Esmeralda would be among friends? But she wasn't. Do you know that not one of them acknowledged her presence? Not even so much as a nod that strangers give in passing. They did not acknowledge her, for to do so would announce to everyone that they were her customers, and this, of course, would open the door to every sort of speculation.

Esmeralda sat alone during prayer time, but when it came time to sing in the choir, she was the center of attention. The other singers would gather around her. I would watch her the entire time. It was like this for every mass.

We went straight home after mass. I was so hungry and excited at the prospect of my aunt's cooking. Every other day my father and I were left to fend for ourselves, but on Tuesdays, while she was still filled with the grace of prayer, my aunt invited us downstairs to eat. I remember my stomach rumbled so loudly on the walk home that my aunt turned and glared at me.

"Carlito, go find yourself some granadas fruit. Your stomach talked throughout the entire mass. It was so embarrassing. Hurry home and help your father prepare for dinner. Remember, you are his only child, the only one to care for him as he gets old. It is your duty, and as you know, he is not strong." This was the future I had to look forward to. My aunt and uncle had three children who would care for them someday. There was only me for my father.

"Yes, Auntie," I said, and hurried home. I did not get much farther ahead than the rest of them. My right leg was already crippled from polio. The best I could accomplish was a steady hobble. Nor did I find any pomegranate fruits. There was really nothing to do in terms of getting Papa ready for dinner. A fresh shirt and trousers: I had readied these items the night before. The sound of my leg dragging was what bothered her. Her left eye blinked and twitched whenever another parishioner came over to talk. My aunt could not concentrate on the conversation; the scraping of my shoe against the dirt set her face twitching in a climactic symphony of blinks and jerks until she grew frustrated and ordered me to hurry home.

As soon as I reached the door to the house, I stomped my feet loudly and lit a candle to scare away the roaches. As usual, they were holding a congregation in the middle of the kitchen floor and scurried away with their meager pieces of food. I went to the cabinets where I knew the silverware was, and once again I alerted them by knocking on the drawer before I opened it. The roaches scrambled out as soon as I pulled open the handle. One was brave enough to jump on my arm. I took out the silverware and began to lay the pieces on the table. That was my chore every Tuesday evening.

At my aunt's dinners, I was not allowed to sit in the good seats. These were wooden chairs with velvet cushions. She had acquired four of them from mah-jongg winnings. She had her eye on the remaining two at the town shop to complete her set. My aunt, in all her poverty, was obsessed with gambling. She always lived in the future. "When I win the big jackpot you will see," her sentences always began. She wanted so badly to replicate the lives of the rich parishioners at church. She had hungry eyes for every detail of clothing, every handkerchief, or every earring they wore. She had numerous items at the various shops in town that were soon to be paid off. She paid them in installments. A gaudy ring, a tapestried lounge chair, a bureau made of cherrywood, all of the items incongruous to her meager clothing, her meager house. It never struck her that the large ring could never help her achieve a semblance of wealth, when her sandals were worn and obviously resoled. These things saddened me beyond explanation.

For dinner, I borrowed two stools from my aunt for Father and me. If I stood anywhere near her precious chairs, even if I did not intend to sit in them, she would shove me aside. That was how it was that night. I was peering over the blur of arms and dishes being placed on the table, when my aunt elbowed me in the neck.

"Carlito, here, here. Sit at the end, so that you can attend to your father. Oh, did I hurt you? You are always in the way." She laughed.

She made pancit, the clear noodles, with slices of chicken and onions, and lumpia, the wrapped rolls of ground beef and potatoes, with sprinkles of carrots and raisins to offset the spices. This was a little more elaborate than her usual fare, to celebrate my cousin Julio's good grades in school.

My father and I each received one lumpia and a spoon portion of pancit noodles. My cousins received heaping portions.

"In case you finish," my aunt said, smiling, "there is always more on the table."

But you see, there was not always more, because any glance, any look, toward the extra food would warrant another glare from my aunt, and I already felt unwelcome as it was. Sometimes she surprised us and offered more, but these times were rare and almost always when something had gone wrong in the cooking of the meal. When I was near to finishing, my eyes began to drift toward the platter in the middle of the table.

My aunt was like a watchdog. "Carlito," she barked, "finish your food before it grows cold, then tend to your chores." I looked to Father, willing him to say something, but he quietly ate his food. My stomach growled, irritated at the teasing I had given it. I willed my father to find his voice, to speak up. My eyes burned, urging him silently to ask for more food for the both of us. He was her older brother after all, but he never looked up from his plate. I became a keeper of secrets, a silent witness to my father's humiliation. Finally, when I could stand it no more, I had one of my few moments of bravery, when my hunger overcame my aunt's wrath.

I asked, "*Tita*, could I have another helping?"

She smiled frightfully at me. "Too much food makes one lazy, Carlito."

I saw her game then; I tasted its bitter rules. "Is that why you take a siesta each afternoon?"

There was not even time to move out of the way. Her chair scraped loudly and she stood, grabbing me by my ear. "How dare you, after I have fed you this wonderful meal! You are an unruly child, Carlito. Do you know what that means?" my aunt asked.

I shook my head.

"It means you do the opposite of what good people tell you to. We are your guardian angels." She put a hand to her chest. "You should listen to us. Yet you have a devil watching over your shoulder. A deeveel, whispering to you."

I looked over my shoulder in terror. Throughout this my father sat with his head bowed as my aunt raged on.

" 'Do that, Carlito.' 'Say this, Carlito.' That is what the devil whispers to you," she spoke in a fury. "You should see my friend Sanctisimma Bulaklak's boy. So well behaved, his *yaya* brought him up with discipline. Too bad your papa cannot afford a *yaya*. If you had one, she would watch over you like a mother hen. She would not allow such abuses from a smart-mouth such as yourself."

I knew her friend Sanctisimma Bulaklak's boy; he was my age, a simpering, pale-faced boy with a constant runny nose. He was not allowed to play in the dirt or to run too fast. He sat with his legs crossed and his hands folded. I saw him often being led by his *yaya* through the market. They dressed the boy like an old man, wearing a Western-style shirt and bow tie, in our tropical heat. But in my aunt's eyes, he was the Santo Niño, the infant Jesus himself.

His *yaya* was a young woman who went to school in the neighboring village. A *yaya*, as I understood it then, was a governess who gave special privileges.

"Do you know what his *yaya* does if he is bad?" My aunt was in a rage now.

I thought quickly of the last time I saw the boy's *yaya*. I had come to ask if he wanted to come play, we needed an extra person in our game of hide-and-seek. The boy and his mother, Sanctisimma, were not home, but the *yaya* was, with Mr. Bulaklak's face deep in her unbuttoned blouse, and I said the first thing that came to my mind. "Feed Mr. Bulaklak milk?"

"What?" My aunt chased me out of the house, her fingers curved like talons and her face more ferocious than any demon I could ever imagine.

I was so hungry when I left that I ran over to the San Lupe house. They were a wealthy family that lived a kilometer away. I knew an older woman, one of the housekeepers, and if I came at the right time, she would bring leftovers for me and for Father. I was lucky that night. Aling Patricia was sweeping near the back door when I arrived.

"Oh, Carlito. Your aunt did not give you a second helping again?" She clucked her tongue. "Tsk, tsk. That woman. Oh, come. The missus did not finish her pie, and I think there are plenty of empanadas to bring home to your father."

"Thank you, Aling Pat." I smiled.

"You wait here," she instructed.

I was not waiting more than two minutes when a side door opened and I saw him. I saw Esmeralda's lover, Tirso. He strolled out with a cigar in his mouth and a woman on his arm. They were followed by two other people, and they chatted as they strolled away from the garden. The woman turned quickly so that her back was to me. I did not have time to stare at her face, but I knew it was not Esmeralda. For one thing, the woman's hands were pale and she was wider around the hips, and when she turned sideways, her chest was flat like my straw mat.

"Carl, Carlito, Carlos," Aling Pat called. She came and nudged me with her shoulder. Her hands were full, with fruits and two baskets of steaming food. "Oh, I will need the baskets back tomorrow. I asked the missus, and she said she was going to throw the food away. Here, there is lechón and gingered beef in there. Ha?" She grinned. "You will have a feast tonight."

"Thank you, Aling Pat." I smiled. "Who are those people?"

"*Ha, sino?*" She squinted. "Well, you know Tirso Batungbakal, and that is his lady friend, Catalina Marquez. They are to be engaged soon. Then there is Cory Carvajal and Dennis Oberes; you have seen them before, have you not? They are friends of the San Lupe children. *Hoy*. Hurry home. Your food will spoil."

I thanked her and pretended to walk toward home. As soon as she went back into the house, I went in pursuit of Tirso's group. I was standing in the garden, searching for which path they took, when they walked up behind me, too fast for me to hide. To my horror, the woman was now entangled with Tirso. Her arms were wrapped around his neck like a serpent, and Tirso was not struggling. I was in such a state of shock that I could not move out of the way, and they bumped into me. Tirso looked down with a frown, and then I saw the recognition in his eyes. He knew my family well from all his visits to Esmeralda's house. Whenever my father sat on the front porch, Tirso would hold up a hand in greeting. I could see he wanted to say something to me, but I turned, stumbling, and hurried home. All the way home I kept wondering how I was going to tell Esmeralda that her lover had betrayed her.

I arrived home and hurried to my room. Father was fast asleep. I had gained enough confidence to knock on Esmeralda's door. But I had forgotten about her customers. As I glanced through my window into hers, I saw that I would have to wait. Esmeralda's first one of the evening was already seated at the table. A rich woman, I could tell by her clothes and her simple strand of pearls, which she looped nervously around her long fingers.

I sat down and opened the basket of hot food. I would make Father a plate just as soon as I spoke to Esmeralda. The tenderness of the beef, with the sweetness of the onions, thin slices of ginger, and green peppers, exploded in my mouth. I shivered at all the flavors assaulting me.

Her patron's voice was timid, embarrassed. "I need a cure, a cure for happiness. I have too much of it. It scares me."

"But people search all their lives for this. What has caused you to feel you are undeserving of it?" Esmeralda's voice was tender. She had a way of speaking, coaxing the hurt out of someone's heart.

"Undeserving?" The woman's voice faltered, shaking the hard edges from it. "I had never thought of it that way. Undeserving. I have lived all my life with things given to me. This ring you see? My grandmother's. The money for these clothes? My father owns many trade ships, to carry cargo from one port to another. It grows each day, bigger and bigger, this business, until I feel it will swallow me. I have never known a day of unhappiness, but Padre Ramirez says that someday it will come and I must prepare myself. This terrifies me, for I've never experienced one moment of hardship. What will it be like? I cannot stand the waiting any longer."

"Padre Ramirez said this to you?" Esmeralda asked in astonishment.

"Yes, the day my father and he fought. Father refused to increase his donations to the church, and in passing the padre said to me; 'Ah, Elena, you are so pure, so protected. I am sorry you had to hear such things.' It was as if he had read into my most troubling thoughts. He said it sadly, as if it were a bad thing. He said, 'You have had too much happiness in your life. Poor child, what will happen to you when the bad things come?' I thought nothing of it at the time, but slowly the thought has crept into my mind, piercing my heart like a ribbon of thorns. I feel I can no longer breathe.

"It came slowly at first, a simple question. I had never known unhappiness, what would it be like? The next time I saw the padre was during confession. I asked him what he had meant by that remark of having too much happiness. He sighed and said, 'Your jubilation elevates you to the highest clouds. But what will the fall be like? For surely everyone falls.' "

Esmeralda leaned forward and took the woman's hands. "The padre is preoccupied with humility. It is his calling in life to be humble, the lowest of the ladder. Surely you have heard it said, 'The meek shall inherit the earth,' 'The last shall be the first'? These are the padre's teachings. You come from different arenas. He must not have realized that he was frightening you. Have you not scraped your knee or been spanked for misbehaving? Those are bad things. We all live through them. You have experienced bad things, Elena."

"No, those things have never happened to me," Elena whispered, her eyes in agony. "You see?"

Esmeralda shook her head. "Still, why anticipate bad things? We all experience these things, both the rich and the poor."

Elena snatched her hands away and placed them on the table to steady herself. "I never talk to the poor. They frighten me with their hungry eyes. They live just outside our house, just below the rise. Every day they watch me as I step in and out of our carriage, when I go to the market. It's as if they are waiting for me to fall. I do not want to become like them; what a terrible way to live. I have no friends. No true friends, whom I can confide in. Please, Esmeralda, have you not some potion, some prayer, that would end all my happiness? Something that would sprinkle a few raindrops of bad luck, to soften my fall?"

Esmeralda sighed. "Elena, there is nothing coming your way that you cannot bear up to. But if it is an immediate cure you want, if you are brave enough to face the bad luck all together, then I have a cure for your happiness. There is a flower that blooms only in Ilalim. You must pick this flower each day, and each day you must ask a different person for water to put in this cup. Tell them it is water for the flower. You will have no trouble finding the flower, for it blooms in abundance there." Esmeralda took down a copper bottle engraved with words in a language I did not recognize. It was labeled *Kontra sa kaligayahan,* "To counter happiness."

"But the town of Ilalim is full of . . ." Elena paused.

"Yes, the poor. And who has more bad luck than they? By giving you their water, they will transfer some of their bad luck onto you. And it shall bloom like the flower you choose. But first . . ." Esmeralda held up her finger and took down a matching copper flask. She held it up to the ceiling and closed her eyes for a moment in prayer, then placed a few drops of red liquid from the bottle into the cup. She peered up at Elena. "Truly, this is what you wish? For bad luck? A cure for your blessings?"

"Oh yes." Elena let out a big sigh, clasping her hands together excitedly. "I do wish it, with all my soul."

"Then go, and remember what I said. Only from Ilalim, and water only from the home of a town person."

Ahh, she was so clever, Esmeralda. That woman was forced each day to speak to what she feared most. Soon these people were inviting her into their homes, and they no longer became terrifying to her. They became her friends. The cure for her happiness was not bad luck, but to make her happier inside.

Esmeralda had a second visitor soon after the scared woman, so I was forced to wait. I wanted to run in and tell her what I had witnessed at the San Lupe house, how I had seen her Tirso and this other woman. But again, I had to sit and wait, and with my confidence and the food I brought home, both emptied of half its contents. When I looked down into the pot of gingered beef, I saw that I had only one slice left for my father. I got up to give him the full plate of roasted lechón. But there was no time. I had to sit back down again with a plate of hot lechón on my lap as her next visitor entered.

At first her room seemed eclipsed in blackness, but I realized it was just the robe of Padre Ramirez. The candles wavered violently as his robe cut through the stillness of the evening air. He came in, and though he could not know I was in the next window, I stood to attention. His presence had that effect on me.

"You have not gone to confession in three days, my child." It was odd for me to hear him call her "child," for the padre was only a few years older.

"Yes, Father, I apologize, but my customers have doubled in the last few months. I think perhaps it is the cooler part of the dry season. Many ailments seem to arise this time of year."

He smiled at her bottles with displeasure. "So Sister Mildred is right, you have been entertaining my parishioners again. You have been leading them astray."

"I merely listen to their troubles, Father."

"That is my job."

"Yes, Father."

He took her hand, startling her. "Esmeralda, I do not mind you giving them cures for their back pains, or their stomach troubles, but when you begin to absolve them of their guilt by telling them they have done nothing wrong, you go too far. We have discussed this before, have we not?"

"Yes, Father."

"Is it your customers or Tirso Batungbakal who consumes your time?" The padre's mouth was smiling, but his eyes narrowed. I remember thinking at that moment, if one were to cover his smiling mouth, he would seem very angry.

"Tirso does not take up all my time." She lowered her eyes.

"Esmeralda, how many times must Sister Mildred and I stress to you that he is from a different world? You see how you enjoy helping people? Your calling is with the church, beside me. The church took you in when you had no home. You owe them your life. This Tirso is a bad influence. I see no future for the two of you."

"A girl can still dream, Father." She blushed with her own secret beliefs.

"Think on what I have said. Give it time to penetrate your mind. Now, I am here to ask for some medicine for my arthritis. That heating lotion you carry?"

"Yes, of course." Esmeralda stood to grab a simple bottle from her bureau. "Shall I apply it to your hands, Father?"

"Yes, that would please me." The padre held out his hand. On his ring finger he wore a heavy gold band, a gift from one of the parishioners.

Esmeralda heated one of her bottles over a small flame, then rubbed the ointment onto the padre's hands. Her ministrations must have worked miracles, for his fingers were always smooth and never once did I see him in agony from his arthritis. Why, his fingers were so nimble that he was able to play the organ in church.

"Think seriously on this matter, Esmeralda. There is something spiritual within you. That is why people gravitate toward us. They need guidance. Now, if you were to spend your powers on more worthwhile occupations . . ." His voice drifted. "Why, with you by my side, we would be unstoppable."

"Unstoppable, Father?"

"Take, for instance, this morning. Mrs. Concepcion confessed to stealing her husband's money for gambling. Her winnings she saves up, for the time she is to run away with her lover."

"Padre, really. Are confessions not supposed to be a private matter?"

"Ah yes, perhaps I become overzealous. But these are things we could discuss together at length. I value your thoughts on these matters. Drop this playing at witch doctor. You waste your time, and theirs. You distract my people from their prayers. How can one concentrate?" His last words were said with such fervor, he had to pause and fan himself.

Esmeralda was startled by his words. She stared at her hands.

The padre cleared his throat. He straightened his robe. "At times, my dear, I may seem too harsh with you, but I only wish you good things. You were made to serve the church. It is not a dishonorable thing, to serve God."

"But, Father, some people prefer to worship the Lord in private."

"Sinners! Why else would they hide in the dark? These people must be guided. They do not know any better. Look at yourself. My child, you may have good intentions, but do you really think you are helping people? You lead them to depend on you, when they should be coming to me. I am schooled in these matters. Their donations to you could be indulgences given to the church."

Esmeralda bowed her head. "I give half to the church and the other half to replenish my supplies, to buy my food, my clothes."

"Only half. You see how sin clings to you?" The padre looked deep into her eyes, and for a moment I forgot he was a priest. For a second, he appeared only as a man in love with a woman he could not have.

"Yes, Father. I shall try to give more."

AFTER THE PADRE left, I tried to regain my earlier confidence. It took great effort. I found myself finishing the entire plate of steaming lechón for strength. I watched as Esmeralda took out a pen and paper. Each time she smiled to herself, I thought, Yes, go tell her now. A simple frown, even when she dropped her pen, would crumple my fortitude. What finally convinced me was a glance down the street. I could see Tirso at the bottom of our winding hill. He would be at her door in a matter of minutes. I threw myself from my seat and rushed to her door. She opened it before I could knock. She must've heard my footsteps and thought I was Tirso.

"Carlos. What a pleasure it is to see you. Come in."

I nodded, glancing up at her, but I was so overcome by her presence that I could only stare at her leather slippers and how they encased her tanned feet. It was a few seconds later that I noticed I had the sweet sarsa sauce smeared across my chin. I wiped it away hastily as she led me to her table. I looked with fascination through her window into mine. I turned my head and stared in wonder at her bottles.

"I have been longing to speak to you, Carlos. Have some tea." She pushed a small stone cup to me.

The cup was smooth and warm. It was the color of pale amber, with cracked lines running through the exterior. I chanced a glance from the cup to her. Her smile made my eyes water. This was a silly reaction, I know, but I was so happy to be there. I looked like an idiot with my awkward fumblings.

"There is a certain matter I wanted to speak to you of, Carlos, that of your father."

I was surprised at her words and momentarily forgot my own.

"He appears to be very sick, yet I never hear him cough or cry out in pain. Are the doctors certain it is tuberculosis?"

I nodded, still unable to speak.

"And he has had this symptom since your mother passed away?"

"And sister," I croaked.

"Ahh, and sister." She nodded. "And you, brave boy, have taken on the role of father, and he of child."

I looked at her, and my mind raced, trying to grasp what she was saying, not understanding but knowing, just knowing, there was a great truth in the words that skimmed past my head.

"Has he always been this sad?"

"Yes," I answered, feeling a fragment of weight break off in my telling of it.

"And you, such a great burden to carry. Have you never told your father how tired you are?"

"I need to tell you something," I said, blocking her line of questioning. It was making my stomach swoon.

"Of course, but let me say these few more things. Do you not wish to play like the other children? Do you ever wish that your father would leave his bed?"

"Yes, but he is so sick." My voice shook. It surprised me, how strained my throat felt.

"Then you must tell him, Carlito. How will he ever get better, if no one needs him to?"

"I cannot tell him that. He would spank me." I don't know why I said those words. My father never spanked me. "I saw Tirso today," I blurted.

"Did you?" Her eyes shone with affection.

"Yes, he was with another woman. I came to tell you they were holding hands, at the San Lupe house. I thought you should know. They are getting married," I finished, gasping for breath.

She did not seem in shock. "Tirso must attend many functions because of his family's social circles. In these functions he must escort young women. It is difficult to explain, but—"

She never finished her words. There was a knock on the door. Tirso strode in. He had in his hands two boxes wrapped in pale blue, with yellow ribbons. He was smiling so honestly with affection for her that my conclusions wavered. His expression changed when he saw me.

Esmeralda stood behind me and placed her hands on my shoulders. "Tirso, you know Carlito. He lives next door."

"Yes," Tirso began. "Carlito, I wanted to ask you—"

"I must give my father his medicine. Thank you, Miss Esmeralda." I scrambled out of my seat and hobbled out the door before they could speak any more.

Esmeralda called out, "Come visit again, Carlos."

I went straight to my room to listen to what they said next.

"I saw him today at the San Lupe gathering," Tirso began. He laid her presents carefully on her wooden table.

"Yes, he told me."

"I was with Catalina Marquez. I was her escort." Tirso's voice was urgent.

"Yes, that is what I tried to tell him."

"She means nothing to me, Esmeralda. I do these things for my parents. You know that."

"Of course I do."

And that was that. She was so blind with her love for him. What I said to her was already forgotten, but what she said to me, about my father, was like a little seed. I paid no attention to it at first. What was foremost on my mind was that I save her from any lies. I did not realize until then how pressing it was that she find out the truth about Tirso, that I find out the truth. It could have been as he said, escorting a woman from his social circle for his parents' benefit. Maybe I was the one conjuring things in my head. My aunt had accused me of this often enough. So I went to the only person I could think of to clear the situation. I went in search of Catalina Marquez.

THAT TUESDAY EVENING was already long in years. The occupants of our house were quickly falling off to sleep, yet I felt an urgency. Looking back now, I can see that I was frantically setting in motion what I feared most. I was setting in motion all the reasons for Esmeralda's disappearance. But how could I know this? I only knew that I could not bear to sit and listen to Tirso's fraudulent voice and Esmeralda's quiet murmurings.

Catalina's home was near the San Lupe house. I acquired this information in the guise of messenger boy. I went into town, to a tavern I knew. I asked the room in general where the Marquez home was. In the corner, a large man was hovering over a smaller man. They appeared to be quarreling over a debt. The smaller man appeared very frightened. This larger man turned at my mention of the Marquez name and asked, "Who needs to know?"

"I do, sir. I have a message for her."

"Well, why did you not say? I have business with her father. Give me the message."

"I cannot. It is only for her ears."

The man surveyed me, picking his teeth with a toothpick and tasting his finds with a grotesque smacking of his lips. I thought if I stood there any longer, I would watch the man regurgitate his entire dinner from his teeth and eat it again. "What, you wish to ride with me, then?"

"No, if you give me directions, I can—"

"Arrive after everyone has fallen asleep. What kind of message, boy?"

"An important one," I answered, watching his eyes as they measured my worth.

"Let us hope you do not waste her time. My carriage is outside. Tell Pancho I am coming and that you ride with us."

We rode in silence, I with my hands grasping the sides of the coach as it bumped at a furious speed, and the big man laughing every now and then at my constant adjustments.

And that was how I arrived at Catalina Marquez's, by way of luxury coach. I followed the big man, whose name I soon discovered was Gabriel.

Gabriel lumbered into the room. "Tell the Catalina there is a messenger boy here," he boomed to the servant. "And Arturo, do not try to uncover his secret," he warned the servant. "It is only for the mistress's ears."

Arturo inclined his head.

Gabriel turned to me and said loudly, "There you are, boy. Give the lady her secret message, then." He laughed out loud as he walked away, turning back to survey me a couple of times, only to laugh to himself again. He disappeared into the sea of elegantly dressed people.

The house was filled with guests; apparently these people kept different hours than at our house. Each room was lit with tall scented candles. Bottles of wine and food were laid out on tables.

"Come . . ." The servant gestured with a wave. "What is it you need to tell the miss?"

"I promised to tell only her," I replied solemnly. He seemed annoyed by my response but led me farther, in his tightly gaited stride. I tried to keep up and nearly tripped over my own leg. As we walked I eyed the grand portraits that lined the carpeted halls. The plush cushioned rugs engulfed my sandaled feet in blessed silence. I was led to a second floor, crowded the same as the first, only with younger guests.

We paused at the top of the stairs until Catalina acknowledged us. She was seated at one end of the room, smoking a cigarette, a glass of red wine in her pale hand. She wore a turquoise gown that clung to her flat chest. She nodded at Arturo, and he approached her. She leaned back as he explained my visit. She peered over his shoulder at me, then dismissed Arturo with a wave of her cigarette. He walked back to me and placed a hand on my neck to guide me forward. I remember how his hand lingered a little longer, his fingers dipping just beneath the collar of my shirt, before he turned and left abruptly.

She was leaning against a tall serving counter trimmed with soft tan leather. She raised a brow at me, poured a generous glass of red wine, and handed it to me.

"I do not drink wine, miss."

"Take it. In case you become thirsty. Arturo tells me you came with Gabriel."

"Yes, ma'am."

"How did you manage that feat? Gabriel has no patience for anyone but me. That alone piques my curiosity. But tell me. You have a message. Who is it from?"

I took the glass and held it. "It is not a message, really, but a warning."

"A warning, oh. Well, now I am really curious. Who dares to warn me?"

"Are you to marry Tirso Batungbakal?" Before she could reply, I said, "He is already taken. I came to warn you that he sees another woman."

"Taken?" She inclined her head, her face wearing an amused frown. "And why should you care about me?"

"I have seen you with him, at the San Lupes'. You seem like a nice lady. I do not think it is right what he does. No woman should be treated that way. I thought you should know."

"Such a gallant lad."

I did not like her words. The tone was mocking.

"But what do you think, that I was born yesterday? I am not blind. I know that Tirso has other women, all men do. That will stop once we are married."

She blew smoke toward me and smiled. "Besides, you lie, boy. You come for a different reason. One I do not care to know." She laughed at my stunned expression. "Finish your drink. Stay as long as you like. There is chicharron, bibingka, sweet saging, and other meryenda on the table."

So that was it? Her response to my announcement was to point to the direction of fried pork skin and sweet bananas? I scratched my head in confusion as she slunk away through the crowd. It was hard for me to think; I had never seen such food, and in such abundance. I proceeded to gorge myself with the sticky cakes sprinkled with shredded coconut. I choked on the vinegar and garlic sauce made for the fried pork rinds. I had never tasted anything so rich before.

I became the center of attention for a group of her friends. They were playing a game, and I was pulled into it. The game was simple. We each had to repeat words to a sentence, adding on a word until the story grew longer and longer. We were laughing hilariously, and their cups continued to be refilled by invisible hands. I did not pick apart until later how the group had nudged one another repeatedly, whispering things such as "Look how the peasant boy eats. It is as if he has eaten nothing but dirt all his life. This must be like paradise to him. How sad." All along I thought I was laughing with them, but they were laughing at me. I was their sport.

An hour later, after my stomach had begun to ache from too much of the fried bananas dipped in sugar, Catalina chose to approach me again. "Boy, tell me. Does that witch have as fine clothes as I? Truly, I do not see what Tirso sees in her."

"Esmeralda's beauty is not in her clothes. And she is no witch," I defended her heatedly, and immediately I realized Catalina had me, for neither of us had mentioned Esmeralda's name until then. That was the night I took my first drink of wine. I drank more than I should have, with my belly already filled with the food from the San Lupe house and then Catalina's display. I felt the heat of the room. The noise of the party made the room seem smaller to me. My tongue felt thick in my mouth. I went in search of a way out. In my wanderings, I mistook one door for an exit and surprised the butler, Arturo, who was locked in an embrace with a servant boy. He did not jump away; in fact, he seemed to wear a smug smile. The boy, however, took that opportunity to walk past me and out the door.

"Who are you looking for?" Arturo asked.

"I took a wrong turn somewhere," I said lamely, gesturing behind me at nothing in particular.

"Come find me before you leave. I may have something for you."

"All right," I said, backing out. I remember the lighting in that small room, which I think now was merely a hallway. It was odd, the light made Arturo's face seem longer, paler. I remember the intense heat that overcame my body. The laughter coming from the floor below seeped through the floorboards and licked at my feet. It followed just behind my ears. When I finally found the back door, I was dripping with sweat. I was almost certain it would not open, but it did, and the cool air hit me like a benediction.

Once outside, I could hear someone gasping. I expected to see someone doubled over from drinking too much wine. Instead I saw Gabriel, my traveling host, with his sleeves rolled up. He was walking toward his coach, where he had a plate of lumpias on the roof. He took a bite of one, placed it back down, and walked to a man who was bent over. He hit the man cleanly in the jaw and the man fell to the ground, still clutching his face.

Gabriel snorted as the man fell. "Not so loud now, are you, my friend?" He was about to kick the man when he noticed my presence. "Boy, did you find the Catalina?"

"Yes." I nodded, then added in my confusion, "Thank you."

"Well then?" he barked. "Why are you standing there? Do you have business with me?"

"No," I answered, and in my eagerness to get away I stumbled over my lame foot and fell. I was so nervous that I got up and heaved all the rich food and wine out onto the flower beds.

Gabriel laughed, then coughed, then forgot about me altogether as he gave the man his undivided attention.

I learned later what I had already guessed, that this Gabriel was Catalina's most trusted lapdog.

I SPENT THE following Wednesday trying to sort through the pain in my head and the images from the previous night. Had I accomplished anything? Had I succeeded in scaring the woman away from marrying Tirso? If I had known that I was sitting on a wagon at the very top of a steep precipice, I would have jumped out and run away to another town. Blind as I was, I decided that nothing eventful had happened the night before. How wrong I was.

When I came home from working in the cane fields that evening, my head was still in a fog and my back was so brittle that it took longer to climb the stairs to our room. Esmeralda's first customer was already seated.

Her customer was dressed in heeled sandals and she wore a yellow dress, with arched sleeves and a square neckline. The woman was Catalina Marquez.

I ran quickly to our other window to be sure, and there outside, leaning against a fine carriage, was her guard dog, Gabriel.

What had I done? *Think,* I ordered myself. *What did you say last night?* Before I could remember, Esmeralda began their session.

"Tell me, how can I help you?" Esmeralda poured a cup of tea.

"What kind of tea is that?" Catalina countered with a sneer.

"Ginger tea. It helps to soothe."

"I only like black tea, and it must be the finest. Not this peasant tea." She turned her face away in disgust. "I have no time to waste. Let us make this short. I have come to see if you have a cure for a witch."

I cringed at her words, remembering now how easily I had given her Esmeralda's name. Esmeralda seemed taken aback by the woman's attitude, but she was used to people coming in with fierce snarls on their faces, only to leave with content smiles. She was not daunted. "So this witch?" she prompted.

"Yes, she is poor, an orphan from what I understand. She wishes to steal my fiancé. He is a wealthy, handsome man, from only the finest of social circles. His charms are universal. I can understand how others would be attracted to him. Even this poor girl from the gutter."

Esmeralda hesitated in the act of sipping from her cup. She looked into the woman's eyes steadily. "He loves this witch?"

"He is under her spell. It is not the same thing."

"And he has asked you to marry him?"

"He shall. His family approves wholeheartedly, that is really all that matters. His parents are the ones who hold his purse strings. And Tirso, my husband-to-be, loves his money."

I watched as Esmeralda struggled with her emotions. "You would marry a man who cares for another?"

"Yes, if he is the man I have set my future upon. This witch I speak of would rather drag him down with her poverty. His family would never approve of her. They would disown him. What kind of love is that? Would you not rather see the man you love living in fine clothes and eating good food?" Catalina smiled angelically, her long nails drumming on the oval table.

Esmeralda could not speak. She was flustered. She spilled her tea. She dropped a jar of her flowers. Petals spilled onto the floor, mixed with sharp pieces of clay. "I am sorry. This is not the kind of problem I can cure. I do not think there is a cure for your intended."

"Oh, there is a cure for *my* intended. There is no cure for *your* intended." Catalina stood. "Let us make this our first and last visit." She opened a beaded purse and threw out four pesos onto the table. The coins spun loudly on the table, then fell to the ground.

I thought Catalina would leave then, but her next actions made me think she had lost her mind. She pulled apart the clean tight braid of her hair, then she proceeded to rip her own dress. She grabbed a bottle of Esmeralda's lotion and threw it on herself, all the while screaming for Esmeralda to have pity on her. "No, please, do not hurt me, Esmeralda! It is not my fault Tirso asked me to marry him and not you." She rushed out, stumbling down the stairs. Our neighbors came outside to see what the noise was about. What they saw was Catalina running to her coach, sobbing.

Esmeralda never moved. She watched Catalina's performance with horror.

On that night, a storm began. The following day people could not stop speaking of how poor Catalina Marquez had to grovel at the feet of Esmeralda Cortez. They could not stop talking about how Catalina had to actually beg the woman to leave her fiancé alone. What nonsense, I thought. But can you believe how readily everyone accepted this? The senator's wife was Catalina's biggest supporter. Between the two of them, they made a big show of the wronged fiancé.

"We must oust Esmeralda from our community. Our husbands and brothers and sons are fooled by this witch. She leads them astray."

The gossip raged like a fire in a dried-up wheat field. It consumed everyone in sight. Esmeralda's customers stopped coming. I realized then how ready everyone was to turn on Esmeralda, how anxious they were to discredit her, as a liar, a man stealer, a whore. She knew all their darkest secrets. She was a threat to them.

Mildred, the nun, visited her that night, with a great show to the villagers of the pious nun pitying the poor sinner.

The nun sat with a knowing look on her face. "Do you remember now what I have told you? How this path could lead only to heartbreak? And now the entire village has turned against you. If you follow me now, if you admit to your sin and marry yourself to the church, all will be forgiven."

"Please, Sister Mildred, I cannot hear this right now." Esmeralda's voice was strained.

I felt bad for what was happening to Esmeralda. I blamed myself. I wished at that moment that I could open a box and put all the badness back into it. But what I started was something that had been breeding for a long time.

"No, we must talk on this matter now. You shall go to church and pledge yourself as one of us. There is nothing else to be done, your reputation is shattered. It has been from the day you were born, an orphan, an unwanted child. You started with a black mark against you. And I tried to steer you the right way."

I watched Esmeralda's eyes grow dim. "And who put that black mark there, *Mother?*"

Sister Mildred looked stunned. "Esmeralda, your mind grows weak in all this chaos."

Esmeralda's gaze did not waver. The tone of her voice was firm, yet there was almost a pleading to it. "You could clear my name. You come from a wealthy family. If you were to stand up and take the responsibility for becoming pregnant with me twenty-one years ago, my standing would change. I would then come from a good family, you would be the black sheep.

"Tirso's family might change their minds. They would be happy to know I came from a decent family, and one connected with the church. Are you willing to take the burden from me? Are you willing to take responsibility for your part in all of this?" Esmeralda pleaded.

Sister Mildred sat stiffly, her hands folded in her lap. "You do not know what you speak of." She wore a smug look. She reminded me of my aunt at that moment.

"But I do know. If you told Grandmother . . ." Esmeralda paused at Sister Mildred's sharp look. "If you told your mother, she might be happy to find she had a grandchild. You could still change things, if you spoke to her. Explain what happened so long ago. She is a powerful woman, she could save us both."

Sister Mildred stood quietly and smoothed her robe. She looked at Esmeralda. "You think she does not know of your existence? Who do you think insisted that I place the baby on the church doorstep? Even when I begged and told her that the father . . ." Sister Mildred's eyes looked wistful for just a moment. "You were my child long ago, but too many years have passed. We are both grown women now. We are no longer anyone's child."

"You are wrong. You are still *her* child." Esmeralda's voice lowered to a whisper.

"You would do well to pledge yourself to the church. This is the only help I can give you."

Esmeralda sighed after her mother left. "No one to stand up for me. Not one person. Such a sad, silent town."

Padre Ramirez came to visit her soon after. Sister Mildred must have reported the news to him. He came with a humbleness of attitude that was sickening, for throughout it all, his eyes gleamed with greed. I was never so surprised as when she asked him to leave. When the padre left I thought to myself, She has sealed her fate.

A few customers came to visit her, but they were like sprinkles of sand on a smooth floor where once there had been a beach. Esmeralda listened to their troubles. It was only after the last one had left that her confidence collapsed. She put her head down on the wooden table. That was how she looked when Tirso walked in unannounced. He stood at the door for a long moment. The expression on his face was one of torment. When she stirred, he strode to her side and took her hand in his. She pulled it back slowly.

"Why did you not tell me?" she asked.

"I had hoped to make plans for us. I had hoped to entertain my parents until we could elope secretly, and they could tell everyone I died, or moved abroad."

"But now it is public knowledge. This woman is claiming to be your intended, and I have lost everything for trusting you."

"Forgive me, my love, you must know I would never do this. Somehow, it all unraveled before I could catch the loose thread." He tried again to put his arms around her, but she pushed him away. "Tell me, what can I do?"

"Go." She pointed toward the door. "Decide who it is you are to marry. Do not come back until then."

Tirso stared at her a long time. He tried a few times to hold her face in his hands, then he said, "It is already decided. I am to be married next month."

"In my church?" There was a sob in her voice. I hated him for putting it there.

Tirso closed his eyes and brought his fingers to press them shut. He seemed to struggle with himself. When he opened them he took a deep breath and paced the small of her room. "Esmeralda, it cannot be helped. I have thought long and hard on this. I have dug marks into my palms from clenching them when I sleep. I am accustomed to the money. I cannot live without it. I can take better care of you this way. Catalina Marquez is rich. I can buy you whatever you want."

"It was never the presents, Tirso. I want only you. I want us to be married as you promised."

"It is not possible, not in name. That I cannot give you, though I had hoped to."

"I will come to watch the ceremony," she replied. The desperation in her voice was difficult for me to swallow. I sat on my knees with my fists clenched, not caring whether they could see me or not, through our open windows. I wanted to run from that room, to keep from hearing her pain, but I willed myself to stay. I owed her that much, after all that I had started.

"Do not do that, my love. Please, spare yourself. I cannot bear to hurt you further."

"I will come," she said quietly.

"Then know that when I speak my vows, I say them to you."

"No, Tirso. You will not be saying them to me."

"Esmeralda, you know that I love you. Only you."

"I do not know that anymore."

He pleaded once again. "Tell me what to do." I could hear tears in his voice. It stunned me. I did not understand how he could love her, after all that he had done. But there it was in his voice, raw and more sincere than any of his words.

"Leave me, and never come back. Whenever you see me, look away. Never let me catch you watching. If someone mentions my name, tell them, 'I do not know this woman you speak of.'"

He walked to the front door with his head bowed. I ran to the front window so that I could watch him go. It had started to rain. Small spits at first, then a strong gale that shrieked at our windows. When I looked outside, I saw Tirso holding on to a tree. He gripped it, then crumpled onto it. He stayed there in the rain, for hours. I heard Esmeralda's sobs throughout the night.

When he left I breathed a great sigh. It is over, I thought. Good riddance. There will be no more distractions for Esmeralda and me. I was wrong. The disruption I had caused was a small upsurge before the tidal wave.

The next evening I went to Father's room to give him his medicine and to clean out his bedpan. He had grown ill again and had taken to his bed.

"*Sana anák, malakí ka na, para makabílí tayo nang malakíng bahay.*" I wish you were big now, son, so that we could buy a bigger house.

When I heard this, something came over me, I do not know what. It may have been the strain of the past few days. It may have been that at that precise moment, I could see my classmates laughing among themselves as they passed just outside our house. They no longer asked me to play. I was a stranger to their circle. A tree you pass but do not notice, one that at times you lean or spit on, without realizing that it is a living thing. I snapped at my father, "What, am I to take care of you for the rest of my life?"

My father withered further before me. "No, I was only dreaming, son," he said, then turned his back to me and went to sleep.

I felt horrible, and angry, and sad. I left his side and hurried to my window. I was hoping to find some gladness from Esmeralda. I was excited at the thought of starting fresh, without Tirso to distract her. I waited for the sound of her coming into the room. Ten minutes passed before I looked up. I saw her sitting on the table with a picture of Tirso. She had been sitting there all along. She had no more customers. I was confused. I had expected gladness and relief on her face. She was sitting there staring quietly at a candle on the table. I grew sick at the small seed of thought that began to form. She still loved Tirso.

She sat like that all night long. My cousin Eduardo did not play the guitar. Only the sound of Father's harsh coughing broke the stillness of the night.

THE NEXT MORNING, I walked through the markets in a daze. I knew that Father needed his medicine, but I could not bring myself to return home. There was nothing there but sickness and tears. I decided I must go find Tirso and confront him with what he had done. I must instruct him to do whatever he must, to make it right with her. I wanted her to have that look of enchantment in her eyes. I wanted her room to be filled with beauty and anticipation. I did not realize that I wanted those things for myself.

I knew where Tirso lived. His large house stood precariously over a cliff, overlooking the village. When I arrived at his doorstep, I stood on my tiptoes and barely reached the black iron knocker. I accomplished two large thumps before the door opened. It was Tirso himself who answered. Before I could open my mouth, he clapped a thick hand on my shoulder and pulled me in. He shut the door with a swipe of his foot. We stood glaring at each other, he with his arms folded across his chest, and I with Father's medicine bottle clutched in my hand like a club.

"Do you know what you have done, Carlito?"

"What *I* have done? What about you?" I shouted, my eyes immediately stinging with tears.

"Come." He directed me to sit. I looked uncertainly at the rich tan carpet and rattan sofa. The chairs were cushioned with thick ivory-and-tan-colored pillows in a palm leaf design. I sat slowly, at the edge. I glanced down at my dirty hands and feet and almost lost my balance on the little corner that I sat upon.

Tirso sat across from me and stared. He bent forward and put his head in his hands. He clutched at his dark hair. "Why did you tell her of my involvement with Catalina? That was not your choice to make."

"Someone had to tell her." My voice rose over his.

"You hurt her." He held out a hand to me. "The way you told her. She had not expected it. I know you do not believe me, but I had plans for the two of us. I was going to run away with Esmeralda, force my family to accept her or send us money on another island. In that way they could save face, tell their friends I had married an aristocrat from another town.

"You pushed our relationship out into the open. You have made public what I was considering in private. Now I must make a public decision. The only recourse for me is to marry a girl of my status. I cannot embarrass my family by marrying below us. I could not shame them that way, after all they have done for me. I am bound by them. I cannot make them a laughingstock in their own community. That is not how a son repays his family. I would ruin the reputation of my brothers and sisters. There are ties, Carlito, invisible ties that one owes to one's parents. We must honor our obligations, despite our true wishes. We must do this out of respect. You understand?"

On this point, I understood him. "I understand," I said quietly, thinking of my ties to my own father.

He looked at me. "Forgive me, Carlito. Perhaps you know too well what I speak of."

I lifted my chin. "If it were up to me, if I had a choice between making Esmeralda happy and . . ." My voice lost its strength. Would I do the same? I pondered. If I had to tell my father, "I can no longer take care of you. I need to marry this woman whom I love," could I do it? I could not do it even now.

Tirso nodded as he watched me come to the same conclusion.

We two spineless ones sat with our heads bowed.

He stood and walked to the window. He put his hands in his pockets and searched the sky. "I was going to tell her myself. You cannot imagine how many days I agonized for the right way, the right moment. The moment you chose, and the way in which you told her, was wrong. It has killed me to break her heart this way." His face was contorted. I could see he was crying. He wiped his eyes with rough fingers that pressed and shook at his skin. It was as if he wanted to hurt his face.

"I want to go home," I said, standing up.

He continued to look out his window, at the clouds that were culminating in the distance. "I forgive you, Carlito. I know that you love her, too."

His words embarrassed me. I stood with my fists clenched.

He looked at my hands, then my face, and smiled sadly. "Maybe someday you will be a stronger man than I. Take no offense, Carlito, but you have done enough damage. Do not come again, unless it is a matter of life." He sighed, and I was surprised that I felt his sorrow. As I walked to the door he added softly, as if to himself, "Or death."

The evening before Esmeralda's disappearance was the eve of Tirso's wedding. It was also Good Friday. The engagement had been announced, and then the wedding date was rushed. This was at Catalina's insistence. I think she was afraid, and rightfully so, that Tirso might give in to his heart. The entire town was invited to the wedding, and that night was the dress rehearsal for the ceremony.

I watched Esmeralda from my bedroom window. All morning, the preparations for the wedding were visible. The wagons that carried the floral arrangements—orange and red orchids with streaming banners of gold congratulating the bride and groom—drove by our house. The equipment for the musicians, the tables and chairs for the banquet to be held outdoors, taunted us from the beds of the *karetelas*. In every house, the chatter of what to wear for the next day drifted in the warm breeze. Little girls sat giggling outside their houses, weaving together a large wreath of white *sampaguita* flowers to put on the church door.

I suffered soundlessly with Esmeralda. She never left her room. She would stand, then sit, then stand again. She dropped her magic bottles. She wrote letters as if she had to mail an urgent message, and then she tore them. When she was finished, she fell to the floor, crying among the broken glass and scattered letters.

My aunt, who had never wasted one glance toward Esmeralda's room and rarely came to visit ours, did both. She came in the guise of visiting my father. Then she came to crouch beside me.

"You do not even tend to your father. You waste precious moments watching that whore," my aunt snorted. "Her time has come. I knew it would, entertaining such men. Why, even your uncle cannot keep his eyes off her. All this talk has only served to further excite the men, even you, a mere boy."

I did not answer her, for I knew that was what she wanted. Suddenly my aunt gasped. "*O, itó na,*" she said. Here it comes. "Get away from that window. What comes next is none of our business. Draw the shades, and do not repeat what you see. Dante," she called to my father, "order your son to mind his business." My aunt hurried downstairs to watch from her bedroom window.

I almost choked at what I saw next. Catalina's lapdog, Gabriel, was at Esmeralda's door. I moved from side to side, unsure of what to do, of what would happen next. I had a bad feeling. It happened like lightning. Esmeralda opened the door. Gabriel shoved her aside and locked the door behind him. He leered at her. He told her who he was. Then he slapped her down and told her his mistress wanted to ensure there would be no interruptions for the wedding. Esmeralda fought back, but Gabriel pulled out a knife.

My aunt came back up and pinched me. She whispered in my ear so that my father could not hear, "Stay away from the window, Carlito. I am warning you. If you bring shame to this family, I will throw both you and your father out. You will be the cause. Do you understand?"

I jerked away.

My aunt gasped, "Ay, ay."

I ran for my father's bolo knife. It had a long curved blade, with a brass handle and short chain-linked tassles. It was sheathed in a bamboo case and hung from the doorknob. It was a gift long ago from my mother's family to my father. I took that knife and stumbled down the stairs. The knife was heavy and reached my ankles. I had to be careful not to trip over it. Before my aunt could stop me, I ran outside to Esmeralda's house. I kicked her thin door open with my good foot.

My aunt was stuck to our window, watching me from our house. "Carlito," I heard her say in alarm.

Gabriel turned in surprise at my entrance. He glanced at my heaving chest, the large knife in my hand. "What will you do with that? Slice me a piece of roast pig?"

"Carlito, run." Esmeralda grabbed for Gabriel's arm.

"I will slice a pig tonight, but it is not for roasting," I answered, my voice as deep as I could make it. Then I found my real voice, and I shouted at the top of my lungs for my father. I forced that entire section of town to open their shades and listen. "Father, he wants to kill her!" I screamed. "Father, help me."

And do you know, my father somehow found the strength to rush to our side?

"Is that my son calling me?" Father asked, repeating the question, until he came to stand beside me. He took the bolo from my hands and waved it at Gabriel.

"*Tito* . . ." My cousin Eduardo followed my father into Esmeralda's house with an ax.

"Eduardo, stay away from there," my aunt called, following my cousin.

As my father struggled to pull Gabriel from Esmeralda, Eduardo jumped on Gabriel from behind.

People gathered outside of Esmeralda's house. The men of the village hovered near her door. They came to help my father.

I untangled myself from the colliding bodies, ducking out of their way. I glanced back once as Esmeralda fought to scratch Gabriel's eyes out. "I shall bring back help," I promised. Then I rushed to town.

I went straight to the church. Tirso was rehearsing for his wedding. People stared when I entered. I did not need to say a word. Tirso saw my face and followed me out immediately. His future in-laws and his entire family called for him to stay. Catalina stomped her foot in a tantrum. She pulled at his arm, insisting that he stay. Tirso pried her fingers off gently but firmly.

We rode his coach back to my house. His fists clenched and unclenched. I was afraid that I would come back and Father, Esmeralda, and the rest would be dead from Gabriel's knife; but, amazingly, they had held the big man at bay. Father was wielding the bolo knife, and cousin Eduardo was holding a chair before him, the way a lion tamer would do. Other men had gathered and were blocking the doorway. These men would not lift a finger for Esmeralda, for fear of their wives, but helping my father was another matter. My father had helped many of them at different times, and they had what we call *utang na loób,* a "debt of the inner soul."

Tirso brushed past the men, and I followed behind.

Gabriel sneered as we entered. "Ah, the Catalina's pretty boy. She will not like that I must kill you, but it is in self-defense." He laughed wickedly. "See what I have done to your whore?" He gestured to Esmeralda, unconscious on the ground.

Nothing chilled me more than the smile that appeared on Tirso's face. He stared at Gabriel with deadly intent. I was frightened for everyone. After all, Tirso was Golden Gloves boxing champion of Blanco Negros.

Gabriel moved forward in wide steps, reminiscent of Japanese sumo wrestlers. Tirso leapt forward like a cat. Gabriel swung heavily with his right, Tirso ducked it and weaved to his left. Gabriel swung again, his body lurching forward, chin first. It was just in time to meet Tirso's fist, on his jaw. Tirso threw three quick jabs with his right hand, lightning fast, *pow, pow, pow,* and then gave an incredible wallop with his left. There was a loud crack as Gabriel's head snapped to the side. He landed on the floor with his eyes still open. It was such a hard hit, I knew immediately Gabriel was dead even before he hit the ground.

It was in defense of innocent people. Everyone witnessed this. There was no argument. The *policía* came and took Gabriel's body. Father embraced me and told me for the first time, "I am proud of you, my son."

In the end, I could remain silent no longer. I could not allow myself to be just like the others, like my aunt. I could not be that which I despised most.

The crowd dispersed and I went to my window to watch Esmeralda and Tirso, but again my father surprised me. He said, "Step away from there. Give them their last moments of privacy. Come. We have much to speak of ourselves."

THE WEDDING OF Tirso Batungbakal to Catalina Marquez was still to continue the following morning, my aunt announced to us. I dressed in my best shirt and short pants, for those were all I had. I combed my hair down with Father's pomade, but my curls fought back. I was the first to arrive at the church. I watched as people filtered in. The evening had a sense of gaiety and laughter in the air. I had never seen such clothing. Many of the guests, I later learned, wore imported clothes from France and Italy. Some were designed locally with silks from Thailand and Burma. Catalina's gown was from Paris.

The ceremony began with no sign of Esmeralda. I watched as Tirso, standing in the front of the altar, searched the pews for her. Everyone was seated. Padre Ramirez had just finished a long discourse on the merits of a good wife when the doors opened and Esmeralda walked in.

She wore a sleeveless ivory dress made of stiff silk that fitted her body and fell just short of her ankles. The simple V neck of the gown emphasized her golden skin. It showcased the amber necklace I had seen Tirso give to her when he first made promises of marriage. She had no other adornments than her beauty, and that day she took our breath away. The guests looked from her to Tirso and back again. Even the padre stumbled over his words.

Tirso said his vows just as he had promised. He looked over his bride's shoulders at Esmeralda when he recited the words. The guests whispered viciously back and forth. Esmeralda's face was calm and serene. At that moment the sun passed through the stained-glass windows and she was bathed in a halo of gold. She looked like an angel. She was at peace amid the accusing whispers.

"Look at that gown. Only the bride should wear white."

"Look at how it fits her body. Indecent."

"How dare she come. Was she invited?"

"Why, even the padre is upset by her presence."

"No shame. She has no shame."

Their words began like a small tremble, a minor disturbance, but as they grew, the chattering became so that the priest had to shout over the whispering. That was when the ground began to move.

The vows were almost completed when the floor jolted and rolled. People began to scream, "An earthquake!"

I fell over onto the pew before me, then slowly I felt the floor moving downward. It sank whole, without any of the walls collapsing. We were covered in darkness. Next came the loud splintering of the wooden support beams overhead and the sounds of screaming as the beams fell.

When the rolling stopped, candles were lit. Everyone appeared miraculously to be in one piece. It was later, after everyone was pulled out, that the rumor began to circulate. Esmeralda was trapped below. Tirso himself went down to look for her. It was not until several hours later that they had to call an end to the search. In the morning they searched again, but the structure was unstable, more of the beams began to fall, and they pulled Tirso out. He struggled like a madman to stay below.

In the daylight the church was an eerie sight. It had sunk completely into the ground. It was nothing more than a mound of rock. The crucifix set atop the church was the only part exposed. It looked like a big grave.

I NEVER SAW Esmeralda again. It was concluded that she died in the disaster. One evening as I was sitting at my window reminiscing, her door opened and my heart leapt with joy, but it was only Tirso. His face was haunted. He touched her things, her silk scarves, her candles. He picked up pieces of her torn letters. He slept in her bed, his face swollen from crying. He had been true to his words. He had honored his obligations to his family, and he was miserable.

I waited until he was gone, and then I too was drawn to her house. I entered timidly and gazed at her bottles. I read the labels on each one, thinking of all the cures and potions they contained. But as I held these bottles in my hands, I came to see that they were nothing more than coconut oils and petals in water. I came to the same conclusion as Tirso. There was no magic in these bottles without Esmeralda.

After a week, Esmeralda's customers began to visit her home. I was appalled at first; I wanted to chase them away.

"Let them," my father said gently. I watched as the senator's wife came and stole away with the bottle that had the stopper of the two snakes entwined. The gambling man found the bottle Esmeralda had prescribed to his wife, the one that had given her courage. He smashed the bottle with his cane. The padre came and took the heating oils, then stole away in the night. And ever after, these people remained the same. They walked our town of Blanca Negros like ghosts, searching for guidance.

Only Father and I changed. His illness, which had been misdiagnosed as tuberculosis, was as Esmeralda had hinted, only a broken heart. It healed the moment we spoke to each other, and he found his strength again. He told his sister how unkind she had been to us. He took on two jobs. He went to a new church and prayed for my mother and sister himself. And me? I was at Bonita beach with my friends, learning to be a child again.

No one questioned that Esmeralda was buried somewhere in the rubble of the church. But I was not so sure. When I returned home the night of the earthquake, I noticed that someone had opened the birdcage and her two yellow birds were gone. It was something, I knew, no one else in the village would have been considerate enough to do. Only Esmeralda herself. I once asked my father about those birds long ago, when she first received them as a present from Tirso.

I asked, "Father, what makes those two birds different? We have the very same ones living in the trees. I feel sorry for them, locked away like that."

Father had answered, "Ah, but they are the lucky ones. They are always assured of being fed. The others must fly day and night searching for one piece of bread."

I remember my response. "But the others are much stronger without being hand-fed."

So you see, perhaps I was not to blame after all. A mere child. Who is to say it would not have turned out the same had I not interfered? But one thing is true. My infatuation with Esmeralda started small ripples in the quiet ocean of her life that soon turned into a tidal wave of misfortune.

The church of Santa Esmeralda is buried there still. I bring the white *sampaguita* flowers to place on the cross whenever I visit.

~ AFTER FATHER FINISHES HIS STORY of Esmeralda, our cellar is quiet. My worries about my hands have lessened. The gnawing pain in our empty stomachs is forgotten for the moment. The sounds of the shelling in the distance have stopped.

Aling Ana nods her head. "Yes, that is what I would do. I would leave. I would not stand for the shame."

"Who is saying she could not stand it? It is quite possible she died," Mang Selso says, shrugging.

"Yes, but then who let out the birds?" Mang Pedro asks, rubbing his chin with his hand. He breathes deeply and closes his eyes. I wonder if he is having another one of his visions. "I see her living long after the church expired," he says.

"Well, anyone could have let out the birds," Mang Selso muses.

"Not in that town." Aling Ana shakes her head. "Unless it was Carlito himself. Ah, but to love like that." A memory seems to trail across her face, leaving a glow.

"Yes," Mrs. Yoshi adds. "She must have loved him greatly. To endure and witness the marriage of the man of her heart to another. To want to see him happy still. I bet she lived quietly in a different town and fell asleep each night dreaming of him. She would always have that to comfort her."

"Yes, that is how I always imagined it," Father says with a quiet smile.

"What a weight you carried on your shoulders," says Roman, the journalist. "The obligation of caring for your father, too much for one person, one boy." Roman smiles at me. He nods to my father. "I agree, Mang Carlito, all must share in the obligation of feeding this family. For that is what we are now. A family."

"Yes, even if we do not always get along," Mang Pedro says. "Tomorrow I shall accompany you to search, Carlito. Tomorrow we will bring back food. I can see it."

"Thank you, Ped," Papa says.

"What else do you see, Mang Ped?" my brother asks, fascinated. Mang Ped's visions always hold him enthralled.

"What do you wish me to see, Roderick?" Mang Ped asks with twinkling eyes.

"What time is it, Carlos?" Mama asks with a tightness in her voice. We all know the meaning of this. My older sister, Isabelle, has not yet returned.

Father's smile fades. "Late. It is late." He pats Roderick on the head absently.

"Pedro, have you had any more of your visions regarding Isabelle?" Mama asks anxiously.

Mang Ped shakes his head with sad eyes. "Not yet, Louisa. But let us hope. Perhaps something will come in the form of a dream."

Roman studies Mama as she makes the sign of the cross and repeats the Lord's Prayer.

"What I would not do for chicken adobo." Mang Selso's wife sighs, fanning herself with a newspaper.

Mama is offended at the change of topic. Her brow wrinkles. My sister is more important than chicken adobo, yet it feels better to talk of something else.

"Mmm, yes. Cooked slow so that the sauce has dried and the garlic sticks to the chicken like a crust," Mang Selso agrees.

I wipe the sweat from my brow and pull at the back of my damp shirt.

Aling Ana closes her eyes and breathes in her memories. "First you chop the garlic, sauté it, then you add the cup of vinegar, half a cup of soy sauce, and the chopped chicken. A little bay leaves, salt and pepper." She throws one hand in the air. "That is all. It does not take much. My favorite dish."

"Mine too," Mama admits, placing a hand to her belly.

The room quiets as everyone soaks in the image with reverence. It is silent except for the sound of the fanning. Then like a thundercloud the earth shakes, explosion after explosion, throwing us forward. Pieces of the floor above crumble. We crouch together, unable to move.

"The house will collapse!" Ate Lorna cries. I count ten in all, before the explosions begin to move westward. The women are sobbing. My nose runs. I turn my face to the wall. It is a few minutes before anyone speaks again.

"If only we had the power to create a potion. One that could send a plague to all Japanese," Aling Ana says. Mrs. Yoshi keeps quiet as the others agree.

I have trouble falling asleep because Mama will not stop worrying about Isabelle. I see my sister in my dreams, lost in a fog.

IN THE MORNING I hear Father's angry voice. "*Gago*," he exclaims. Stupid. "He never listens. That boy will get himself killed!"

"Shh, Carlito, *baká matakót ang mga batà*," my mother whispers. You might scare the children.

My cousin Esteban snuck out in the middle of the night. They thought he was going to use the bathroom, because of his dysentery and because that was what he told them; but now he is gone. Papa is certain he has gone back to my uncle's house in Ermita, Manila, because he could not stop talking about this last night.

Father is even more upset because my sister, Isabelle, has still not returned. She is not at any of the neighbors or with any of our relatives. He asks Mica Yoshi one more time, though he has already asked. "And she told you to go ahead of her and she would meet you here, at home?"

Mica pulls her long black hair into a bun. Her pretty eyes slant down at the outer ends. She frowns and crosses her arms over her belly. She speaks softly, like the movement of a butterfly's wings.

"Yes, Mang Carlito. I know now that I should never have left Isabelle. But she said she wanted to stop by the Bonifacios' and see if she could ask for food." Mica looks miserable, and Mrs. Yoshi holds her close.

"You should have waited. I wish you had waited," Father murmurs.

"Carlito, do not blame Mica. You know that daughter of yours. When she has her mind set on something, nothing will sway her. Isabelle is exactly like you," Mama says. Even though Mama is worried for Isabelle, she is angry with her as well.

Father does not respond to this talk. It is a sore subject between Mama and him. He is dressed to go out, in search of food. He wears a straw hat, sandals, and a short-sleeved shirt that the moths have eaten through. He looks fragile beneath his clothes. Roman and Mang Pedro are ready to accompany him. Ate Lorna has stopped asking me about her husband, Domingo. She watches me with scared eyes. I think she is afraid of what I will say. I am thankful, because I am not yet ready to tell her.

Mama's eyes fill with tears when Father is ready to leave. She hugs him and he whispers something. She smiles and hits him playfully, but I can see she is frightened.

"We shall look out for Isabelle as we search for food." Father kisses her one last time. He nods to my brother and me. "Watch over your mother," he tells us.

"Yes, Papa." We nod.

Mama wipes her face quickly and says loudly, "Okay, we shall be here waiting."

After they leave, the room is so quiet that it hurts my head. Mama sneaks upstairs to fill water and gather tea leaves. Ate Lorna goes along with her. Baby Alma is asleep on a blanket while her brother, Taba, has laid all Ate Lorna's trinkets on the ground. He is pretending to be a vendor and that the glass beads and wooden jewelry are worth something. Roderick watches curiously, looking from the dull baubles, two bottlecaps, and scratched colored glass to Taba's face.

They are not gone long when a loud *boom!* sounds outside and the ground rolls. Roderick puts both hands to his ears. I shout for Mama and race toward the ladder. I can hear her and Ate Lorna. They hurry back down with the tea leaves, the clay kettle clinking. The explosions come closer and closer. We cover our heads. *Boom, boom!*

"*Dios ko,*" Mama calls out to God. "*Dios ko!*"

Mrs. Yoshi stumbles over to comfort Mama, stopping Aling Ana, who was about to embrace her. Mama is hysterical. I watch as she kicks out and pulls her hair.

"*Tamà na!*" Mama pleads. Enough! "Carlito, Carlito," she calls out for Father. "Isabelle is dead, Yukino," she sobs to Mrs. Yoshi. "I know she is. She would never stay out this long!"

"Louisa, the children," Mrs. Yoshi reminds Mama.

Another loud explosion, much closer this time. I feel our house shake above us. I can hear the wood and the bamboo splintering. Everyone screams. We crouch again into a corner. Another explosion, and then another. We do not know what to do. There is nowhere to run.

"We will be buried alive!" Mang Selso exclaims.

Another explosion, but a little farther away, then another, farther. The danger has moved on for now. No one speaks. Mama cannot stand; she sits against the wall with her legs thrown before her like a rag doll. She covers her face with her hands, and I rush to her. Roderick and I hold her hands.

Mrs. Yoshi lights a small fire in the corner of the room and places the clay pot over tiny bamboo sticks. She uses a wooden broom to open the ceiling hatch.

"Ma?" Roderick asks.

"Be quiet now, Roderick," Mama tells him.

Baby Alma is awake and crying. I cover my ears at the sound.

Ate Lorna picks up the baby and speaks soothing words. She avoids looking at me. Last night, she could not stop asking me about Domingo. Today, she wants to pretend I know nothing. When the tea is ready, Mrs. Yoshi passes the cups to everyone. We wait.

IN THE AFTERNOON Roman and Mang Pedro return. Roman was able to purchase two cans of red beans in exchange for one of his tools. Mang Pedro was not so lucky.

"Last night when I had a vision of us returning with food, I did not realize my own hands would be almost empty," Mang Pedro jokes, handing Mama a few sad-looking bananas.

"Thank God, thank God." Mama makes the sign of the cross and looks over their shoulders at the door, waiting for Papa.

Roman looks around. "He has not yet returned? We each went a different way. Perhaps there is a line at the warehouse he spoke of."

Mang Pedro looks very concerned but keeps quiet.

"Yes, that is possible." Mama's hand shakes as she brushes a strand of hair. She busies herself opening one can of beans and slicing the green bananas Mang Pedro found. My stomach rumbles at the sight. I feel the urge to shove everyone aside so that I can have it all. When she hands me my plate, my face reddens in shame.

~

IN THE EVENING cousin Esteban returns. He comes stumbling down the stairs. This time he is crying. His tears stream down the sides of his runny nose. His lips are swollen and wet. His face has become a sad waterfall.

"Steban, what is it?" Mama asks, putting her hands on his shoulders.

"They took my papa away," he says between hiccups.

"Who took your papa?" she demands.

"The Japanese soldiers. The Makapili pointed their fingers at him, and they took all the men on our street. I hid behind the houses and ran here. They have accused him of aiding a guerrilla."

My mother puts her hand to her chest. She picks up her coat and heads for the door.

"No, Aling Louisa, you cannot go outside. It is too dangerous." Roman blocks her way.

"But I must find Carlito, and Isabelle. It is much too late. I know something has happened to Isabelle. I must find her."

"I can go. I am smaller. They will not notice me," I tell them. My words fall like dust that no one hears.

Mang Selso busies himself with taking care of his father. He brings a warm cloth to the old Spaniard's head, but the old man pushes his hands away. "Ay, basta," the old Spaniard snaps. Enough.

Roman places his hands on Mama's shoulders. "We must wait until evening. What if he returns soon? Then we will have yet another person wandering the roads. If they are not back by morning, I promise, I shall go in search of them myself."

"And I will come," I answer.

Roman smiles. "If your mama says that it is all right, we shall go together."

This quiets my mother for the time being. She glances at Mang Selso. I know that she wishes for him to volunteer. But I am the better choice. Mang Selso would only stumble around in confusion. And he is more terrified than the women by the sounds of battle. He refuses to look at my mother. He stares at his hands instead. He no longer tries to cut the anger with one of his jokes. I can tell Mang Pedro, on the other hand, wants to protest but again remains silent, as do Aling Ana and Mrs. Yoshi.

Roman studies Roderick. "How about we play match the sets?"

Roderick's lip is shaking, but he nods his head and shuffles the cards and lays them on the table for Roman to cut. Roderick relaxes and begins to ask him questions about being a newsman. They are still playing when my eyes grow heavy with sleep.

~

THE NEXT AFTERNOON Ate Lorna stands up in alarm. She slaps her son, Taba, on the back. "What is that? Spit it out, Taba. What is it?"

Taba's eyes water. He coughs out something grotesque, covered in spit. It is half a fishbone.

Roderick's eyes widen and he sits up.

"What were you thinking, hah? Do you want to die?" Ate Lorna shakes him. Taba opens his mouth in a silent cry.

Roman has his hands in his pockets. He steps forward with a sheepish look on his face.

"It is my fault. I told him that story of Mang Minno, the old fisherman. Do you know of him? The old man from Bohol, who lived near the forest, right at the junction where it drops to meet with the Bohol-Mindanao Sea?" he asks the room.

We shake our heads.

To Aling Ana he says, "Yesterday you spoke of power as if it were a good thing. You said you wished we had some kind of magic that could rid us of the Japanese soldiers. I have never seen it used for good. Think of the Japanese soldiers with all their power. It has eroded their hearts and their souls." He turns to Mama. "Mang Carlito spoke of when he was younger and his father depended only on him. He wanted to be free of his father's obligations. I was just the opposite. I would have given my right arm if it meant I could have just a moment of my father's attention. I needed his guidance so much. This want, this overpowering need for his approval, it tripped me, it spun my thoughts. I was willing to do anything, and that was how I met Mang Minno."

~ mang minno

IN OUR VILLAGE of Baclayon in Bohol, there was always talk of an old fisherman who carried a powerful amulet. People said he could command the sea with it. Some mused that he was really the Jonah mentioned in the Bible, that the story of Jonah and the whale was really his story, but who can say? The conversation surrounding him was always dark and consummated in the smallest of whispers. It was taboo to speak his name, blasphemy.

The stories were always different. He could send a swarm of bees to sting an enemy. He could make himself like one of the trees in the forest. If you heard someone whisper your name at night or whistle, you should never answer back, for it was he calling. I only heard pieces, for the grown-ups would always shut their mouths tightly when I walked by. It possessed me. I wanted to know the whole of it, so I went in search of him.

I stand before you now an accomplished journalist at twenty-three. I write for the *Manila Herald,* and I assure you I am quite content with my achievements. But long ago, I used to tell elaborate lies where I was always the hero. Anything to impress my father.

My father was rich. He gave me everything you could think of to give a son. But he kept the one thing I desired most. Ah, there is always the one thing, isn't there? But it wasn't of material value. All I wanted was my father's time.

At fourteen I was already this tall, this broad in the shoulders. I never had to work hard at attracting women, of any age. It made for some very interesting situations. But to my father, I was invisible. As for my mother, she was like a delicate bird, always elusive. She would perch beside me for a few seconds each day. She never stayed long enough to talk. Everything she said was a cliché, or a laugh, one line, a pat on the head, and then she was gone.

My parents were always distant, as if we were shouting at one another from opposing cliffs, with no bridge, no way to get close. I was carted to social gatherings every other day. I was left to play and bunk with strange children until Mother and Father were ready to return home. I was bought extravagant gifts to occupy myself. Grandfather was the only one who was affectionate to me. But an old man who sits by the window each day is not much of an instructor on the ways to become a man.

I prayed in my heart for a real father, since the one I had been given was a failure to me. That was my deepest wish, and my deepest sorrow. So it is not surprising, really, who answered my prayers.

WHEN I FIRST became interested in Mang Minno, I knew this much, that he made his living catching and selling fish and that he had become very wealthy from it. Enough to buy his way into our social circles. He even had a family, a wife and three children. They were all very embarrassed by him. To them he did not exist. He refused to live in the grand house he had bought for them and insisted on the treehouse by the sea. After a time his family became very prominent in the elite circles, and one day his eldest daughter, Amalia, came by and asked that her father not visit anymore. She asked his permission to tell her friends that he was a distant uncle and that her father was dead. Can you imagine how that must have broken the old man's heart? To have your own daughter ask this of you?

I shall never forget his name, for Minno reminds me of a fish—*minnow*, you see?

ONE DAY AT the market I stumbled across two fishermen taking their siesta with cold coffee and their catch stored in nearby baskets filled with ice and shaded from the sun. They were trading stories about Mang Minno. One man shivered and discouraged the other from saying anything further. When I asked them to tell me more, they quickly took their belongings and bade me good day. Their quiet served only to intrigue me more.

People told me Mang Minno was crazy, that he worshiped the devil, and that that was how he came back with so many fish each day. He had bargained his soul in exchange for money for his family. I was confused, you see, for I had always associated being a fisherman with Jesus of Nazareth, the fisherman of souls. I was not afraid.

THAT AFTERNOON I went in search of Mang Minno. I scoured the fish markets. I waited for hours, but he never showed. Then the thought struck me. Where better to find a fisherman than his special fishing hole? I asked the market owner, Mang Saro. "Where does Mang Minno hunt for these fishes?"

Mang Saro looked startled. "Why do you want to know? Stay away from him. Besides, there is no one special place for him. Everywhere is special, you see? He calls them, they come. Black magic," Mang Saro whispered with large eyes.

"What do you mean?" I scoffed. I could see my tone offended him.

"The *anting-anting* he wears, it brings the fish. But he is too old now. It weighs on him, you see? As he gets older. If he does not give away the medallion soon, it will drag him down."

When I questioned him more, Mang Saro clamped his mouth tight on a soggy cigarette and turned his back on me. I tried to goad him further to see what else he would let slip.

"You're frightened of an old man? I shall tell everyone how much of a coward you are."

Mang Saro turned and tossed the cigarette stub at me.

"Hey!" I shouted.

"Get away from me, unwanted boy. Tell your grandpa to teach you manners. Go—" He gestured with his hands, his face like one who smelled something disgusting.

I remained with my fists clenched.

He placed his hands on his hips. "What, what will you do? You are tall, yes, but you have none of your grandfather's character. Go home, mama's boy." He laughed. Mang Saro obviously knew more about goading than I did.

I left with my tail between my legs.

I WALKED HOME at the end of the day frustrated, but more determined. I went through the woods, using a shortcut. As I walked, I began to have the sensation that I was lost. The woods seemed alien to me, though I had walked them a hundred times. Has this tree always been here? I asked myself. This hill, why have I not noticed it before? I stopped and looked around, frightened. I shook the feeling. *This is foolishness. You have made a wrong turn somewhere. Don't be such a sissy.* But the hair on my neck was standing on end, and my heart was playing at a tempo that made it hard to breathe. I could hear whispering and movement. And I know you will not believe it, but I heard the kind of whispering that one would imagine a fish would make when talking to another fish. Doesn't that sound crazy?

Then I realized what else was bothering me. The forest, usually blanketed with rows of chattering mynah birds, scurrying lizards, and snapping crickets, was quiet. Not a bird could be seen, though I squinted my eyes at every coconut tree. The silence was unnerving. All was quiet, except for the fish sounds. It was like the cackle dolphins make, but deeper in pitch, liquid somehow. I began to hear other noises as well. I heard something like a waterfall, or rainfall, or a stream. Soon, the sound of running water was everywhere, the taste of it in my mouth.

I took a step to go, but my foot sank into swamp water. I looked down, incredulous. All around me was a kind of bayou. I was taking quick, short breaths at a time. When had the forest ended and the water begun? I couldn't remember leaving the forest. I stayed very still, all the while my mouth tasting cool water, my ears hearing running water. I turned in a circle. I could feel the panic rising, and then I saw him. He was staring right at me, as if he had been there all along, waiting for me to pick him out from the tall swamp grass.

He was dark, like the warlike Igorot tribes of the Cordillera Central. He wore an old gray shirt, rolled up to reveal strong forearms. His face was wide, his dark eyes dull, yet watchful.

"*Sino ang tumatawag sa akin?*" he asked. Who is calling me?

"M-Mang Minno," I stammered.

He nodded slowly, then looked down into the waters. He canted his head, as if listening. When he looked back to me he said my name: "Roman Flores."

I nearly fell backward. That was when I saw the shadows in the murky water, dark ink taking form around my feet. Fish all around me, weaving in between my feet. Mere fish, but they alarmed me. There was something different about them. I could see they had thought, and that was what frightened me the most. They gathered around and watched me expectantly, a swirl of metallic colors. They did not scatter as I turned and surveyed them.

A group of twelve in particular hovered near me. There was a difference in their appearance from the others. Each had a bright stripe of violet down the length of their backs. Their fins cast the kind of glow a candle gives off. They appeared to watch me with great interest.

"What is it you want, Roman? State what it is. The tribunal is listening."

"The tribunal? Uh . . . I come to ask . . . I want to become a fisherman." My hands shook as I watched the purple fishes.

He stood still at my words, then looked off toward the forest of trees. The trees had reappeared somehow. The only way I can describe it is it was as if the forest had become flooded by the ocean, the same forest, only filled with water. I could feel my feet solidly on the ground, but when I looked down I could not see past the murky waters. He studied my arms, the set of my shoulders, and the way my arms were soft from lack of work.

"Go home, Roman. Do not speak my name again." He turned, and as he started to walk away, the fish moved from around me and followed him.

I was so amazed by the sight that for a moment, I lost my voice. By the time I found it, he had almost disappeared into the trees. "Wait, Mang Minno. I would give anything to become like you. My family is starving." It came naturally, this lie.

I explained how my family worked without sleep, job after job. I think the desperation in my voice was what gave him pause. He seemed to pick through the truth in my words. He moved toward me, his dark eyes almost violet. The tribunal surrounded me again, touching noses. They looked upward at me, as if discussing my case with one another. They seemed to come to a decision, and though still surrounding my feet, they looked toward him.

Mang Minno nodded to them. "Perhaps, perhaps." His voice became gentle. "Come back tomorrow. Sleep tonight, and in the morning let the sun wash over you to clear your thinking." At his words the fishes swam violently between us. "Silence!" he bellowed. I thought he had gone mad. "I am weary,

Roman. But I must be certain. Come back. I ask only this: If you decide to return, remember the feel of the sun upon you."

"Yes, sir. How will I find you?"

"The same as today. Begin at the edge of the forest where the rays of the sun do not touch the ground, then call out my name. Farewell." He turned and walked away.

"Tomorrow." I cupped my hands together and called out to him. Already he was at the edge of darkness, surrounded by trees. No sooner had the words left my mouth than the forest became as it had always been. There was no water at my feet; my legs and pants were completely dry. I turned in a tight circle, and there were all the green-billed *malkoha* birds perched in the trees, grooming their long tails and chattering happily. I took a deep breath and ran home.

THAT NIGHT, ALL was as usual, and as I eased into the simplicity of our evening I began to wonder if I had imagined it all. I went to my room to check my bed, to see if it had been slept in. There was always the chance I had fallen asleep and dreamt it entirely. The maid called us to dinner and I sat down to eat, mentally scratching my head.

She had prepared my favorite dish, lugao with manok, the warm rice and chicken stew. I stirred the bowl, and the green onions and slivers of ginger appeared hidden in the thick porridge. I squeezed a slice of lemon over it and added a jolt of the pungent fish sauce known as patis, my mouth already watering. If you put just the right amount, the salty flavor of the sauce complements the sweetness of the ginger; too much and you have to throw out the whole bowl and start again.

I was still pondering my afternoon, allowing the steam from the bowl to rise and cool, when my parents walked in. My father sat down at the table and flapped open the day's news with a quick snap of his hands. He was dressed in a light gray Western vest with matching trousers. He and my mother were both dressed to go out for the evening. I glanced over their clothing with annoyance. They would be leaving us again.

I looked at my older brother, Roger, absorbed in his bowl of lugao. He spoke without looking up from his stew. "Daniel Romero is going to study in the States, Papa. When will we look into the schools I shall attend? Daniel's father is buying him a car."

I rolled my eyes. My brother and I were different, like milk and cola. We could stand each other only in front of our parents.

"We shall see, Roger. Concentrate on your studies," father answered through his paper. My brother pulled out a book at the table and started his studies.

Father peered over his paper at me. "There will be a social dance tomorrow at Aling Lumina's. Do not forget to come, Roman, not like the last time." He thrashed his paper. My eyes followed the servants as they walked back and forth. Our maid, Sara, was getting big around the hips. I watched as the extra weight on her behind tried to find a place to protrude in her small uniform.

My mother coughed to distract me. "Sara, please get a bigger-size uniform. I will not have you displaying yourself to my boys in this manner."

Poor Sara. She was sixty years old, not exactly a point of sexual interest to a fourteen-year-old. She blushed painfully and muttered, "Yes, ma'am.'"

I looked at my mother in irritation. She did that, spat things out without thinking of people's feelings. Like the time my brother brought home his first girlfriend, and my mother said as she was still smiling and waving good-bye to the girl from our window, "Her nose is as flat as the *banig* the servants sleep on. Can you not pick a prettier girl, Roger?"

"*Itay,* how long has it been since you have gone fishing?" I asked my father. "I hear there is a really good fishing spot just outside of the forest."

"What do you need to fish for? We have plenty of fish at our store."

"Oh, I wasn't thinking of myself. I thought maybe we could go have a look. Maybe send our fishermen there. We could go if you like, test the spot. We could sell whatever we trapped at our stores."

My father laughed. "We could not catch enough to make a difference. That is what we have workers for. Really, Roman, sometimes the ideas you have. Very uneconomical. If you want fish, just tell your mother. She will have the workers bring some home on their next run." We owned a market, and Father was not interested in anything that would cost instead of earn us money.

My father shook his head and went back to his paper. My mother had gotten up and was rearranging her hair in front of an oval mirror. My brother was bent over his book, and I marveled at how his spoon made it to his mouth each time without spilling onto his clothes. Yet I felt someone watching me and looked up to meet my grandfather's eyes.

"I was at the market today, Roman. I spoke with Mang Saro. He told me you were asking about a fisherman."

My grandfather was a keen observer of me, and I became so nervous that I bit into my spoon and yelled.

My mother rushed to my side and laughed. "I thought you had swallowed a bone." She took her hand and squeezed my cheeks.

"No, just the spoon," I explained, pushing her away in irritation.

She laughed and mussed my hair. "All right, a grown-up now, are you? No crying to Mommy?"

I snuck a glance at Grandfather; I could feel his eyes boring into me. "I wanted to know more about the fishing hole I mentioned to Father. I thought it might be a good place. Someone mentioned a fisherman who goes there often."

"A fisherman, you say? I knew a fisherman once, by the name of Mang Minno." My grandfather took a drink of his sangria; the slice of orange soaked red from the wine floated in the crystal goblet like a raft in a red ocean. He watched me closely as he said this. "He was a good friend of mine. In fact, you could say we were the very best of friends."

My head snapped up at this new development. My mind raced like a water snake. I knew my grandfather guessed every question before they even formed in my head.

"When did you know him?" I asked, ladling more lugao into my bowl and pretending to concentrate on the amount of patis to add. My palms and the undersides of my arms had broken out in perspiration.

"When did you hear of him?" he countered.

"When I spoke to the other vendors at the market."

"And what exactly did you hear? Tell me all of it."

"Nothing, *Lolo,* just that he is a good fisherman." I did not fear anyone, but if anyone could make me uncomfortable, it was my grandfather. I shifted in my seat and considered dropping my mother's precious plate collection to distract him. I weighed the time that would be wasted to discipline me and thought better of it.

Grandfather's eyes softened, but his voice remained gruff. "Leave it to me to teach you. Who do you think taught your father how to fish? Do not bother Mang Minno again, he has no patience for outsiders."

"Yes, *Lolo.*" I nodded in disappointment. I promised Grandfather I would not search for Mang Minno, and at the time I felt it in my heart to be true, but that is the way it is for liars.

THE NEXT AFTERNOON, I willed the clock in the suffocating heat of our classroom to reach one. Our teacher lectured on José Rizal, our national hero, and his battle in 1896 with the Spanish ruling class. What good did it do him to fight? I wondered if I could be so brave. To fight for something when it meant sacrificing my own life. He was killed in the end. I imagined myself as him, the bullets hailing down upon my body. My family on their knees, sobbing and regretting my death.

As soon as we were let out, I started walking to the forest. I hadn't forgotten my promise to my grandfather, but neither could I forget my promise to Mang Minno. Nothing could sway me. Not Pepe Rosales's invitation for a swim at his pool, not Paulo Cruz's bag of makapuno, though the thought of the small white balls of powdered fruit rolled in sugar made my stomach speak. I walked with a vengeance. When I got to the edge of the forest, where the blanket of branches blocked out the sun, my feet remembered the previous day, and they slowed their pace. I hesitated just outside of the darkness. I could feel my heart in my throat. I turned to look over my shoulder at my classmates, who were walking in an unorganized body. A part of me longed to go with them.

As I stood there contemplating, a cloud drifted over, blocking the sun and shading me. I remembered Mang Minno's words when I asked him how I would find him. *Begin at the edge of the forest where the rays of the sun do not touch the ground.* I looked up at the dark cloud in a panic, then back down to my feet, covered in darkness. Before I knew it, I was standing in the perimeter of the forest, where the sun did not tread. I saw my classmates off in the distance, fading from sight, then the entire area became enclosed by trees. All became eerily silent as the previous day. It was as if the entire forest were listening. I became so afraid that I called out, "Mang Minno."

There was a great sound of gushing water all around me. I felt as if a tidal wave were towering just behind, ready to swallow me.

"*Sino ang tumatawag sa akin?*" Who is calling me? He asked this even as I stood there before him, easily recognizable. His bare feet were set solidly apart, with the water lapping at his strong calves and rising slowly. His eyes, dark and opaque, squinted menacingly.

"*Ako lang, Mang Minno. Si Roman Flores,*" I called out. It is just me, Mang Minno. Roman Flores.

"Roman, so you have returned." His eyes blinked slowly shut, then open. It seemed a trick of the dark, but the lids of his eyes seemed to converge together the way a lizard's do. He turned quickly as if he floated on the water. "Come, I will show you how I call the fish."

"Call?" I stuttered, splashing and hurrying to catch up with him. He glided forward effortlessly. Feeling the need to speak, lest I lose myself to shaking, I looked sideways at him. "Are you as they say?"

"And what do they say?" His voice had the texture of the liquid mercury we had studied in chemistry class. It was elusive yet stationary, hovering just over my head, but I could not grasp it.

"Are you truly the Jonah in the Bible, who was caught inside the whale? The man God sent to preach to the city of Nineveh?"

He jerked his body sideways and looked at me then, an expression of great horror on his face. The fishes in the water grew thick in number and swam violently. Mang Minno shouted a laugh like a rushing waterfall. "No, I am not Jonah. But I know of him. I am not allowed to walk his waters."

The bitterness of his voice touched me like the fingers of the dead. I shivered. He took me through the waters to a part of the forest I had not known existed. I lost my footing, and for a moment I was submerged. I opened my mouth at the sight. All around were big fishes, giant even to a boy my size. Fishes the size of the caribous, the large water buffalos that pulled Father's carts in the fields. Small fishes as small as the little bothersome lice I detested. I gulped the water, clenching my eyes shut, expecting the flavor of mud and seaweed. But it tasted sweet, like the rice wine Father favored.

We walked up a steep rock that emerged from the water to a jagged point. I marveled at how quickly my clothes dried from the absence of wind. We stood at the precipice of the cliff, and Mang Minno slowly placed his hand on a thin rope tied around his neck, which he pulled up from beneath his shirt. I strained and pretended to look forward, but all the while my eyes were glued to the corners, watching his every move. Finally a bulk appeared at the neck of his shirt. I braced myself, waiting for the blazing amulet that it was rumored he carried. You cannot imagine my face. I blinked several times to clear my vision when I finally saw what it was he had tied to the end of that necklace.

It was a fishbone, as big as my hand. It was caked in dirt and something resembling phlegm. The bone itself was thick and smooth, the texture of ivory. The backbone had six pieces radiating from the center, three on each side. The end of it appeared to have been broken off from a longer piece. He took the bone and placed it whole into his mouth. I shuddered at the sight. He pressed his lips together and puffed his cheeks out, in much the same way a person whistles. A deep haunting sound with no bottom came forth. It pierced my ears and shattered the air into movement. Immediately great gusts of wind began to blow. His eyes moved from side to side, though he looked straight ahead. He took a breath and blew one more time. This time the sound reminded me of a trumpet. He pointed out to the ocean. "There, look, Roman."

In the water were thousands of ink shadows taking form beneath the surface. I blinked and they became fishes. There were the great *lapulapo* fish, the orange-and-white *dalagang bukid,* the ghost white *sapsáp,* and thousands of tiny silver-and-gold *dilis,* to name just a few. My legs wobbled at the absurdity of it all. I was scared. I hadn't felt fear until that moment, for it was then I realized he had in his possession a great power.

The fish had voices. They sang and called out in a million different tunes. They faced us, rows of them, listening, waiting for his instructions. The tribunal hovered around Mang Minno like guardians, their purple fins glinting in the sun.

Mang Minno laughed at me. "Well, what are you standing there for? Do you expect them to jump into your basket? They will, you know, if I tell them to."

I had forgotten the basket I carried in my hand. Our cook, Octavia, had given it to me that morning. I opened the basket and looked inside stupidly. Mang Minno shook his head and pointed a leathered finger downward.

"Open the basket, and throw it into the water."

I did as he told me to; my hands were shaking terribly. The basket sank into the clear water, and to my excitement and horror, the fishes moved into the bag, forming a polite line as if getting onto a bus. Mang Minno laughed at my expression of shock. He clapped my back and I nearly fell forward into the ocean of fish:

"Go home, Roman. Go home and tell your family they will soon be rich."

I was not sure if I even bade him good night. By the time I thought of it, I was walking in the sunlight with two bags full of undulating fish.

OCTAVIA GREETED ME at the door, her apron smeared purple from preparing the salty bagoóng spread and chopped tomatoes. My brother, Roger, loved to heap the mixture over his rice. Octavia's face registered shock. She looked at me, then down to my basket, then back at my face. No one in our household had ever seen me lift a finger in work. It was not necessary. Father would grow angry if he saw my brother or me even attempting to help a servant. "That is not what we pay them for; we have other servants to do that," he would say.

That was why when Octavia beheld my clothes reeking of fish, and my hair plastered against my face with sweat, she almost screamed.

"Who has told you to do this?" She looked around at the empty room accusingly. "Your father will have our heads. We will be out on the streets come evening. Who has allowed this? Oh, my goodness. I have five children to feed." She wrung her hands, her voice rising shrilly.

"No one told me to do anything," I barked at her hysterics. Then, more gently, I said, "Give these to Rolando and Ariel to bring to our store." They were our houseboys and did a number of odd chores. They were also my age. My father detested the idea of my socializing with them, so I did, at every opportunity. She shouted for the two of them, and within seconds you could hear the muffled padding of bare feet on our hardwood floors. My mother did not allow them to wear shoes inside our house. She was afraid they would scar the floors.

Rolando appeared first and grinned from the hallway. He nodded at me and I grinned back. Next came loud thumping sounds that would have made my mother faint if she had witnessed their origin. Ariel stomped into the kitchen, each foot tied to half a coconut shell, so that he was at least five inches taller. He had them strapped on in much the same way one walks on circus stilts or the American roller skates. The hollow half of each shell faced the ground. The fibers were perfect for glossing the hardwood floors. Rolando and I burst into laughter at the sight of Ariel. This was not an uncommon way to wax the boards, yet you had to know Ariel to appreciate the sight. He was the biggest clown and always in trouble within our household.

"*Hoy*"—Ariel nodded—"*maraming isdâ. Ang galíng mo namán.*" Hey, look at all that fish. You're good. He smiled appreciatively. His two front teeth were missing from our rock-climbing incident several weeks back, giving his words a lisping quality.

"The two of you, stop standing there and take these to the market," Octavia said with a frown, but I could tell she was hard-pressed not to laugh at Ariel's outlandish appearance.

"Okay, okay." Ariel wiped his hands and dropped to untie his coconuts. He looked up at me and nodded once with a jerk of his head. "*Sama ka?*" he asked. Come along? Only two words, but they promised a great deal of mischief and wrong routes before we got to the market.

"Okay," I answered, but just at that moment the front door opened and we could hear my parents enter the house along with my brother. Ariel and Rolando did not even stop to look at me, they walked straight out the back door to wait for Octavia to split the fish into four baskets.

My parents walked into the kitchen, and Octavia brandished the fish in her hand to distract them from my appearance. I watched their expressions. My mother was surprised. "Such healthy specimens. Where did you find these? It is as if someone has hand-fed them every day. Look at how their scales shine." She held up a squirming blue fish with bright gold stripes. "We shall bring some to Aling Lumina's party tonight." My mother laughed.

My father was so impressed. "Was this the fishing hole you spoke of? This catch is exceptional. You must show me where you caught these." He was so thrilled, he stopped my brother as he walked by. "Look, Roger, *talo ka palá ni Roman. Tingnán mo ang na huli niya'.*" Your brother bested you. Look at what he has caught.

My brother looked at the fish my father held up.

"*Tay,* you will get my clothes for Aling Lumina's dirty," Roger said, scowling in disgust. He made a big circle around my father and hurried down the hall to his room.

My father handed Octavia the rest of the fish. "*Oo ngâ anó,*" he exclaimed. Oh, yes. "Get dressed for Aling Lumina's party, Roman," he ordered as he rushed off to get ready.

In the hallway, I saw my grandfather. He stood at the doorway of his room as I passed. I did not look at him. I felt his eyes on me, stronger than the day before. I could feel his disapproval lashing me with every step I took. I chose not to meet his gaze. I gloried instead in the memory of my father's short compliments. I had brought home a prize catch. I felt like a man. I shoved my chest forward as I walked by. I must have been a real sight, my chest like a small twig, thrust forward against the wind that was my grandfather's eyes.

ALING LUMINA'S PARTY was in full swing when we arrived. My brother's friends were milling about the front of the house. They were talking to a group of young girls, and Roger went straight to them, like an arrow shot out of our car.

"Behave yourself tonight, Roman, ha?" my father warned. "Not like the last time." He and my mother disappeared in embraces and loud greetings.

"I will," I answered, but they were too far away to hear. I walked up the stairs slowly, with my hands in my pocket.

"Hi, Roman. Hello, Roman," the girls from my brother's group called out to me.

I inclined my head. They giggled, and I saw my brother put away his comb.

I went inside and found my friend Eduardo Rosales near the punch bowl. He was nearly as tall as me, but narrow in the shoulders, long in the arms, and short waisted. I looked around the room. It was filled with teens. Everyone was huddled in their safe little circles. I felt a mad urge to take this girl and that boy from their safe circles and mix them up. The same way I wished to throw my American football against my mother's imported china plates during dinner.

The sky when I looked out the window, past the swaying leaves of yellow acacia and palm trees, was a watered-down blue. As if the oil had separated from the color in the bottle and all the ink had spilled out. Clouds drifted eastward, tinted coral by the fading sun. The others eyed me suspiciously, the older boys trying to look tough yet having to look up past my shoulders. They were wearing dress shirts and ties, or the traditional *barong tagalogs* made of fine pineapple thread. I came with a shirt but no tie, and Father had berated me the entire way. I held my jacket tucked under my arm.

"Another boring night," I said to Eduardo. I was about to walk out of the room when I saw Aurora Martinez, Mang Minno's youngest daughter, walk in. My brother and his friends jostled one another, sneaking glances her way. They looked like a bunch of fools talking in poses they had obviously practiced at home.

Eduardo grinned stupidly. "You will never guess what I just heard."

He waited for me to ask what it was. I gave him a look.

"I overheard Aurora Martinez wants you to ask her to dance."

I scowled. "She never even looks my way." I chanced a glance in her direction.

"Well, you know what they say: When someone likes you, they avoid you even more."

"She must be in love with me, then," I said wryly. "Anyways, where did you hear this?" I tried to hide the hope in my voice.

"Her friends Theresa and Felicita."

I looked at Eduardo, encouraged, "Yes?"

"Yes." He shrugged. "She said she thought you were dangerous."

"Dangerous, and she likes that?"

"Remember that time you ran off to visit those caves in Cavite without telling your mother?"

"And all the police were searching for my kidnapper?"

"And the time you dove off the top of that waterfall and split the back of your head like a broken water trough?"

I looked over at Aurora, standing near the punch table surrounded by her friends. She didn't seem particularly interested in what they were saying. I looked back at Eduardo. He shrugged again, but this time with a grin.

"Okay," I said.

"You're going to ask her to dance?" Eduardo grabbed my elbow.

I pulled his fingers off me. "I'm just going over to see what's going on."

As I approached the table, Aurora's friends began sneaking glances at me, and to my surprise they scattered and left Aurora standing alone. She turned immediately and picked up a plate. I excused myself and did the same.

"Hello, Aurora," I said, studying the food.

"Hi, Roman." She spooned some rice onto her plate.

We stood surveying the rest of the table. Finally she spoke again. "Did you just get here?"

"Yes, but I am probably going to leave soon. I was thinking of borrowing Aling Lumina's boat." I don't know how I even thought of that, except that perhaps I was trying my best to seem wild. I wasn't even sure if Aling Lumina had a boat.

"Don't you like the music?" she asked, looking down at her shoes.

"Would you like some lechón?" I asked, impaling a crispy piece of roasted pig.

"Yes, please." She lifted her plate, and I placed several pieces onto the blue-and-yellow china.

I reached for her wrist as she pulled her plate away. "Here, let me put some sarsa on it," I offered, ladling the thick spicy sauce over the pork.

We became nervous from the contact. We studied the table again. I saw that one of the large fish I had caught had already been grilled and sliced open. It was presented on an oblong plate with red sauce and onions, garnished with green and red bell peppers. I took my fork and reached for a piece. I dropped the fork. The eye had moved.

"What was that?" Aurora asked, picking up my fork from the table. It still had a piece of fish attached to it.

I looked at her. "Did you see it, too?"

"See what? I meant, why did you drop the fork?" She placed the silver delicately on my plate and speared a piece of fish for herself.

I winced and took a step back, waiting.

"Would you like some sauce, Roman?"

I couldn't speak. I shook my head. She frowned, smiling unsurely. She closed her eyes. "Mmm, taste the fish, Roman. It is wonderful. Did you truly catch this yourself?"

I raised the fork to my mouth, all the while expecting the white meat to move. It did not, and I decided I must have been imagining it. I put the morsel in my mouth; the taste was fresh, the sweetness took your breath away. I swallowed. "This is good," I said to her. Then, suddenly, my mouth began to burn, worse than the time I had eaten an entire bag of chili peppers. My eyes watered, and I looked around in a panic, then grabbed the large spoon in the punch bowl and drank from it.

Aurora laughed. "What are you doing?"

I couldn't answer her. Suddenly her image blurred and I could see water all around me. I shook my head. Aurora appeared before me, concern on her face.

"Roman?"

"It is nothing," I began, but another image blocked hers out, this time stronger. I saw the sky the same color as the ocean. There was no horizon to separate the two. It was dusk, and the water was silver blue. I heard laughter, a man's laughter. I saw a man running in terror toward the water, away from someone, from me. I shook my head.

"Roman, are you all right?" Aurora put a hand to my shoulder.

The image disappeared at her touch. I took an unsteady breath. My whole body was shaking. "Do you want to dance?" I blurted.

"Yes," she said.

I took her hand and walked out onto the dance floor. My brother and his friends stopped talking the minute we walked past. I couldn't help but smile, but I was still shaken.

I placed my hand stiffly on her waist and almost jumped at the softness of it.

"Roman, you're shaking," she said.

"You smell like flowers," I told her.

"Thank you. You smell like . . ." She paused. "Fish."

I looked at her in surprise and we both started laughing. I could feel Roger glaring at me from the sidelines.

"Did you want to borrow Aling Lumina's boat to go fishing tonight?" she asked excitedly. "I think that would be great fun. Would you take me?"

"Of course," I answered before I could stop the words from swimming out of my mouth.

"When, when shall we go?"

"After the next dance? I need time to look for the boat."

"Fine, let me just gather my things." She rushed off as soon as the song ended. Her girlfriends were waiting, and they surrounded her like a harem, laughing and chattering away.

I walked past my brother, who called out to me. I went straight to Eduardo. He was stupid with excitement.

"Oh, my God, you really did it, Roman. You are king of the mountains. You are the head carabao."

"Something's wrong. I ate the fish and I heard laughter."

"What?" Eduardo asked.

"Mang Minno, I heard his voice. He was laughing."

"The old fisherman? But how do you know what he sounds like?" Eduardo was staring at me.

"She wants to go for a boat ride. She thinks I want to go fishing in the dark."

Eduardo looked at me as if I were crazy. Our parents would have convulsions if we left the party. It was just not done. "What do you mean? Why would she think that?"

"Because I told her. Does Aling Lumina have a boat?" I asked, hoping she did not.

"Let us go and see." Eduardo wrinkled his brow in agitation. I blinked at him. That was one of the things about Eduardo. He never questioned the stupidity of my requests, just helped me to achieve them.

"All right." I shoved my hands in my pockets and followed him out. I glanced back at the table of food, but the fish sat properly on its plate.

THE NIGHT WAS hot, with the scent of jasmine. The orange moon sat low above the ocean, a ball of fire smoldering against the black. The water lapped softly against the dock. Behind us, the gay lanterns of the house flickered, music played, and laughter filtered out to us.

There was a *bangkâ,* bouncing gracefully, anchored to the pier by a loosely knotted rope. The waves lifted and placed it, carried, then gently nudged the pier with its bow, in a soft drumbeat. I placed a foot in the small rowboat. The music stopped, and the water below pushed against the pressure of my shoe. I looked at Eduardo.

"Your father will be angry . . . no, furious. He will want to send you away to a private school. It will be so private that the students themselves will have trouble finding it. You'll be in purgatory, the kind Mrs. de Leon lectures about, with the souls walking around with no memories, always trying to find their thoughts. The souls that starve, with plenty of food, only when they eat it, it is not enough. Never enough—"

"Eduardo . . ." I brought him back to me. "We are not going anywhere. I will hide the boat. We will say Aling Lumina does not have one."

"Oh . . ." Eduardo's face crumpled, and he breathed a deep sigh. I could feel his eyes willing me to change my mind, to force him to go on this adventure. I would not meet his stare. I had made a promise to myself to behave, to try to win my father's affection the way Roger did.

I stepped into the boat. The inside was filmed with seawater, and my foot did not catch immediately, but the water took to my new shoes quickly enough. "Father will love this," I mumbled. "Eduardo, throw me the rope."

There were two sets of oars, still wet. They slid sideways and thumped against each other. I thought to hide the boat among some tall weeds, when Aurora called out to us.

"Wonderful, you have found a boat. I think it will fit the five of us. What do you think?" They skipped over to the dock.

I pursed my lips together and made an effort to turn up the corners. "Let's go." I held out a hand to Aurora. Eduardo turned to help Felicita and Maria Consuelo, but I had already shoved the little boat away. The girls screamed, nearly falling into the water. Eduardo and the girls watched us from the pier, half smiles pasted on their faces, unsure if I would return for them.

"Too many people!" I shouted back.

Aurora sat with her mouth open. I was ready to toss her over if she complained, but to my surprise, she began to laugh. "I have always wanted to do that."

I began to row, and as I cleared the pier, I saw my brother standing solitary on the pier, watching us in the dark. Aurora looked at me. I shook my head in silent answer. No, of course I would not go back for Roger. He would only nag me the entire way. "Let him tell if he wants," I said loud enough for Roger to hear.

The air caught a chill as we drifted farther from shore, and you could see a soft mist swirling just above the warm waters. I took my coat and put it around her.

She shook her head and offered me my coat back. "I like the breeze. And I want to help you row."

I took the coat, and my hand brushed hers. I felt myself smile in the dark. I could smell her fragrance, light and flirtatious. Her black hair reflected the moonlight. I felt a bottomlessness to my stomach. She reached past me for the second set of oars. When she bent over to pick them up, her face brushed near mine and I swallowed hard. My eyes could not break free of her gaze. Her eyes were dark pools of ink. Her lower lip was full and pink, like the flesh of a grapefruit. I longed to taste it.

Aurora's brow lifted in consternation. "We have forgotten our fishing nets."

"It doesn't matter," I answered, breaking free of her spell and feeling like a fool. "The ride itself will be enjoyable."

She did not seem to notice, but the water propelled us forward as if it had a specific destination in mind. We went down a ways, following the smooth lines of the shore.

"Or, well, maybe we can use this basket," I said to my own surprise, for I did not remember seeing the large basket when we had first stepped in.

"Perfect." She clapped her hands. "Where was it hidden?"

I tried for an explanation, but I could not help staring at the basket in wonder. Aurora didn't seem to require an answer. Her face was smudged from the dirty oars, but she wasn't concerned.

"Look at the houses," she breathed. The houses were small golden lanterns that dotted the darkness. "We should stop." She pushed her hair back distractedly. "Where is the basket, Roman?"

I handed her the basket and she lit a match.

"Where is the candle I gave you?" She whirled around, her silken hair catching my cheek. She took the candle and the wick came alive from the match. She peeked into the water. "I don't see anything, Roman. Here, you are the fisherman." She handed me back the basket. She did not notice, but the moment I took the basket, the water came alive with motion.

"Oh, they have been here all along." Aurora laughed. "Look at all the fish. We have come to the right place. Throw the basket in, Roman."

She took the breath from me; where had I heard that last phrase? I tried to remember, but I was transfixed at the two violet orbs that peered out at me from the shadows of the tall swamp grass. The boat floated about, and the moonlight danced just before the shoreline of thick trees. It was then that I saw him. Mang Minno stood silently, violet fins threading around his feet.

"The tribunal." I mouthed the words. I almost panicked and turned the boat around when I noticed that the glowing eyes were not directed at me. He was staring at Aurora, his daughter.

"Roman." Aurora put her hand on my shoulder. "Throw the basket in."

I did as she instructed, terrified, already knowing what would happen. The basket sank downward, and I heard her gasp. She thinks it will be lost, I thought, but the handles remained floating. I was rooted to the wooden seat, watching the basket.

"Well, pick it up." Aurora smiled at me uncertainly. I looked at her with trepidation, flexing and clenching my hands, which were each propped upon my thighs. She seemed to catch my unease and glanced at the basket curiously. The moment I reached my hands out to the handles of the basket, I swear to you, the basket practically jumped into my hands. I swallowed and pulled up, dreading what I would see. I was in shock. With all the different types of fish swimming and mingling about our boat, the container was filled only with *bangos,* the milkfish that our cook, Octavia, always marinated in vinegar and garlic before baking.

"Only *bangos,*" I said with wonder.

"Ooh, my favorite." Aurora laughed.

My attention snapped to her, and then back to the shadows, where I saw the violet orbs recede into the dark.

"We should be getting back. Getting you home, that is." I gestured to her.

"It makes no difference, Roman, they won't even notice that I am gone."

I only liked her until that moment, but those last words, they echoed my own heart. I fell for her then. "We can return again," I suggested.

WHEN WE DOCKED in the little pier, the guests were already leaving, carrying plates of take-home food. They looked like ants marching away from a picnic. The servants balanced flat woven containers over their heads. Eduardo was waiting at the dock, like a true friend. Some of my brother's friends passed us on our way in. "Your father is looking for you," they said in the same tone they'd use to say, "Oh, boy, you are in for it."

Eduardo's father was the first adult to see us. He strode over, rolling his sleeves. "Sorry, *Tay.*" Eduardo's shoulders rose to protect his ears, his father's favorite target.

"What did I tell you about following Roman around like a lapdog?"

He stepped around me, hitting Eduardo on the ear, then clamping a hand on it and pulling him forward.

"Ow, ow." Eduardo sucked air through his teeth.

"He will be your downfall. How many times have I told you? If he asked you to jump into a flaming volcano, you would do so, hah?"

I looked at Aurora. Her two friends had also waited on the dock. They were starting to sniffle, their eyes red.

"Aurora, how could you leave us? I lied to your mother and told her you were in the party somewhere." Felicita folded her arms.

I interrupted, "Do not worry, I will take the blame. Tell them I promised only to take you around the house, but that I changed courses in the middle, and there was no way to turn back."

Aurora was appalled. "I will not let you take the blame."

I did not have time to respond, for we were now standing at the door. I braced myself for a scolding. I could see my father sitting composed, the lines of his face deceptively smooth. My brother sat beside him solemnly. I narrowed my eyes at Roger's betrayal. My mother sat beside Aurora's mother, who did not seem concerned in the least.

I felt Aurora's breath warm and soft beside my ear. "I told you my mother would not notice."

Aling Lumina looked up at me, and her eyes measured Aurora with brittle kindness. "Aurora, you should not be going out alone with young boys unchaperoned."

Aurora went straight to her mother, who glanced over at her, then resumed the conversation. "As I was saying, Lumina, you really should come to Manila with me. There is a social club there just built. And the American soldiers frequent it often." She sighed dreamily.

I was the only one left standing before the doorway. I waited for my father to stand so we could hurry home and have the punishment done with. I wondered what rules he would conjure this time.

My father snorted at my expression. "What, are you expecting a punishment? What purpose would it serve? I am tired of worrying over you."

I turned away from him to offer to walk Aurora home, but my father's next words set me on a different course. "Why can you not be more like your brother, Roger? He causes me no grief. He brings home good grades. But you, you cause my hair to go white. Each time you do something, it is like shoveling more dirt over my grave. What is it you want from me?"

Aurora tried to intercede. "I asked him to take me out—"

"Stay with your mother, child," my father interrupted, turning to her with a pitying smile. "Do not waste your time on Roman. He is like a magnet, attracted to misbehavior."

I never received so much attention from my father as when he was angry with me. I was so furious at that moment; I thought I would light the floors on fire with the heat of my anger. I hated my father, hated him so much that I pounded my fist into my hand.

"Oh, Roman. We will have none of that here, ha?" my mother warned. "Be a good boy, wait in the car. We are expected at your *tita* Connie's tomorrow. Rest yourself now so that you are refreshed, and she can see how handsome you have become."

I looked at my mother in disbelief. "Don't you care about anything but how we look?"

She sniffed and rolled her eyes at Aling Lumina, as if to say, "You see what I have to put up with?" I knew deep inside she was mortified and would not be able to live it down for the next five months, at least.

"I am not going to any party tomorrow, or the next day. I am sick of going to parties. I am sick of you showing us off, pretending you care, and then forgetting about us." I turned on my heels and walked out the door.

"*Hoy, hoy!*" my mother shouted in alarm. "Mauriano," she said to my father.

"Let him go." My father's voice was filled with exasperation and finality.

I ran out into the night, the embarrassment of my tears goading me on. My legs moved and bounced off the ground like those belonging to a marionette. I ran to the top of a steep hill and looked out upon the village below.

In the distance I could see the phenomenon of the dancing fireballs on Lake Sumpa. They looked like small tennis balls from where I sat, and this was at two kilometers. We were forbidden to go there. It was said that at close range they were the size of human heads, and upon closer inspection the fireballs wore faces of the damned. These faces cried tears of fire, and they wandered, begging the Lord for forgiveness. They grazed just above the water, and if you called to them, they would come rolling toward you, pleading to you to pray for them. If you wanted to wish bad things upon someone, you could do it there, before them, and that wish would come true.

"I wish I were someone else's son! I wish I had a different father!" I shouted to the lake below.

The moment I said this, I felt a shock run through my body. My eyes blurred, and once again I saw a vision. It was the same man, running from someone, from me. He tripped, he fell into the water. "Please, no," he cried out, holding up an arm to protect himself.

I heard Mang Minno's laughter. "No competition. There is no one to rival me." A blinding white light, and then the image was gone, leaving me exhausted and perspiring on the hillside. I shuddered and stood up quickly on shaking legs.

OUR HOUSE WAS silent when I arrived; only the sliding of the long hand of our clock could be heard. I took off my shoes. When I walked past my parents' room, I heard my father snoring. The light to my brother's room was turned off as well, but the moonlight illuminated his bed. I could see the even rise and fall of his chest. As I walked by Grandfather's open door, he called out to me.

"Roman, come here." His voice was deep, compelling. I felt his strength reach out across the dark.

I walked into his room, holding my shoes. He was sitting up in bed with his legs crossed. I stood in the middle of his room, with the glow of the moon encompassing the two of us.

"Yes, *Lolo?*" I asked impatiently.

"Where have you been? You smell of fish. Your brother was worried about you."

"Roger? The only reason he was worried was that I left with his favorite girl."

My grandfather said nothing; he let me stew in my annoyance.

"I'm tired, I want to go to sleep now," I said.

"Sometimes people, like your mother and father, become consumed by other things. They forget what is important."

"I know, I know." I brushed his words away.

"Yes, you know everything." His voice softened. I guess he felt how futile it sounded, my parents caring anything for me. "Why don't we go fishing this week? It has been a long time since I have done that. I used to be quite the fisherman at your age." My grandfather chuckled.

"Sure, *Lolo,*" I said distractedly. "Good night."

"Good night, Roman. Don't forget to say your prayers."

"I won't," I lied. I had long ago stopped saying them. They never seemed to be heard. I was angry at God for not giving me a real father.

I DID NOT sleep that night, and in the morning I passed my friends on the way to school and went straight to the forest. I felt a pull, deep in my chest, as if an invisible hook were tied to my soul, dragging it forward. I walked with my thoughts hovering around my head, random thoughts about my father, my family. The sun was already warm upon my face. Large red-and-gold butterflies fluttered before me, as big as my hand. From behind a tree, a red mouse deer peered at me with its large doe eyes. It raised its ears and flicked them nervously before hurrying across the carpet of pine needles and diving into a cluster of emerald-colored ferns.

Before I knew it, I had stepped into the shade of trees. The water rushed around my feet as if from a newly opened dam. I looked up to find Mang Minno eyeing me from a small clearing of trees. I remembered the visions, and my confidence wavered. I could see the sunlight just beyond my reach. He approached quickly, closing the gap between us.

"So, you are a wealthy young man after all. Or shall you tell me that you were merely there last night to chauffeur the rich children?"

I bowed my head. "I thought if I told the truth you would not want me as an apprentice."

He wore an amused smile. "Never apologize for a lie. It helped you to meet me, did it not? Do not ever show that you have been found out. Keep a straight face, throw the other person off balance. Make them doubt what they know. You could have told me that you had rich friends. Lying can be very useful. It can win you a card game, elevate your standing, it can avoid hurt feelings, give you the advantage over an opponent. It is"—he paused—"an underused gift.

But certainly lying and anger are trivial matters here. What difference would they make to mere fish?" He laughed.

But they were not mere fish, I thought.

"Did Aurora like her *bangos?*"

"She was very happy."

"Those are her favorite." He smiled, and for a moment the opaque fishlike quality of his eyes became light, very humanlike, very normal. But only for a second.

"I thought you would be angry at me for taking her out there." I was talking nonsense, saying whatever was on my mind.

"Aurora is safe in my waters. But keep her to this area. Do not take her past the dark waters. The sun can sometimes be blinding."

"I won't." I shook my head. "I meant to ask you, when I ate the fish last evening—" I stopped, thinking how to explain how my stomach had churned while the others had consumed it with no such concerns.

Mang Minno chuckled. "Did you think you could eat them, too?"

I stood dumbfounded at his words.

"Do not worry, they are not poisonous; anyone who eats them will be fine. It is only you. Masters do not eat their servants, do they?"

"Sir?" I asked, bewildered, but he was already walking ahead of me. "I had a vision. There was a man, running away from my sight. And laughter."

"Shall we fish?" he asked. He wore a smile, but his eyes challenged me.

"Yes, I would like that very much." I felt better immediately at the mention of fishing. We spent the entire day calling them. There were more exotic species, ones I had not seen before. There was one he called a stonefish, for its brow and fins were sharp edged like rocks. Tiger-striped puffer fish with their square heads gazed at me, ready for my instructions. Several poisonous sea snakes appeared, and I jumped back, disturbing the water. Mang Minno laughed and grabbed one of the snakes, and the slithering creature became instantly paralyzed and stiff as a stick. Mang Minno pulled it out of the water and broke it in half and then into quarters. He fed the pieces to his violet-finned tribunal. They slapped the water happily with their tails.

He taught me how to use my two hands to clap, and then he would whistle, and when I dipped a finger in the water, the fish would swim to us.

"All they need is a guide, you see? Come, I will show you a different way." He waved me forward with his hand.

I would have followed him, but I noticed the orange blaze of the sun as it descended behind the mountain in the distance. Had I spent my entire day with him? "I have mass tonight," I blurted.

"Ah, mass." He studied me. "Do you wonder at times if your prayers are even heard?"

"Sir?" I asked, shifting my weight from one foot to the other.

"In church, does it ever seem to you a kind of game? Hypocritical. Be humble, they say, yet people come in their best clothes. Give penance, yet as they close their eyes and kneel, they compare who is better dressed, the beauty of someone else's wife, the sway of her hips, they think of anything but prayers."

"I have to go," I answered.

"Of course." He bowed his head. "I will see you again."

I WAS LATE for mass. My footsteps echoed to the high ceilings and cupola portraits of angels, and Jesus in the garden of Gethsemane. I found our pew. I knelt and made the sign of the cross before entering. The minute I did this, I became disoriented and almost lost my balance. I moved past my brother and stood beside my mother. They were standing and holding the Book of Psalms in their hands. She reached out and pinched my side, just under my arm, and twisted my skin beneath her fingers. I gritted my teeth.

I grew dizzy as the priest raised his hand in the sign of the cross and said his blessings. My ears burned at the words. The benediction seemed louder than normal. My fingers had broken out into a scaly rash. It happened immediately after I had dipped them in the holy water and pressed them to my forehead, my chest, my shoulders, and my lips in the sign of the cross.

When the wine was passed around, I felt a coldness go through my body. I took the goblet from my grandfather, and I knew at that moment something was terribly wrong. I placed the cold edge of the copper to my mouth and took a drink. My throat closed and I began to choke. I spat out the wine and dropped the goblet. A gasp went through the entire church and I ran out the door.

It was worse outside. The vision came to me again, the one of the man running into the water, with terror in his eyes, away from me. "Please," he begged. The laughter came again, as if it were from my own mouth. "I have no rivals. I share my waters with no one." What happened next dropped me to my knees. I saw hands, but were they *my* hands? They reached out and pointed to the terrified man. "Eat," my voice said. And that was when I saw the tribunal, and I realized that the pointing hand was not mine, but Mang Minno's. I was witnessing what he had done, as if I were in his body. The tribunal surrounded the man, and then in an instant, a hundred fishes attacked him, and the waters ran red.

I screamed and put my hands to my eyes, and the visions fell away. I found myself kneeling in front of the church. The mass was still going on inside. I stumbled away and ran for home. I remembered all the warnings the other fishermen and vendors had given me. "Stay away from him," they had said. "He is dangerous. He uses black magic." All the way home I heard Mang Minno's laughter.

I WAITED FOR my parents to return from church. You would have thought the punishment from my father would be so severe that I would not be able to sit for days. Do you know, he was too busy to take the time even to punish me? He had a business meeting that evening; he and my mother went straight to this engagement. I lay in bed wondering at what had happened to me when Roger peeked in.

"Did you swallow the bread?"

I shrugged. He waited at the door a moment. I waited for him to say what it was that was on his mind, but the next sound I heard was the door to his room, shutting behind him.

My grandfather came to me. "You are feeling better?"

I nodded.

"Good."

"I swallowed the bread," I lied.

He squinted at me, as if my image had become out of focus for a moment, then he turned and went to his room.

I LIED ALL the time after that. I lied to Father Ambrosio about going to confession. I lied about going to school. When I did attend class, I copied from the person in front of me. I exaggerated the truth in order to make a story more engrossing. I became compulsive about lying; I could not stop. I no longer chased my father around, begging for a morsel of his attention. I had someone else whose praise and advice I valued. It did not matter that he frightened me. I distorted the truth from myself.

I WAS GROWING closer to Mang Minno and yet more afraid. I brought up the visions that had been plaguing me. "The other evening, I had these images. I saw a man running away from me. But he was not running from me. He was fleeing from you," I accused Mang Minno.

Mang Minno smiled at me placatingly. "Yes."

I lost my words. I did not expect him to confess the truth. "You killed him."

"I allowed you to see that. I meant to test your courage. You have proven yourself, Roman."

My head spun. I had never received such blatant praise. I relished it. It started at my feet and filled my chest. I forgot about the man and the red water.

"When will you show me how to use your whistle?" I gestured to the bone he had beneath his shirt. He touched his dark hand to the rope that held his talisman. I had grown familiar with the withered leather of his palms and the thick ropes of pale green veins against the dark skin.

He was quiet.

"There is still too much brightness. The eclipse of Agraria falls on All Souls' Day this year. The darkening comes once every twenty years. This is the only time the amulet can be transferred to the successor. Ten days from now."

I became excited. All Souls' Day, also known as Todos los Santos, happened on the evening of October 31. Halloween, they call it in the States.

"I am ready."

He chuckled. "That is not for you to decide. Do not answer so quickly. This position I hold carries much responsibility. There are three tests you must pass."

"I will pass them. What are they?"

"You must bring an innocent to witness the proceedings. You must warn them that they may lose something by coming."

"That is all?"

"You must turn your back on all relations." He watched me carefully as he said this.

"What is the third?"

"The third is the tribunal's acceptance and the final transfer itself. Sometimes, even when all three are met, the transfer does not hold."

"It will hold," I said with a set of my chin.

He watched me gravely. "It means living in isolation from your friends and family. The more you demand of the fish, the more they demand of your soul."

I WENT HOME that evening in good spirits. I brought two bags of fish and dropped them off at our store. I meant to leave them with our store clerks, but my father was there and he called out to me from the back room.

I sighed, expecting him to reprimand me for leaving the church the other evening.

He hurried up to me, very animated. "Roman, your fish are the talk of the village. Everyone has come back begging for the same. They claim it is the sweetest fish they have ever tasted. You must gather more."

"I could show you where I caught them. We could go together," I offered.

"Oh no, not this week. Next week, perhaps. You know me, I must watch the store. But you must go. You have become a big name." He regaled me with stories of how the customers were begging for more. That they claimed the fish was unlike any they had ever tasted. "So fresh," they said. His smile was like a candle that immediately lost its fire. His face wrinkled back into concentration. He opened the cash register and became engrossed in counting his money. I waited, still smiling, not understanding that I had been dismissed. I looked around at our baskets filled with ice and fish. I studied the woven containers overflowing with pineapple, langkâ, kalamansî, and bayabas. All this food that would bring us money, and still he had no time for me. He only had time for making more. I wanted to tip the baskets and crush the fruit. I wanted to take the fish and throw them into the dirt. I chided myself for falling for his enthusiasm. After all Mang Minno had given to me, I was ready to give it all up just to be in my father's light. And here he was, ignoring me once again.

My mother walked in, her mango-colored slippers flapping against her heel and back onto the floor in lazy fashion. She nodded to me.

"O, bakit nárito ka pa?" she asked. Why are you still here? "Go home, the store is closed. We could have used your help earlier. There is only the money left to count." She went to my father and bent down to count with him. I sighed; how easy it would be to turn my back on these people.

THE NEXT SEVERAL days I woke burning, and my hands would not cool until I had touched the waters of the forest. I avoided Grandfather at all costs. He had grown suspicious and watched me like an eagle waiting to swoop up a monkey. He no longer invited me to fish. He spent his days in prayer with his door locked. I had dreams that he stood over me at night, but when I woke, the room would be empty.

ON THE MORNING of the eclipse, the day was strange. It was only six, yet the morning was unusually bright. A glare permeated the sky and sucked the color from it. There was no sound, as if the earth were holding its breath in anticipation. My fingers were burning especially hot, and I rushed out the door, thinking, This will be the day. I must not be late. I almost did not recognize her standing there, until she called my name.

"Roman, I have not seen you at school." Aurora smiled thinly. "You missed my party last night. I saved you some cake." She held out a tiny brown bag with a pink ribbon laced through the top.

"Thank you." I reached out and took the bag. She looked pretty in a peach dress with white orchid prints. She wore her sweater around her shoulders, like a cloak, buttoned only at the top, her arms free to hold her books.

"Will you be at school today?"

"If I catch enough fish," I said distractedly, looking off toward the forest. The eclipse would start at noon, and I had yet to think of a way to bring Roger to the forest, or Eduardo. Either one would do. Both were as innocent as babies.

"I could save you a seat in Mrs. Martinez's."

"No, don't bother."

She looked down at her books.

"Aurora, I'm a busy person now. Maybe it would be best if you—"

She nodded. "I'll see you, Roman." She turned, her body folded inward over her books, and I watched her go.

I was not afraid of her leaving me. I had come to realize that her attraction to me had everything to do with the fish. If I stopped, I would lose her completely. If I continued, she would always be there.

"You're really becoming a jerk, you know that?" Eduardo came out from behind some bushes. The branches snapped back into place like a whip. The cicadas called shrilly in anger.

"Edo, wonderful. I was going to look for you. Only I'm really in a hurry. I—"

"Don't have time," he finished my sentence for me. I had been neglecting him also. "I came to tell you that you missed our presentation together in class. That's the second time. You also missed your promise to watch over my mama's booth at the carnival with me."

I closed my eyes tight. "Eduardo, I have more important— I'll talk to Mrs. Martinez. I'll ask her to only mark me for it and not discredit you."

"She let me make it up. I just came to tell you that I wanted out of the science project we are supposed to do next month. Pepe Barreras and I have already started one together. Find another partner."

I blinked at him. Eduardo had never told me what to do. He was not one to make such decisions. "Sure," I told him. "Again, Edo, I am—"

"Sorry. I know."

"Let me make it up to you. Come with me to the forest today. We can watch the eclipse. I am going to see Mang Minno, and it will be a great adventure. I must warn you, however, that you may lose a piece of clothing or something important in the process."

Eduardo looked at me. "Have you not heard anything I have said?"

I opened my mouth and then shut it. I shrugged. "Eduardo, the forest."

He waved away my answer and turned to go.

I looked around in frustration. I needed to find my brother. He was my last chance, though I suspected he too would be unwilling. We had never been great friends. I almost expected Grandfather to drop from the sky to lecture me, but I knew he was still at home. I had seen him myself when I passed his room.

He was up early with candles lit, praying on his little altar. He was on his knees, holding his crucifix in his hand, when I left the house. He was probably praying for my grandmother. He did that during their anniversaries. When I say anniversaries, I mean they did not have just the one day when they were married. He honored the anniversary of their first meeting, the anniversary of their first Christmas, the anniversary of their first kiss, and the anniversary of her death, as well as the birthdays of each of their children.

I walked toward the forest without fear; it felt like home to me. My instincts had grown acute; within seconds I knew someone was following me. I disappeared into a shade of trees, and as the forest filled with water, I jumped out in front of my stalker.

Roger stood with eyes large and terrified. He looked at me, then back at the ground, where the water was now up to his thighs. "Roman, there's a tidal wave c-coming," he stuttered.

I crossed my arms over my chest. "What are you doing? Did Grandfather send you?" I was annoyed, because I had not invited him, as Mang Minno instructed.

Roger looked at me. "Roman, do you not see the water?"

"Of course I see the water. It is because of me the water has become like this."

"What are you saying? Are you mad? Let us go." He grabbed my arm and took a few steps before he realized nothing looked familiar to him. "Roman!" he shouted desperately. "Where are we?"

"Let me go." I shook my arm free. "You're acting like a fool. Mang Minno will think my family is made up of idiots. He already knows I have a father who does not keep promises."

"So Grandfather was right. You do know this man. He is evil, Roman. He has no soul. Here, wear this." Roger took a leather necklace with an image of a saint from his pocket and tried to put it over my head.

I shoved him away.

"Roman, I know it is hard. I know Papa isn't much of a father."

"What do you know?" I shouted. "You are his pet. But not for long. The minute I get the amulet, that will all change." I clamped my mouth shut, furious at Roger for luring me into spilling my secret. I kicked at the water.

"The amulet is real, too? Grandfather said—but I didn't—does Mang Minno . . . ? Will the fish . . . ? The ones we . . . ? At the store?" His words were a jumble of dead-end questions.

"Go home, Roger, or you may lose something more than your words." I gave him the designated warning without meaning to, and he gave me the desired response of the innocent.

"I will stay."

He had answered correctly, like a pig to the roasting pit. It set a tingling in my spine. "Here, I will show you the way out." I pulled at his shirt, and he let me lead him, but a large shadow of a bird loomed over us. It was then I felt his presence.

"So you have brought Roger." Mang Minno stood before us.

Roger would have fallen backward had I not been holding on to his shirt.

"Roger, it is all right, you're okay," I soothed him. He was hyperventilating, his intake of breath tripping over his fear. "Rog!" I shook him. "I am sorry, Mang Minno, Roger is not the person I have selected to witness my baptism. I did not invite him. I shall find someone before the designated time."

"The time is already at hand. He has come willingly. He shall do."

A small moan escaped Roger. He was watching Mang Minno like a man who knew. And funny, Mang Minno seemed to look at Roger with the same respect.

"I brought the book." I pulled out my Bible from my shoulder bag. Mang Minno had requested that I bring it for the ceremony. It was a gift during my first Communion. It had come along with a set of pewter rosary beads, which I had stuffed into my pocket.

"Roger, are you ready to see your brother confirmed?" Mang Minno chuckled. He mistook Roger's swallow as a nod.

"Then let us hurry to the cliff. We must be standing there as the world dims for the celebration of the dead. We will be at the pinnacle of darkness."

Roger was made nearly comatose by those words.

"Come, it is just a figure of speech. He's really a nice man," I whispered, pulling my brother along.

Once we were on the cliff, I expected the ceremony to go along in much the same way my confirmation had. Probably I would lay my hand on the Bible, promise to not disclose any secrets, and confess my loyalty to the fishes, and then Mang Minno would step down from his spot and I would be given the *anting-anting*. I waited with anticipation, my hands in my pockets.

The air was electric, as before a strong storm, when the earth waits to be cleansed. Suddenly it began to dim. The sky rumbled, and it turned dark purple, close to black.

Mang Minno raised his fist. "Now, now is the time. My soul is weary. I can no longer carry the weight of my *anting-anting*." He inclined his head to the tribunal, hovering just at his feet. "The tribunal has accepted me into their school." He spoke in a booming voice that reverberated like thunderclouds. He was Moses shouting the Ten Commandments to the people. You see, even after all that I knew, I still thought of him as good. "Roman Flores, do you accept the responsibility of becoming a servant to Agraria and to his fish, and yet king to them all?"

"Yes." I nodded solemnly.

"Do you swear to serve only one master?"

"Yes," I said, wondering curiously at his phrasing.

"Where is your Bible?"

I handed it to him, raising my hand in expectation.

"Do you refute these teachings?" He lifted the book above his head, and I saw that the hand that held the book was shaking with pain.

"Sir?" I frowned, unsure if I had heard correctly.

He gave me back the book. "Throw it into the water. Shout your promise to your new master."

"Roman," Roger gasped.

I did not throw the book but gritted my teeth and repeated the promise. The water split open and formed an arc around the cliff. It rose over the large rock, and we were again submerged to our waists. I saw a large mass looming beyond the horizon, a hundred meters away.

"Come, master." Mang Minno took out his fishbone, and instead of blowing into it, he held it to his lips, whispering feverishly in some language I did not recognize. But the dark mass remained in the distance. "Master," he called, "why do you hesitate?" Then Mang Minno shouted in anger, and I took a step back. His eyes were a brilliant violet, yet they appeared shallow, as if Mang Minno were not present at all, but his soul trapped just below the surface, beneath the opaqueness. "You, what are you saying there!" He pointed at Roger.

"He's not saying—" I tried to explain, turning to Roger. But I stopped, for Roger was indeed saying something. He was holding a crucifix and saying a different prayer, in the ancient language of the Morro people, the people of the mountains. I turned from one to the other in confusion. Only Grandfather knew such prayers.

The rules had changed, and no one had warned me. Mang Minno was spitting as he called out his incantation, and Roger, who seemed to find some solace in shutting his eyes, was shaking uncontrollably but still reciting his prayer.

With an angry cry, Mang Minno grabbed at my brother's crucifix. His hand was lashed suddenly with cuts, as if by a whip. But he held on and ripped the crucifix, throwing it to the ground. He shoved my brother down, and instantly tears came to my eyes at the sight of my brother.

"Come, Roman, we shall call Agraria on our own." He reached out to me; his voice was like a hiss, slicing through air.

"No." I kicked him away. I helped Roger up, and we started to back away. "Rog, are you hurt? Can you walk?"

"I shall try." He got up and placed his arm around my shoulder. "Get behind me and run home."

"I won't leave you." I held on to him. The mass in the water set the earth trembling and began to roll toward us. It was huge, the size of at least six tourist buses in length. As big as our two-story house in height and width.

"Come, master!" Mang Minno shouted in a crazed voice. "The boy has made his promise. The tribunal has accepted. All that is needed is a drop of his blood to seal it. The other will give his soul. He has come willingly." Mang Minno walked toward me with the fishbone held in his hand like a dagger.

I watched the dark mass in the water, transfixed by the sight. The ocean broke open, the way it did for the cargo ships in Manila Bay. I saw the speed at which it was approaching; there was no way we could outrun it, whatever it was. I pictured a thousand man-eating fishes.

The fish surfaced and it was monstrous, with large eel-like parasites attached on its sides. It opened its mouth and a million fishes came forth, like a plague. The tribunal swam around Roger and me in a tight circle. I was paralyzed.

"Minno!" I heard a loud voice boom from behind us. My brother and I turned to see my grandfather come forward, a spear in his hand.

Mang Minno gaped with genuine fear. The confidence leaked out of his voice. "Prudencio." His eyes were human again. They softened as when one sees an old friend. But the tribunal spoke to him, and his eyes turned hard again. "This is no longer your concern. But perhaps the tribunal will still accept you if I speak to them. We can live forever, Prudencio, stay young forever."

"Not my concern? Surely you are mistaken. Are these boys not of my very blood? You have gone mad if you think I would let you harm one hair on their heads. Their souls are already logged in a different book." He turned to Roger. "You have done well. You said the counterprayer as I taught you."

My mouth fell open. I was in a panic. How would I ever get my feeble grandfather and my brother out? It was truly a nightmare.

My grandfather patted my head. "Have you no faith in me yet, Roman?" He pulled out a necklace from the chain around his neck, and I saw that he had the other half of Mang Minno's fishbone. "This does not belong to me, though it was once given to me. I kept it, knowing that such a day would come. I did not know it would involve my own grandchildren, but perhaps it is fitting." He took the bone and blew into it, and the creature in the ocean came forward.

"*Lolo*, what are you doing?" I gasped.

"We refute you!" Grandfather roared, and handed the bone to me.

"Yes, take it to your lips, Roman," Mang Minno shouted.

My grandfather looked at me quietly. "Throw it into the water, son."

I nodded and threw it into the ocean. The water exploded, the waves as high as a house. I thought it would consume us, but it did not. Mang Minno took his necklace and held it out to me. I looked at it. It was covered in spit. I turned away, disgusted. He screamed and the necklace tightened around his neck. The fishbone weighed him down; it pulled him to his knees. "Prudencio," he called out to my grandfather.

"You were long ago dead to me, my friend. Go to your rest." Grandfather's tears surprised me.

Mang Minno leaned forward into the water. He bared sharp teeth at us and laughed. His jaw thickened and lengthened. "It will not end with me. I shall find another."

"No more." Grandfather raised his spear, and I saw that it was the one that Aurora had hanging in her father's old study, Mang Minno's old study. "Remember how we found Agraria? With this spear? Blessed with holy water and the prayers of your family when we were both so engulfed by poverty? Your favorite spear, the one you said was blessed by God Himself." He threw it down, and it stabbed right through Mang Minno. The second it touched him he turned into a fish, and not even one of the tribunal.

He had once told me that those who retire become part of the tribunal, but I thought it had been only a figure of speech. I did not know he meant literally. He raised his head one last time, and I saw that he had become a bottom feeder, a catfish.

The fishbone moved from his neck, which was now replaced by gills. It came to life and broke free of the necklace. It swam like a living fish toward the half we had thrown into the water and formed a full skeleton. The bones swam toward the monster in the ocean, and the monster opened its mouth and took in the swimming skeleton. The monster submerged itself immediately, leaving only a circular disturbance in the smoothness of the ocean.

The water finally receded, and we hobbled home without too many words. The eclipse was over, and the light came soothingly upon our backs.

"He was my best friend." Grandfather sighed. "Roman, you may never win your father's affection, but you should rejoice in what you do have. A brother who would risk his life to save you, and a grandfather who cares." He pointed to the edge of the forest, where Aurora waited in the sunlight with her books.

"I thought she was only interested in me because of her father."

"Have a little faith in yourself," Grandfather said.

FROM THAT DAY on, I no longer agonized over Father's disinterest. I merely accepted him for who he was. I learned to be thankful, to value that which I did have: my grandfather to teach me the kind of character it took to become a man, and my brother's companionship.

The three of us became inseparable. We began fishing in the sunnier parts of the ocean. We found our own fishing spot, without any shade, and we became brown from the sun.

~ WHEN ROMAN FINISHES HIS TALE, it is early evening. I know because the room has cooled. The cellar is filled with silence. Roderick is in awe. He watches Roman's hands as if he will pull out an *anting-anting* in the shape of a fishbone. Roman chuckles and messes my brother's hair.

"Imagine if we had that bone, Jando," Roderick says to me. "The fishes we could call. I bet we could ride in the belly of a whale."

"*Stupido*," I tell him. "Did you not understand any of it? That man was bad. He wanted to take Roman down into the water forever, away from his family."

"I would not let it make me evil," Roderick says.

"Go to sleep now, you two," Mama says. "Those things belong to the darkness. We must rely on God. We must ask Him to make us strong, unafraid. To give us the strength to band together, to defeat these devils." She makes the sign of the cross. "God will guide us through this."

"Yes," Aling Ana says. "If we stay strong like Roman and his grandfather did, there will come a day when this war shall end and we will have the sunlight on our faces again. Will you visit the beaches and search for your own watering hole, Roderick?"

"Yes." Roderick brightens. "And Alejandro can come along if he wishes." My brother sneaks a look at me.

"Maybe I will find the watering hole first," I joke, and we elbow one another.

Mang Selso snorts. "I was quite a fisherman myself in my youth. I challenge anyone to a fishing contest the first chance we get." He winks at Roderick and me.

"We accept the challenge. Right, guys?" Roman asks Roderick and me. He holds out his hand to each of us, and we shake it, cementing the deal as fishing partners.

"All of you, be prepared to lose," Mang Ped joins in. "Do not forget I grew up in a fishing village." He is lying on his back, his eyes already shut, wearing a big grin.

"Excuse me." Mrs. Yoshi straightens her posture. "But I believe all of the men should be prepared to be put to shame. Besides, Pedro, you would cheat with your premonitions. You would know exactly where the fish swim." She puts an arm around her daughter, Mica. "Tell them, sweetheart. Is there a better fisherwoman than your mother?"

"I know of none." Mica glows with pride.

"Whoa-ho!" Mama grins at us. "Did you hear that?" We laugh and settle into our mats.

Mang Selso, still smiling, attends to his father, Tay Fredrico. The old man has been coughing hard. There is a dry scraping in his throat that makes us cringe. Mang Selso covers him with an extra blanket. "*Tay,* here. Some water. Drink."

"No." The old Spaniard pushes the tin away.

Roderick and I stay awake as long as we can, discussing Mang Minno. I think of the three of us fishing together someday, me, Roderick, and my sister, Isabelle. I send God a prayer to watch after her and Papa wherever they are. I close my eyes and try to imagine where she could be.

THE WRISTWATCH I took from the dead man reads nine in the morning. Papa and Isabelle have not returned. I try to imagine the height of the sun upstairs. I imagine it slants, trying to break through our blackout curtain. My head aches from hunger.

"So late, so late now . . ." Mama sighs as she prepares the last can of beans.

"We fought, that was the last time I saw her. Always fighting, your *ate* Isabelle and me. She claims that I am too bossy, always interfering, that I am jealous of her . . . how does she say? Her 'opportunities.' How can I be jealous of my own daughter? Even a mama dog will protect her young to the death. What more of a mother? Would I not give both my arms for her if I had to, Jando?"

"She did not mean it, Ma," I tell her.

My mother smiles a half smile. Only one side of her lip goes up; the other side is not convinced it is happy. "She meant what she said. She is not stupid. She knows exactly what she says at all times. This is not the first time she has said such things to me." Mama rubs her arms. I see where the skin sags below her underarms, how her cheeks pull and droop past her jaw. I wonder when Mama grew old. She turns her face away from us. I watch her throat move as she swallows her fears.

"Ma?" I call to her.

"I am the grown-up, I should not have said such things to your sister. Now—" Mama's voice cracks, and she holds her palms open. "She did not come home right away because she was punishing me. The things I said to her. They were for her own good. She wants to study medicine, good for her. But why cause so much trouble for herself, trying to be a doctor? Be a nurse instead. This is more acceptable. For a woman to become a doctor is like climbing a ladder full of people on top, fighting to kick you back down. If she becomes a teacher, or even a nun, the door is open, wide open. They will take her with big arms and happy faces." Mama shakes her head.

"But so silly, stupid, the things we fight about. She makes me so mad. She thinks only of herself, of the things she does not have. She is always watching what the other girls have. I never complained to your *lolo* or *lola* when I was her age. I knew my parents were not rich. Anything we had I was thankful for.

"But Isabelle has hungry eyes. She is never happy with her situation. I tell her, 'Think about others worse off than you. At least you have a family, at least there is a roof over your head.' And do you know what she said to me? 'Why should I be content with what I have? What is wrong with reaching higher, wanting more?'"

"Ah, but that is the way of the young nowadays. Especially with the younger girls." Aling Ana pulls her blanket closer around her. "Before this war, they had every possible opportunity. The young women were seduced by all the roads they could travel. They could become lawyers, doctors, whatever they wanted. They could live abroad, start a business. It was too much for them to eat at one sitting."

My mother sighs. "If only that were the only problem with Isabelle. But between the two of us, there is more. Her father spoils her with ideas. He encourages her to climb high, reach for the heavens. But who is there to catch her when she falls? Me. Who has to explain to her that not as many doors are open as she would like to think? Me. So what do I get in repayment? I am the bad person. The one standing in her way. Have you ever seen a daughter who hated her mother so, Aling Ana? Curse this morning chill."

"Louisa, you are too hard on yourself," Aling Ana chides. "These things occur between mothers and daughters. Their relationships are more fragile than fathers and sons. They compete with one another, grow jealous. They compete for the father, the husband's attention. Such is the way with all women."

Mama smoothes her hair into place, curving it behind her ears. She frowns a little at Aling Ana's last words, but Mama does not like to make too many waves in the ocean. She told us it is important to be good to one another, especially now. She said the time has come when we must each lean on the other, so it is important to have patience. Although I think she feels differently with Mang Selso. "Yes, perhaps you are right, Aling Ana. I am frustrated with my thoughts of Isabelle. I love her too much. If only I could make her understand that." She stops rubbing her arms and paces the floor. "This infernal heat."

"Ma . . ." Roderick looks at her. "Ma," he says again.

"What is it, Roddie?"

"You just said it was cold."

Mama looks at Roderick as if he is the one who is delirious.

"She will be all right, Ma." I stand and take her hand.

"*Ay, anák*," she says. Oh, son. "If it weren't for my stupid words, your sister would be home. I should have ground my teeth together to keep from fighting with her. I forget she is just a child, only seventeen."

"Isabelle knows you love her, Ma," I tell her, but she doesn't hear me. I am worried about Mama. She acts as if she has a fever that has gone to her brain. Papa said that this sometimes happens when people are in closed areas for too long. Like in a ship full of people who have been in the water for many months.

"Ay—" Mama yanks at her hair. I try to pull her hand back, but she moves away from me. "It is my fault, my fault. Maybe she lost her way." She is starting to shout. "The soldiers, maybe she came across some soldiers. She is so pretty, like a flower. How would she go unnoticed? If anything should happen to her . . . And now your papa. Where can he be? What if they have accused him of something?"

"Louisa, stop this talk," Mrs. Yoshi says.

Roman stands and goes to my mother. He puts a hand on her shoulder. "Aling Louisa, perhaps it is best if I go in search of Isabelle and Mang Carlito now."

The lines on my mother's face straighten. "You would do that, Roman?"

"Yes."

"I can go with him, Ma." I stand. "I know all the places Isabelle can be."

Mama twists a small handkerchief in her hand. "No, Jando. I have already let your sister go, and then your father. I could not bear it if you did not return."

"But Ma, how will Roman know where to look?"

"It is not safe," Mang Selso says. "It is only a job for a grown person."

"A grown man." Mama looks at Mang Selso accusingly.

Mang Selso has had enough. He stands. "Why are you blaming me? Carlito volunteered to go. Why should I be responsible? What of the other men? They are here safe with us. Why do you choose to pick on me?"

"They have done their part!" Mama shouts, her eyes narrowing. "And you call yourself Carlito's best friend."

"I am," Mang Selso says defensively. He makes a fist. "Carlito and I have shared many things together."

"You refuse to share in the danger," Mama says with disgust. "But you are more than willing to share in the food he brings home."

My brother pulls at my mother's skirts. She looks down at him, not seeing anything but her anger. "Mama, I can show him," Roderick offers. "I can show Roman where to go. Alejandro is injured. His hands. I can go."

"I'm older than you. I should go," I say.

"No!" Mama shouts so loudly, all talk ceases. She covers her mouth and runs up the ladder, slamming the hatch.

I move to follow her, but Roman puts a hand on my shoulder. "Let her go, Alejandro. She cannot keep up with everything that is happening. None of us can."

I go to sit by Roderick. He looks up at me and shrugs. We sit with our backs against the wall. After a few minutes have passed, Mama comes down. Her face is dry, her eyes swollen. We look at her expectantly. She tries to speak; it takes her a moment. "Jando, you will escort Roman. Keep your eyes open. Show him the places that Isabelle likes to visit. The Cabrera dress shop, the Bonifacio farm, the little bookstore on Escota if you get that far."

"The Bulosans," Mica offers timidly.

"Yes, the Bulosan hacienda, where the horses are," Mama agrees. "Roman, keep him safe. Hide when you see soldiers. If it is too dangerous, if there is shelling, come home immediately. As soon as it gets dark, return home. Do you two understand?"

"*O pô,*" Roman answers. Yes, ma'am.

I watch Mama's face. I am very worried about her. I should not leave her. Papa would not leave until she felt better. But Papa is not here. As soon as we find him and Isabelle, Mama will be better.

Mang Selso watches as we gather our things. He is seated next to his father, Tay Fredrico. He avoids our eyes and tries to tuck the blankets closer to his father.

But Tay Fredrico shoves them away. "Too hot," the old man grunts.

I turn to say good-bye to Roderick, but he is asleep. I decide to tell Ate Lorna about Domingo, in case anything should happen to me. She sees something in my face and shudders.

"Ate Lorna, there is something I must tell you."

She picks up the sleeping baby, busying herself with baby Alma's clothing. "Go ahead, Alejandro, go with Roman. You can tell me tonight."

"But Ate Lorna," I insist.

"Alejandro, it will be dark soon. You had best be on your way." She turns and picks up the sleeping baby.

I stand before her and try one more time. Roman shakes his head. "Come, Alejandro, she is right."

WE CLIMB THE ladder into the kitchen. It seems strange that we no longer occupy it. We move quietly through the house, like visitors in a funeral parlor. When we open the door, we pinch our eyes shut from the glare of the sun.

"This way." Roman grabs my shoulder. "We will avoid the soldiers better this way. Let us look where I last saw your father."

"I should have told her," I say out loud, thinking about Ate Lorna.

"She already knows, Jando."

"The smell of gunfire, but no soldiers." I search our surroundings. I do not focus long on the corpses. It is no use burying them. We do not want to waste our strength, and if we bury them too shallow, the rats unearth them the next day.

"The wind carries the battle from the city," Roman tells me. "Look—" He points excitedly in the distance. Japanese planes fly, red circles blazing on their wings.

I shade my eyes with my hand and nod.

"I wonder how we are ever going to find Father," I tell Roman.

He is listening to something. He puts his finger to his mouth. There are footsteps trailing us. Roman signals for us to take cover behind a group of banyan trees.

"Soldiers?" I whisper as we crouch low.

"Perhaps. Maybe just deer, but better to stay hidden."

I nod. I try to convince myself he is right. But I know there are no more deer to be found. Deer will usually stand still or leap the other way. This one is following us. My heart is in my throat, and I can feel my skin tingle all over, especially on my arms. The sounds become louder and we lean back, away from sight. I pull out my father's hunting knife. Roman has a big stick in his hand, the kind they use to play baseball in the United States. The sound comes closer until it is right in front of us, and I choke when I see who it is. It is Aling Ana's nephew, Feliciano. He is a Makapili, a Japanese sympathizer. I feel my heart hit my chest.

"He won't hurt us. He knows my sister," I whisper.

Roman shakes his head and points. Behind Feliciano are a dozen Japanese soldiers. They walk with bayonets, prodding three captives with their blades. The men groan in pain at the jabs and try to keep balance with their hands tied behind them. A fall could mean a vicious beating. We wait an hour to let his group pass. We are about to leave when another group comes our way.

I stretch my neck to see if Papa is one of them and breathe a sigh of relief. He is not there. We hear more footsteps and gasp. Ate Lorna's son, Taba, has been following us. He walks noisily without a care. When he comes within passing distance, Roman reaches out and grabs Taba, but not quickly enough. Taba shouts out.

"Mama, ay, they are killing me! Mama, help!"

My stomach sinks at the sound of many footsteps. When we look up there are bayonets glinting down at us. We get up slowly. Roman puts one hand on my shoulder and the other on Taba's.

"Up, up!" the soldier shouts. "Guerrillas." He alerts the others.

"No, only looking for food." Roman brings his hand to his mouth back and forth. The soldier shakes his head and points his gun, then turns and hits Roman in the mouth with the wooden stock. Roman falls to the ground, his lip cut open. Taba begins to sob loudly, and I put my arms around him. The soldiers pull Roman up. "I'll come. Let them go," Roman pleads.

The soldier laughs. "Why let go? So can contact other guerrillas? You, and you and you. Get in line."

A soldier pulls Taba away from me. Taba's screams pierce our ears. I have to tell him in a big voice not to cry or they will kill us. Taba's eyes grow big. They push Taba in front of me and I say, "See, I am right behind you."

"I want to go home. Home now," Taba cries. He doesn't care who these men are. When the men ask him to stop crying, he only cries louder.

"Stop it, Taba. Remember what I told you." I push him a little with my hand.

"Don't push me. I'm not going!" Taba screams. It pierces my ears.

"No!" The soldier slaps Taba, and Taba sucks in air, immediately quiet.

Roman walks in the front of the line. There is no hope now of finding Papa or Isabelle. We will die, be butchered like Domingo Matapang. I wish now that I had told his wife, Ate Lorna, that the husband she kneels in prayer for is already dead.

part 2

ISABELLE
KARANGALAN

~ THEY HAVE GORED DOMINGO MATAPANG like a cornered bull. I could see from the light of the moon when the bayonets made contact with his body. I have watched from this hiding place, a thin tree with branches that are as starved as I am. The soldiers tried to pierce him in the chest, but he wrestled them to the ground. I had to put my fist in my mouth so I would not scream; that was when I saw the blood come pouring out. They struggled until they stabbed him in the thigh, and still he fought. Somehow he managed to run away from them. They shot at him and he went down. When they got to where he had fallen, he was already gone. The soldiers were in a panic to find him. They whispered back and forth, then went quickly back to their commander.

After they left, Domingo appeared from the shadows. He refused at first to fall, staggering about until he collapsed a few feet from my tree. I have waited another hour, not daring to make a sound. The branches have torn my skirt, and my legs have gone numb. I feel as if the soldiers can hear every movement, from my stomach moaning to the sound of my breathing. My body is drenched in sweat.

New soldiers have come to relieve the first group. They watch with rifles slung across their backs. The captives still hang by their thumbs.

I was on my way home when I saw my brothers led to this field. I hid in these bushes to see if I could think of a plan to free them, but no plan ever came. I thank the Almighty for setting my brothers free. But I know it was not because of my prayers that they were saved. I think God is very angry with me. I have not been an obedient daughter. If I were, I would be home now.

I slowly inch my way down the tree. I let my legs drop first as I hang on to the branches, my body close to the trunk. The bark is rough edged and pulls at my shirt and scratches my thighs and face. The resin brushes against my skin and emits a fragrant aroma. I am terrified it can be smelled by the soldiers. There is no way out but to pass Domingo's body. I take a deep breath. The twigs and branches crackle with each step. The sounds are thunder to my ears. The ground is dark with his blood. I move to step over him when his hand reaches up and grabs my ankle.

"Isabelle," he gasps. "Help me."

I almost scream. I try to shake his hand from my foot. "I—I cannot carry you. There is nothing I can do. I will get help," I whisper.

"Bella, I will die."

"No." I pry his hand from my foot and fall back on my butt. His eyes will not let me look away; angry eyes filled with disappointment and accusation. *Selfish,* his eyes say to me. No different from the words my mother often uses. I look away from their glare. I step back into the shadow of trees. He cannot see me, but he knows that I am here. He has the ears of a predator; he watches the darkness surrounding me. He moans my name, asking for help. I put my hands over my ears and tell myself to go. I pity his wife and children. But I will not help him. How could I possibly carry him? The best that I can do is find help. His eyes focus in my direction, holding me captive with guilt.

"No," I whisper fiercely.

He stops his moaning and listens.

I know I should feel compassion for him, but I don't. He has brought this danger upon himself. He knows how I feel about guerrillas. They harm our people more, by bringing the wrath of the Japanese. Easy for them to perform their hit-and-run missions, while we, the civilians, must bear the repercussions.

The anger of his words cuts me. "Then go now. Go quickly, they will come soon."

I scramble up and jump over his body. I run through the tall grass. My feet tangle and I fall through the ferns and land with my hands splayed out before me, skinning my knees. I can see the Japanese soldiers talking a hundred feet from us. They point in our direction. I look back at Domingo.

"Help me, or go. Do it quickly. You will get us killed with your indecision," he orders.

I hate him. I hate him for making me feel guilty. What has he ever done but worry his wife and cast suspicion and danger upon our house? He is a guerrilla leader, yet for all the kindness my family has bestowed upon him, he risks our lives by hiding under our care. And now, now he is calling out my name like an imbecile.

I have a whole life ahead of me. As soon as this war is finished, I will be a doctor. Domingo has chosen this kind of life for himself. I have not. Yet even as my mind thinks this, my feet are running back to him. I pull his arm upward without thinking. Domingo grunts horribly and grits his teeth. He pulls himself to a standing position.

"Can you walk?" I ask.

"Go, I will walk." His tongue sounds thick in his mouth. He leans on me heavily, and I push up to bear his weight. His feet are like pedals that will not work. Shots are fired. Whether they are meant for us or for the other captives, I do not wait to find out. We hurry north toward home. We have many more kilometers to go, twenty-four kilometers, fifteen miles at least. We must pass through the city where the fighting is concentrated. We stick to the outskirts and keep moving.

WE HAVE BEEN hiding for several hours. We are just south of our hometown of Santa Maria in Bulacan province, maybe eight kilometers away. Yet our town seems hundreds of kilometers away. Domingo wishes to head farther north-west, toward his camp in the Zambales Mountains. Our clothing is damp from the evening downpours. We are cloaked behind a large grouping of ferns and climbing vines with purple flowers. It is not a very good hiding place, but Domingo cannot move any farther. He will die, I think. Twice now, Japanese patrols have marched by on their way south to Manila, and twice they have overlooked us. I fear our luck will soon come to an end.

Our beautiful city is burning. The scent of broken churches, charred flesh, and a fallen people carries like ashes in the wind. They are burning great fires, and the evening sky mingles with the heat and flames a blood red. A bad sign. This is the story at the end of the Bible. This is Judgment Day.

The ground shakes continuously from the sound of the Amerikano tanks. Overhead, the Amerikano planes buzz by, great birds swooping down with a vengeance. But who is winning? I cannot imagine the Amerikanos will win. How can they? They have lost once before, and how will they resupply them-selves when their country is so far away? The Japanese need only jump north and they will be home. How I wish they would both go home.

"Isabelle," Domingo whispers hoarsely, "leave me now. I will make contact with my men."

His eyes are drained, void of their usual fire.

"*Napápagod na ako,*" he says. I am weary.

I do not argue. I do not think he will make it through the night. "You will be all right here?" Such a stupid question. I beg him silently to tell me that he will. I look at him. He does not look so threatening now. But when he was in good health, and his eyes burned with that ferocity, he became something else. He has grown a beard, a full one, and his hair is long and wavy, touching his shoulders. Few people know that he is a senator's illegitimate and unacknowl-edged child. His father is a Japanese sympathizer. My father is more of a father to him.

Domingo's bleeding has stopped for now. He has deep cuts, one near his hip, one on his thigh. A long gash starts below his right ear and continues winding to the nape.

"I am lucky," he says, seeing my concern.

"I thought you were dying."

"It only appeared that way. Because of the blood. It is not so bad. I have been in worse situations," he tells me.

"What about the bullet?" I ask. "I saw them shoot you."

"When they shot me, their aim was bad. I twisted and they only managed my shoulder." He winces. "A flesh wound. Nothing more."

I am still not convinced. He has lost a lot of blood. When I move him too quickly, the one on his left leg starts again. I have seen horrible things this day. I have seen babies; oh, I cannot describe it. Little babies, in a ditch, some of them half-alive, with their tiny fists reaching for absent mothers. Domingo saw them, too. We tried to save one who was still breathing, but when I picked it up, I realized it would soon be dead.

I watch as he presses his hand down on his shoulder wound. He glances up at me, his eyes drained. "I will manage. Make your own trail. Stay away from the roads."

I look toward home. I wait for him to thank me, but already he has closed his eyes. I get up uncertainly and mumble, "Good-bye."

"Thank you," he breathes.

I hesitate.

"Go," he orders.

I jump at his words and crash through the ferns. When I am a few meters away, I look back and see how flimsy a hiding place it is. If one looks closely, Domingo's sandals can easily be made out. I keep moving. I remember what he has told me, and I cross to where the trees are thickest, away from the well-traveled roads, always careful not to make any noise. My eyes scan everything, the thick vegetation, the hanging vines as thick as my arms that entangle me from the shadows, the baby tree that my eyes mistake for a solitary soldier. I am dizzy from it all.

After an hour I come to a clearing, and with the help of the red moon I see a definite path. I hurry in the opposite direction. I come across a running stream. I fall down on my knees and throw water onto my face. I drink and drink; the taste of the water is so good. Something brushes against my leg, my schoolbag. In my bag is a tin cantina.

~

WHEN I RETURN, Domingo is clutching his knife. I have frightened him. He looks at me incredulous, angry.

"I found some water," I explain.

He grabs the cantina. "Stupid girl," he says.

I feel the anger rise in me at his words. "I could have—"

"Sit down before you give us away." He studies me grudgingly. "Sleep, I will keep watch."

I WAKE WITH my heart pounding; I look around, unsure of where I am. Domingo is sitting up, clutching his shoulder. His eyes are shut tight, and a look of pain covers his mouth. He has bandaged his wound with pieces of his trousers. I feel stupid for not thinking of it myself. I wait for his face to relax before I speak.

"Does it hurt much?" I ask.

"My men are waiting. You must leave, Bella."

"Tell me where you are going and I will take you there. You cannot make it by yourself."

"No, you must return home. Now."

"I can't," I tell him. "It must be Father's blood running in me. Whatever it is, I cannot leave an injured man behind."

He looks at me for a long time. "Then we must go, now."

We continue northwest, climbing gradually up the mountains until my home is just a small dot below.

Domingo's neck has become infected. It has turned his skin into a patchy bright red. His cheeks fall inward, and he looks like a dead man who does not yet know he has died. We move slow as banana slugs. Domingo insists on walking on his own. It is amazing. He does it from pure willpower and the help of a thick branch he has found. We sleep for six hours in the safety of a hollow tree trunk, and at dawn we start again.

We stop to rest often, passing through thick trails in the forest, overgrown with ferns, *apitong, molave* trees, all competing for space. Rattan plants assault us with their long thorns. The great banana leaves bow down as we pass. They are sad, too. Lianas drape down as thick as my legs. Tiny *nik-nik* flies attack for blood. Now and then there are *waling-walings,* queen of the orchids, sprouting at the most unlikely places. I have to wave away the flying roaches that drop from the canopies and land on my hair.

We continue northwest, toward the foothills of Florida Blanca, below the

Zambales Mountains. He tells me we are searching for a cave. I point out various caves that I see or ledges that look as though they are the path to caves. But I already know that Domingo's cave will not be anything like I imagined. I feel scared, and lonely, and proud somehow. And yes, stupid. Stupid for not going home when I had the chance. I think of my mother. What would she say right now? I can almost hear her. *Why did you wait so long to help him? Could you not see he needed your help?* She would not congratulate me for deciding to help. She would see only that I did not help sooner. *You are always so proud, Isabelle. You do not know everything. See what happens when I tell you to come home and you do not listen? See what happens when I tell you to be like me and you try to be yourself? When I tell you better to be a nurse, and do not reach so high and think you can be a doctor? You are wrong, Isabelle, always wrong. You do not know your own self. Look what has happened to you now. Do you even know where you are going?*

I think of the things I said to her. I worry at the thoughts I have. At times I wish she were dead, but I don't mean it at all. I guess what I wish is for all the fight she saves up for me to die. I wish I could be as close to her as Mica is to her mother. Mica's mother plans things with her. She spends long moments in conversation with her.

I love Mama, but I cannot stand to be in the same room with her. She is always trying to smother me. She won't let me do the things other girls my age get to do. Mama is always defeating my hope. Always stomping it out before it can even grow into a dream. Anything I begin to desire, I already know she will feel opposite about. And even though my father encourages everything that I do, Mama always finds a way to dissuade him and turn him against me.

Like the time that Papa said I could study abroad if I received good grades. Then, as the grades came each year, better and better, I know that Mama started to whisper in his ear like a little bird. She turned his support into fear, until Papa decided not to let me go. He said it was something he had thought hard on and had changed his mind about. But I know it was because Mama was the one who had thought long and hard. When she did this, I wanted to pull my hair out. I wanted to run outside and scream at the top of my lungs, and tell the neighbors what she had done, but I couldn't even leave the house because she wouldn't let me. "If you leave now, do not come back," she said.

Mama responds to minor things in dramatic ways. I never want to be like her, such an actress. I strive to be like my father. He is always calm and happy. Mama worries about every little thing. She watches me closely, like a hawk circling for food. If I do anything out of the ordinary, she comes down to swoop me away. She never lets me discover things on my own. Everything has to be done the way she was brought up.

For instance, I am not allowed to walk alone, I must have a chaperone. She has imaginary kidnappers waiting around every corner to pounce on me and take me away. When I tell her they wouldn't want me because we are not rich, she simply grinds her teeth and tightens her jaw. I wish Mama would come around to the Western way of thinking.

My cousin Maria Elena and her mother never fight. Maria Elena is part of my grief. Her mother lets her do anything and everything she wants. Maria Elena can go unescorted to parties; already her mother has sent away for different applications to different schools. She brags about the schools in Europe and the other schools in the States. She tells me of her plans to attend these universities once the war is over. Maria Elena was never interested in these places until I told my mama that I was. Maria Elena is just like her mother; they pretend not to brag when they are doing just that. She pretends that really she would rather attend school here, but her mama insists that she test her wings. How else will a baby bird learn to fly? she says to me. Especially if she is chained to the mama bird at all times?

Maria Elena says these things, knowing fully that it is what I want most in life. We have the same birth date, born the same day, exactly the same age. So you see, we were competing even before we were born. My mother would compare the way each of us sat in their wombs. "See how high my baby sits, like royalty. She will marry a prince or a rich man someday."

And my aunt would say, "My baby sits lower, close to the earth, so strong. Not even the wind can sweep her off her feet." I know this because my father told me. He wasn't telling me to show how silly my mother can be. He was telling me to show how proud she was of me. I just understood the other meaning. I was so mad at Mama when I left to visit Maria Elena the other day. I am mad at her still.

WE HAVE WALKED for over five hours, nearly twenty kilometers, and I have forgotten our destination. Domingo collapses against a tree. I help him to stand. "There." He points up toward a steep ravine, and I think he is delirious, for I see nothing but the evening sky.

I help him, my legs shaky from bearing too much of his weight. "Are you sure this is the place?" I ask, suspicious that he is fevered.

"*Oo,*" he says, squinting. Yes. "Come," he breathes, and jerks his chin. The path is straight upward, thick with saw grass and entangled branches, leaves with giant stalks. As we approach I become aware of movement all around us. I tell myself it is only the trees, the forest creatures. And then I see them. Filipinos appear, stepping forward from the dark, like trees come to life.

"*Hoy, pare.*" Domingo nods to one in greeting, calling him short for *kompadre*, "comrade," "friend."

"*Si Matapang ba iyán?*" someone asks. Is that Domingo Matapang?

"If not, you are a dead man." Domingo's voice changes.

The man smiles and urges us forward.

I have no strength to protest. I reach for Domingo, but he tells me with his eyes not to help. The little pebbles go stumbling down the hill as we climb.

"*Sige.*" Go on. He grits his teeth, and the men crowd around to help carry him. He refuses at first, and then he gives in with a sigh.

Another half hour and we meet a second circle of men. It takes us almost fifteen minutes to go a few feet. We have to stop frequently, for Domingo is bleeding again. Our guides look at us with concern. Domingo tells them that he has not had food in several days. When we reach the top, I see a dozen eyes peeking at us from the surrounding green. I see a dozen more with guns and spears pointed at us.

"Domingo," I say.

"*Si chief, si Matapang.*" It is the boss, Matapang; someone says Domingo's last name.

"*Oo ngâ!*" someone exclaims. It is! Then the ferns close in on us, and the men come down to greet Domingo. The canopy of trees blocks out the moon. I cannot even see where I place my feet.

They study Domingo with great concern. "Alert the doctor," someone orders, and a man runs on ahead.

They escort us to the top of the cliff, and I gasp, for the height is dizzying. I fear I will go over. We do, but there is a rope, a thick one anchored to the ground and to the side of the mountain. We grab on and climb down a steep drop. There is a ledge, and a small path that hugs the mountain, and then a large cave.

All at once they speak. A man rushes forward and greets Domingo. They shake hands. Domingo is happy to see him. "Palaka," he calls him. The name means "frog."

Palaka glances at me and nods. His eyes are strange; they push forward, giving him a look of great curiosity.

Domingo searches the faces. "Where is Miguel?"

No one speaks. Domingo asks a second time, this time looking only at Palaka.

"It is too late, he took a group to meet with the Amerikanos," Palaka explains.

"You let him go?" Domingo asks.

"Let him? He disappeared in the night. He talked all day about how we should meet with the Amerikanos, so that they would give us guns. In the morning he was gone, along with thirty of our men. Hippolito Capistrano, Euterio Aquino, Vicente Rivas, you know his group. When he returned"— Palaka shrugs—"he had a new gun."

"And the men?" Domingo asks.

"All dead. The Amerikano guerrilla would not see them without a sponsor, someone who could vouch for Miguel. So of course he turned them away.

"On their way back they became lost. The terrain was not familiar. They were chased by Japanese patrols. They stumbled into a war between Bangungot's guerrillas and Calderone's guerrillas."

"The fool," Domingo spits. "Miguel the ass. Those were valuable men."

All the men voice their grievances about this Miguel Ochoa. How he taunted that Domingo was dead. How they had begun to believe this. Someone had claimed he had been bayoneted. They are in awe of Domingo's return, and they watch him with reverence, as if he is a walking miracle.

As the men gather around, a young man approaches with a basket of odd needles and broken knives. He lights a small fire and holds the blades over the flame. He opens up Domingo's shirt and cleans his wounds. Palaka nods to me and gives me water to drink. Something passes between us in that instant, when he hands me the cantina, but then it is gone. The hairs on my arm stand to attention.

I drink like an animal, choking and coughing at my thirst. Palaka reignites Domingo's anger. He fans the fire with more stories of how they are sick of Miguel, how he wants only to be top dog. At times Palaka whispers things meant only for Domingo's ears. He shifts his eyes suspiciously at me, so smooth, like an expert knifer, a *cuchillero.*

Palaka gives Domingo a large blade, and Domingo pushes it up his sleeve, where it is hidden from view. His movements are stiff, and he grimaces when he turns. I flinch at the thought of his wounds.

It continues for an hour, the ministrations with Domingo. I feel far away from him. With all these people surrounding him, I feel so alone. He has not once tried to introduce me. In fact, he has ignored me from the moment we arrived. I cannot help but feel slighted. After all, I carried him, I gave him water. The men wear the same look in their eyes, a mixture of desperation and pride. I see now why Domingo is their leader. He has a presence, even in his wounded state. He is calm; he looks to no one for guidance or comfort. He has it all within himself. The others do not. He is offered a cigarette; someone quickly lights it.

A man pushes forward. "Oh, boss, sir." He stops in front of Domingo, and I am mesmerized by his movements. He jerks his chin in hello, a series of quick motions. He blinks and licks his lips. The man shifts his weight from one foot to the other. He sticks a hand inside his pants pocket, then removes it quickly. His hand shakes, tapping his leg with the same quick rhythm.

"Oh, Inocencio." Domingo clenches his jaw as he leans forward and holds out a hand. I am the only one who notices his pain. I can see in his eyes that he has good feelings toward this skittish man. "Have you finished off the emperor's army with your shooting?"

Inocencio blushes; he gives a big toothy grin, revealing teeth that are crooked and chipped. "*Si boss namán,*" he tells Domingo. You joke.

"I have told you all before. All we need do is put Inocencio where he can get a good shot at the Japanese and he will take them all out," Domingo says, laughing.

I can see that all the attention has taken a toll on him. His complexion is bland, the eyes dull and his breathing labored.

"Yes, well, if he plugs his rear end, he might get something done," Palaka shoots back. "He has been eating too many tomatoes. We found a whole crate of tomatoes and K-1 rations meant for the Amerikanos that landed in the wrong place. It took ten of us to pull it out of a swamp. You should have seen us. We were sweating like pigs. It is a good thing they were canned tomatoes. I told Inocencio to stand guard over the treasure. But what do you think happens the minute I turn my back? He ate five cans' worth, and since then he has not stopped shitting."

Everyone roars with laughter.

Inocencio looks offended. "It burns like someone is shooting a cannon out of my tail," he admits. He glances at me, then covers his mouth.

Everyone notices this and looks in my direction. I am uncomfortable with their stares. There is a strange tension in the air. I wait for Domingo to introduce me; instead he changes the subject.

"I need a shave badly," he announces.

"I got it, boss." Inocencio runs off for a mirror. Someone else brings a razor and scissors.

Domingo waves away the scissors. "No, just the beard. Trim it a little. I don't want to look like a houseboy." His beard is shaved quickly and the mirror given to him to study himself. When they are done, Domingo looks more presentable. Not as fearsome, but he is not happy with the work. "You have cut too much. Take this away." He lifts the mirror in the air. A hand is at the ready to take it from him.

Domingo shakes his head. "Inocencio, have you been practicing?"

Inocencio's face brightens. "Yes, sir. I think I am faster than you now. Shall we try, sir?"

"No, I will rest. Palaka, can he beat you?" Domingo asks.

Palaka curls his lip in derision. "Only when he dreams. Go on, get your rifle," he tells Inocencio.

I watch in fascination as Inocencio runs off like a jubilant child. He brings back his rifle. He and Palaka sit cross-legged on the ground, opposite each other, and they are blindfolded. The men begin to crowd together. Domingo counts to three, and in a flash of hands, they begin to take apart their rifles. The cave becomes filled with shouting and laughter.

I cannot believe the speed at which they take apart their weapons. Their hands fly over the stock, the safety, in a frenzy, their lips pressed in tight concentration. I cannot help but laugh. Inocencio beats Palaka by a quick second. Palaka protests that Inocencio had a false start. They are about to put the rifles back together when the men begin to whisper and look toward the opening of the cave. Domingo's eyes grow dark, and he sighs heavily.

A man walks in, thin, with a sly face. He looks from person to person, then swaggers into the cave like a wolf who has his pick of sheep. He walks deliberately slowly, studying each person's face.

"*Kompadre*"—he nods to Domingo—"*buhay ka palá.*" Comrade, you're alive. His eyes are not fully open, the lids lowered.

"Ah, Miguel, the one who does not follow orders." Domingo nods back. I am amazed at Domingo's transformation. His face has shed the painful grimace, and his eyes are alert. He leans back in his chair and lights a cigarette. He puts his arm around his chair and stretches one leg out. He seems a man of leisure.

"We had a change of plans. I thought, Why wait for an invitation? We were able to get to the Amerikanos much quicker. We now know where they stand. They want nothing to do with us," Miguel explains, taking a cigarette from behind his ear.

"Of course, what had you to lose except thirty of my men?"

Miguel looks accusingly at the others. They look back with blank faces. He shrugs. "I am convinced more would have died had we waited to follow your plans. At least we now know where the Amerikanos stand. They do not want our help. To hell with them."

His voice is edged like a sword, and I picture his wolf fangs beginning to show.

Domingo throws back his head and blows smoke upward. "I have come to show you I am not dead. I return, and what do I find? Someone who would play leader. If there is going to be a meeting with the Amerikanos, it will be through me, and only me." The smoke dances and twists.

"Of course," Miguel says easily. He leans against the side of the cave with his arms folded. "Best to sleep now and go over plans once again in the morning."

Domingo gestures to me. "I must take my sister home. She cannot follow us."

Miguel smirks. I feel his eyes on my neck, on my cheeks, my lips. "I can watch her here."

"No," Domingo says. "We have seen what happens when things are left to you. I will take her home, then we shall discuss matters in the morning."

"Of course, you are boss." Miguel smiles tightly. "Perhaps you should tell me if we are to attempt to meet the Amerikanos again. The name of your sponsor. What is to be discussed in case . . ." He pauses. "You should be delayed a second time."

"I will not be delayed." Domingo meets Miguel's eyes for emphasis.

"No, of course not." Miguel's smile is insolent, and I suddenly become alarmed.

"And you will not be in charge again."

"Ah . . ." Miguel crosses his arms. "Finally you say what is in your heart. It is a pity that you choose to do so now, in your weakened state."

"Weakness comes from the heart. You are a good example. You care nothing for our cause and only for your own glory."

"Phh, I am no fool," Miguel says, sneering. "I saw how they carried you here. Like an infant. There is no strength left in you to lead a group, much less to challenge me." He watches Domingo with a smug expression of triumph.

Domingo continues to blow smoke upward. In fact, he has not even stood up. He smiles, takes his cigarette, and studies the smoldering end. "It is amazing, is it not, what five days without proper water can reduce a man to? Even more amazing how several drinks can revitalize one so quickly." He gets up so smoothly that it takes my breath away.

Miguel's face shows obvious astonishment. He seems unsure. I remember now the stories I have heard of Domingo. They say he is very good with wielding a knife.

Miguel has no shame. Immediately he holds out his hands in protest. "We have allowed ourselves to become too upset here. Let us think things over. I was encouraged, you see. Palaka said that I should lead the men since you were gone."

"You bastard!" Palaka shouts.

"You lie too much," Domingo tells Miguel.

"Domingo, are we not on the same side? Wasn't it you who said there should not be d-division among our group?" Miguel says, beginning to stammer.

Domingo thinks on Miguel's words. He puts a hand to his beard and touches it distractedly. "Perhaps you are right."

"Good, yes. Good." Miguel nods.

"I will take my sister home and then I will return. I will cool my thoughts. Isabelle," Domingo calls. "Gather your things and wait at the entrance while I discuss the rest of this."

I nod and move toward the opening. My heart is pounding in my temples.

Miguel reaches out his hand to Domingo. "God go with you," he says.

Domingo takes his hand. "And also with you." In a flash his knife comes out of his sleeve. They struggle and push away from each other. They circle the room, and the others crouch forward and move about as if they are watching a cockfight. I am not sure if I am breathing. I look around for an object to hit Miguel with. I see the faces all at once—the cheering, the looks of amusement, of concern. My head spins.

Miguel's face looks hideous, filled with fear. His eyes bulge out and his mouth is open, showing clenched teeth that open and chatter. His breathing is sickening to hear, a snorting that starts at the throat and goes up his nose, reminiscent of a wild boar's. He holds a small knife, which he swings from hand to hand. His eyes are fixed on Domingo.

Domingo is calm. He watches Miguel like a lion, not exerting his energy. Waiting. When Miguel lunges forward, Domingo grabs his hand. They struggle, and Miguel pulls his hand away quickly. The blade from his knife slices Domingo's palm open. Thick drops of blood fall to the ground, stealing the breath from my chest.

But Miguel looks down at his chest in surprise. There is a large circle of blood in the middle of his belly. His thin white shirt is pasted inward, as if it were being sucked into his stomach. I am stunned. Domingo was so quick.

"Stop it, stop it," I tell Domingo.

The men watch as Miguel falls, and though I did not like him on sight, I feel sorry at his helpless figure. It does not seem right that he should die in front of angry faces. He looks up at us for help, with small gasps. His eyes bulge as if straining to see the tops of the dark cave. "*Nasaksák ako,*" he explains over and over again, in between sharp intakes of breath. I was stabbed.

"Domingo," I plead.

Domingo steps forward to finish Miguel. When he does, Miguel lurches up and grabs for Domingo's injured leg. He bites through the wrappings on the thigh and does not let go. Domingo drives the knife deep into Miguel's neck, and Miguel drops instantly.

WE LEAVE THE cave with assurances from the others that they shall wait for Domingo. Domingo does not allow me to help him down the mountainside. We descend another way, farther to the north of the first trail, but where it is not so steep. He walks with his head high and his back straight until we are gone from their view. Then he collapses upon me, and I carry the brunt of his weight. The struggle has sapped his energy. His skin is an ash color. The wrappings on his shoulders and thigh that the amateur doctor prepared are soaked red.

At the second circle of men we are met by a slender woman. She runs easily up the steep mountainside to us. She wears a rifle strapped across her back. I squint to see her in the dark. On her hip is a sheathed knife. She is gaunt like the rest. But her eyes, which seem to capture the sparkle of the moon, are large and gold, and her lashes are very long. She is a mestiza, half Spanish, with chocolate hair, a high brow, and thin lips. She grins openly at Domingo until she sees me, but the sight of me does not stop her. She walks up to Domingo and embraces him, leaning back to kiss him full in the mouth. He holds her easily and for a long time. My body stiffens and my thoughts go in a hundred directions. A mistress! Domingo's face, his entire body, speaks differently to this woman. I have never seen him act this way with his wife, Ate Lorna. I cannot tear my eyes from them. Their movements are unguarded, natural. They have been together long, I decide.

She speaks rapid-fire. "Thank God, there were rumors the Japanese had caught you. I was so worried. The day you were to return I waited all evening and late into the next day. I refused to believe they had caught you. I was half-crazy. I screamed that we must all go in search of you. No one but Bartoy could speak to me—"

"I am here now," Domingo says gently. They no longer touch, but his eyes seem to caress every misplaced hair around her face. He studies the whole of her while she talks. It hits me like a bullet. They are in love.

"There is much to discuss. The Amerikanos wish to use us as guides. A submarine just dropped crates of ammunition and food for them. Some cartons fell into the bay; we can send divers to see if anything can be saved. Those damned Paghamon guerrillas wish to meet again. Our agent with the Kempeitai is under suspicion. The Japanese colonel has grown suspicious of her. I fear for her safety. The men need to go on maneuvers; they have been going crazy with waiting. And there is the matter with these damned paper guerrillas. Bandits, the lot of them. They are multiplying now that the war is coming to its climax. They are giving us a bad name with the Amerikanos. Who is this?" she demands, looking at me. "This is not Lorna."

"Nina, this is Isabelle. I have spoken to you of her many times. This is Mang Carlito's daughter."

She looks at me. I look back, equally irritated. A slow, languid smile starts at the corners of her mouth at my refusal to look away. I do not smile. Then, just as quickly, she dismisses me. I bristle at the exchange.

"It was Miguel's fault," she explains. "But I must speak to you about Palaka."

"We will have no more trouble from him," Domingo says. "Palaka was easily impressed by Miguel. Miguel is dead now."

She nods in understanding. "Was it a good fight?"

"No, of course not." Domingo is annoyed with her question.

She notices his slow speech. Her eyes begin to take account of his injuries. I can see she is worried, but she does not show it to the others.

Domingo sees her concern. His voice is gentle. "It is all right, Nina. I will escort Isabelle home. I shall return tomorrow," he promises.

"I shall come," she says.

"No, you must watch over the others."

I feel the irritation in me growing, pushing through the thickness of my exhaustion. I helped him here just so he could betray Ate Lorna with this tramp.

A boy my brother Alejandro's age comes racing up the hill. He is unhindered by its steepness. He grins stupidly and holds out a hand to Domingo. They shake. Domingo claps a hand to the boy's shoulder and his eyes soften. He nods to the boy. *Do Domingo's eyes water? Is it a trick of the moonlight?*

"Bartolomeo, have you been taking care of the troops?"

"Hello, sir," the boy says, his face beaming. "Yes, I have been watching everyone as you asked. Everyone is accounted for. Except Pogi, he has not yet returned. It has been almost two weeks now."

"You have done an excellent job. Continue the good work. Do not worry about Pogi, he is a smart dog. He will find his way back. He always has. I will return shortly."

The boy notices me for the first time. "Hello, miss." He gives me the same toothy smile. I press my lips in an attempt at a smile, but I do not feel it from the heart. Bartolomeo snaps his attention back to Domingo. He salutes with his left hand. "I will keep up the good work, sir."

"I know, Bartoy, that is why I do not worry. I must go," he tells everyone. Domingo puts a hand out again and places a palm on the boy's head. He has a strong affection for the boy, more than I have seen him give to his own son. I turn away as he embraces the woman once more.

"Captain, Captain!" Inocencio runs down the hill. "You are leaving? But what is the plan?" He is very agitated. "Sir, you have not told me the plan."

"Sorry, sorry. You are right, Ino. Where is my head?" Domingo steadies himself and puts two hands on Inocencio's shoulders. "You are to follow us to the third circle of guards to ensure our safety. Then you are to come back here, and await my return."

Inocencio is instantly relieved. "Very good, sir. That is a good plan. A very good plan."

I glance at the boy and the woman; they keep straight faces, but there is obvious amusement in their eyes.

Inocencio follows us down the hill with his rifle in hand. His eyes shift continuously left to right. I feel comforted despite his strange behavior. At the last circle he tells Domingo, "Now I will return to Nina and Bartoy. We shall wait for your return, sir." He salutes Domingo, also with the left hand.

"Excellent." Domingo returns the salute.

I watch Inocencio as he walks away.

"Does he not cause more trouble for you?" I ask.

"He is the deadliest shot I have ever seen," Domingo answers.

WE HAVE LEFT the last circle of guards. We walk silently for the next two kilometers. Finally, I grow tired of the silence and I look at Domingo's face, then turn away before he can see me.

"Say what is on your mind, *buliit*." He calls me by a nickname, meaning "littlest one."

"I hate what you did to that man." I push the sweat and stray hair from my face.

He watches my expression. "I could not walk away with the thought of him hovering behind me for eternity. He was bad, Bella, he had to die."

"How do you know you are not bad as well?" I challenge.

"Oh, I am bad. Make no mistake. But I can be trusted. There is a difference."

"You killed a Filipino," I tell him.

"Yes, he was Filipino." Domingo's face is without guilt.

"You should have stayed. Let someone else escort me."

He looks surprised. "That would not have been wise. I would have had to hurt them had they done anything untoward."

"I can take care of myself."

"This is not your common group of people, Bella. Their allegiance is held together only by their own vendettas and the threat of my retaliation. There are many who are good, but the other half are unsavory, crude men."

"Why is *she* safe with them?" I cannot take the sarcasm from my voice.

"Nina? She can shoot a forty-five-caliber more than well, and she has a tongue that could stop a charging bull. She can read a person's shame and speak publicly of it if they take even a breath against her person. Also, she has the reputation of having been Serafino Beltran's woman, and now . . ." He lets his words trail into the thick air.

"And now she is yours." I cannot help but sneer for Ate Lorna, who is not here to do so for herself.

Domingo stops walking and blinks at me. Obviously he has not had to explain this situation before. He tries to speak, then stops himself. He goes through this several times; each time concludes with him looking off into the distance. "It is difficult to explain, Isabelle."

"To yourself or to me?" I ask. "The boy is your son?" I see his unease at the question I pose, and I am glad.

"The boy is not my son. He is an orphan like me. Only his parents did not desert him, they were killed by the Japanese. Executed before his eyes."

I feel ashamed suddenly at how I acted toward Bartoy. I chastise myself for not smiling back at him. "And the woman?" I ask.

"And the woman is none of your concern."

"So you met her after you were married to Ate Lorna?"

He glances at me and sighs. "I knew Nina Vargas long before I met your *ate* Lorna. She was the woman of Serafino Beltran, the first leader of our troops. I knew them both before the war. The three of us grew up together. Serafino and

I were rivals for her attention. The only reason she fell for him and not me was that he met her a week earlier. We were from the same orphanage. I was sick with the flu the week she arrived. But we all knew secretly, though it was never spoken, that Nina and I were the better match. I knew how to speak to her. She listened to me. Serafino was a very jealous man. He did not know how to revel in her beauty, to celebrate it. He wanted to keep her locked up. It made him miserable. At times he could not act sanely if she was with him in a room full of men. He was forever forcing her to dress up like a mouse. I used to joke that he might as well sew her up in a rice sack permanently so he never had to worry.

"We had gone our separate ways as adults. It was actually my idea. Serafino did not understand why I wanted to abandon them. I told him I wanted to go in search of my father. But secretly, I thought it best not to have my most valued prize dangled forever in front of me. I would start to resent Serafino, if I didn't already. But she was always on my mind, this woman I could not have. Despite Serafino's invitations I would never spend time with them except in passing, to share a drink, and then the war broke out. We were all three thrust together again. It was as if we had never been apart. That is how strong our bonds of childhood were. If only the bonds of our people were the same. But we are divided.

"During the first year after General MacArthur's retreat, and General Wainwright's surrender of Corregidor, Serafino was killed. I could have predicted it. He was a brave man, but always very brash, temperamental. You need a cool head if you are to be a leader. Not all wars are won by fighting and dying. He was assassinated by the Japanese. His head was sent to Nina and his troops. Nina and I remained good friends. We kept our distance, afraid we would betray his memory, and I was already married, but it was inevitable, our coming together again.

"When I first met your *ate* Lorna, I had hoped that she would be the same kind of woman. One who would follow her man into the jungles, to the death." Domingo sighs. "But I should have known. Lorna is a wealthy man's daughter. She might have been willing to break ties from her family, but to ask her to live in the jungles . . . I do not blame her. Nina and I, we are cut from the same cloth. We understand things through the same eyes. Your *ate* Lorna is a good woman. And I, I am a bastard."

I do not like his answer. It is more than I wanted to hear. In fact, I prayed that he would stop in the middle of his explanation. It is what I feared most. I feel pity for Ate Lorna. How can she compete with this woman?

"You did not have to kill that man. You could have let him go."

"Let him go?" Domingo laughs. "What do you think war is about? Do you think it is just a bunch of grown men playing at leader?" He shrugs. "Possibly this is true, but there is also much struggling with the lower levels. Even, as you witnessed today, within the group. Have you ever played chess, Bella?"

"Yes, but it is not the same," I insist.

"In some ways it is not. But do you see how one pawn, in order to get further ahead to the other side, must jump or, as they say, eat the other?"

I do not answer. I watch him. I ask myself, *Is this man good or bad? Would he kill me in a certain situation?*

"Miguel and I became two pawns facing one another. If I did not jump over him, he would eat me."

"So your murder of Miguel, it now allows you to follow your plans? It does not matter that you have killed a man? He is now off the board?"

Domingo becomes frustrated with me. He clicks his tongue. "Your heart is so tender still. I could not have him threatening me from behind at all times. Wondering at what moment he would choose to try to rise up against me. There are people who look up to me, who watch me for guidance."

"So you are a god now." I am frightened, yet I cannot help my mouth from saying these things. It has always been this way with me. My thinking and my mouth have been the matter of many arguments with my mother.

He is silent for a long moment. Except for his occasional grunts, and the weight I help him support, we say nothing. After a few kilometers he says, "I should not have let you see that, what happened back there."

"It is too late," I say with such resentment that Domingo pauses. "You could have told me that I risked my life in order for you to meet with your mistress and then kill a man. You have made me an accomplice to your sin. Ate Lorna will never forgive me."

"Enough. I will not make excuses for what I did. I would do it again. What did you think? That we were going to a tea party? These men are trained to live through days in the jungle without food, without hope. They fight for a better Philippinas than the one we have at this moment. We've been reduced to animals, and so we act as such. Do you have a better answer on how to win this war?" His face is red, the same as my mother's when we get into these exchanges.

I look at him, his wounds soaking through his thin clothing. The exhaustion that breathes through his whole body. I feel the weight of his responsibilities, the lives he holds in his hands. But I am still angry with him, and about this woman Nina Vargas; I wish to humiliate him for what he has done to his wife.

"Why is it that with all these men at your disposal, you do not try to help the prisoners at Santo Tomas, or Bilibid?"

He studies me, his eyes showing impatience with my flippant tone. "And what would I do with them once they were set free? How would I hide them? There would be hundreds of Filipinos and Amerikanos. There would not be enough weapons to give them. How would I feed them when I can barely feed my own? How would they keep up with us in their weakened states?"

I feel my face redden with embarrassment.

He sighs. "We cannot free the prisoners and then retreat. Do you understand? It must be all or nothing. We cannot approach the situation halfway."

After several hours, we find a grove of papaya trees and yellow acacias. We try to catch our breath. I think of home and wonder what they are all doing. Domingo's eyes constantly shift left and right; I feel as if my entire body will unravel at any moment. He seats himself on a rock and unties his pants. I look away quickly, then glance back. He pulls down his pants and inspects the wound on the thigh. The rag is soaked with blood. It smells bad. When Domingo peels away the dressing, the wound oozes a greenish color. He clucks his tongue and shakes his head.

"Miguel's bite has infected it further. He would take me with him to the grave."

IT IS ALMOST morning when we reach the foot of the mountain. We are again near my hometown of Bulacan. The indigo of night is fading fast, and the moon is farther away. If I close my eyes, I can pretend I am home and that I can return to school.

Domingo has become feverish from the exertion. Soon he is talking in a delirium. I cannot leave him this way. His strength has left him completely. We are not resting more than an hour when we hear footsteps, many of them. When I peek through the bushes, I see women of all ages walking in single file, heading toward Manila. Japanese soldiers walk beside, herding them forward like carabaos. They are mostly Filipinas, but there are two Amerikanas. One, with faded yellow hair, falls on the ground. She looks odd with her dark skin and pale hair. The soldiers prod her with bayonets. "Up, up."

The Amerikanas have been separated and walk behind the Filipinas. I am so stricken that I accidentally put my hand down on Domingo's leg and he cries out, muttering in his delirium. His eyes are blurred, and he does not recognize me. I put my hand to his mouth. "Quiet," I tell him. "Sleep."

"Sleep," he murmurs.

The soldiers stop to listen. Any moment now they will find our hiding place. I give Domingo one last look and run out into the clearing. The soldiers see me turn around, but they do not know where I have come from. They think only that I was walking and stumbled across them.

"Young girl, *daraga, daraga.*" A Japanese soldier smiles, trying to say the Tagalog word for "young girl," *dalaga.* He waves at me, flapping his palm downward, to come. I swallow and will myself not to look back to where I have left Domingo. I look around at the trees so that I will remember where he is. I see a thick grouping of ferns. "Near the ferns, and the large *narra* tree," I repeat as the soldiers shove me forward.

"Come, come. I not hurt you." The soldier smiles with dead eyes. "We go to nice hotel in Manila, nice place. Give you food and drink. Nice for you," he says. I look at the women. They stare at the ground. "You are hungry?" he asks as the soldiers surround me slowly.

My body begins to shake terribly. The muscles of my mouth tremble. *Of course I am hungry. Can't you see the way my skirt hangs from my hips instead of my waist? We are all hungry. Ever since you devils came three years ago and wanted to control the rice production. You controlled it so well that our rice tripled in cost and created a black market.* "Yes." I nod. "I am very hungry."

"Good, good." The soldier smiles.

Two soldiers run past me and look at the spot where I came from. My heart is pumping cold blood through my veins. *Please God,* I pray. They come so close, but they do not find Domingo. I pray that he remains in quiet delirium. There is nothing he can do. The soldiers have guns. We begin to walk again. I am part of the line now. I think back to three years ago. I was a different girl then. And the only reason I needed to be home by dark was that my parents wished it so.

My friends and I have the same interest. I was accelerated two grades because of my good studying, and I was to attend the university before the war broke out. My friend Karing is also to go to medical school. I have known her since we were babies. I have not seen her since last year. Her family was taken away and brought to Santo Tomas prison because her father is an Amerikano and that is where they keep all the Amerikano soldiers and their families.

My best friend Mica's father was killed, and at times I feel guilty for having all of my family still living. I wish she were here with me now. It used to be that the three of us were inseparable. Now I do not even know if Mica made it home safely the other evening. I told her to go alone. It is my fault. I insisted she was being a baby and could make it home alone. I did not think she could be hurt because she is Japanese.

My eyes burn with tears. We were so close to home, Domingo and I. Now I am walking farther away again, back toward Manila. This is madness. I think of my little brothers, Alejandro and Roderick. I force myself to believe that they made it home. We walk for over an hour, the sky a cloudless blue. The sounds of war explode ahead of us. Another two hours and the sounds of battle swallow us completely. The explosions drop us to our knees. Twenty meters away there is machine-gun fire. Planes fly overhead, and I stare in horror as we walk into the city. Manila is on fire.

HALF THE BUILDINGS have crumbled to the ground. The Japanese soldiers scream for us to get up, but some of the women do not hear, and the soldiers come and pull them up by the hair. The beautiful churches are half standing. We follow the soldiers along the back of the *luneta*. We go to Pilar Street, where a soldier points a dirty finger, to the grand Villamar Hotel. The hotel is at least ten floors high. It is a simple square stone structure. For just a moment the smoke is blown away, and I can see faces peering out the window like specters.

We run as explosions fly overhead. A woman drops to the ground and sobs hysterically. She recognizes her children and her husband dead on the street, killed by a sniper. The soldiers echo her frenzy, and two of them drag her toward the hotel. She is beyond reason, kicking and cursing, clawing at the soldiers. We are surrounded by the dead. Bodies are strewn in the streets, some without arms or legs.

There are babies on the ground, their tiny frames riddled with bayonet points. What crime could they have committed? The sickly stench of rotting fills the air sweet and thick, worse than I have ever imagined. Death is everywhere, and I breathe it in.

The inside of the hotel is like being in a dream, beautiful and opulent with imported rugs, paintings of colonial Spain and our islands. High chandeliers and wooden polished handrails, dulled by the print of many hands, grace the interior. A shock to the senses after the devastation outside. The electric lights that line the hall blink dimly, then brighten as the ground shakes and then stops. We are taken up many flights of stairs, through several corridors, and pushed into a dark room. The door is slammed shut and locked. We listen to the retreating footsteps and the sound of more locks turning.

I let out a breath of air and lean my back against the wall. I hear a muffled thumping against the wall and put my ear to it. The sound is close, as if it were just on the other side. It seems to come from lower; I follow the sound and stare at my knee as it bumps against the wall. I am trembling uncontrollably.

The women begin to whisper, slowly at first. They speak of the woman outside who became hysterical.

"She was taken to another room," someone whispers.

"Will they feed us, you think?" a woman asks with sarcasm.

My eyes take a moment to adjust to the dark. She is older than me, in her mid-twenties, perhaps. If it were not for the long dirty hair stuck to her face and the hollow of her cheeks from starvation, she would be beautiful, I think. She wears a gold band on her finger. She wears an olive dress, sleeveless, with a straight skirt belted at the waist. It is splattered with dried blood, dirt, and grass stains. She is not wearing shoes, and her feet are badly blistered. Her arms have deep scratches, and I notice a large bruise on her jaw and along her neck.

No one answers her.

"Where were you coming from?" she asks me.

Again no one answers.

"You there. Young girl."

I look up. "I was on my way home to Bulacan." Even now I do not disclose the fact that Domingo was with me. I am terrified someone will hear.

"But you were in Paombong when we found you, west of Bulacan. Why were you so far away?"

I shrug. "Where are you from?"

"I am from Nueva Ecija."

"Even farther," I answer. Nueva Ecija is north of Bulacan. I hear the edges of my voice. It sounds brittle, callous.

"Yes." She gives a tired smile. "I was searching for fruit yesterday. I left my baby by herself in her basket. My husband went out to hunt for food two days ago and did not return. The Japanese found me, the same way we came across you today."

"What is your name?" I ask.

"Jocelyn," she says. "Jocelyn Kuago, and you?"

"Isabelle Karangalan."

She chuckles. "Such a name. It suits you. *Karangalan* means 'honor' in Tagalog, but you know that, right?"

I nod.

"One of honor. I like that. Why did I not think of such names when we named our daughter? Something strong. Instead I chose Lily."

"I like Lily," I say.

"Yes, so do I. I should not say such things. It will not be good for her to hear me say such things.

"Do you know why we are here?" Jocelyn asks.

"Shut up," one of the women says, and starts to cry. "We are here for food."

"Believe what you wish, but she needs to know. It has already been done to us, surely you do not think we will still get food?"

"Why are we here?" I look levelly at her. A vein in my neck pulses wildly, and my mouth goes dry.

She nods, as if to say, "Good." "We are here to serve the soldiers when they relieve themselves from the battlefield. You understand?"

I nod numbly. "And the little ones?" I ask, because there are several little girls with us who look to be between nine and twelve years old.

She nods again, and I look away.

"They are trying to rid Manila of her people. They want to break the only thing we have left, our spirits. I will not let them. No matter what they do to me. Isabelle, do you understand?"

"Yes," I whisper.

"Come here." She pats the floor beside her.

I get up, and I feel the soreness of my joints, the hunger in my belly. It takes such an effort to cross the room. I lean against the same wall and slowly lower myself next to her.

She holds up her left hand and kisses the ring on her finger, then takes it off. "Here, wear this. They will think you are married."

I frown at her. "I cannot take that. Your husband."

"Don't be silly. They want the *dalagas* first. The virgins. Put it on."

I take the ring from her finger and start to cry for the first time. She pulls me to her and smoothes my hair. I fall asleep to the sound of my stomach moaning.

WE HAVE NO windows in this room. It is not the typical hotel room, but a supply closet of some sort. It is dark. The light no longer filters through the bottom of our door. A million cries escape our throats when we hear the heavy sound of boots.

"Oh, God," we hear women sob from the next rooms. It is the first time we realize that the other rooms are filled with women also.

We are at the end of the third floor. I pray even though I know it is horrible, I pray that there are enough of the other women in the first room to satisfy them. When the door to our room opens, my mouth widens. A torch is brought in and held near our faces. The flame cuts through the dark, slashing at our eyes with its heat and searing our ears with its breath. I see my expression reflected in the terrified faces of the others. The ones with young daughters hold them tightly in their arms. I wish for a bomb to fall on us, but God does not answer my prayer.

Jocelyn and I hold hands. Five soldiers come in and pull the closest girls to them. Immediately the girls begin to cry. One of the soldiers laughs and puts his arm around the waist of the smallest girl. She looks to be about eleven years old. The girl's mother stands and tries to grab her daughter back, but the man hits her with the back of his hand. Her arms flail as she falls to the ground. The other girls are dragged out by their hair.

So this is how it will be. They take the Amerikanas first. Then they take a fourth woman who looks to be in her early twenties. They scan the room until their eyes land on me, and I begin to shake.

The soldier points to me. "Up."

Jocelyn holds up my hand with the ring. "She is married. No longer a *dalaga*."

The soldier frowns. "You, then." He grabs Jocelyn by the shoulder.

She gives me one last look. I do not find the words to thank her.

There is screaming coming from different rooms, more desperate than ours. I shut my eyes and hold my fists to my ears. The door opens again and one of the girls is thrown back. She is too tiny, all bones, and the soldiers will have nothing to do with her. A different girl is groped, then selected.

After another hour, we hear new footsteps at the door, and again the rooms are opened. They pass our room. This continues on and on, every hour, as the soldiers are relieved from their posts. It must be very early in the morning when our doors open again. The three girls are thrown back in the room. One is bleeding profusely beneath her skirt.

"*Dios ko, Dios ko, anák ko*," the woman says, weeping. My God, my baby.

"I am hurt." The young girl walks to her mother and collapses.

"You, *daraga*, come with me." A soldier points to a younger girl. Both the girl and her mother begin to sob.

"No, oh no," the mother says over and over. My heart aches for the girl.

"Shut up." Another woman covers her ears. "They have chosen her, she must go."

"Come, come. I am tired. I need to sleep." The soldier speaks perfect English with no accent, so I am surprised by this.

"I will go." I stand. I do not bother to show him the ring. He looks at me in surprise, and then he nods. "Okay, okay, good. Hurry."

Think of good things. God, why have you deserted us?

The soldier takes my wrist and leads me down the hallway. We pass other soldiers, who tug at my skirt. He must be higher ranked than they are, for he shoves their hands away and they move away from him. He takes me to the fourth floor and opens a large suite. My mind spins. *Rake his face.* I look at the vase on the table. *Smash it over his head. And what if he does not die? Then what?*

He is watching me think through this. He is young for an officer. He locks the door to the suite and sits to study me. My breathing is coming so fast that I cannot think. I look to the door and to the open window.

The soldier moves toward me. "Be still." He brushes the hair away from my face, and my skin grows cold.

I am about to be butchered. I look him straight in the eyes. I know I should not do this, but it has always been this way with me. Once I feel fear, I can stand it for only so long before I become angry. He seems taken aback by my glare.

He tilts his head back a little and chuckles. "What will you do? You wish to hit me? I would treat you nice." He takes the back of his hand and rubs his knuckles against my cheek. It takes great effort not to bite his fingers. I am so tired, and my body will not stop trembling, from fear or anger or exhaustion, I do not know. All I want to do is sleep. We continue to stare at each other.

There is a knock at the door. The soldier grunts an answer in Japanese. His answer is met with silence and then two more quick raps. The soldier curses and strides to the door. I look around for a weapon. When I look to a nearby table, I cannot believe my eyes. There is a desk, and a copper letter opener, dull but pointed at the end. I take it quickly and put it in my front skirt pocket.

There is arguing at the door, and when the soldier steps aside I am mesmerized. I don't know what to think. A Makapili stands there, wearing a cloth mask with slits for eyes. He gazes at me, and I hate the traitor on sight. He points a finger at me.

"This is the girl. The high commander asked that I keep her aside for him. She was mixed back into the crowd by accident," the Makapili explains.

"Too late," the Japanese soldier snaps. "I have already picked her."

The Makapili shrugs. "I shall tell the commander, then." He bows to walk away.

"Wait—" The soldier reaches out a hand to stop him. He looks back at me while the Makapili waits at the door. The soldier walks back to me and rubs my back. His hand follows the curve of my back, down past my skirt. He reaches underneath my skirt and rubs my rear.

I grit my teeth, my hand resting on top of the metal letter opener. He sighs and pulls away from me, and we stare at each other again.

"What I would do with you," he says in English, and grins. "What you would like to do to me." He laughs and wags a finger at me. "Here—" He pushes me forward. "Take her. It is probably best. Warn the commander not to turn his back. She has blood in her eyes."

"Yes, Major," the Makapili says, and ushers me out of the room.

We walk through the hallway again. It is filled with more soldiers coming in from the fighting. I keep my head bowed and watch them from beneath my veil of hair. I see them in a blur. The hallways seem slanted to my eyes, as if they are on an incline. The dim lighting flickers with the distant explosions. I am lost in the voices of the Japanese soldiers and in their stares. They reach out to touch my arm, my chest; one wraps his fist in my hair and I gasp at the pain. He smells of death and sweat. His breath is foul.

The Makapili puts his hand out, but the soldier shoves it away. "She is reserved for the commander," the Makapili says firmly.

The soldier takes his hand from my hair and grunts. He says something in Japanese to the others. Their eyes trace the curve of my breasts. I hold my breath. It makes my skin crawl. They glance condescendingly at him. One of them gives a sarcastic snort, not quite a laugh. A chuckle, with the eyes scoffing.

The Makapili leads me upstairs to another room. I feel a sickness in my stomach. I want to scream. He opens the door and I turn to run. He blocks my way and I stare into the slits of his mask. "Why are you doing this?" I despise the sound of my voice, raw and helpless. "You are a Filipino," I remind him.

"Shh, come." He grabs my wrist and turns on the light. When he shuts the door I move away from him and look around the room for the commander whose present I have become. The room is cool and empty, with a window thrown open. The curtains flap in the wind, ushering in the scent of gunpowder and ashes from the burning buildings.

There is a large canopied bed, with smooth ivory silk and gossamer nets to keep the mosquitoes away. A jade-colored vase with pink lilies makes my heart turn. On a corner table lies an open cedar box of cigars. I watch as the Makapili unties the mask from behind his neck and begins to pull it off. I picture a devil behind the mask and my first reflex is to flee, but he is too quick, and when his mask comes off I see that it is Feliciano Bautista, Aling Ana's nephew.

"You!" I shout.

"Shh." He puts his finger to his mouth and comes to put his arms around me.

"*Hayop!*" I scream—Animal!—and slap his face. He scrambles to put his hand on top of my mouth. We wrestle and I fall over a low table and my knee hits the corner of the table painfully. I begin to cry, and he pins me down.

"Isabelle, I will protect you. But you must listen to me. You must stay here. Do you understand?"

I think of all the times I helped him with his homework. The times my father let him come to visit. I think of my family dying somewhere from hunger, from our enemies, my young brother hanging from his thumbs. And this man, this traitor, dares to touch me. I have no care; I pull the letter opener from my skirt. I mean to plunge it in his neck, to gouge an eye. But again he is too fast for me, and he grabs my wrist and slams it on the ground twice until I let go. I curl my fist and strike him hard across the face the way Father taught us, when he would hang a sack of rice and teach us to punch it.

Feliciano falls back, holding his face. I find the letter opener and lunge for him. He leans forward and slaps me. My nose begins to bleed. I scramble free and stand up to fight him.

"Isabelle, forgive me. Please." He holds his palms in front of me.

I stare at him. "You coward, you traitor. I would rather die."

"You *will* die. Your family will die, if you do not let me help you."

My heart twists at the mention of my family. "Do not let the Japanese hurt them, Feliciano. My family has been good to you. We have always welcomed you into our home."

"I haven't forgotten. Let me find a way to get you out of here. Will you listen when I think of a plan?"

I nod slowly.

"Stay here. If someone knocks . . ." He stops, not knowing what to say. "I will be back soon, okay?"

I nod and watch him hurry out of the room. I push my hair away from my face with the back of my hand. So tired. The minute he leaves I rush to the window and look down. I am on the fifth floor. There are no balconies. I would die instantly. My mind begins to play tricks on me. Perhaps it wouldn't be so bad to give in to Feliciano. He could protect me. At least I would pick a lesser demon to lie with. Better to lie with a Filipino than the enemy. Even if the Filipino is a traitor.

I hit my forehead with the base of my palm and begin to cry. I avoid the bed and curl myself into a ball. *What are you saying? What are you thinking? You do not know. He could have been the one that pointed a finger at Domingo, at Alejandro. He could be the worst of all of them.*

IT IS DARK in the room when I wake. I have no sense of time. When did I last see Domingo? Is it tomorrow already? There is a loud explosion, followed by a second. I don't know where I am. I crouch low, waiting for the bomb to land. It takes a moment before I realize it is someone kicking at the door. Still I am not yet myself; I think for just a moment it is the door to our house. But this is not my room. There is a large carpet on the floor. I feel it uneasily with the palm of my hand. My mind stretches. *Think, think,* it says. My heart begins to beat quickly, like the wings of a hummingbird, strong like the rumbling of a volcano. Then the picture forms and I realize where I am.

"Feliciano?" I call out.

Someone is yelling in Japanese, and then in thick English he says, "Open this door. Who has key?" The kicking grows louder, more crazed.

I stand, crouch down, then stand again. I put my hands to my ears, wanting to die. I want my mother. I run to the window and throw it open farther. I will wait for the door to break open, and then I will jump.

Someone is running down the hall. I begin to cry and throw my right leg over the window. But the door is kicked open, and before I have time to think, three soldiers rush toward me and pull me back into the room.

"So this is girl Makapili has saved for me?" A heavy Japanese comes forward. He is dirty and his face is caked with dirt and sweat. I watch with fascination as a pool of sweat forms in the crevice of his upper lip. "Good." He nods and begins to undress. The other two soldiers do the same. They take off their underclothes, and I catch a glimpse of their private areas and look away. My face burns. One goes to the window and shuts it, checking the lock.

I cannot move. What a fool I was to think Feliciano would help me. He merely said that so I would go willingly to this room without a fight. *Fool for trusting him. Fool for sleeping. Now I will die.* My stomach twists and I pace the small area between us. The other soldier lights a cigar, and soon the room is filled with the heavy sweet aroma. They watch me with disinterest. They talk of conditions at the battlefront and of the orders that are coming from the emperor himself. The leader waves his hand for me to come forward. I stand my ground.

He lights a cigar and repeats the gesture, his face bland with impatience.

This is not happening. I am to study medicine at the University of Santo Tomas. I was accelerated two grades for my intelligence. I catalog all the classes I am to take, all the books I must buy. The soldiers come closer to me. I remember all the friends who will attend, their faces smiling. The commander reaches out and touches my breasts as if he were sampling fruit at the market. My body cringes and my mind shouts, *Improper!* Their hands are all around me, touching. My throat convulses and I fold within myself. My hands are moved away as I try to hold off their advances. Oh God, their laughter, and the smell of their filth. I cover myself with my arms. It only incites their violence. They pry my arms open. I hear a tearing sound. It is my soul. I feel the last of my strength drain, and I am paralyzed. Their hands are so strong, so thick; their faces blur before me. I hear the tearing of my blouse, my skirt.

"No, stop it. Please." I slap and slap at the hands until I feel a strong blow to my face. My strength leaks out. My pride lies in a pool of sorrow with my clothes.

Their skin smells of sweat and smoke and the blood of my people. *My blood will join theirs.* I repeat this like a prayer, though the meaning of it I do not know.

Their laughter withers my skin. My legs are spread and held. I scream in anticipation of the soldier's flesh. It comes like a shock, a stab; my stomach convulses in pain. It wants the intruder out. I taste blood on my tongue. I feel the weight of each of their bodies as they hover and grunt over me. They force kisses on my neck, they avoid my lips. A hand pinches my nipple, twisting it. Pinning my thigh with a thick knee, grasping at my hair at the last minute, then mewling like a baby before slumping over me entirely with heavy breathing.

I become detached from my own skin. *I am a virgin no more,* I repeat to myself. People will know this when they see me. I look into their eyes, but there is nothing, no hope, no compassion, only hate and blackness. I see the face of war.

Such an awful thing to happen to this poor girl. She is so alone, and then I remember, the girl is me. The girl *was* me. I cry because there is nothing left for me to do.

The door opens and I hear them as they begin to pick up their clothes. I hear the jingle of belt buckles and the flapping of sleeves. I begin to drown in the darkness. In the hallway I hear the sound of running footsteps and then Feliciano's voice as he swings open the door. He says, "Major, Major, that one is reserved for the commander." He has to repeat this several times.

"Yes, me. I am commander here."

"No, for Kurohiko." Feliciano gives a name.

"Too late for Kurohiko," the commander announces, and his companions laugh.

The laughter slices at my body like a whip, and I shudder.

Feliciano looks down at me, stunned. His face is stricken with disbelief. It would be comical really, if not for the situation. I feel like I will suddenly laugh at his face and scratch his eyes out at the same time. He helps me up, grabbing my upper arm tightly, pinching the skin. "*Dalaga,* time to take you to the commander. Come, come." He touches me with his devil hands. I slap him again and again.

The leader gets up slowly and buttons his pants; he watches us with no expression, then leaves the room abruptly. My legs are wet, drenched with their garbage.

I push Feliciano away. *"Hayop!"* I scream. Animal! I run to the window. The heat hits me like a fist, and the stench waters my eyes. I put my leg over the rail and stare down at the street below. *If I were to dive headfirst like when we visit the three waterfalls in the province, perhaps I would not feel it.*

"Isabelle," Feliciano says. He runs to me and clasps my wrist, gently at first, then strongly. "My God, Isabelle, forgive me. Please."

I pull my leg back in. My thigh scrapes against the cool metal. I shake so hard against the window frame that I can barely hold on.

"Monster!" I scream. I wrench free of his embrace. I feel my hand as it thuds against his head, his face, his eye.

"You must trust me. Trust me," Feliciano says. "I did not know this would happen. I tried, Isabelle. I tried to bring you somewhere safe, but I was detained."

"Traidór," I scream. Traitor! He lets me claw at his neck, gritting his teeth until he can stand it no longer. He grabs me by the wrists. I crumple to my knees with him still standing holding my wrists, my arms held above me.

He is encouraged by my submissiveness and places my torn blouse around my shoulders and keeps his arms there. "We must go now. I know a place. Soon it will be dark. The soldiers are tired and drunk. Fewer questions will be asked. If someone should stop us, you must let me talk. I will take you somewhere."

I struggle away from him. He brings me my skirt. I see my undergarments lying on the floor.

"Shh, shh," he whispers with his lips near my temple. Then he takes out his mask from his back pocket and pulls it over his head. He holds his hand out to me. I take the devil's hand because I do not know what else to do.

How I wish to stab him. He enjoys this game of being my protector. He ushers me through the dimly lit hallways. A few of the rooms are open. My gaze wanders into a room as we pass. A girl is seated on the edge of the bed, and our eyes meet. Her hair is pasted to her neck from sweat. Her dress is torn. Her eyes have no life. I see my image in her. She is already dead inside. A soldier zips his pants and hurries out. Just as quickly another walks in and blocks my view; he glances at me as he unbuttons his shirt and kicks the door shut. We hurry down the hallway, Feliciano pulling me forward. He plays the Makapili again to his audience of filthy soldiers. They study us as we walk by.

"Hurry, the commander is waiting." Feliciano shoves me. "You have kept him waiting long enough."

I almost fall when he does this. I have no strength left in me. Again the corridor of endless hands and endless rooms. We walk downstairs, through more passageways that twist and turn like a snake. I close my eyes. So good to just sleep.

"Isabelle, stay alert." Feliciano nudges me. He pulls my hand, and I try to keep my eyes open. Suddenly I feel the outside air hit me, and I take a deep swallow. The scent of rotting flesh and smoke fills my nose. It is evening now, maybe eight o'clock. Was it just this morning I left Domingo? When was the last time I ate? I look away to the side street just as Feliciano tells me not to look.

There are bodies of women, one piled atop another. The bodies are bloody and stiff. I walk slowly forward. I have to see. My eyes focus on a hand with a pale circle around the ring finger. I recognize the bloody olive dress of the woman who gave me her ring. *What was her name?* I turn and heave, but nothing comes out. I stumble forward. I must give her back her ring. I must put it on her finger. Feliciano grabs me roughly and shakes me. "Come, come, do you want to be just like them?"

"I *am* just like them." I stomp my feet. "And you, you are just like them." I point back toward the building. Something changes in his eyes at my words. *Does he flinch a little? Are those tears? Does he pity me now?* He clenches his jaw, but I see he is crying.

"How dare you cry for me!" I tell myself not to say these things to him, but I am helpless to stop myself, just as I am helpless to stop this storm of madness. I am a moth caught in a downpour.

Before this, I was so proud, so confident. I was on my way to medical school. My friends and I would gather after class and talk about the studies and cases that made our blood pulse, that opened our eyes. Now, all I wish is to close them. I am a stray dog, unsure which outstretched hand to trust.

"Get down, sniper." Feliciano points to one of the rooftops of the buildings. "Stay close."

I break free of Feliciano. I look in a daze for the sniper. Amerikano or Japanese? What difference does it make? I step out into the street and open my arms wide to embrace his bullet.

"*Gaga!*" Feliciano shouts. Stupid! He grabs for me.

Lightning streaks the sky, and the thunder joins the sounds of gunfire. I wonder where my family is and if I will ever see them again. Each step I take, no matter the direction, feels as if I am moving farther and farther from them, irrevocably. I run and glance down at my legs, as if they were separate entities from me, moving, while I am just a passenger watching.

Feliciano puts his arm around me. I resent this. He is taking liberties where he would have never done so before. I resent even more the way I clutch his hand tightly and the way my other hand grips the back of his shirt. We are running through back streets, through narrow spaces, crawling under fences, tasting the gutters. Everywhere I look there is complete madness. Death is on the ground. In the sky the planes fall like angels. The ground rumbles from the Amerikano tanks. Buildings are on fire. The long wide streets of Manila are straightways for the big guns. There are dead babies on the streets, as common as bird droppings. I see a little girl crouched in between two small houses, with gunfire so low that it almost shaves her head. She sits on her haunches, hugging her legs. I stop and Feliciano drags me forward with the momentum of his running.

"We must not stop. Cannot stop for anybody. Too many," he shouts.

My heart aches for my people. I don't understand why God gives more power to some and less to others.

We go many kilometers without stopping. Buildings are crumpled on the ground, others left standing like metal carcasses. We leave the city for the outskirts.

"Here, here, see?" Feliciano points, but all I see are fallen palm trees, a dry creek bed. We are on the outskirts of the Malate district. Then I see it, a small abandoned house. We rush into the house, and I pause. I look to the heavy wooden roof. It has the feel of a death trap. Feliciano lights a candle and ushers me in. He singes his hand and drops the match. I take pleasure to see pain cross his face. He notices my smug expression and says gravely, "I would take any pain away from you if I could."

"Don't say such things."

"Before the war I had plans to court you. To ask permission from your father."

I place my hands over my ears. "Stop it. Do you think I could care for you still?"

He stands very still. "But you *did* care for me?"

It is enough, my pause, the denial that does not come quickly to my lips. "I grow tired," I say.

"Let us rest. It is safe here for the time being." He acts suddenly like the host.

"Of you. I grow tired of you." I imagine myself twisting my words like a knife into his chest, but instead of pleasure I feel only sadness.

"Of course." He nods. "Rest now. I shall watch over you while you sleep.

Right here—" He points to the doorway. "I shall be seated with my back to this door. I will not fail you again. I would die first."

I leave his promise hanging in the air between us. I give him one last look, then walk to the other end of the empty room and rest against the wall. We sit facing each other, and though I am afraid of what nightmares may lurk the minute I close my eyes, I find I can keep them open no longer. I close them with a sigh. Though I resist, an image comes to me. A proud-faced young man. I remember how Feliciano looked that last fall before the war broke out. Showing off with the other boys in school. How he strolled up to me in front of everyone in the courtyard and announced that he needed a tutor in mathematics. He had heard that I had gotten a near perfect score in the last exam. Would I be available? He would pay me, of course. I remember being surprised because he was the highest-ranked student, but my ego had readily accepted his request. Of course I would tutor the smartest boy in school. I remember his eyes, the way they had bordered on mischief, but I was not quite sure, for he kept a straight face. So different now from the eyes I feel studying me. A hundred years those eyes have aged in their steady observation of me. I see no trace of the boy in them. I fall asleep wondering if he still sees the girl I once was.

THE DREAM, WHATEVER it was, was pleasant. It lingers, and I try to hold on to the feeling, but it eludes me. I wake with a smile on my face as Feliciano shakes me gently.

"Listen to me, Isabelle. I must go back, or else they will notice I am missing. You must stay here and not stray. You will get yourself killed if you leave. Do you understand?"

My body rebels at the familiarity of this situation. *Stay and be raped again. Leave and be raped again.* I do not answer him. I notice the scratches I have left on his face. I follow the lines from his eyes to his neck. They are deep lines. I feel the urge to trace them with my fingertips.

He talks gruffly to me the way Father does when he is trying to infuse me with courage. "It is up to you. If you want to live, you must stay here. If you want to die, then you need only open the door." He eyes me to see if he has made his point. I stare back at him without feeling. A coldness has crept back into my body. I do not answer him. "It is up to you," he says. He stares at me for a long time as if he wishes to say something. The lines of his brow crease deeper, then he turns suddenly, opens the door, and leaves.

I watch him through the window of the house. Something in me screams,

Don't leave me here! The lightning lights up the streets, and his shadow is swallowed by the night. I am stunned. I cannot believe he has left me alone. I scour through the house, through the kitchen, afraid of what I might find, hopeful to find anything, anyone. I pull open kitchen drawers and find nothing, just emptiness. I find an overturned armoire in one of the rooms. It is heavily laquered with ornate handles. There are clothes scattered on the floor. These people are dead, I tell myself.

I am surprised to find clothing. Despite the heat I pick up two sweaters and put them both on. I find no food, but there is a knife, an empty flask, and two bottles of beer. I am so thirsty that I break the bottle and drink. I put some in the flask and place it in my pocket. *Has he really left me alone?* I peek through the broken windows. My eyes scour the dark. The sky rumbles and explodes in a shower of rain. I throw open the door and set out running.

I am a rabbit broken loose from the jaws of a snake. I throw my head back, letting the rain drizzle into my mouth, and laugh. I laugh until my whole body shakes with the tears I shed. I run farther away from the sounds of fighting to an open field. I do not know where I am going. All I know is that I must continue north to get back to Domingo and my family. I run without thinking. The rain has eaten at the dirt, turning it into mud. It reveals something beneath the dirt. The ground every few feet is filled with gopher holes. I run a few feet, then stop suddenly. I feel my bones shake against the cage of my skin. I look down slowly, I see a piece of metal in every hole. These are not gopher holes. My mouth falls open, the way my youngest brother's does when my father hits the back of his head and tells him to spit out whatever bad thing he is eating. All around me, dozens of land mines.

My knees bend in horror, and my fingers touch the ground softly. *"O Dios ko,"* I breathe. Oh God. *Think, think, calm down.* I turn slowly, the way a snail would, afraid even to swallow. I squint at the faint traces of my footsteps on the ground. Already the rain is eating at them, blurring them back into the mud. I put my foot out slowly and trace my last step. Painstakingly I do this, shaking as I place my weight. I am almost near the beginning when I see a horrible thing. A beautiful white doe, just a baby. Its ears are alert. It stops just at the edge of the forest, and our eyes meet. Its small tail whips nervously. She raises her nose and it trembles, sorting the different smells in the air. Does she smell it, too? The thick burning, the powdered dirt, the indelible smell of our people dying.

Her stub tail switches quicker, back and forth, like the pendulum on a broken clock. My eyes are fixed on her legs, set firmly but lightly on the ground.

Stay there, please, I beg silently. Our eyes are locked; I feel the sensation of a thousand beads of sweat break my brow. I am too afraid even to swallow. The deer looks back over her shoulder. *Yes, go back,* I plead in my mind. She is so beautiful, so perfect. I want to reach out and wrap her in my arms. I pray that she dies on the spot so that she does not move.

My horror is complete when her gaze starts to wander from mine. I feel my scream lost somewhere above us, lost in the lightning and thunder. It mingles with the screams of a thousand women, a thousand mothers, and children, and husbands and fathers, and brothers. In a heartbeat the little doe goes bounding to the center of the mines. I turn and leap in the opposite direction, picking my scream from the air and giving it voice. There are a series of explosions, and I am thrown against the base of a tree. I hit the trunk full in the chest. I choke until my breath surges back. The dirt falls around us, black and charred. There are a hundred cuts on my arms, and my face is stinging as though it is being attacked by bees. I stagger up on legs that feel broken in two.

I walk for at least a kilometer when I realize that I have gone the wrong way. There are no buildings to mark which way I am going. The church of Santa Teresa is no longer standing so that I can say, *"Yes, the back of the tower faces north, and the front, with the Latin words inscribed, is south."* There is no church standing at all, so I do not realize until I have passed the old cemetery that I am heading in the opposite direction from which I desire. A Japanese patrol approaches, six of them. I throw myself into a pile of corpses. Their poor frames are stiff and cold. I shut my eyes tight and breathe through my mouth. When the soldiers are gone, I slide down slowly from their bodies. I gasp as a hardened hand scrapes against my lips.

I keep my eyes upward to the trees, for any sign of fruit. But it appears the soldiers have already gotten to the fruit. I find a bayabas on the ground, its sweet yellow fruit bruised and mushy from a fat little worm living inside. I try to pick out the worm, but it swims back into the meat of the fruit. I eat it with the worm intact. My stomach rumbles from the hunger pains.

Thoughts without purpose creep in and out of my head. I do not know why, but I think of my mother's hands. The soft skin, callused on the inside, the veins soft and protruding on the outer side. I remember how cool they are on my brow when I am sick. How they feel when they braid my hair or rub my back. I long for her familiar caress on my shoulder when I pass her in the hall-way. She was right. All along she was right. When she told me not to stay out late, that bad things would happen to me, I laughed in her face. I called her old-fashioned. I taunted that I was not like her, that I was not afraid of anything.

When she told me evil comes out after twilight time, and that people should be indoors, I called her superstitious. I had no right thinking I could be any different, any stronger. I am a fool, and I deserve what has happened to me.

I have wronged her. I have been her greatest foe, and she my biggest protector. Her heart is so pure, like a child's. She gives without thinking. She longs to have beautiful things, I see it in her eyes, but she always thinks of us first. Before the war she spent each day sewing or peddling our plantains, so that the fried sweet banana smell was stuck indelibly to her hair. Each night she prepared tusino, the red marinated pork, adding a touch of rice wine vinegar to sweeten the flavor. She brought them to the houses that had special ordered them, and the remainder she peddled in the streets. She did this until her fingernails were pink and brittle from the preparations. And all of her proceeds she used to purchase my school supplies, Alejandro's shoes, a toy for Roderick.

My mind is not working. I do not recognize any part of the woods. I thought this way was north. I tell myself to forget about north, what about west, pay attention to where the sun has set. Pay attention to where the ocean is. But in this forest the trees hide the moon, and the rain and dark clouds fool me. I see no ocean, only branches extending like arms as far as I can see. I spin myself in a circle, my eyes remembering nothing and my legs shaking from hunger. *Domingo is probably dead. Save yourself. Save myself for what? Save yourself and drink from the small flask you took. You may be saving it for someone who no longer needs it. Perhaps I no longer need it. Perhaps I do not want to live. You cannot leave Domingo.* I collapse on the ground from all the thoughts fighting in my head.

"Isabelle?" I hear a whisper.

I stop my crying and look around. I see no one. I feel the hairs on my neck stand. *There are no ghosts in the forests,* I repeat to myself.

"Isabelle," the voice whispers once again. I am so frightened that I run forward, heedless of the Japanese patrols. I am falling through branches and tripping over rocks. A hand is placed over my mouth and I am dragged farther into the bushes. I fight with all my might. Hands reach out to grab me. I am flipped over and someone sits on my belly. It is Feliciano; he bends his face to me, and I raise my hands to claw at him. "Stop it. Patrols," he whispers. I am paralyzed by his words. Japanese soldiers pass not more than ten meters from us. We lie for a long time this way. I am conscious of his heartbeat against my chest. His face is close to mine and he stares at the ground, listening. When it is safe he pulls away from me; he seems embarrassed.

"The moment I left you I knew that I should not have. I fought myself until

I could stand it no longer and hurried back. You were running straight to one of their camps. There will be more. We must find somewhere to hide."

"I do not know where to go. Home is the only place I know."

WE WALK FOR an eternity in the rain. We are like two drowned carabaos. My knees are bleeding from constantly falling forward. We are nearing Bulacan, my hometown, when I smell food. The scent makes me crazy, like a wild animal. I hurry forward with renewed strength.

We look with silence at the plundered houses, the broken windows, the doors thrown wide open, as if the enemy were standing mockingly before us. The trees, every one of them, their fruits picked, regardless if they were ripe or not. There are no stray chickens walking the road, no carabaos lumbering about, no pigs squealing and jostling one another. Our countryside is like a dying dog. Helpless and flat on its side, cloaked in death, with no strength left to lick its injuries.

Once I see our house I become happy and sad at the same time. Gone only three days, yet I am changed. My heart longs to go back to feeling pure. I can still smell the soldiers' sweat on my skin. I evade the dark thoughts that threaten to consume me. They hover just beyond my reach. I know that if I start to think of what has happened, I will die.

The shower has ceased, but the temperature has turned hotter, and the ceiling of clouds overhead presses low. Rain again soon. A thick breeze scatters dust upon us. I think of the passage from the Bible that says wipe even the dust from your feet to show you have turned your back on this place. That is what has happened. Hope has turned its back on us. My nose begins to run.

We step inside and the house looks the same. My heart pounds in my throat. *Pull open the floor latch. What if everyone is dead?*

Feliciano hesitates. "I shall go now, Isabelle. I only wanted to see you home safely. I am not welcome here."

"Your aunt, Aling Ana, is here. She will want to see you." I feel a tinge of confusion at my own words. Do I feel concern for him? Have I now become his defender? No, I tell myself. I am only repaying him for seeing me home safely.

"She does not care about me. You forget what I am."

He is right, I have forgotten. "I will tell them how you helped me."

He considers my words, unable to hide the exhaustion in his eyes. The wonderful smell of lapsang souchong tea flows up to us. Aling Ana's favorite flavor. Feliciano nods to say he will stay. My heart soars. There is the sound of arguing below; we stop to listen.

I hear Domingo's voice, angry and righteous: "Be careful what you say, old man." Domingo has made it home safely! I thank God.

"See?" Mang Selso shouts out. "You see how he threatens me? I am telling the truth, Domingo, you bring danger upon this house. We cannot harbor a guerrilla, much less a commander. Let us take a vote, if we shall allow you to stay or not. You must not be selfish. Think of others for once."

"Do not lecture me about selfishness, you coward." Domingo is in a rage. "You hide behind your father's illness, an easy excuse to keep from the fighting. My guerrillas fight your battles while you sit in the safety of this cellar with the women."

"I am too weak to stand. How do you expect me to fight?" Mang Selso sputters.

"I fight. I can poke my skin and feel my bones. There is no meat left on this body. Yet I fight. You want to win this war? All of you. You want our country back? Then you must stand up and do the same. This war will not pass you by. You cannot wait it out in this basement. Everyone must fight, man, woman, child, everyone."

"But the danger is great," Aling Ana says.

"Yes, you will risk your lives, but what kind of life is it to cower at the enemy's every word? There will be no more discussion of a vote. I shall stay here, to rest, then go in search of the children. Try to move me and see what happens," Domingo says.

The children? Who else is missing? My heart twists, and I turn to Feliciano. He bows his head sadly.

Mang Selso directs his argument elsewhere. "Do not listen to him. He does not care about the danger he puts us in."

Domingo does not let him escape. "I am in danger night and day. Yet I still live. If we were all to rise and fight together, we could overtake them."

"Many would die," Mang Selso challenges. "Easy for you to fight and hide. We are the ones they torture when you ambush their patrols. Who is the real coward?"

"I have to hide. We do not have the strength to fight them at once. You love to look down your noses, but who do you call when they harass your family?"

"You don't fool me." Mang Selso's voice rises foolishly. "You were nothing but a small thief before this war. An embarrassment to your father, the great Senator Matapang, the Japanese sympathizer. You are two of a kind."

There is much shouting, and we hurry down the ladder. Everyone rushes to one end of the small room. Domingo has Mang Selso against the wall, his hand on his throat. He is heedless of Mang Selso's father, Tay Fredrico, who leans out of the way. It is wrong of Domingo. The elders must be respected. The others have their hands on both men, trying to pry them apart.

Domingo can barely speak; his voice is deep with anger. "Do not ever compare me to Senator Matapang. Or I will slit your throat."

"Let him go!" Mang Selso's wife shouts. She pulls weakly at Domingo's arms. One move from him and she would topple like a house of sticks. "Did you hear what he said?" she asks the others. Domingo whips his head to the side and scowls at her. She drops her grip on him. He releases Mang Selso and the older man falls to the floor, coughing.

"Enough," Mama declares. "Those who will not share this house with Domingo must leave. He is my guest." Mama loves Domingo; she protects him like a son. He respects her like a mother. She surprises me, the fierceness that comes out of her chest and rises to her face, to her thin arms.

I wait for them to notice me. I am scared, terrified that Mother will see the difference in me. Slowly they disperse, and there is a gasp as Mrs. Yoshi and Ate Lorna see me. Mica runs and embraces me. I pull away from her embrace, and there is confusion in her eyes. I feel dirty. She looks hurt at first and then, like the stubborn girl I have always known her to be, she throws her arms around me and hugs me harder.

"Isabelle," she sobs. The pain wells in my throat until I no longer care. I hug my best friend with all my might.

"I'm so sorry—"

"No, I am the one," I say. "It was my idea that we split apart."

"It does not matter now. You are safe, sister." Mica has no siblings and has always insisted on referring to me as such.

Mama turns to see the faces all staring at me. She follows their gaze and sucks in her breath sharply. Her hand flies to her mouth as the tears flow immediately.

For just a moment, I feel a panic rise within me. Mica lets go slowly, with one arm still on the small of my back. I look behind me, wondering where else I could go. Is it my imagination or does Feliciano stand closer to me? It feels protective.

"Isabelle, o anák!" my mother cries—child!—but I am numb. She looks at my clothes and my face. I do not need to explain. Her eyes search my shifting ones. I cannot look at her directly. I see the hurt in her eyes, hurt for me. I wonder why I was so afraid that she would judge me. She hugs me to her. I can smell her skin, like faded flowers, and a distant smell of the green plantains she used to cook.

"Thank God," I hear echoed through the room. I study the faces around me, Aling Ana, Mang Selso and his father, and Mang Pedro.

I move from Mama's embrace and wait for Feliciano to move out of my shadows. The group gasps when they see who it is.

"Feliciano, nephew." Only Aling Ana gets up. Feliciano moves away from her.

Domingo has his back turned as Ate Lorna bandages him. He smiles at first when he sees me, but the smile melts when he sees Feliciano. "Isabelle, what have you done? He is a Makapili, a Japanese sympathizer."

Before I can explain, Domingo takes out a knife and lunges for Feliciano. Feliciano kicks out at him, and they are wrestling on the ground, stumbling over the others. Feliciano is not injured, and he has the advantage.

"Stop them, Ma!" I shout, but neither Mang Ped nor my mother can tear the two of them apart. Mang Selso will not help; he would be happy if they killed each other. Feliciano shoves Domingo away, and I run and stand in front of Feliciano, though he tries to push me aside.

"Isabelle, move," Feliciano orders.

I steel myself as Domingo approaches. My conscience screams at me, *You have become Feliciano's defender!*

"Do not hide behind a woman's skirts, traitor," Domingo says.

"You are the one who hides." Feliciano moves from behind me, and I run forward and embrace Domingo.

"Stop it, please. He saved my life. I was raped. He helped me to escape."

There it is, I have said it. My chest hardens with the pain of my words. I shove the feeling back down. I cannot let it out. It is too hurtful. Too big, it would kill me. The room has grown quiet. All that can be heard is Feliciano's and Domingo's breathing. I feel the room swing sideways.

I SLEEP FOR hours, I know, because I hear the voices drift in and out; I hear the rain, muffled as it pelts our house above. I am conscious of the stifling heat inside the cellar. When I wake, Mother is wiping my face with a cool rag.

"*Ate, ate,*" Roderick asks, holding my hand, "are you all right? Feliciano caught you when you fainted." He gestures with his chin toward Feliciano, seated against the opposite wall. He sits separate from the rest. He and Domingo have come to a truce for the moment. They avoid each other's eyes, their jaws tight.

"Good thing you did not *umpóg* your head on the floor." Aling Ana frowns.

"Imagine, staying strong, only to become weak at the last minute," she chides. "Have some tea. This is good tea, the finest. You will never have such tea again. I brought it from my house."

A cup of tea is handed to me. I sit up slowly. She is right, the tea is exquisite, but maybe any tea would taste this way after two days without proper water. My throat constricts as soon as the liquid touches it.

"Here, comb your hair." Aling Ana holds out a pearl-inlaid comb with three etched flowers on the handle and in the center of each a ruby. "A lady, especially a young woman, should always be properly dressed." She looks at my clothes with apparent disdain. "And if not the clothes, then at least in her appearance. She must make do with what she has to appear presentable. That way a potential husband can still find it easy to gaze upon her." She emphasizes the words *potential husband* and inclines her head toward Feliciano.

I take the comb from her hand. It is heavy, and my hand dips down at the weight. I comb my hair and pull a few loose strands from her comb before presenting it back to Aling Ana.

She shoos away my offering with a wave. "You keep it now, it is yours. A young woman should always have beautiful things." She avoids Mang Selso's eyes, then adds more gruffly, "I did not know your hair was so dirty." She and Mang Selso bicker constantly about her riches, but Aling Ana has always taken a liking to me. As if she were a favorite aunt or godmother. She is not the same with my brothers, a little more tough with them.

I look at my mother uncertainly. She smiles and raises her chin to say, *Keep it.*

"Thank you," I whisper.

Feliciano is watching me. I feel his eyes, and I turn to him. He turns away with a troubled look. Domingo has caught our exchange. He studies me, then Feliciano, and I feel his anger building again. He sits with his back against the wall and his hands dangling over his knees; he clenches and unclenches his fists. He stares at Feliciano until finally Feliciano meets his gaze. I try to think of words to break their connection.

"Domingo, I was worried that I would not return in time to help you. How did you manage to get here?" I ask.

Domingo's face softens slightly. "You were a great help, Isabelle. I managed to stumble forward, hiding and resting from tree to cemetery to banana grove, until I caught up with an old man who was in possession of a wagon. He was carrying the bodies of his family, pulled forward by a skeleton of a mare. I asked him if I could ride along with him, but I don't think he even heard me. His face was a mask of shock. So I simply climbed on and lay with the bodies of his wife and sons, praying that no soldiers would see us and check. If not for you and that old man, I might have died."

Domingo stands abruptly. "But I have rested enough. I will go in search of my son and Alejandro."

It is only then that I realize my brother and Domingo's son are not with us. Nor is Papa or Roman. "Where are they, Ma? Where is Papa?"

No one answers.

Mama struggles, then looks at me painfully. "Your father went for food but did not return. Your brother and Roman went in search of the two of you but did not return. We think Taba snuck out with them. That was this morning. I knew I should not have let them go. Mang Pedro, have you had any more dreams of where they might be?"

Mang Pedro sighs deeply but shakes his head. "My visions are weak now. Not like before when I was younger. They come only when they wish, and very cloudy. Not at all like before. I have dreamt nothing of the boys. Though I have opened my mind all day."

"I should not have let them leave," Mama says.

"It is not your fault, Aling Louisa." Domingo glares at Mang Selso. "The men should have been the ones who volunteered to go, instead of the children. They are at fault."

Mang Selso's wife pinches him to keep him from saying anything. Feliciano watches my mother. He turns to Domingo. "I know of two Japanese encampments nearby."

"I will find them on my own, without the help of a traitor."

"Domingo—" Ate Lorna clutches his arm. "Perhaps we should listen. After all, he saved Isabelle. Perhaps he has had a change of heart. Perhaps he no longer sides with the Japanese."

Domingo scoffs at her words. "Does a devil lose his horns?"

Ate Lorna looks at Feliciano pleadingly. "Am I right? Have you had a change of heart, Feliciano? Have you broken your ties with the Japanese?"

Feliciano is quiet, I think his eyes water, but he looks away, so I cannot tell. "I no longer side with them. When I saw what they did to the women, to Isabelle."

I shudder at the memory and clutch the comb Aling Ana gave me until my knuckles hurt.

Domingo shouts, "Do you forget the others he has pointed a finger to and turned over to the Japanese? His masters." He paces the floor; he looks ready to fight. He points at Feliciano. "Isabelle is the only reason you are still alive, boy."

"I don't need her protection," Feliciano says with a sneer.

"Enough!" Ate Lorna cries.

Feliciano looks at my mother. "I will go to the encampments, to see if I can find them."

Domingo laughs in a frightful way. "You are not going anywhere. I know your tricks. You think I would let you bring the Japanese back here?"

"Come with me then, unless you are frightened," Feliciano challenges.

"Maybe you will just tell me where the encampments are right now." Domingo stands swiftly and pulls Feliciano up by the collar.

The others shout for them to stop. Feliciano pulls out a pistol and brings it to Domingo's head. "Or maybe I shoot you now, and I find them on my own."

"Stop it! Look what they have done to us." Ate Lorna falls to the ground, hysterical. "We are ready to kill one another at the slightest insult."

My mother walks in between the two of them and puts her hand in front of Feliciano's gun. She speaks softly. "Please, we will need you both in order for us to survive. Let us wait another hour. We have had such bad luck with sending people to find others. Though my heart screams for Alejandro, we need your strength. We cannot afford to lose you both. You two are the strongest. We may need you to search for food. We can barely walk. Let us wait. Rest, Domingo, you have been through much. If they do not return, perhaps you should both go in search of the children."

They shove each other away and walk to opposite corners.

My brother Roderick asks in a small voice, "Have the Japanese killed Papa?"

All the talk has frightened him. I call him over to sit near me. He crouches beside me and places his hands between his knees as I rub his back.

"*Hoy*, Roderick." Mang Selso lifts a chin to my brother. "Do you believe in ghosts?"

"Ghosts?" Roderick asks skeptically; still, he scoots his back closer to me.

Domingo sits tensely beside Ate Lorna. He does not like her fussing over him. He will not allow her to brush his hair or clean his face with a towel. She has just bandaged his wounds. His skin looks gray, and I heard him whispering to her about going to meet his group after he finds Alejandro and Taba; but Ate Lorna would hear none of it.

"Well, Roderick? Do you believe in ghosts or not?" Mang Selso asks.

"I don't know." Roderick shrugs.

"What if I paid you five centimos?" Mang Selso takes out five coins and they clink in his hand. "See here? What if I paid you this to visit the house of a certain Mang Bidding in Aklan? Would you go?"

The province of Aklan runs rampant with stories of witches. *Asuwángs*, they are called, beings that sleep in the day standing up and at night come alive, grow wings, and detach from their lower bodies in search of unsuspecting blood donors.

"*Selso, ha, huwág mong itakotin ang mga batà,*" Mama chides him gently. Do not scare the children. But I know she is thankful for the distraction.

Roderick takes no time in considering the question. Immediately he shakes his head earnestly. "*Hindî Pô, duwág ako, hindî katulad ni Ate. Hindî siyá natatakót,*" he says. Not me, sir, I am not like my big sister. I am a coward.

I smile at him and brush his hair from his brow. "I would protect you, Roderick, I am not scared. Besides, there are no such things as ghosts."

Mang Selso narrows his eyes; he knows he has captured Roderick's attention for the time being, and he smiles knowingly. "Do you know why there are no telephone poles set in the province?"

"Why?" Roderick smirks, crossing his arms in front of him.

"Because the *asuwángs* do not allow it. Their wings would get caught. So they send their helpers in the morning to cut the phone wires down. That is why they have remained for so long undiscovered."

Mang Selso's father, Tay Fredrico, chooses this time to laugh and babble about spirits. It shakes Roderick's confidence even more. He looks at the old Spaniard as if he were already a ghost. My mother sits beside me as I murmur soothing words in my brother's ears and nudge him playfully. My heart longs to be little again and sit in my mother's lap, but instead I sit like a proper lady, conscious of Feliciano's eyes on me.

Feliciano's aunt, Aling Ana, sighs with disgust. "Selso, you should not speak of things you know nothing of. You might disturb the dead. Do you want to hear a true story? Nothing silly about witches flying in the night. A true story of ghosts?"

Her tone is so serious, it sets my hair to attention. I raise my arm before me and look at the hairs.

"*O anó? Natatakót ka rin ba?*" she asks me, the laughter coming from deep in her belly. What? Are you scared now, too?

Even though she treats me nicely, sometimes I hate her bossiness. Sometimes I agree with Mang Selso, who says she is a nasty old woman who enjoys bringing out others' embarrassment and setting it all on the table for everyone to feast on. I can feel her studying me now.

"Do not hold this pain of what has happened to you close to your heart, Isabelle. You must let it go. No matter how painful. It will ruin you. If you keep silent, if you swallow it, it will eat you like a cancer."

I close my eyes and rest my head on Mama's shoulder.

"I tell you now, better to spit it all out, cry a hundred days over this matter, an entire year, than ruin your life over it. You must acknowledge it now, so that it has no power over you. I do not assume to know what you are going through, but I do know something about hate. That is what you are feeling right now, is it not?"

My brother Roderick grows anxious at the silence. "Mama," he moans.

Aling Ana searches in her purse and brings forth a coin. Her hand is wrinkled and thin. There are deep cracked lines against the shiny brown of her fingers. She holds the coin out to Roderick to stop his crying. "*O, itó.*" She nods. Take it.

Roderick looks over at Mama, then scurries forward like a little mouse and takes the coin. Everyone looks at her in surprise except Mama and me.

She laughs a hard, hacking laugh at their expressions. Her teeth appear, and I am jolted as always by the color of them, red, dark crimson. As if someone has punched her in the mouth. She chews betel nuts compulsively.

"You think I am ugly, stingy? I was not always this way. I know what most of you say: 'She has so much money, owns so many stores. Why doesn't she use any of it? Why does she keep saving it for a rainy day when that rainy day may never come?' The reason is I never intend to spend that money, not on a rainy day or ever. It is not mine to spend. I do not deserve that money."

Aling Ana pulls her blanket around her shoulders, then takes her two fingers as a roach scutters by and squashes it. We grit our teeth at the sound. She takes the cigarette from her mouth, studies the burnt-down stub, and takes one more puff. She turns the lighted end, fading like a coal but still lit, and taps it to her tongue to kill the flame.

"*Inay!*" Roderick shouts. Ma! He turns his head quickly against my arm.

Aling Ana looks at him with amusement. "Shh, it is nothing. Only a little flame. That cannot hurt me. I have been through so much more. This little fire, you think that will hurt me? I will tell you about something much more painful. Will you sit still and listen, Roderick?"

My brother nods, his face still turned halfway in toward me, as if Aling Ana will pull her face off next.

She reaches out a hand to Feliciano, but he moves away. She looks at him for a long moment, then her shoulders sag in defeat. "I have failed in my care of you. But this story concerns your mother and your father, so you must listen."

At the mention of his parents, Feliciano glances up sharply. He never met his mother; she died soon after childbirth. His father is a stranger to him, the village drunk. Feliciano told me once how he wishes to be everything that his father is not. In this regard, and in many other ways, he is similar to Domingo.

Aling Ana looks again to me. "Do not hold on to the bitterness, Isabelle, it will eat at your body like worms, and you will ruin your future because of it. I was not always this unhappy. I know what people call me behind my back, cheap, stingy, rude. Once, long ago, I was happy. I had many dreams, too. But I became bitter, and by the time I realized it, I had almost wished my whole life away."

~ ghost children

IT HAPPENED ON THE EVE OF OUR SEVENTH BIRTHDAY, this tragedy, when the great monsoon arrived, chasing out the dry climate and ushering in the tempestuous rainy season. My mother was like that wind system; she altered the course of my fate that night, the evening my twin sister, Janna, died.

As the season went from parched to wet, I too changed inside, from innocent to bitter. It was fitting that the sky was weeping; it should mourn every time a child dies and the well of a mother's love turns empty. They called that one Monsoon Minang; they did that even then, named the storms and floods that wreaked havoc after people who had similar temperaments. There was a young soprano at the time by that name; she was known to throw tantrums at the slightest flutter of a butterfly's wings. They should have named that one Monsoon Mirabelle, after my mother.

That evening when my destiny changed is a tattoo needled into my soul. I shall never forget it. The wind was already shifting, yet the night was thick with heat. Clouds rolled across the sky, illuminated by the moon. No one moved unless it was necessary. My aunts sat on corner chairs, fanning themselves with rolled-up newspapers, too exhausted from the heat even to play a game of sungka. Our windows were tied down to keep out the gales, but still the steaming gusts of air managed to get under the bamboo and nipa shutters and bang them against the house, like something wretched demanding to be let in.

I sat anxiously at my sister's bedside, but I was told not to bother her.

"She is resting, Ana, for your birthday party tomorrow. Let her sleep, so that she will be strong and refreshed," Mama said.

I remember the exhaustion in Janna's eyes and the warm rag that smelled of sukang illoco pressed against her brow. The rice wine, Papa believed, would chase the ills away. Janna's hair was a matted clump, like the energy around her.

It hovered like a low mist in the jungle, that badness surrounding her. It carried the scent of the graveyards, of wild weeds and dankness, and it swirled around us, chilling me.

IN THE MORNING the crow of the rooster intruded into my sleep, and along with it came the crooning cries from Mama: "Janna, come back. Come back to me."

Her sobs pierced my slumber. I dreamt that a rooster had flown away with Janna, and Mama was chasing after it, calling, "Come back, come back." When I awoke, excited for our party, I was told there would be no celebration, Janna was dead. All of her blood had vanished, the leukemia had claimed her. She lay stretched out on her bed, next to the brown, rosy-cheeked doll she loved so much.

"My beautiful baby," Mama sobbed.

I saw no beauty, only a gray version of myself.

I CLUNG TO Papa's legs, moving aside for Mama's skirts as she paced the floor in a trance. I trembled as the black of the padre's mournful robes floated by in a swirl of smoke and funeral incense. The cloud of smoke was housed in a silver vessel, which he swung from a chain as he recited prayers that sounded more like incantations.

Janna and I had always been given matching dresses, matching shoes, and matching hairstyles; would it be the same with the sickness?

"Papa, am I sick, too?" I begged to be comforted.

"Shh, *hija*, it is time to be quiet." Papa patted my head distractedly as he swept up pieces of a broken vase he had thrown in his sorrow.

"Mama, what happened?" I tugged at her skirts, but I could have been a fly on her back.

The padre pulled me aside. "Your mother is grieving, child, be still."

"But what about me?"

No one answered; I had been forgotten. I should have been put to sleep each night like a treasure, with my favorite blanket tucked in on all sides. I should have been comforted and sung to sleep. Instead, I became a ghost child myself.

Mama was inconsolable. Having twins had made her special. Without the set she was just a rice farmer's wife with rotting teeth and clothes to stone clean in the river. She had nothing to separate her from the other women in our village of stilt houses along the Rio Grande.

THE EVENING BEFORE my sister's burial, we had the "viewing" in our *salas*. It was not much of a living room, but still we called it that. Janna's body was placed in a wooden coffin lined in pink satin. Chairs and mismatched boxes had been borrowed from the neighbors and arranged as seats in neat rows in front of the body. Even now I hate the feel and look of pink satin. I cannot even have a cup of coffee in my front parlor without the taste of death surrounding me. It curdles my skin.

During the rosary, in between the beads of Hail Mary and Holy Mary, Mother of God, I tried to avoid the coffin. I could see the outline of Janna's body with her hands folded atop her blue dress. The only dress I would not have a matching set to. Looking at that coffin was to see myself lying there. It is not true what they say about the dead, that they look as though they are asleep. She looked strange, far from sleep, a wooden carving of my sister, with waxen face and bright orange lipstick striped across her lips. Her mouth was a beacon in a sea of pink satin. I prayed that the lips not turn up in a smile.

In all the chaos there was no one to console me. Thankfully Ate Yu saw this and sat beside me. She was my mother's only true friend. She lived with us, free of rent in exchange for her help around the house. She was full-blooded Chinese but had been raised in the Philippines. She spoke fluent Mandarin and Tagalog. She held in her hand a statue of Kuan Yin, the Chinese goddess of mercy, carved in white jade, and on her neck she wore a crucifix.

"Why do you have both?" I asked.

"*Ai-ya,* don't you know me by now, little pig? I wear both to cover double the prayers for your sister's ascent into heaven," she explained, brushing my bangs away from my brow. Her name, *Yu,* meant "jade," and since her statue was made of it, I thought of her as the goddess Kuan Yin herself, or Sister Jade.

"You are ready now to say good-bye to your sister?" Ate Yu asked. "It is our turn before they close the box and lock her away forever."

I felt as if I were choking, and my mouth trembled to stay calm. I could not get enough air. I had seen how people were saying good-bye, touching Janna's hair, her hands, kissing her on the cheek. I did not want to do those things.

"Why are they touching her, Ate Yu? What if they catch her sickness?" I asked.

She put her hand on my shoulder. I felt myself steady under her touch.

"That sickness does not pass to others. It is internal." She pointed to her chest. "What they do, when they touch her, they are saying good-bye. They are asking for *tawad*. You know what that mean?"

"Forgiveness," I said.

"Yes, you smart girl. You must tell her, 'Sister, I forgive you for any wrongs, and in turn, please forgive me if I have wronged you.' Otherwise, how will she get to heaven with so many apologies and obligations weighing her down? She will be like a bird with an anchor bound to its feet, unable to fly to paradise."

"But why must I ask for forgiveness? I did nothing wrong."

"I know, little pig. Do it out of respect."

"Out of respect." I repeated these words like a prayer, trying desperately to keep my breathing normal. I began to cry when I saw my sister's face.

"Oh, look how she misses her twin," an older aunt commented. There was a murmur of agreement in the room. I was not grief-stricken, as everyone thought. I was terrified.

Ate Yu took my hand and fed the words to me. I followed, repeating what she said in between gasps of breath.

"Janna"—gasp—"forgive me"—gasp—"as I . . . No, I can't"—choke—"as I forgive you."

"Now touch her," Ate Yu urged.

I was paralyzed. "Touch her," Father urged.

"Touch her," Mama hissed.

"Touch her, touch her," the room chanted.

I reached out my hand and quickly tapped hers. I was shocked at how cold Janna's hands were. My aunts later told me that I had screamed out, "This is not my sister!" but I only remember being led to one of the chairs and watching as Mama stepped up loudly.

It was like one of those dress-up shows, an opera. Mama wore the red dress that Janna had admired so much. It was hideous, and so was my mother's face, with her hair like a bird's nest and her eyes swollen with shock. The room quieted and my mother began to moan Janna's name over and over again. I covered my ears and let the tears fall. My mother crumpled into a ball, making great sobbing noises from her chest. It was an awful sound, as if someone were kicking her in the stomach. She fainted once, and twice she fell to her knees.

Papa had to pull her up. "Contain yourself. People are staring, Mirabelle."

"I do not care. My baby, my baby, oh, Janna. *Ako na lang sana.*"

People gasped at her last words and made the sign of the cross. It was very bad luck, what she said, to wish that it had been she who had died instead.

"*Janna, Janna, patawarin mo ako. Janna anák,*" Mama begged for forgiveness. Father hushed her sternly and warned, "*O Mirabelle, huwág mong ipatulò ang luhà mo sa mukhâ niya.*"

"Why does Papa tell her not to let tears fall on Janna?"

Ate Yu bent closer. "Very bad. Tears must not fall on dead. Otherwise spirit not able to rest. Janna will be bound to earth by tears, and spirit will return again and again to owner of tears, until matter is resolved."

Mama did not care. She kissed my sister's face again and again, the tears falling on her brow, her hair, the blue dress. When I saw this, how Mother's tears were raining on Janna, weighing her down, I panicked.

It was then that I heard my two aunts talking. They were like two clowns, always giggling and whispering. Tita Lulu and Tita Babelyn were my father's two older sisters. They both lived with us in our cramped three-room house. Ate Yu kept her belongings in their room but slept in the *salas* at night.

My aunts did not share in the housework, but they contributed greatly to all of the village gossip. They had fake faces, showing Mama kindness and calling her *ate*, "big sister," but once they were alone, I heard the snide remarks they shot like an arrow in her direction. They had no shame. On that day of our deepest sorrow, the two of them snorted, elbowing each other while Mama writhed in agony on the floor, her red dress bleeding color onto the ground.

"Psst, Lulu . . ." Tita Babelyn took her two fingers and slid them quickly across Tita Lulu's shoulder. "You know, I spoke with the *mangkukulam,* and she claims that Janna's blood was weak. Ana has all of the strength, but her spirit would not share any of it. And that is why Janna died, she ran out of blood."

"What if my blood is weak also?" I asked, giving them a start.

"Oh, Ana, we are just talking. I only meant that this will not happen to you since you are much stronger than Janna was. You know, she was always *ubó-ubóhin.*" She poked Tita Lulu's thigh and gave her a conspiratorial wink.

"But Janna was not *ubó-ubóhin.* I never saw her cough once." I frowned.

"Oh yes, I saw her cough a lot. Here, always here." Tita Babelyn slid her fingers insistently down the front of her neck. "Go play now." She canted her head. "What?" she said to the air. "Oh, Ana, your mother is calling you."

"She is not. You always do that when you want me to disappear."

"Ana, ha! Go away, then," Tita Babelyn said, growing tired of me.

Tears welled in my eyes. "I'm telling Papa what you said."

Tita Lulu became like a hawk. She glanced quickly to my father and mother. "Ana dear, do not cry. Your *tita* Babelyn does not know what she is talking about. Here, I will choke her." She pretended to choke Tita Babelyn. "You feel better now? You want to choke her yourself?"

"Ay! Lulu, ha!" Tita Babelyn choked back a giggle. "Jesus mariajosef, look at your mama's gown, it is too bright. She should not have worn that. How embarrassing," she exclaimed.

She was trying to bait me, I knew, but I could not resist answering back, "I like it."

Tita Lulu shuddered. "I am shutting the door tonight. You know the spirits are allowed to walk the earth for the next three days until their bodies realize they have died. You remember how Janna liked to play with your handbags, Babelyn."

"Ay, let me sleep next to you," Tita Babelyn pleaded.

THE NEXT DAY, I watched as Mama lit a candle by the window and said a long prayer. She then turned a glass upside down on a board of letters. My aunts tittered in their corner perches. When Mama raised her hand over the glass, it jumped under her hand and whipped from side to side. It frightened me how her eyes pulsed with excitement. "Janna, are you cold, *anák?*" she asked the room.

No answer; the glass stayed put. "Come visit me," she pleaded. "Tonight, I will place your doll out." Still no answer. She sighed heavily, and I crept back into the shadow of curtains. She glanced up quickly at the sound.

"Ana, oh, good. Come sit with me. The *mangkukulam* said that Janna's spirit will have a stronger bond if you sit with me."

I grabbed my belly, feeling the urge to go pee. It did not comfort me to know that the neighborhood witch doctor had instructed Mama on this game. She was a frightful woman with sharp eyes.

"Come, come . . ." Mama patted the chair beside her.

I crept to her. I could hear my aunts murmur that Mama had lost her mind. It straightened my back and my confidence. I sat in the chair and looked at the board.

"Place your left hand on the glass," Mama instructed. I did so, but the glass did not move. Mama put her hand over mine and said, "Janna are you here?"

The question made me sit straight. My attention was caught by the glass as it pulled our hands forward and spelled out "yes." I stared at the board in horror.

"Is she here? Is her spirit in the glass?" I whispered.

The glass circled the board, pulling our hands back again to spell "yes."

"Oh, Ana, she is with you," Mama breathed in awe. The glass wove back and forth across the board.

"I don't want to play." I stood, disrupting the flow of the glass. It toppled and shattered to the floor with the force of someone throwing it.

"Look what you have done. Janna, come back, *hija!*" Mama screeched. Her face was crumpled into an ugly mask. Where was the beautiful mother I had known? In my haste I tipped over the chair and ran out of the room. Papa grew angry at these games, and he left the house more and more.

Mama became a sleepwalker. She was no longer aware of those around her. She immersed herself in mah-jongg. During one game, she managed to win a place for Janna's body in a rich opponent's mausoleum. It did not matter that Janna would be among strangers.

"At least she will not be cold," Mama said.

The first night Janna was moved into the crypt, we could not find Mama, and in the morning Papa found her asleep on the cold mausoleum floor. After that, Papa rarely came home.

Thank goodness for Ate Yu; without her I would have been a filthy child, for Mama had stopped caring for me. I was helping her one day in the kitchen to peel the seam off a basket of peas and cut off the ends.

"Not like that, too slow. Like this . . ." She leaned close and showed me how to pluck one end off and then start the strip from that end to the other. I nodded, but not before she turned up her nose. "What that smell?"

"What?" I said, continuing to peel.

She sniffed around our general area, scrunching up her nose in distaste. "That, that smell." She raised her head, leaned the other way, and then she came closer and closer, until she sniffed at my head. She blinked and stared at me in disbelief. "Oh, Ana, you smell like poo-poo. And oh! Look at your neck, covered in rash. Wait, that not a rash." She spat on her hands and rubbed my neck. "My God, when last time you take bath?"

I shrugged, my eyes stinging.

"Oh no, baby, come here." She hugged me. I could see her eyes hurt for me, and I pushed her away. "Come on, we peel those later, first we peel you."

I followed her and she scrubbed me as I sat in a clear tub of water that soon turned a dark gray. I did not lift a finger to help. It had been a long time since someone had cared for me. I was raw with emotion.

"Little pig, I cannot always pay attention. You need to care for yourself, understand?"

I nodded; of course, I did not do what she said. Several weeks passed before I reached the same level of filth. I had been walking indoors and out in my bare feet; afterward I would put the same dirty feet in my school shoes in the morning. One day I was sitting in dance class with my legs crossed. Our teacher, Mrs. Peralta, had us warm up by doing several kicks like marching soldiers. When it came time to practice the *tinikling*, she told us to take off our shoes. My feet by now were drenched in sweat, and when I took off my shoes you cannot imagine the stench that filled the stuffy room.

"Ewww, what is that smell?" asked Jeanette Agbayani, the school beauty.

"Yuck," I spoke up, scrunching my nose. That was my first mistake. Children are smart, and soon the entire class was staring at me. "Ana stinks like cow dung," Jeanette had the girls chanting.

I was pent up with self-pity and unspoken emotion; before I knew what I was doing, Jeanette's nose was bloody and a good clump of her thin hair was in my fist. I had made a terrific bald spot in the front of her head. It was a bright red, and Jeanette was screaming. This time Papa was called to school. When I saw him my heart swelled with gladness.

"Ana, ha, your mama is already losing her mind, and you decide to cause more trouble?" He stood there, the glare of the sun on his wonderful face, and I felt very far from him, very small.

I WAS TERRIFIED at night, in the room Janna and I once shared together. I thought certainly her spirit could not rest from all the tears Mama had let fall upon her body. I thought of how cold her hand had felt. I had *bangungot* at night, and no matter how I tried, I could not break free from those nightmares.

Without Janna, I became ordinary. Even my name, Ana, became plain. As Janna and Ana we were "the twins." "So lucky" my mother was to have been blessed with us, people would say. They believed we felt the same things. When Janna got the flu, people would say, "Ana does not look so well. She is feeling her sister's sickness. They feel the same things." And I would get soup or tea, just like her. I missed my sister so much, my heart felt like a rock in my chest, but when night approached and the room grew dark, my imagination turned her into something cold and scratching against the windows. I imagined Janna like a vampire coming back for more blood, my blood.

IT WAS MANY months before Mama could even speak of her death. For a long time she phrased questions and discussions as if Janna were still alive. She would say, "I shall take the girls with me," not, "I shall take Ana." It made me feel sad and forgotten. She kept to her bed for months without speaking.

~

It was only a year later when the dark cloud began to lift. Papa slowly came back to us. In fact, we had all grown accustomed to Mama not speaking, as if she no longer lived in the house. So it was like a miracle. One morning Mama had awoken and she was lively again, chattering and charming at the market-place. She made small talk with the fruit vendors. She took my hand and swung it in hers. I was finally able to breathe again.

"Ana, I have a surprise for you when we get home," Mama confided.

I could not believe my ears; to have months with no words from Mama and then suddenly to be in the warmth of her presence was like standing in a ray of sunlight. When we arrived home Mama gathered Ate Yu, my aunts, and Papa. Papa seemed pleased he already knew the secret.

"Well . . ." Mama clapped her hands nervously. "I was not sure until today, but you know my friend Mang Daniel at the embassy? The one who has connections to the orphanage?"

I was confused; I had imagined a party or a visit to my *lola*'s house. Mama rarely visited her own mother, but the orphanage?

"Mang Daniel told me about a woman by the name of Karasova; her husband was Russian, but he had abandoned them. She died recently, and her daughter was orphaned." Mama looked directly at me, and I smiled back unsurely. "She is your age, Ana, her name is Corazón, and she is coming to live with us. Ana, you will have a new sister. Just think, you will have someone to play with. You can wear the same clothes. You can walk to school together."

"Like I used to do with Janna?"

"Don't you want to be happy again?" Mama snapped. Then she gentled her voice. "Corazón is eight years old, just like you."

I ran to my room and looked at myself in the mirror, pretending to talk to my sister. "Janna, they want me to forget you," I cried.

If my name was any plainer without Janna, it now became ridiculously so next to Corazón. *Corazón* in Spanish means "heart." *Ana* in Spanish or any language means "Ana."

New sister came in holding Papa's hand and looking down at the floor. I hated her immediately. She had brown hair with gold colors that sparkled like the sun on water. She had fair skin that turned a glowing tan; mine would just turn a dull brown. She had doe eyes—"hazel," my aunts cooed; "the color of leaves," my mother bragged. She was very shy. When Father introduced her and urged her forward, she turned to him in a panic and grabbed on to his waist, hiding her face.

"Crybaby," I whispered under my breath.

"*Ay, ang gandá,*" my *tita* Lulu breathed. How beautiful. "Come here, darling. Don't be shy. This is your home now. Come meet your new mommy and sister."

I glared at Tita Lulu, but she pretended not to notice.

"This is your sister, Ana." My mother spoke in a scary singsong voice, the intensity of her eyes frightening to me.

I walked up to new sister and simply stared. We were the same height.

"Ana, say hello," my mother chided, giving me a push.

I couldn't speak. I thought they would mourn my sister's death for a lifetime. I was shocked to find it took only a year.

AT BEDTIME I pretended to read my book as Corazón changed into a silk pajama pants and top. The set was a deep emerald silk, with pale pink lilies embroidered around the mandarin collar and around the legs, like clinging ivy. She had matching slippers. I thought someone must have loved this girl very much.

"My mama bought this on a trip to China. We have our own trade business in China, Malaysia, and Singapore. When I get married it will all be mine. Until then, my lawyers are to care for the running of the stores. I am to receive a generous allowance each month." She walked into the room and sat on the edge of Janna's bed. She took her suitcase and opened it on the bed. "I have three of these, see? White, red, and this one. I bet they would fit you. Would you like to have one?"

I looked at the smooth silk of the pajamas on her and the others folded neatly in her suitcase; they were so lovely. The white one was embroidered with cherry blossoms and a small bridge. The red had a yellow dragon with a gold-and-purple tail. Each set had matching silk slippers that were stuffed into the folded shirts, with the heels sticking out. I felt like a traitor to Janna's memory.

"Why would I want to look like your twin? I already have one. You are going to sleep in her bed, and at night her ghost will come and sleep next to you."

"I am not afraid of ghosts. My mother said they can't hurt you. Only the living can. My mother has been dead for two weeks now, and even though I pray and pray for her to visit me, she never comes. What was your sister like?"

I got into bed and pulled up the covers, looking over my nose at her.

"My sister was the best girl in the world. She looked just like me. We told secrets and played games. We have a treehouse. Only the two of us know where it is."

"Can I come to your treehouse?"

"Maybe," I mumbled in an attempt at kindness.

She smiled and got into Janna's bed. "Ana, I hope we will have secrets together, too."

I pretended to be asleep.

SHE WAS THE perfect angel, my aunts exclaimed. I was sadly finding that this was true, until a week later, when Corazón's clothes ran out. Her maids had forgotten to send over the rest of her clothes. I have never heard such a shriek come from a girl. I ran to our room. Corazón was standing with the back of her palm against her lips, crying. She was in her underwear. Ate Yu was standing back, holding the top of her head where Corazón had yanked at it.

"Ma," I called gleefully, "Corazón pulled Ate Yu's hair!"

My mother came running in. I thought, Now she will get a good spanking. But to my disbelief, she swept up Corazón in an embrace. "What is it, darling? What's wrong with my little girl?"

"My clothes! I don't want to wear those." She pointed to Janna's clothes. "I-want-my-clothes." She stamped her feet, her face contorted. She sneaked a teary glance my way, then hid her face in her two hands with shame. "My mama said to always dress like a lady," Corazón sobbed.

I was fascinated at the dramatic display. I sat on my bed and snickered.

"Is that all, sweetheart? So easy to fix. We will send for your clothes today." My mother embraced her again. I felt the absence of her arms. She had not held me in months.

Corazón struggled out of her grasp and threw herself theatrically on the bed. "I want my mama!"

ON HER FIRST day of school, I avoided Corazón. I would walk and she would follow me like a shadow. I would sit and she would sit two feet away. I would stand and she would do so quickly. In a suffocating frenzy, I dodged through the others until I lost her and slipped into class. It was only when Jeanette Agbayani, Miss Popular, tried to pick on Cora that I took notice and gave Jeanette a black eye to match the bald spot I had given her previously. But I didn't like the feeling. It reminded me too much of how I used to protect Janna, and I didn't want to feel that vulnerable ever again. So I decided the best thing was to get rid of her.

After school, I told Corazón that since we were now sisters I would take her to the secret clubhouse. I took her to the main *kalesa* stop. She was so excited, chattering unstoppably as we waited for the one horse- or donkey-drawn cart. Behind us a woman at the corner was selling bibingka, the sticky rice cakes with a layer of brown sugar on top. Beside her a boy was playing the *kulintang*, pounding the kettle gongs with wooden sticks and calling out, "Pandesal, bibingka . . ."

"Here's the *kalesa* now." I pointed.

"Oh boy, is it far? Should we send word to *Inay* and tell her we will be late?" She had taken to calling my mother *Inay* now.

"No, do not worry about it." I waved down the man. He stopped, looking at me suspiciously. I leaned forward and whispered that I would pay for the entire ride to take Corazón to her house.

"*Bayad* . . ." He held out his hand, and I paid him. "*Saán siyá nakatira?*"

I gave him the name of a village far away. I waited for her to get in, then gave the man the money. Corazón's eyes became as big as pork buns when the *kalesa* started to move and I was still standing on the roadside. She didn't scream or anything. She just held on to one of the metal posts and looked sadly at me as the *kalesa* drove away. I had instructed the man to take her to the next province, a good five hours away.

When I arrived home everyone peeked around me.

"Oh, how was your first day at school, Corazón?" my mother called out.

"She's not with me." I walked past my mother, wishing she would reach out to hug me.

"You did not wait for her?"

"Was I supposed to?"

"This was her first day of school!"

I shrugged. "Maybe she ran away."

"Ana, I know you're hiding something from me," my mother snapped.

I began to cry. I wanted to say, "All you care about is Corazón," but the words became lodged in between my hiccups, until they were pushed down deep where I could not find them.

"Come here, Ana," Tita Lulu said.

I walked slowly to her. I hated the way she smelled, like old mothballs and tiger balm, but I wanted so badly to be held.

"You know you are special to us. Corazón is not like you. She has pale skin like a ghost. Yours belongs to a true Filipina." She gave me crocodile words, as my father would say. Fake words, but they made me feel better.

Ate Yu went to my mother. She knelt beside her. "*Ate,* go and rest. Take a hot bath to relax yourself. I will prepare it."

I followed Mama, wanting to apologize, but when I got there I heard her talking.

"Even if I had taken Janna earlier to the doctors, as I know everyone is whispering, we would not have had the money to pay for it. Say what you will, this gambling puts food on our table."

I frowned to myself, because I knew she was alone. I edged my way to her bath and saw her talking to the rising steam. She heard my footsteps, turned abruptly, and gasped, "Janna, my baby."

"It's me, Ana," I said, sniffing. "Mama, don't worry. I will take care of you."

"Oh, Ana. Only you. I thought it was Janna." She looked away from me. She did not reach out a hand to braid my hair or tuck my shirt in. I knew then that I no longer existed for my mother. Her heart could not handle my sister's death. It was as if I had died with her. I was like a walking ghost. A rose thorn woven into her clothes, poking at her. A sore reminder of the child she lost.

MY FATHER DID not return with Corazón until three in the morning. I heard my father's footsteps, angry like hot coals, stomp up the stairs, *poom, poom.* The door to my room swung open with a bang and my father stood over my bed with Cora beside him.

"You tried to give me away." Corazón's face was swollen from her tears.

"Ana, ha. You cause everyone trouble." Papa threw back the sheets and spanked me five times. My thin sleeping attire was no match for his hands that were thick with calluses, and I immediately began to sob.

"No, Papa!" I heard Corazón cry. I looked over through my tears and saw her disheveled hair and the outright fear. She had probably never been spanked in her life. I screamed louder with each spanking. I received ten in all. My father was no fool, and he knew the dramatic display I was creating for my new sister. When my father was done, Corazón came to me and hugged me, but I pushed her away.

"Leave me alone; your face is all wet." We both went to bed crying.

MY HEART DID soften a little toward Corazón after that. But you see, even then my mother without knowing ruined any chance of Cora and I ever accepting the idea of becoming sisters. Just when my mind began to let her in, my mother would do something to shove her back out.

A few weeks after our truce, Corazón and I played quietly with our dolls in separate corners. This may seem cold to you, but that was progress for us. I usually could not stay in the same room without taunting her. That day my mouth was silent, closer to a smile than a sneer. It was Friday evening, and my mother had her mah-jongg visitors over that night. My heart was content for once. It was now more than a year after Janna's death, and although I had not forgotten her, my soul was restful. The rock at the bottom of my stomach had begun to float. I listened as Ate Yu brought out my mother's new set of mah-jongg tiles. The cheaper ones came in flimsy boxes with plain-colored backing on the tiles. These tiles my mother had bought soon after Corazón moved in were like a work of art.

"And why not? I am entitled to use a little of her allowance. We have given her a new home, a new family." Mama explained loudly to my aunts how she had come to use all of Corazón's July allowance from her inheritance to purchase the tiles. My mother always spoke loudly because she was afraid to lose the listener's attention. When they were children, Mama's elder sister had been dubbed the smart one and Mama the beautiful one. This was how my grandmother had raised them. As if a woman could not be both beautiful and smart.

The tiles came in a wooden box with an arched top. It had a latch of wrought iron and a key. The box itself was lovely, deep red flowers on intricate vines hand-painted against a black background. From a distance, it gave the box the illusion that real vines and flowers covered it completely. Each tile had the same flowers painted on the back in dark olive and red.

As the four players sat down to play, my mother, Tita Lulu, Tita Babelyn, and Mang Albert, I could hear the clink of the pieces as the players laid them out on the table to check that the suits were complete.

Mang Albert sat in his favorite spot with his wide back folded and creased like that of a hippopotamus. He smoked so much that the ceiling directly above him had a large yellow stain the size of a frying pan that radiated outward. He always came with his wife, Aling Karing, who sat beside him to watch. It fascinated me to watch Aling Karing, who was a big-breasted woman with narrow hips. She and Mang Albert traded places every few hours. Aling Karing would slip her hand under her own shirt during the games and touch her breasts. Tita Babelyn swore they cheated with hand signals, but my mother still invited them, and Tita Babelyn still agreed to play.

As we sat playing with our dolls, I heard the conversations from the mah-jongg room, in between the exclaimed, *"Pong!"* when a person matched three of a kind, or *"Chow!"* when they got three numbers in consecutive order. The tiles, as they were mixed for a new game, rumbled like rain against a tin roof. I could see the players mixing with their hands palms down, as if they were massaging the table in big sweeping inward circles.

"Hoy, alám mo," my mother confided in a shushy voice meant to be a whisper but was not a whisper at all. "When Corazón is older, she will give her mother's business to us. Joker!" my mother shouted, slamming down a tile, hoping for a wild card.

"Has she said this, Mirabelle?" Aling Karing asked. *"Pong!"* She laid down three of a kind face up.

"Well, of course she has." My mother coughed.

I glanced at Corazón to see if she had caught any of this, but she was busy finding a matching outfit for her doll.

"She is a beautiful little girl. *Parang anghél,*" Mang Albert said. Like an angel.

"Oh, and her skin. Like cream," Tita Lulu, the traitor, said. "She has a nose like the queen of Spain, proud and perfect."

My mother lowered her voice, but I still heard. "*Hoy,* do you think Ana will ever be pretty? She is so plain, huh? Her hair too curly."

"Ate Mirabelle, namán," Tita Babelyn said with a giggle. How bad of you.

I knew my mother fished for compliments this way, saying something negative so that someone would raise her up by contradicting her with just the opposite.

"Oh no, *ate,* of course she will be beautiful," Ate Yu said.

Maybe that was all Mama was doing that day, fishing for compliments for me. But that did not stop my chest from turning in pain when I looked at Corazón. Until then I had not thought about how we looked. Until then I hated her only for trying to take Mama away. Now I envied her perfect skin with the little freckles. I noticed the dimples she had when she smiled, and the golden hair, and then I saw her nose. It was so straight and perfect, like the American dolls, like the Russian doll she had tried to give me when she first arrived.

Corazón chose this moment to turn and smile at me. Her cheeks were rosy from playing, and she was happy to be next to me. "Ana, do you want to have our dolls talk together?"

"I hate you," I said, and pushed past her to play alone with my Filipina doll in the garden.

I became obsessed with Corazón's nose. I would lie awake at night and push at the bridge of my nose from both sides, encouraging it to grow straight. I went so far as to steal a wooden clothespin from Ate Yu and clip my nose together at night. After a few days my nose became sore to the touch.

The evening before a school voice recital, as I secretly watched Corazón's profile, I ran to the bathroom and looked at my nose sideways until my head hurt from crossing my eyes so much. That night I stayed up as late as I could, pinching my nose harder than the clothespin, using my own hands, alternating hands when one grew tired. I will have a straight nose by morning, I told myself.

In the morning when I ran happily to the mirror, I had a dark red line going down the entire face of my nose. It was still as flat as ever, but bruised and thick from swelling.

"Ana, what has happened to your nose?" my mother gasped at the breakfast table. "You look sick. What will we do about your recital tonight?"

"I bumped into the wall last night," I explained, eating my breakfast. I caught the knowing looks and the poking elbows my aunts gave each other.

"I think she looks pretty." Corazón tried to put an arm around me and smoothed out my long braids, but I wriggled my body out until her arm fell away.

That night at the recital I put on my best performance yet. I sang "Bayang Magiliw," our national anthem, to the rooftops. I pretended I was the loveliest bird. The crowd stood and clapped, but they were laughing as well.

I heard a man in the front row say, "What a voice, but look at that nose. What is wrong with her?"

"Leprosy," the woman next to him replied.

I heard that all night long, and many years later in my head.

As we grew older, my feelings did not change toward Corazón. If anything, I treated her worse. It embarrasses me now to think how much I enjoyed the pranks I played on her. But none were worse than the ones I played after our seventeenth birthday. I still remember the pretty napkins laid out on two long buffet tables. They were peach colored, with embroidered lavender around the edges. Corazón had sewn them. She had learned to sew like the best seamstress in the village.

How did we find the money for such an elaborate party? Well, of course my mother suggested it. She kept on dreaming out loud in front of us. She would say things like "Oh, my girls are growing up. I wish I had enough money to give them a proper party." She said those things knowing Corazón could not resist.

And when Corazón offered to use her own money, my mother then pretended it would be an embarrassment. "Oh no, I could not allow it. What would people think?"

She did this until Corazón said, "Mama, you can say it is your money. That you have saved up for it." You see how clever my mother was? She was able to give us an elaborate party and tell the guests that it was from her own purse.

Even so, it was a special evening because it was our coming-out party, our debutante ball. It was a grown-up party, with music and young men. All the parents were invited to come view the possible future daughters-in-law.

Our house was not big enough to hold all the people my mother had invited, so Mama had nagged until my father had built a pavilion with a canvas roof outside in case of rain. There were tiny lanterns the size of apples hanging on wires around the dance floor, which was just the ground swept as clean as possible of dust. Ate Yu had swept all day, while my two aunts laughed and gossiped away.

I had worked and saved for a Western-style gown, and when it came packaged in a brown box from "Stevenson's of New York," I could barely breathe. The gown was too long, but Ate Yu helped me to hem it. It was beautiful, powder blue with large puffy sleeves that ended at my elbows. I had purchased matching gloves that stopped at my wrists.

My best friend, Nene Villanueva, was one of the first to arrive. She held my hands as she came through our door. "Oh, Ana," was all she said.

I shooed her words away playfully with my hands. We peeked through my bedroom window as the young men began to arrive. "Come, let us see our choices." Many of the young men we had never met. It was my mother who had sent out the invitations, to the nearby schools and to our neighbors. We giggled as each boy came through the door and promptly went into the dance circle to pick up a cup of punch and study the crowd, looking for friends.

"Too tall"—we laughed—"too short, too dark, too pale . . . oh, look at that one. Is that a boy?"

"I might want to dance with the one in the light blue *barong;* we would match," I said.

"Oh, and that one with the nice smile." Nene covered her mouth.

"I have two picked out so far. See that one there with the white *barong?* Look at the way he throws the punch down his throat. And that one, look at those shoulders." I sighed.

"Huh, what if he throws whiskey down the same way? And the one with the shoulders, I bet he could punch very hard when he is angry."

"Oh, Nene." I hugged her.

"Where is Corazón?" Nene smiled; she and Corazón had gotten close at school. They had similar interests in sewing and schoolwork.

I rolled my eyes. "She asked Ate Yu to help her finish the last of her fitting. Papa offered to buy her a dress. And Tita Babelyn says she has enough money to buy all of Stevenson's, but she still wanted to make her own dress!"

Nene smiled. "Well, that is kind of sweet, don't you think?"

I could not answer her, because a young man walked into the courtyard and I stopped breathing. "Who is that?" I shouted, then clapped a hand immediately over my mouth. My father walked by the room with a look of disapproval.

A boy strode in. He didn't walk but strutted like a rooster. Even the other boys could not help but stare. He had a beautiful smile and eyes so wonderfully bright. He was comfortable among the others, who stood fidgeting and checking their clothes.

"That," she said proudly, "is Jamie Bautista." She smiled. "Is he not gorgeous?"

"Ay, what a horrible name, that is a girl's name."

"No, it's not, it is short for James. He has three elder sisters, and they have called him Jamie since he was little. I think it is sweet."

"Let us go down now. I want to test out my new dress."

"Ana, not before you are announced," Nene gasped. "Your mother will be furious."

I didn't care. The more I thought about it, the more I liked the idea. I would make a grand entrance by rushing down myself. So I did. Nene watched from my bedroom window, her mouth turned down in disapproval. I could feel my heart thumping with excitement through my body. I took a deep breath, steadied myself against the door frame, and then strode into the courtyard full of young men.

My mother was across the courtyard, instructing the servants on where to put the basket of tiny chicken legs and the honey dipping sauce. She was dripping more of the sweet sauce onto the large grilled fish baked with tomatoes, and onions stuffed into its belly. She turned, still speaking to someone with a smile on her face, when she saw me approach. I heard a plate crash, I heard the servants scramble around to make order once again, but I paid no attention. Someone told the band to strike up the music, and "the band," a group of three guitarists and a singer, began to play.

The man had a sweet voice. He sang about a young girl who had grown out of a field of wheat and grew into a precious field flower, a *dalagang bukid,* and how a young widowed farmer had picked her from the stalk and rescued her from her ladder of thorns.

I walked into the courtyard and felt powerful. The boys were looking at me with admiration and confusion. I smiled, walking among them, not really stopping anywhere. I turned and saw Jamie Bautista grinning openly at me. I lifted my chin and looked away. I let myself get lost in the music, swaying from side to side, pretending I was the precious flower in the song.

I told you Jamie Bautista was bold, but I didn't realize how charming he was as well. For what he did next, a normal boy would have been reprimanded for. An ordinary boy would have been labeled as coarse or inappropriate, but not Jamie. He wooed the crowd, he made a game of it. He strolled next to me with his hands behind his back, and every now and then his feet skipped a little to the music. He walked around me, playing to the music as if he were the farmer somehow, studying the rose. Our eyes followed one another, and he bowed and somehow managed to look like the humble farmer asking the flower for a dance. I could not help but laugh and the crowd clapped and I gave him my hand.

He was so charming, he received a dance from the debutante without asking for one. He made up for it by taking my hand and kissing the back of it. He knelt with one leg on the ground and let me walk around him once, as if letting me contemplate his modest proposition. I was in heaven. What were the names of the other two boys I had chosen from my bedroom window? I could no longer remember.

Again Corazón managed to outshine me, and I had helped her. By coming down first, instead of side by side with her, I had allowed myself a small show of glory. But it was nothing, you understand, to how it left her the only one to come down the staircase announced as "the daughter," and as if that were not enough, her dress was magnificent. It was a rose gossamer over a simple design of raw silk. She had left one shoulder bare, and from the other shoulder diagonally across her body she had embroidered sequins and mother-of-pearl beads in swirls that fused into the small train of her dress. I hadn't noticed her in weeks because she had worked so hard at the gown. She would often sit out in the garden as she sewed, with the sun blanketing her. Her skin that night was a gorgeous brown. The highlights in her hair were streaks of gold. The only makeup she had was the red lipstick that seemed to glow against her skin. Her hair was clasped with a single pearl clip and the rest left to fall long down her back. People sighed when she walked down the stairs.

"Wow," was all Jamie said. "Two beautiful daughters, your family is lucky.

I'm glad I noticed you first." You see how he was? He paid her that one painful compliment, like when taking a blood test. One simple stab of the needle and then it is over. I hardly felt it. But that was it.

He did not get in line when all the boys surrounded her. He did not do so later when all the others had had their first dance with her. He stayed by my side all night, and when Corazón was brought over by Jamie's mother and introduced to him, he took her hand and bowed to her. "Sister," he called her, as if he and I were already promised to each other.

But then his mother insisted they dance and that she and I talk. I became excited, already a proposition from an interested mother. It was so difficult to take my eyes from Corazón and Jamie dancing, they were such a striking couple. He with his straight back and graceful stride, she with her blushing innocence.

"Ana, tell me about yourself." Jamie's mother smiled. I could see she was studying my hair; she even reached out and combed a few strays into place. I smiled graciously. She had Jamie's eyes, or rather he had hers. The long eyelashes, the color a lighter brown, unusual in a full-blooded Filipino. Their family was middle class like ours, meaning we were poor but not homeless. We had a few luxuries, if you could call them that, such as furniture and a little extra money to gamble with, Corazón's.

"I am seventeen today. I like to sing and I take voice lessons."

"Ah, for how long?"

"I've taken lessons for ten years now."

"Oh, very long time. You are so lucky that your family can afford this."

I nodded. "Mhmm," I said.

"This is a very beautiful dress, did you make this?"

"Oh, no. I worked very hard to save for it. I had it sent from the United States."

"This is a lovely party. Did you help to cook any of these dishes?"

"Oh no. I only know how to make a few things."

"Yes, yes, of course. You are young yet. All fun right now. Enjoy yourself now, right?" She laughed encouragingly.

I laughed with her.

"Look at Jamie dance. I was a good dancer when I was young. He gets that from me," she whispered with her hand held to one side of her mouth, as if her words were only for my ears, and then she winked.

I was so overjoyed. His mother was so easy to get along with. And then I realized; it hit me on the head like guava falling from a tree. When I get married, I will also get a new mother. A mother-in-law, of course, but just the same.

She would love me as her own daughter. My heart had wings. I could have spun around in a circle, but instead I stayed in place, showing Jamie's mother how mature I was. She told me how she loved to cook; she confided, in fact, that she was an excellent cook. I became encouraged, I thought of all the dishes we could create together. When she excused herself and walked away to speak to my mother, I bit my lip and waited for Jamie to come back.

I was so happy that I congratulated Corazón on the beautiful dress she had sewn. She glowed and thanked me.

She hugged me. "Happy birthday, sister," she said. I could see in her eyes there was still hope that we could be close. "Perhaps later we can open our presents together," she suggested.

"Sure, sure." I nodded, pulling away from her embrace, but I was too excited about Jamie to listen to her at that moment. I took Jamie's arm and we excused ourselves. I left Corazón standing alone.

She did not stay that way for long. I saw the boys get in line again to ask her to dance. Oh, there were boys interested in dancing with me as well, but I would not leave Jamie's side, and after a while they saw how I was about him.

A young man came into our party late. He was very handsome. I saw that Corazón was immediately attracted to him.

I remember asking Nene, "Who is that man?"

"Matthew Parris. Corazón talks about him endlessly."

Something possessed me at her words. I was only curious about him until that moment, but I knew when to pay attention to valuable information. I looked at Nene keenly. "I want to meet him later."

As I studied our new guest, I saw that he and Corazón were alike. He was half French. But they looked the same with their fair golden skin and high brow. He had lighter hair than she did. A dark gold and, in fact, you could not tell he was half Filipino until you saw how his blue eyes turned up a little at the ends and you looked closer at his lips, which were fuller. He had very sensual lips, that one, and oh, how he made the other girls swoon.

He had been brought up in Puerto Princesa, and his father was a well-known lawyer who traveled much. He was a real, as they say, ladies' man. I saw how his gaze strayed from Corazón to the other girls at the party even as he stood before her engaged in conversation and despite the fact that she was the prettiest one there. He looked at me many times, until Jamie stared him down. Corazón did not seem to notice any of this. Or perhaps she did not mind. Maybe she was just happy to have found someone like herself. This man is not so good, I thought to myself.

If I were a good sister, I would have warned Corazón about this before she fell in love with him. But you already know what kind of sister I was back then. Instead, Jamie and I, we sat in the shadows, away from the twinkle of the stars. And I forgot for the moment my interest with Corazón's admirer.

"How is it I never crossed paths with you all this time? You live just three kilometers from me." He shook his head.

"What makes you think I would have been free then?" I teased.

He liked that, I could tell, my boldness. And that night, I was bolder than ever. I felt as if I owned the stars. As if I were the one who had filled the moon with crushed pearls just for my own party. I stood. "Well, I had better get to the other guests now."

He looked up in confusion. "What do you mean?"

"Well, I've already wasted enough time on you, and you haven't tried to kiss me once. By the time you decide to, I could have danced with every boy in this room. So I might as well start now." Really, I do not know what came over me that night, to talk that way. I think I felt that since he did not know me, I could be the kind of girl I had always wanted to be, the kind of girl in the romance books my aunts read.

He laughed, throwing his head back, and grabbed my wrist and swayed our hands to the side and back while he studied his shoes. He took my hand and silently led me to the back of a large *narra* tree. "May I kiss you, Ana?" he asked with those wonderful eyes.

I nodded, too breathless to speak. But before he could kiss me, we were interrupted by that man, Matthew Parris. I was not sure where he came from. But he pretended not to see Jamie.

"Ana, isn't it time you gave me that dance you promised me the other night?"

I was in such shock that I couldn't speak. We had not even been introduced, yet he knew my name. How inappropriate, to suggest I had been alone with him, and during the night at that. I was so stunned, I didn't know if I should slap him or laugh at the ridiculousness of it all. My silence made it appear that I had been caught in a lie. I turned to explain to Jamie that I didn't even know him, when Jamie walked off with a small curse.

I watched as Jamie crossed the dance floor, straight to Corazón, and asked her to dance. My head swam with how fast it had happened, and here was Matthew waiting with that smile. I wanted to run to Jamie and explain, but my pride would not let me do that. It would also have been inappropriate, chasing a man I had just met in front of our guests. I nervously took Matthew's hand and headed for the dance floor. I was angry, jealous, confused, and flattered. Yes, flattered that the two best-looking men were vying for my attention.

What I should have done was turn and walk away. What I should have done was run. Matthew led me out to the dance floor next to Corazón and Jamie. She would not look our way. It is funny how youth can block out instincts and a handsome face can block all thought. I forgot about how I had decided this Matthew Parris was a bad man, for the minute he turned on his charming ways to me, I too fell for his charms. His eyes were so blue. I felt as if they were the sky and I were a single cloud sitting in all that great expanse. It turned my thoughts upside down to be looked at the way he looked at me. I felt like one of the little monkeys that hang by their tails from the coconut trees.

He was tall, so he had to bend his head to talk to me. "You are so beautiful in that dress," he whispered in my ear. I laughed nervously and looked over his shoulder. I saw my friend Nene standing in the sidelines, frowning.

"Did you and Corazón have a fight?" I asked, not sure what to say.

He chuckled. "What makes you think Corazón and I have anything?"

"Well, I . . ." I didn't know what to say, so I looked over at Corazón and Jamie dancing. They were talking in whispers. She looked sad, and I almost felt bad for her, until Jamie lifted her chin with his two fingers. My hate rekindled, like a new log thrown into the fire. Why was she always there to catch the goodness that filtered through me? Why was I always left with the dregs of jealousy and hate? How had she managed to look the victim, when I was the one innocently minding my own business with Jamie Bautista? I did not want this blue-eyed man who dripped honeyed words from his lips. Though I didn't exactly think that when I looked at him.

I was furious; our night was coming to a close. The evening was supposed to represent our futures, and look what bad luck was already showing. Me with my feelings all in confusion, and Corazón dancing with the man I had just found and was not ready to let go of. But most of all, I was angry at all the bitterness in my heart. I didn't want it. I felt she had brought it there. She always did that, brought me bad luck. I told myself if my sister, Janna, were around, this would never have happened.

WHEN IT CAME time to open our presents I was so upset, I was ready to pass and open them in private, but Corazón insisted. We sat in the middle of the courtyard, and the presents were brought to us. There were many colorful presents, and most of them were for us to share as sisters. Like the picnic basket we received, and the matching tea set made of porcelain. I wanted to throw the tea set on the floor and say, "This is to represent my break from this woman. She is not my sister." Instead I smiled and we posed for pictures with each present opened. Do you know how it feels to be forced in a situation with someone you despise?

I felt I was walking barefoot on lava. When our mother came and stood behind Corazón instead of between us, it did not go unnoticed by me or our guests. She was punishing me for my earlier dissension, for coming down the stairs unannounced, but it only added to the fire. Mama was selfish that way. Once you offended her, you needed to crawl on your hands and knees to regain her favor. She could have chosen to forgive me, a rash young girl of seventeen, but she didn't. She dug my wounds deeper, embracing Corazón and speaking only to her, showing everyone who the favored daughter was, as if I didn't exist. My mother knew the pain she caused me. She knew the rift between Cora and me.

It was just one more thing to add to my feelings toward Corazón. I felt as if everyone had turned against me. I noticed how Jamie sat on Corazón's side, avoiding me. I wanted to run to my room and shut my door at the whole party.

Even her gown began to annoy me more and more. My blue expensive gown had become wrinkled as the night wore on, and one of the sleeves kept slipping off. Corazón's gown had kept its freshness. Each time I turned around someone was complimenting her on her talents as a seamstress. I ached to spill my glass of punch on her gown. I envied how the iridescence of the fabric caught the candlelight. I wanted to put out its brightness, so I did.

As the next card was read, the next present passed to us, I pretended to lean over at the gift as if I were curious. I could see Nene's eyes grow large. She shook her head at me. I heard my name announced first and reached over and— "Oops!"—the punch spilled all over that remarkable gown. Corazón stood with her mouth open, brushing away the punch. Everyone rushed to help her. But funny thing, she wasn't concerned. She was more excited about the present she held in her hands.

That was when I realized that the presents had ended and what they had saved for last, probably my mother's idea, was our own presents to each other. What I held in my hands was the present Corazón had bought for me. It was a big box, as large as a double-layered sheet cake to feed two hundred people. The box was wrapped in bright yellow, and the ribbon was blue. She had added a little accent of small yellow roses to the ribbon.

What she held in hers was the stupid set of wind chimes I had bought at the market at a bargain, with the intention of keeping her awake at night. It was the first present I had ever bought her.

I felt much better after spilling the punch, and I could see from the corner of my eyes the pink streaks of punch growing permanent roots. Cora did not seem to care.

"Open yours first," she said excitedly.

I pulled apart the ribbon and ripped open the pretty paper, forgetting to thank her. When I opened the box, even I was shocked. She had sewn me a gown. It was a pale pink, with a pearl sheen to it. It was made of raw silk and was almost identical to the one she wore. It was breathtaking. "Do you like it?" She clapped her hands. The guests exclaimed at the beauty of it.

"Yes," I said, dumbfounded, and feeling embarrassed now at the gift I had given her.

"I am going to open mine," she said, laughing. When she opened the plain brown wrapping, her eyes lit up. She was so happy, you should have seen her. My shame flared inside me. I felt as if the corners of my soul were eroding. I wanted to shake her and say, "Look, look at the attachments, cheap wire. Look at the metal, not good at all, just tin." But from her expression, you would have thought I had bought her rare black pearls. She shook it, and the wind chimes did sound pretty. But as I looked at the faces of the guests, I could see they were watching the two of us intently. As if our true feelings were revealed to them. I could see the disappointment in Jamie's eyes, though he tried to hide it. He told Corazón it was a lovely present. The only one smiling was Matthew. Smiling not with his mouth, but with his eyes. A secret kind of smile, as if he were saying "We are two of a kind, you and I."

And that was how our first night as "young women" began. Jamie did not come by to try to straighten things out between us. And Matthew, I avoided him so much, he somehow found a way to make friends with Corazón again. I was so exhausted from the party that I said good night to a few guests and walked upstairs to our room. I heard Corazón as she came up the steps. Her feet were always light and graceful.

"Oh, she is already asleep," she said to Ate Yu. She laid the gown she had sewn for me in a box beside my bed. "Good night, sister, thank you for the present." I heard her hang the wind chimes outside her window. And do you know, those wind chimes actually sounded lovely? I remember how she used to care for them; whenever the weather threatened, she would take down the wind chimes to preserve them.

THAT WAS NOT the last we saw of those young men. Many of the ones who were too shy to approach us at the party came to call at our house. In fact, for months after, our house was the busiest one in the village. Matthew Parris came often to visit Corazón, and I avoided him like typhoid fever. I did not like how out of control I felt whenever he was in the room. I already told you how he mixed up my thoughts like my favorite dessert, halo halo. I felt like the crushed ice mixed with too many sweet beans, ube, langkâ, and other such goodies. Jamie never visited. The next time I saw him was at the harvest festival known as the Lami-Lamihan Festival.

CORAZÓN AND I were to perform in a dance contest. There was every conceivable type of contest at the Lami-Lamihan. There was the cooking contest, a tree-chopping contest, a *tinikling* contest. The *tinikling* was my favorite. I loved the sound as the two large bamboo sticks met and separated on the ground. The typical beat is for the two bamboo holders to hit the ground twice, then bring the sticks together on the third beat and repeat again. There are usually two wooden bars set crosswise underneath, so that the carriers do not hit their fists on the ground when they strike.

It challenged me, skipping in and out of the two sticks without the sticks catching my feet. This was the dance I chose to do. I had intended to perform it with Nene, but she had slowly become closer with Corazón after our party. You know how friends are, fickle. I did not have any plans that night of sabotaging Corazón's performance. I had already licked my wounds from the party. It was just a joke, you see. I did not think it would hurt anyone. Well, maybe I was a little bitter over Nene's abandoning me for her, but I swear that wasn't on my mind that night.

Corazón had decided to do the candela dance. *Pandanggo sa ilaw,* "the dance of light," as it was called. The dance where one lights candles in little tin or glass containers and, depending on her expertise, more candles are placed on the dancer's body. The candles are placed on the shoulders, the palms of the hands, and the top of the head. An amateur, for example, would have only the two candles carried in the palms of her hands. Corazón was an expert. She was graceful, so it was an easy dance for her. As I watched her practice that morning, the idea came to me to make it a little more challenging. So I placed more wax in the candles, so that the weight she had practiced and grown accustomed to would be different.

As we walked around the festival, watching the different contests, my mind was somewhere else. I think maybe I was practicing the dance steps for that evening, but it is so long ago that I cannot say for sure. Corazón was excited; Matthew was to participate in a tree-climbing contest, so she and Nene rushed us over to the section of coconut trees. We watched as they introduced Matthew and he took off his shoes and rolled his pants up to his ankles, and then he took off his shirt and the girls called out and giggled. They announced another name, and the girls shouted once again. Nene nudged me. "Did you hear? Jamie Bautista is in the contest."

I shrugged but moved farther forward to better see. Matthew was grinning and playing to the crowd, flexing his arm muscles, but he was not as impressive as Jamie. Jamie worked with his father in the fields night and day, so his body was very lean and muscular. I thought my eyes would go crossed from staring at his body too hard.

Mama used to tell us that if we stared too long at something we were not supposed to, like a boy's pee pee, our eyes would go crossed and stay that way. Anyhow, that is how Jamie caught me when he turned to wave at Corazón and Nene, who were shouting out his name like a couple of yellow-beaked parrots. I blushed, and he smiled.

"Oh, see, you still like him," Corazón and Nene teased.

"Shut up," I said, biting my lip. But I found myself shouting for him when the gun went off and he started to climb the tree like an expert. He hoisted himself up so quickly, using his bare feet. He made it to the top and cut down all the coconuts, dropping them into a net bag tied around his waist. The first thing he did when he received his little trophy, a wooden miniature of a man climbing a tree, was come over and give it to me. I guess that was his way of making up for our lost time. From then on, he and Matthew stuck by our side. I must say, that is the best time I can remember ever having with Corazón. Maybe because we were both too preoccupied to fight.

We visited the various little booths until the intoxicating scent of turon crooked its finger at us. The sweet bananas were hot from the frying, and the flaky pastry shell sprinkled with sugar and melted into the mushy filling stopped our wanderings, and we bought two each. I enjoyed myself so much that I forgot about the extra wax I had added to Cora's candles. And by the time I remembered, it was too late.

It had grown dark, and the festival was now lighted everywhere by orange and green paper lanterns. The dance arena was roped off by a small square section. I had just finished doing my dance and received much applause. My only competition was Corazón. As I got off the stage, Matthew came to congratulate me, hugging me a little longer than usual. And when he bent to give me a kiss on the cheek, he sneaked his lips a little closer to mine. I quickly moved away from him and grabbed Jamie's arm before he could see what had happened. I sat cross-legged with him holding my hand as Corazón came out. I even clapped as she brought out the candles, until I remembered with dismay what I had done.

As always, her beauty received involuntary sighs and jealous whispers. She smiled sweetly, walking with her natural grace to the row of candles on the floor. She began by swaying to the music, lighting the first candle and then weaving in and out as she did the rest. The idea was to start easy and place one candle on her head and continue to dance, then two on her shoulders, the insides of her arms near the hollows of her elbows, and then finally two in each hand. The ones on the insides of her arms were her own creation. She added those for difficulty and maybe to show off a little.

When she bent to place the first one on her head, the audience smiled in anticipation. I saw a slight look of confusion cross her face. I think she realized then that the weight she had grown accustomed to was different, but still it was proceeding nicely. Next she placed the two on her shoulders, and the one on her left appeared a little wobbly. The audience held its breath, but she overcame it and everyone clapped. Next she reached for the ones for the insides of her arms, and I could see fear cross her face. The weights were very different, and as she tried to balance and compensate for the two new ones, the candle atop her head, now burning with hot wax, fell off and singed her hair, and the ones on her shoulders fell on her arms. The audience gasped, and many ran up to help her.

I was the only one who stayed seated in shock, but that must have given me away. Jamie and Matthew ran up to see how she was, and when Jamie returned he looked at me accusingly. "Someone added more wax to each candle." Before I could respond he walked off.

"Are you all right, Cora?" I asked stiffly.

She moved away from me, but not before she gave me a sore look. The same look she had given me when I paid the *kalesa* driver to take her away, the same look as when I tried to lose her on that first day of school. She never said a word; just that look said it all. I ran after Jamie and grabbed his arm.

"Jamie, where are you going?" I pleaded. My whole body ached for him to need me.

"Let him go, Ana." Matthew had come to stand behind me.

The trouble was, I couldn't. I had replaced my obsession for my mother's attention with my rivalry for Jamie's affection. I wanted to be chosen over Corazón.

"I cannot believe you, Ana," Jamie said, running a tense hand through his hair.

"What do you mean?"

"Don't play stupid. Why do you do such things? Unless I'm blind, your sister is nothing but kind to you. Yet you play these evil games with her. Just when I think I know you, when I'm just about to fall for you—"

"You're falling for me?" I asked.

He stopped and sighed, his hands on his hips. "Will you stop this nonsense with your sister? What is it all about?"

"I—" The words would not come out. I wanted to explain how I never wanted a new sister. How she stole my mother's love, and then my best friend. How she was always undermining my happiness. But all that came out was, "I'll stop." They were hollow words. I think God heard this and knew. Promises should be sacred; I think I cursed myself by making one I did not intend to keep. Maybe I should have told Jamie this. Maybe if I had told him, he would have helped me to stop. But it was too late. It was already in my blood, already in our fates for me to continue to the end.

THE FOLLOWING WEEK, my mother was very excited. She said that Mrs. Parris, Matthew's mother, and Mr. and Mrs. Bautista had requested appointments with her. By the way they requested these meetings, we knew that this could mean only one thing. They were interested in talking marriage.

My mother and father set their meetings with the two families on the same day, only an hour apart. Mrs. Parris came first. We should have waited in our bedroom; we should not have hid behind the mural screen in the next room.

Mrs. Parris was obviously there to represent her husband, who was away on business, and to propose marriage for Corazón. That's how it was back then; the young men did not always have a say, as they do today. My parents asked her to sit, and she was offered tea and pandesal, the sweet milk bread that sometimes comes with a little sprinkling of sugar or cheese on top. They talked pleasantries for the first few minutes, and then Mrs. Parris put on her glasses and folded her hands on the table.

"As you know, Mirabelle, Manuel"—she nodded to each of my parents—"Matthew is interested in your daughter Corazón. This is a perfect match, I believe, since they are so alike."

It always amazed me when people said that about the two of them. For I did not think they were so alike at all. Oh, I had thought so at first, but I had come to realize that they looked alike only on the outside, with their light skin and golden brown hair; inside they were quite opposite. Matthew was like a beautiful eel, exotic but tricky to catch his true personality. Corazón was more like a white catfish. Pretty, and you always knew what she was up to, cleaning up my throwaways. She was interested in books and sophisticated music, the kind they play abroad, with no singing, just the violin, the piano, and such. Matthew was interested in himself and the women he could surround himself with.

"I of course told him I would be happy with either one of your daughters, they are both lovely. I even thought for a moment that he may be more suited for Ana, but . . ." She laid open her palm and shrugged. "Such is the way of the heart."

I was watching Corazón from the corners of my eyes, and she clasped her hands together and closed her eyes. It made me wonder if she was just as eager to be apart from me. That was something I had never thought of. A tear rolled down her cheek, and I wondered if that would happen to me.

"How good for you," I said to her, and she thanked me.

I thought I would die of impatience for the next hour as we waited for Mr. and Mrs. Bautista, I was so excited. This is it, I thought, now my life will begin. I was so happy to have already spoken with Mrs. Bautista. Corazón had not had that luxury, so the visit with Mrs. Parris had been more stressful for her.

Finally Mr. and Mrs. Bautista came, and to my surprise Corazón waited with me. They were more formal, more curt, with my parents. They did not exchange pleasantries. The Bautistas were not wealthy, but their family was descended from village chieftains, so that was where their attitude came from, but still, I had not remembered Mrs. Bautista that way. At my party she had been very sweet. But people are different when they come to bargain, just as at the market, you must wear your game face. So I was not alarmed.

"Well, Mirabelle, Manuel," Mr. Bautista began. "As you know, we are very interested in a marriage between our only son, Jamie, and your daughter Corazón."

My breath, which I had been holding, choked in my throat, and Corazón turned, pale as a ghost.

"There must be some mistake," she whispered. "Ana, I never," she pleaded to me.

She might as well have stabbed me in the chest with one of the big bolo knives we had hanging above our dining room table. Tears came down my face; they crept into my lips, hot and bitter. I thought back to when I had spoken to Jamie's mother. I chided myself. I should have known, with Jamie's mother. I should have known when she asked me how long I had taken singing lessons and she said "very long," she meant that if it took that long and I still hadn't learned, I must be a really bad singer. How sweet her words had been, but I should have known how hard her eyes were.

Her interest was so engaging, as hypnotic as a snake, waiting for you to put your guard down, then stinging you with its venom. Her words were soft and encouraging to lure me in, but her thoughts were sharp as snake fangs. When she fixed my hair that night, she was thinking with embarrassment how her son could have fallen for such a sloppy creature. I later learned she was appalled at how I had come down the stairs on my own the night of our debutante party.

When she had complimented me on the dress I had ordered from New York, and asked if I had made the dress, she was seeing if I could sew for her son. When she had asked if I had cooked the delicious food, she merely wanted to know if I could cook at all. I chided and pitied myself. Yet even then I should have directed my hate toward that evil woman. But you can guess by now whom my hatred was directed at.

I looked over Corazón through hot tears, and her pleading face became distorted. "Shut up. If you had never come into my life, I would be a happy person by now," I said, and walked out of the room.

She tried to follow me, but I locked the door to our room and told her to sleep with either one of her in-laws.

JAMIE CAME THE next morning. He told my parents he wanted to marry me and that if they did not give him permission, we would run away together. He declared what his mother had done was wrong, that he had specifically told her he wished to propose to me. Yet she had undermined his request and asked for Corazón instead. He stood outside my window and threw small rocks at Corazón's wind chimes. It was awful to hear; the chimes would start their music with a small breeze, and then—*ping! plonk!*—Jamie's rocks would halt the melody.

"Please, Ana. Speak to him," Cora pleaded.

"He's your intended, you have two. Do whatever you want with him," I spat.

Jamie sent letters and asked Corazón to give them to me, but I always threw them away. I was beyond thinking anymore. The doors to my heart had shut. I had only hate inside me, complete hate. I felt as if my life were just a series of betrayals. So when Jamie, the one good thing, finally arrived, I was too hardened. Like a dried-up grape, nothing could bring back my sweetness. At seventeen years old I had given up on the kinds of dreams that young girls cling to. It made me crazy that all I could think of, all my mind was capable of concluding, was the fact that if Corazón had never come into my life, I would never be this miserable.

After the fourth week, Jamie stopped coming. The next time I saw him was at a hayride arranged for the students. It was something that the church set up, and Ate Yu insisted I go. She said I was acting like a fool and that I should go. I went only because I grew tired of everyone trying to force me out of the house. Matthew arrived to gather Corazón, and I was somehow convinced to go with them. That was the final mistake.

As I sat in the carriage and watched them laugh and chatter about the future, I wanted to rip the smile of satisfaction from Corazón's face. I wanted her to be as unhappy as I was. In my mind her questions concerning my welfare became insults. That was when the bad thought formed in my mind. If she really wanted to know how I was doing, I would let her feel firsthand.

Jamie came to the wagon ride. I am sure it was planned: he had flowers for me. His smiling face almost put tears in my eyes, but as I said, I was too far gone by then. I had become another creature altogether. I no longer had the innocent hate that two sisters have, one that later turns to love and fond old memories. I had cultivated an enduring sore, the kind that would go to the grave.

I let Jamie sit next to me, but there was no feeling left for him, and I could see by the brave smile he wore as he tried to engage me in conversation that he saw that, too.

As we sat there with the other young people beneath the canopy of clouds and moonbeams, I conceived a plan in my heart. When the wagon stopped, and we were allowed to stretch our legs and the picnic baskets were laid out for us, I fell behind and walked next to Matthew. He looked at me curiously.

"Still angry with Jamie?" he asked. "Have a heart, Ana."

I shrugged. "Sometimes I long for someone more exciting."

"I know what you mean," he said with sincerity.

We walked in silence.

Matthew spoke again. "Well, I have always thought he was too weak for you." Matthew had a deep fascination for me because I was the only girl he could never charm. He had fooled around with many girls, but I had never told Corazón this. I thought if she was that blind, then better she stay blind. Their wedding was set for August 30, in two months.

I returned to Jamie satisfied. I had planted the tiniest seed in Matthew's brain, and that was all it took.

After that night, Matthew tried again and again to catch my attention. He would tell jokes to Corazón, but all the while I could sense he was really telling them to me. One day I stayed home sick from school. I had asked Corazón to stay after school and gather my homework for me. Matthew came an hour early. I walked into the living room in a sleeveless summer dress. Unbeknownst to him, I had been preparing myself hours before.

"Oh, Matthew, I didn't know you were here. Where is Corazón?"

"Oh, I don't know, she doesn't know how to be on time for an appointment. She has no sense." He grinned.

WE WOULD DO that, dance around each other's words. Always hinting. What of Jamie? Oh, I liked him enough, but looking back, I realize that I had been wanting something even more. Whenever I had thought of Jamie, I had thought of myself as the beloved daughter-in-law. I had pictured many ways I would be showered by love from his mother. Having her betray me that way erased all feelings I had for Jamie.

How could I marry him and be with yet another mother who did not want me? At least Matthew's mother had even confessed that she had thought I would have been a better match for her son. The only woman who probably thought I was better than Corazón was the one she would inherit as a mother-in-law. You see how unfair it all was?

As I expected, it was easy to win Matthew away from Corazón. Do not think me immodest when I say that he practically leaped at the chance to get away from her. We took long walks together and talked about our futures. I told him how I wanted to travel the world, maybe even become a hostess on one of those cruise ships that were becoming so popular. He talked about how he wanted to move to America and become a movie star. We had a lot in common. I saw that Matthew could be a true friend. He held me in higher esteem than he did other women. It wasn't long after that he simply started coming an hour earlier than his dates with Corazón, and the two of us had that much more time together.

One evening as Matthew and I returned home from one of our walks, I heard my aunts telling my mother about the two of us. How it was inappropriate for us to be seen walking and holding hands. They exaggerated, of course; we never held hands. How like my aunts to start a fire as soon as they saw the merest twigs to burn. Little did they know how much easier they made it for us. My mother said nothing to me when I strolled into the house with Matthew.

The next day was a different story. Somehow the entire neighborhood was talking about us. How this person or that person had seen us in a secret embrace. How Matthew was fooling around with his bride-to-be's sister. Such sweet talk for the gossips. I came up the steps and there was Matthew's mother, my mother, and my aunts. Corazón greeted me at the door with a somber face. Tita Babelyn was sniffing; she had gotten a berating from my father before he went off to work and was still explaining her uninvolvement in the entire affair.

"I never said that to Aling Panchita. I merely said that Ana and Matthew are the best of friends. Why would I say such a thing?" she sniffed.

Matthew's mother was staring at Tita Babelyn with the most disbelieving look. "You should be ashamed. Your own nieces. How could you start such rumors?"

Tita Babelyn began to sob. "What about Lulu? She has been talking also."

"Oh, Babelyn, don't involve me in this, huh? I am innocent. Why would I say such things about Ana and Matthew?" Tita Lulu raised her chin and looked away, pretending to straighten her skirt.

"Well, someone said something!" Mrs. Parris shouted. This woman had a strong voice. I tell you, it shook the wooden beams and made the cats scurry out from under the beds. "The whole village is talking about their affairs."

I turned to Corazón then. She looked at me sadly. "Ana, please don't do this," she begged.

Better for her if she hadn't said a word. How dared she beg me! She wanted all of it. Had she ever saved anything good for me? And here she was again, wanting only the good things. I clenched my hands into fists and looked at her. "You have heard what they say. It is already done. Everyone knows. Matthew's mother is protecting me. You can have anyone you want. You already have Jamie's mother."

I remember her face and the shocked look she gave me. "What would I want with Jamie's mother?" She was watching me carefully, the way one would a wild animal or a rabid dog. "What about Jamie?" she asked.

"You can have him, too!" I shouted.

MRS. PARRIS RESCINDED the offer of marriage from Corazón, and at Matthew's request, she asked for my hand in marriage instead. Of course, I said yes. I sealed all our fates, sentenced us all to misery. We were married and I moved out of that house. And do you know, Matthew became a good husband? And his mother, just as I had hoped, we became the best of friends. I hardly visited my family. I thought to myself how lucky, how lucky that I jumped at my only chance when I could. Sure, I did not love him, but I was *loved*. I had everything Corazón had wanted. I had beaten her at every round, yet I felt nothing but a devastating emptiness inside.

YES, I WAS saddened a little when I heard that Jamie and Cora had gotten close in my absence, until finally he had offered for Corazón's hand in marriage. But it was like hearing something in a long tunnel, very vague and distant. I did not realize then that it was my heart that had become hard and faraway. Still, I thought, how funny; even when I tried my best to hurt her, she always came out with what I wanted most. I was invited to the wedding but found some reason to be away at the time. I remember seeing them once by accident. Corazón's belly was big with their baby. I was riding in our carriage, and Matthew had gone into a store. As I sat in the carriage, I saw Corazón and Jamie laughing outside with ice-cream cones in their hands. I remember how beautiful Corazón looked.

Over the next three years Corazón wrote me often, though we lived only two miles away. I never invited her to my home, but she tried all the time to visit me. I always managed to grow sick or be too busy. My mother wrote me once or twice, usually to ask for money or jewelry but never to inquire about me. I never responded. She had some disease of the mind. It made her forget things. One moment she knew who she was and the next she did not recognize anyone. I felt nothing.

ONE DAY ATE YU came to visit, and my heart danced when I let her in. I showed her our grand house. She stayed and chatted with my mother-in-law. Before it was time to go, she took me aside and said, "Ana, your mother not doing so well. Maybe you should visit. Your sister getting very big with baby."

"I have been busy arranging my new home. I will visit as soon as I have time."

She gave me a knowing look. "Things change, Ana. You should make amends before it is too late. Smooth any bad feelings. Be a family again."

"Sure, Ate Yu," I told her.

A few weeks later, Jamie himself came to knock on our door. Matthew answered and invited him in. I could tell that Jamie wanted a word with me alone, but my husband would not leave until my mother-in-law called him out of the room. She was fair like that.

As the two of us stood alone in the room, I watched Jamie's sweet face. Did he notice our silk carpet at the entrance? Imported from India. What did he think of our servant who led him into our *salas*? His voice held impatience for my wandering thoughts. "Ana, Corazón is having trouble with the baby. She started her labor pains this morning. She has been asking for you."

His words jolted me. "Send for the midwife. I don't know anything about delivering babies," I said with alarm.

He paced angrily. "We have a midwife; your sister is asking for your presence."

I turned and my mother-in-law was standing in the doorway. She said in a soft voice, "Ana dear, you should be with your sister."

Just like that, so easy. She changed my mind. I chastised myself for thinking differently. "Of course, *Inay,* I will go immediately. I cannot promise to be of any help, but if you feel this strongly, then I shall go."

As soon as my sandals touched the first step of their house, my hair stood on end. I knew something was wrong. The air in the house, it seemed unmoved, oppressive. I could hear the wind chimes in the back room, and I went to see Corazón. I could hear her low moaning. My mother was there, hovering around the door like a ghost. When she saw me her eyes grew large and she ran from the room. "Janna, no!" she shouted. I shook my head and went in to see Corazón. The midwife walked out of the room to talk to Jamie; I could hear them speaking in hushed tones.

Corazón looked up from her daze. "Ana . . ." She managed a smile. "So good to see you. I have missed you. I am having trouble, sister." Her words, as always, were too sweet for me to hear. I brushed them away, pretending to be concerned with her condition.

"What is wrong, Cora? Are you having twins?"

"The baby wants to come out sideways." She tried to smile, but then her face bunched up and I could see her gripping the bedcovers with her fists. "The midwife has tried everything, but the baby will not turn. I am frightened."

"Don't be silly, the baby will be fine," I said sincerely. I had forgotten for the moment it was Corazón. I saw only a lovely young woman lying there in much agony, trying to be brave. That was the one true time I saw her as I should have.

"It is not the baby I am worried about." She shut her eyes tight again. Her breathing had become labored. It was then that I noticed the sheets were a deep red. As if she had been swimming in a red pool.

"Corazón," I said, "let us call a real doctor."

"Sister, there is not enough time. I tried and tried to have you come over sooner. We have much to discuss. There is no time to call a doctor now. He cannot fix things between us."

"What do you mean, between us?" I asked, watching the bed grow dark with blood. I thought she was fading. I could hear it in her voice, like a candlelight fading from no oxygen. I shouted for Jamie to get a doctor. He peered in the room quickly and then ran out. I watched through the windows as my mother and the midwife hurried after him. I thought how stupid not to have called one sooner. When I turned to speak with Corazón, she had fallen unconscious. I was in a panic. I tried to wake her, but her eyes stayed shut. I checked her breathing by watching the unsteady rise of her chest.

I felt a tension take over my entire body. I felt like an intruder. I paced the floor and noticed how sparse her house was and how dark. I felt a pang of sadness for her. What kind of man was Jamie that he couldn't bring sunlight into his wife's room? Couldn't call a proper doctor? I felt another pang, this time of outrage for my sister. She was used to finer things. I went to the windows to open the shade and let the sun in. She was perspiring badly, and I got a cool towel and placed it over her head. The room was insufferably hot, like the night Janna had died so many years ago. It alarmed me. I felt as if the same energy were hovering around us, trying to claim her. "I shall read you a book," I said loudly to the room.

I walked the entire house and found nothing. I hurried back and went to her bedside. I slowly placed my hand on her moving belly and worried over the baby.

"Cora," I said sternly to her. "Cora, you will kill this baby if you don't wake up." I could feel my hair stand on end at the chill that permeated the room, though it was suffocatingly humid. I was not good in stressful situations, and I felt as if I would pull out my hair. In my desperation I pulled open drawers, looking for something to occupy me. Her rubies and pearls were tucked away neatly in blue and green velvet boxes. Never worn, I realized. Her silk undergarments were folded in perfect rows. In the last drawer I opened, something caught my eye. My name, ANA, written in crooked letters on an envelope. I reached for the letter and realized it was wrapped in a ribbon. I undid the ribbon, and my breath became lodged in my throat. There were many letters attached, at least twenty. When I pushed one of her scarves away, my heart almost stopped. The drawer was filled with sets of letters tied in ribbons. Each stack had a year written on top. Twelve stacks, twelve years of letters, all addressed to me.

I reached out nervously and brought a stack to her bedside. "Cora, please.

Wake up." I shook her. I even pried her eye open with my fingers. Her iris stared out at me, blank and dilated. "I shall read to you. Are you listening?"

I was so nervous, I fumbled with the first envelope until I ripped it open. It was dated the year after Janna died. We were only eight years old. *"Dear Sister,"* it began. *"Why do you hate me so? I have been here two months now and I try and try, but you only seem to hate me more. Are you not longing for a sister again? Do you not want the company as I? I shall make it my lifelong goal to win your friendship."*

I glanced quickly at Cora and felt my face grow red with embarrassment. I read the next letter from the next stack. Two years later: *"Dear Sister, As you know, I enjoy making you angry. But not for reasons you think. I enjoy it because you make me feel as though I exist."*

I skipped through all the letters. I thought, How crazy this girl is, wanting my attention so. But also I started to think, How sad that she had no one. How scary to come live with a new family. *"Dear Sister, How I wish I were as strong as you. When Papa grows angry you are as strong as an old tree. You make him move with your strength. In order for me to move him, I must cry. I understand how this must disgust you so to see such weakness. I shall strive to be as strong as you."*

Five years later: *"Dear Sister, Mama told me I must give her half of my monthly allowance. I don't care about the money. But I am extra glad you don't care about it. Unfortunately you don't care about me either."* I looked at Cora sheepishly after that one.

The one that struck me the most was the night we had found out Jamie had gone against his parents and asked for my hand. *"Dear Sister, Jamie is the best match. You deserve him. He loves you very much. With all the girls wanting him, he has eyes only for you. Why can you not see this? I want to shake you sometimes. But I will support you no matter what your decision."*

My stomach twisted at the memory of that time. I stood up and nervously put the letters away. I shoved them back in the drawer and studied my sister. She did not look good. She looked near death. I remembered Janna the night she had passed away, and I thought how Corazón's skin looked that same sickly gray.

"I won't let you take her!" I shouted to the room. I imagined myself standing between her and the bad energy that was creeping around us. I would not let death take her. "Cora, be strong." I took her hand.

It terrified me that my sister might die. I had thought she would be around to hate forever. I never thought she would leave me. The doctor came bursting through our house, startling me and breaking our connection. He injected her with something, and she came to slowly. We were ushered out of the room, and I went to pick flowers. I think I picked their rosebushes bare. My mind went over and over my new revelation. *She has been as lonely as I. We could have been lonely together. We could have been happy together. I shall make it my goal to make things right. I have a sister!*

When the baby arrived, Jamie called me in. I placed the roses near the window and the sunlight, but not before I noticed the doctor give Jamie a sad look. My heart jumped. I went to sit beside Cora. She blinked at the brightness of the room. She seemed surprised to see me, almost nervous. I realized she was waiting for another one of my pranks or maybe my anger. I blushed in shame.

"I brought flowers for you," I said, smiling.

"Thank you," she said unsurely. "Did you see the baby?"

"He is beautiful. Like you, sister." Her eyes welled at my words. I had never called her sister.

OVER THE NEXT few weeks I came to sit with her. But instead of gaining her strength, she seemed to wilt. As I was visiting one evening, I helped her to walk out onto the porch and see the sunset. I had decided the best way to breach our distance was to forget the past and start new.

"Cora, as soon as you are better we shall spend more time together," I said.

She smiled and asked, "Have you ever wondered why I chose to live with this family instead of the many others that offered to adopt me?"

I shook my head and placed a cool rag to her brow. She was now always cold or feverish, no in between. "Conserve your strength," I said. "No explanations necessary."

"I chose this family first because I thought it was the right thing. *Inay* had just lost a daughter, and I had just lost a mother. But, in time, I began to see that nothing could ever change the damage Janna's death had done to her."

I went silent at the name of my dead twin. Corazón did not seem to notice. She did not falter in her words. She continued. "Papa was always busy, too busy to welcome me as a new daughter, too busy to help shake Mama's sadness, or your sadness. I stayed even after I discovered that I had come to live in an empty house. I stayed because of you. I knew you needed someone just as I did. Mama wronged us both. She grieved over a dead child, when she had two who were alive and starving to be loved."

"Cora, that is all in the past now. Let us not talk of it. Besides, I am willing to forgive you for all the hurts. It is done. Let us concentrate on building a new bond."

Her eyes faded a little at my words. She squeezed my hand. "Oh, Ana. You still do not see," she said sadly. "We don't have much time."

I fixed her dress. "We have the rest of our lives, silly."

She struggled to stay present but fell asleep soon after. She tired easily, and I tucked the blankets around her. That was the last time I saw her alive. She had fallen into a coma and she died that night in her sleep. I left town for a while, visited friends. I told Matthew I had to be alone for a while. I tried to run away from the realization that I had lost something good, that I was truly alone, but when I returned home the sadness was there waiting for me. The pain was so acute that I slept for days, refusing to acknowledge her death. It broke my heart. I had found out too late that Cora was a worthy sister. It twisted my emotions. Regret again filled me, followed by bitterness. The life we could have had. I was truly alone now. "Why did you keep me so blind for so long?" I screamed at God.

I went to visit my mother after that. I had in me all the anger that I had directed toward Corazón all those years. I practiced what I would say, how she was selfish and had neglected everyone after Janna died. She kept all of us from grieving with her theatrics. She had chased Papa away and affected everyone's life. Even Ate Yu, for when Ate Yu had fallen in love with a nice man, who wanted to marry her and take her away, Mama had begged her not to go. But most of all she had neglected Corazón and me. She was not fit enough to care for one child, yet she had adopted another. I wanted to spit these things to her feet. But when I arrived all I saw before me was a frail old woman with no memory of any of it.

THE LAWYERS LISTED all of Corazón's belongings, the two large houses she was to inherit on her twenty-first birthday, which was only two months away. The import/export business her mother had started and had multiplied three times over, so now they had nine big warehouses. All of her mother's jewelry. Oh, I knew she was worth a lot, but she never acted as though she had anything. Then they named the things as they were distributed in Corazón's will. She had nine warehouses of goods, and just one of these would be enough to care for a person for an entire lifetime. She had willed seven of them between her husband and any children they had. Two of the warehouses she had willed to me.

This was not necessary, what she did. As I told you, Matthew's family was wealthy. And my little business of giving voice lessons was prospering. I had many clients. I refused her gift. I told them they must redistribute it back to her husband and child. They said she had anticipated this, and in her will she had stipulated that if I were not to accept, the property would be given to her biggest competitor. Better that I accept, I decided, and give all the proceeds to Jamie and baby Feliciano. But when I tried to do that, Jamie was insulted. "Will you not even grant her one wish, Ana? Are you that selfish? She wanted these things for you."

IT DID NOT happen right away, my hearing the wind chimes in my sleep. It happened weeks after, on the month anniversary of her death. Or perhaps they sounded every night and I did not listen for them until the night of her anniversary prayers. I had almost reverted back to my old bitter self. Only now I was angry not with Cora, but at God. I had trouble sleeping; I heard those wind chimes in my sleep. I dreamed of Corazón and how she used to polish them. How she would unwind the wires carefully and bring them in whenever the weather looked bad. *I miss you, Corazón. Why have you left me?* I pondered. I did not attend her anniversary gathering. I knew it would not bring her back. I didn't want to remember anymore. It was too painful.

The night of her anniversary prayers, around the time that the rosary would have started, eight o'clock, I heard wind chimes. The soft bells were coming from inside our house. Not unusual, unless you considered the fact that I owned none. I was in the living room, playing solitaire, when something made me sit straight. The little hairs on my arms and all over my scalp were tingling. "Go away, thought," I said. "Just my imagination." So I began to tap my fingers on the oak table. I stopped tapping and had pulled the next card from the deck when I realized the tapping had not stopped. I looked a few inches past my card, and there were fingers tapping. I followed them upward, already knowing, the scream caught in my throat.

There was Corazón wearing her funeral gown, her one hand held to her chin as if she were playing cards, sitting at the table and pondering her next move. I backed away from my chair; I remember it falling over. I stood, she stood. I started to choke. She approached me and put her arms around me. *"Yakapin ko kitá hanggáng—"* she said. I will embrace you until— "Forgive," I heard her words whispered.

"No!" I screamed. I was still screaming when Matthew came running in, his eyes searching the room for an intruder.

"I saw her. Corazón, she was here, she was torturing me. I thought we had become friends," I sobbed hysterically.

"Shh . . ." He enveloped me in his arms. He promised to watch me as I slept. He sent word to Ate Yu to come visit us. I think he was concerned that Corazón's death had clouded my thinking. I prayed that night. I asked Corazón to please not terrify me this way. Had I angered her somehow before she died? I told her that I missed her. Wasn't that torture enough?

THE NEXT MORNING I woke with a start. I had decided it was a dream. I walked out into the living room, and there was Ate Yu already in the kitchen, preparing coffee.

"Oh, Ate Yu. That smells so good. Could I have a cup, please? And one for Matthew?"

"Of course," she said, and as I sat down she placed a cup on the table.

I looked up gratefully. "Thank you," I said.

The wind blew at that moment, and the hair on my arms stood on end. The wind chimes that I did not own rattled. When I looked up again I saw that it was not Ate Yu at all, but Corazón. "Forgive, *ate*," she said, and came to embrace me. My heart caught in my throat, and my cup shattered on the floor. Her cold embrace choked the breath from me.

"I forgive you!" I finally screamed out, and the real Ate Yu ran to the kitchen. My scream had woken her and Matthew.

We hurried to Ate Yu's small apartment that day, for Matthew had business he could not cancel and she told me she would sit with me as I slept. She ordered me to sit as she began to fix me a cup of tea. She made sure to turn every few minutes so I knew it was truly her. My mind was in chaos. What was happening? I thought Cora and I had buried our troubles.

"Why do you think this is happening? Am I going crazy like Mama?"

Ate Yu placed the cup of tea before me and crossed her arms. "Does she seem angry? What does she say when she visits?"

"She says, 'Forgive.' I cannot understand it. We had buried our differences before she passed. I had come to love her as a sister. I miss her still. I went to her funeral. I told her I forgave her like Papa and you taught me at Janna's funeral so long ago."

Ate Yu was watching me. "Ana, can you not yet see?"

I glanced up in surprise, my blood pumping in my ears. I looked behind me in terror, expecting to see Corazón again.

"No, no. I mean, can you not yet understand? Think about it. What else did I tell you before?" When I still did not understand, she took my hand. "Come, you should rest. Think about what I have said. I shall read my book. I will be right beside you the next time she visits."

Her words did not comfort me. The fact that she was sure there would be a next time. As she sat down to read, I thought about the things Corazón should ask forgiveness for. I puzzled it over in my head. I went back to the time of my sister Janna's death. What had Ate Yu told me then? What had my father said? *Do not let your tears fall on the dead, otherwise they will return again and again until the matter is resolved.* I had avoided that at Corazón's funeral. *What else? What else, Cora? Please help me to remember. Have I wronged you in any way?* And then it hit me like a storm.

"Ate Yu," I said, "would you please leave me for an hour?"

She stood in surprise. "You are sure? She may return."

"She will return," I said. "But I will be all right."

Ate Yu embraced me. "Yes, you will be."

After Ate Yu left, I did not wait for the wind chimes. I took a deep breath and called out, "Cora, I am waiting." A cool air swept the room and the tinkle of chimes sounded. I turned and Corazón stood framed by the doorway. She looked just like a normal person standing there, only she was stiff, something in her eyes not from this world.

"*Ate* . . ." Her voice permeated the room. Big sister.

"Yes, I have called you."

"Forgive," she said.

"No—" My tears overflowed at all that had passed between us. All the chances. "No, forgive me, sister," I sobbed, and as I walked to her image with opened arms, she vanished.

"Yes . . ." Her answer filled the room. I felt her all around me, as if her love were embracing me. I cried for all that we had lost. All of it not my fault and yet all my fault. "Yes, I forgive," she said like a small song, a fragrant whisper.

I had remembered now what Ate Yu had said the night of Janna's viewing, when she lectured me on what to say to the dead. "You must tell her, 'Sister, I forgive you for any wrong, and in turn, please forgive me if I have wronged you.' Otherwise how will she get to heaven with so many apologies and obligations weighing her down?"

I smiled and hugged my arms to myself. The bitterness had left me, and the thought of Corazón flying free to paradise made me happy for once.

When Matthew came home that night and saw me there, he looked around our room. I could see he sensed something.

"Where is Ate Yu?"

"I told her to go home."

"Corazón came. Is she still here?" He looked around.

"No."

"I can smell the fragrance of her hair," he said, coming to sit on the bed next to me. His bags were packed, and our eyes met. "Ana, you have no use for me now that she is gone. I had hoped, but I know you do not love me."

I began to cry again. All I could do was nod my head. He left, and I never saw him again. He went to live in the United States with his mother; he remarried.

⁓ **ALING ANA BLOWS HER NOSE** loudly into a silk handkerchief. "All those years, all the sadness I thought I had created for Corazón, I had created for myself. All these riches I have? I have never felt they were mine. I had beauty around me at all times. I had a sister who loved me, a husband, and only later, when we had wasted so much time, was I able to see that I had thrown away my chances at happiness. So I have learned to let go of anger, to never let it wrap its talons around me again.

"I should have been a mother to her son, to you, Feliciano, but instead I left you to a father who no longer cared to live. And look what happened. You grew up without any direction. You could not learn about strength from your father, Jamie, so you found it elsewhere, with the enemy."

She looks at Mang Selso. "We must stop this fighting. This rivalry between us. There are others who need our help."

I look away, for I know she means me.

"You remind me so much of myself, Isabelle, with this pain they have given you. It threatens your future. And at the same time you remind me of Corazón, so gentle and kind. Do you understand what I am telling you? Our experiences are different, yet they could have the same ending. Only you are young yet, you still have a choice. Do not hold this bitterness to you. Crush it and let it fly away. Both of you, start anew, leave the bitterness behind."

When Aling Ana finishes, Mang Selso looks humbled. He nods slowly and apologizes to me with his eyes. I feel the truth of Aling Ana's words. It is not the same, her story and what has happened to me. Yet I see that she means for me to understand about choosing to truly live or choosing to stay alive when you have died inside. I take her words and keep them in my mind to inspect later when I am alone. It is my turn to feel pity for Feliciano. He sees this, and his face reddens. I realize again how lucky I am to have a family. I realize now how hard it must have been for Feliciano to have none. Perhaps I might have made the same choices as he, if only to belong to something, to some kind of family. Something changes in my regard for him. It is not complete forgiveness, not yet, but it is as if a window has been opened. A small crack.

Feliciano has come to sit to my right. He has done so casually; no one has noticed but my mother, who looks from him, then to me, with teary eyes. He looks to his aunt pleadingly, and for the first time he addresses her with kindness. "Auntie, please, we must let Isabelle heal in her own time." His tone is not lost to the room. The others busy themselves to give us privacy.

"You are a good boy to watch out for her." Aling Ana regards him with pride.

"Yes, Feliciano. Thank you," Mama says to him.

"But, I didn't—" Feliciano begins.

Mama reaches out and places a hand on his shoulder and repeats, "Thank you for bringing my daughter back. No one else was able to do this." She keeps her eyes on him until he bows his head and accepts her gratitude.

There is rumbling outside, so strong that the ground shakes, and I try not to sob. I feel crazed, nervous. I turn my face automatically to Feliciano, and he puts his arm around me. Domingo stands. "An hour has passed. I shall go now in search of the children." He looks at Feliciano. "You will come with me. If this is some trick, I promise you, you will not live to see the next day."

Feliciano glances at me, then stands. He and Domingo lock eyes. "Let us go."

part 3

DOMINGO
MATAPANG

~ FELICIANO CLIMBS THE LADDER up to the house while I follow behind and stare at his exposed neck. The neck of a Japanese sympathizer. It would be so easy to wrap one arm around that neck and with the other hand slip my blade behind the collarbone to the heart. But he is the key to finding my son and the others. When we reach the door I glance one last time at that exposed skin and gesture for him to again walk before me.

"Thank you," he says under his breath, and opens the door.

My sarcasm is lost on him. I grab him roughly by the shoulder and turn him to face me. "Let us understand two things. If not for your knowledge of the Japanese encampments, I would kill you. If not for your rescue of Isabelle, I would kill you."

He clenches his teeth, turns, and begins to walk west, toward the direction of the cordillera mountain region. My body protests immediately at the pace. My mind spins from the hunger in my belly and the weight of my obligations. It screams for me to be at ten places at once. I am walking in a nightmare.

Hurry, my mind says. Quickly, to save my son, Taba, Alejandro, Roman, all innocents in this game of war—possibly, more than likely, dead. *Do not think that. Never think that.* I am ashamed at my failure to keep my son safe. I am a disappointment as a father. How I long to have him adore me the way he used to. Before Lorna's family poisoned him with their words. The connection is breaking between my son and me. The war has kept us apart. When in his presence I am awkward, a stranger; I do not know who is more terrified. I fumble to put away my rifle, my knives, to hide the wounds and bloodstains that make his eyes grow large. I feel the way I do the few times I have sat down to dinner with Lorna's family. It is a ridiculous feeling, being humbled by a six-year-old child. I feel like a leper when I hold him. I have nothing to offer.

I have become like my father, a vague figure in the life of my child. From the beginning I have not been worthy of my son. I knew it was only a matter of time before he looked down his nose at me like Lorna's family, yet my heart aches for his acceptance. I have wanted desperately for him to love me. My body screams for me to bring him home safe, to try to form a stronger bond with him. If nothing else, I can love him from a distance, the way I have my father.

My father . . . It is crazy, I know, to love a man who wishes me dead. But there it is, my secret. One that I will never admit to anyone. If only he knew the many times I could have ordered him killed. Could have killed him myself. Maybe he wonders at times how he escaped many patrols and attacks on his home, on his office. I wonder what he would think had he known my orders that he was not to be harmed. Would it have made him love me finally? A stupid game I play. A fantasy I hold. One that could come back to hurt me, for he is my enemy, and all true soldiers know you never let the enemy go once you have the opportunity. But the thought remains in the recesses of my mind. Though my father, like Feliciano, is a Japanese sympathizer, would he still be considered dangerous after the war? Or would it then be nothing more than a political preference? Would we then only be on opposite sides of a discussion table? Would I regret through eternity if I killed him, and the war and all its imaginary lines were to end tomorrow? I do not know. So he lives.

There is also Bartoy and Nina to think of. They are more like family to me. Bartoy is the son I would be proud to have. He has the passion and the hopes that I carry with me. And Nina Vargas? She has always been my dream. Never have I felt so accepted by a woman. It still feels new, that she belongs to me. I walk in wonder of her. Ahh, Nina's smile; to be in her warmth is to lie in the sun. How I long for the sun. I have no questions of morality. Morality has cheated me in many ways, so I take what I can. Yet here I am, far from them. I have many concerns: How to protect them? Whom to protect first? Whom to lead? When to rest?

Up above, the stars against the black are incredible. They outshine the sliver of a moon. *Does Nina see these same stars?* Feliciano leads me through the jungles, twisting and turning at a fast pace. He means to test me, but I know the jungles better than he can ever know. How else have I managed to outrun the Japanese raids and patrols? We travel this way for an hour. I study his every move. His eyes scan left to right, he pauses to listen to things I would not waste time with, then moves again. He grows tired at the pace he has started, while I keep up with him even in my injured state. He knows I too am watching, judging him. He does not know the extent of my hate. I fight at this moment not to kill him. I remind myself again that he is my only hope of finding Taba and the others.

I laugh inside at my situation. Who would have thought I would be walking beside a Makapili? If my group saw me now, they would not understand. I wonder at what would turn a Filipino into a Japanese sympathizer. What would it take to turn in your own countrymen and watch as they are tortured? We have similar upbringings, no family to turn to. But I have chosen to help our people, whereas he has sold his soul to the Japanese Imperial Army. I stop my thinking when I see he is studying me.

"Why not just ask me? I know you have been thinking about it," Feliciano says.

"What?" I ask.

"You have many questions about the Makapilis. You want to know what would make me a sympathizer. Perhaps you would ask if I have ever met your father, Senator Angelito Matapang." He asks this plainly, as if discussing the workings of a motorcar. His manner is casual. His arms swing confidently at his sides.

"I already know what it takes to join your ranks. It takes a coward, a traitor. It takes a person who wishes to be led, and not to lead. I have no questions about this. As for my father, do not bait me."

He continues to try me. "I have met your father. He is well respected within the Makapilis. He has many Japanese friends."

"Yes, and he will rot in hell with them."

"He denies you publicly to this day. But everyone knows you are his son. The resemblance is strong. You look more like him than his youngest child. Your half-brother favors his mother's side. Have you met your brother, Eladio?"

I stare at Feliciano. He swallows once.

"Why do you bear their name if you hate them so?" he asks defiantly.

"Why not? I wish for his important friends to know this. I am a stain he cannot wash away." I say these words with much bravado, but inside, inside the pain is rekindled. The same badge of shame I have carried since I was a young boy at the orphanage. At twelve I was adopted. I had mixed feelings. Hadn't I always wanted a family? My foster mother was told my real name, Matapang, yet she hid that name from me. I had always been told it was Legaspi. It was only later, something said in passing by the other kids. A joke, the word *bastard*, and then the confusion. *Your name is Matapang, like the well-known lawyer, very much like the lawyer's. Ask your mother.*

When I confronted her with the question, she caved in easily and gave me the identity of my father. She said it was nothing to be ashamed of, and I believed her. I believed her, and in turn I believed secretly something else. I believed she was wrong when she said my father would never acknowledge me. I thought she said it merely to keep the peace for him and his family. But I was wrong. On my eighteenth birthday I ran away from her and found myself on my father's doorstep. He was not a senator yet, just a lawyer, but he came from a wealthy family.

I remember walking up those stone steps and how my heart jumped when the door was opened and I saw my younger half-brother walk past the door in fine clothes. He was carrying a leather schoolbag. He was clean and well fed. There was happy chatter coming from the back rooms. Just a glimpse, but it was enough. I wanted that life. And when Mr. Matapang, my father, came to the door, I saw an older version of myself. There was no doubt we were blood related.

I revealed my identity to him, and the hate in his eyes was scorching, but even more painful was the love I had unconditionally built for him. It could not be undone in my heart, even when he denied me to my face. All the fantasies I had created around him were still there. I had built a make-believe world where he existed and searched and longed for my return, his eldest son. I have never let go of that image. It taunts me still.

Perhaps that was what I was thinking when I married Lorna. She came from a wealthy family. I thought to be closer to my father's circle in that way. I am ashamed to admit it even to myself. I should have known they too would react like him. An unwanted orphan, a bastard.

Feliciano continues with his rambling. "You even talk like him. The other week, he ordered the Reyes family taken in. I reminded him that these people were once his friends, and asked again if he was certain he wanted them brought in. He said, 'Why not? They are known guerrillas.'"

I smile at Feliciano. His talk has opened up a well of bitterness. I relish my words as they leave my mouth. "And you, you are like *your* father. Jamie Bautista." I watch his eyes narrow. I can see the anger burn in them. His hands are balled into fists. "Yes, I have seen your father, the drunk. The weakling who could not live without his woman. He walks our barrios like a ghost."

Feliciano stops; he takes his pistol from his holster and his hand shakes. "I will shoot anyone who compares me to him."

"Use it or put it away. I grow bored with your threats."

He continues to hold the gun toward me. His eyes are red.

"You are not going to cry, are you?" I scoff. "The man who would give his people to the enemy has feelings? The man who can watch our women being raped can also cry? You are very talented. Who knew you were capable of such feelings? Ah, but I see he is not a man at all, but a boy. A frightened, misguided boy who is very much like his father," I taunt him. I cannot resist. He holds the gun unsteadily now.

"I am not like my father. My father is weak. I am strong. The Japanese and the Makapilis bow to my words. He is defeated. I can never be. But I have already told you. I am done with the Makapilis. After I saw what they had done to the women, to Isabelle."

"It is late, I wish to find my son. It may be too late already. We must hurry."

He searches my face. For kindness, maybe, or understanding. He will find no compassion here. He begins to speak, then stops himself and looks up at the stars and takes a deep breath. "This way. I know of two encampments."

We turn up a ridge, leaving the flatlands and the waist-high cogon grass bending in the wind. We pass the sugar cane plantations, with the cordillera mountains far north in the distance. We climb alongside rice terraces, the ground soggy from the recent storms. The moon is a slice of lemon above us. White orchids freckled with coral and magenta bloom in abundance. I have walked this trail many times with my troops, sometimes at a full run, and long ago with my friends. Feliciano glances back to me. "I tell you the truth, whether you believe so or not. I am done with the Makapilis. I have turned my back on the Japanese. I see now what they have done to our people."

"I am here to rescue my son. I cannot grant you redemption. You have killed many of our people, maybe not with your own hands, but with your finger that has pointed to them and turned them over to the enemy. Does that not eat at your conscience?"

He stands strong at my words, his silence angering me more.

"You wish to impress Isabelle by rescuing her brother. And now that the Amerikanos are so close to winning, maybe you fear punishment. You think that siding with a guerrilla commander will win you leniency. You wish to change sides in the eleventh hour, but that cannot be done. I will not vouch for a traitor. Find some other fool."

His eyes flinch slightly, the jaw clenches a little, but that is all. There is intelligence and a fierceness in him that few of my men possess, but I am not swayed by it. He stares, blinking at me several times, then turns abruptly and begins walking once again. The crickets quiet as we pass, listening in the cloying heat, and then they sound loudly again. The whir of the mosquitoes is constant at my ears. And high in the trees an owl speculates out loud as we pass.

I hear a sound, a voice. I reach out for Feliciano. He turns to me with hope in his eyes. I put my finger to my mouth and purse my lips and point with them toward the shadow of trees. In our discussion we have almost missed a small encampment a hundred meters below us. There are tents and Japanese soldiers standing guard. I count four guards and six soldiers lying down. Feliciano crouches beside me. I watch him from the corners of my eyes, aware of the positioning of his hands and his gun. The soldiers talk easily among themselves. They trust that their guards are watching over them. The fools.

There is a grouping of captured Filipinos at one end, five of them seated against a tree with their hands tied behind their backs. They are blindfolded and badly beaten. A guard walks from behind the trees with a large stick. He questions one woman, and when he is not satisfied with her answer, he pulls her head back and hits her across the face with the stick. The woman's face is no longer a face at all, but a mound of purple flesh. The woman and her group belong to Ocampo's guerrillas. I can tell by the red woven wristbands they wear, their blood pledge against the Japanese. I grit my teeth at the sight. I fight the urge to shoot the woman and take her from her misery. I tell myself to go. Nothing can be done. We must go. I feel like weeping.

I see no sign of the children. I make a circular movement with my finger. We will move around the perimeter to make certain my son is not present. As we complete the circle, a Japanese guard stops to listen. He looks into the trees and calls out to a comrade. Soon they are all craning their necks into the darkness, their rifles at the ready. I look to Feliciano and point backward for us to go.

The words come out pained. "My son is not here."

"What of the captives?" he whispers.

I feel a tear in my soul when I speak the words. "Nothing more can be done for them. We must find my son." *Hold on, Taba. I will find you.*

He looks at me in surprise, then nods slowly in understanding.

WE TRAVEL ANOTHER hour in the same northwesterly direction. The wound in my leg expands and begins to throb with the heat of infection. We climb the side of a waterfall at a furious pace. The sound of rushing water is a balm to my soul. The water sprays the nearby rocks, making them slippery to our grasp. My throat constricts with thirst. I feel a fever starting in my bones, but I do not let Feliciano see this. Instead, I speed my stride, forcing the boy to move faster. He says nothing, but his shirt is stuck to his back from sweat and his breathing has become labored.

Feliciano's group, the Makapilis, keeps mainly to the flatlands, serving as eyes and ears to the Japanese army. They do not traverse the jungles as we do, so his conditioning is not good. He leads us to another encampment, but this time it is the Japanese themselves who warn us of their presence.

They speak loudly, and we hide in a thick cropping of brushes and ferns. The soldiers have grown weary this last year. They talk loudly among themselves in areas they know may house guerrillas. They hope for us to avoid one another. Unless they are a small patrol and we can pick off the stragglers, we let them pass. It is safer for us to let the bigger patrols by unless we are expecting them or we are forced to fight. We prefer to combat them in our own way, after we have studied their habits and have weighed the benefits to an attack. A direct assault can be more costly to our troops if open combat occurs. They are better equipped than we are. It is wiser to plot our raids and come in full force on smaller groups.

Feliciano looks around quickly and then whispers, "This is the only other encampment I know of. It is to grow larger in the coming days to go against Augustino's guerrillas."

I nod and scan the area with my eyes. This is Augustino's territory. I wonder if he knows of the Japanese strategy. I cannot worry about that now. Again, I am aware of Feliciano's proximity to me, of the positioning of his hands to his gun. I count five guards and two men seated in the center of a grove of papaya trees. The men are not regular foot soldiers. They are higher ranked. To our right is a large tent. To the left are metal slabs laid out on the ground. There are five bodies tied to the slabs, three adults and two children. They are laid flat, on their backs, with their hands outstretched as if they were on a cross.

"In the morning, the sun will heat the metal and they will cook to death," Feliciano explains.

"I know this," I tell him through clenched teeth. I see Alejandro immediately. He wears the same torn shirt and ragged trousers with the large belt around his waist. He looks dully at the stars. The fire has gone from his eyes. He is defeated. The sight of him brings my anger full to the surface. To the right of Alejandro is my son, Taba. He moves restlessly. I sigh and send a prayer of thanks that he is alive. The adults have been badly beaten. Roman Flores is among them.

"Wait here," I tell Feliciano.

He reaches out to stop me. "I have a plan."

I wait for his explanation.

"I know these men. The two in the middle are Majors Koiso and Matsura. They will recognize me immediately. I will take you in as prisoner. There is a high price for your head. Your likeness has been drawn, and Matsura carries a sketching in his pocket. You and the Amerikano Holden are highly prized. There is great honor in your capture. They would not plan to kill you until later. They would show you first to our Filipinos to break their spirits further. They would display you to their comrades as a trophy, before finishing you. It will buy us time. Later, while the soldiers sleep, I will untie you and we can rescue the others." He takes a piece of rope from his pocket and a mask and looks at me expectantly.

I laugh quietly. "Do you think I was born yesterday? I am no fool."

"We have only one gun. You must trust me."

"As Isabelle trusted you? A boy whose loyalties change with the wind?"

He keeps his eyes on me and slowly pulls the black Makapili mask over his face.

The sight of the mask unsettles me. It brings a riot of emotions to the surface. I feel my breathing come sharp and quick. I see his eyes through the slits still focused on me. Next he pulls out a white band and ties it around his arm, and still he watches me.

"You must trust me," he insists.

There is truth to his words. We are outnumbered, outgunned. I hold out my hands.

"No, they must be tied behind your back. I will tie them loosely."

"You think me crazy?"

"There is little time."

I take a deep breath and put my hands behind my back, and he begins to tie.

"Loosely," I grunt. When he is done, I look over my shoulder at him. "Let us not regret this. If this is a trick, I will not rest until you are found." I pause for a moment and swallow my pride. "If nothing else, Feliciano, save these three, they are innocent. My son is just a boy. Their lives are in your hands."

He nods, his attention already fixed on the soldiers. The soldiers listen at our approach. The officers stand and grab quickly for their guns. Feliciano bows and presses his gun into my back to urge me forward.

"Commanders, I bring you the guerrilla leader Domingo Matapang."

I jump at the sound of his voice beside me. My skin crawls at his words. I am a lamb to the slaughter. The commanders squint at Feliciano while the guards look anxiously at the surrounding jungle. Feliciano pulls off his mask, and the majors' faces relax in relief. The response alone turns my stomach. Their casual trust in him means many things. He has done much to win their loyalty, but at what cost?

I glance toward the prisoners. Roman Flores makes eye contact with me, and I raise my brows slightly. Alejandro cranes his neck to see. Taba watches with large eyes.

"Feliciano, excellent!" the one named Koiso exclaims. He studies me from head to foot. He calls the other commander, and the man takes a drawing from his pocket. Koiso slaps the paper with the back of his hand. "It is him. But how did you capture him? The general will be pleased."

"I was on my way back from the Villamar Hotel. He was injured. You see?" Feliciano lifts my shirt and points to the bandages along my side.

"But who has bandaged him?" Koiso asks suspiciously. He has a long straight nose. His eyes are small and close together.

"He was with his wife, but I killed her."

At his words, my son begins to cry. "I want my mama."

"Quiet!" Matsura shouts. He walks over to Taba and kicks him in the side. Taba loses consciousness. I grit my teeth so hard, I feel as if my jaw will break.

"You see?" the long-faced Koiso asks Matsura. "What did I tell you about Feliciano? He is loyal to our side. He has proven this many times." He turns to Feliciano. "You will be rewarded by the emperor."

Feliciano bows obediently. "I am honored."

"Place him with the other captives," Koiso orders.

We begin to walk toward Roman and the others. It is perfect.

"Wait," Matsura orders.

My blood pumps fast through my body. We stop.

"Yes, Commander?" Feliciano asks.

Matsura comes toward us. He walks pigeon-toed, his wide hips giving his thin frame a pear shape. His cigarette is stuffed in the corner of his mouth. He takes the lighted end and presses it to my neck. I grunt loudly in pain; the fury in me is almost uncontrollable, but I quench it. He takes a step back and kicks me in the stomach. I drop to my knees.

Matsura smiles proudly. "We have defeated you. With your father's help, we will defeat the Americans as well."

I force myself to bow my head. The burn to my neck is a hot dagger. The Japanese laugh among themselves in approval. Feliciano smiles and nods with them. I glare at him, but he refuses to look my way. He grabs my arm and leads me toward the others. He pushes me to the ground. My shoulder bears the brunt of the fall. Feliciano follows the commanders into the tent without a backward glance.

"Domingo," Roman whispers.

"If I cut you free, can you fight?" I ask Roman.

"I will fight," he answers.

"And the other prisoners?"

"They are near death. The children have not yet been harmed. Alejandro has been very quiet."

"As long as he still breathes."

"But how will you free yourself?"

Three guards approach and we bow our heads. The guards talk quietly among themselves and glance my way. They come for a closer inspection, and I avoid their eyes. They make a show of being unimpressed. With mouths turned down they walk to the middle of the encampment and ready their mats for sleep. I breathe a sigh. There are now only two active guards. One walks a smaller circle around our perimeter, seventy feet from us. The other walks counterclockwise in a larger circle. I wait. The larger circle takes the guard fifteen minutes to walk. The smaller circle takes the other guard ten minutes.

When they have passed, Roman asks his question again. "How will you untie yourself?"

"Feliciano is with us. He led me to this camp."

Roman frowns. "You trust him?"

"We shall see. I mean to take this guard. When he returns from his walk." We wait until the guards intersect again, and I begin to strain against my ties.

I turn toward the tent, and the sound of laughter rings out. The commanders laugh and joke easily with Feliciano. Their voices carry, pricking at my skin. Roman raises his head and looks toward the tent and shakes his head.

Koiso's voice is loud and jovial. His shadow moves, giant and godlike, before a lantern. "You have served us well, Feliciano. You are very brave to take this guerrilla commander on your own. He is said to be very deadly with the knife."

Feliciano's voice is thick with pride. "It was not difficult. The stories of him have grown as they have been passed on. He is just a man. Older than me, starved, with nothing but pride left. We fought, but it did not take much to subdue him. I convinced him that if I took him in as a prisoner, we could raid your camp."

Roman looks at me sharply.

Laughter bursts forward from the tent. "And he believed this? The fool." Koiso crows like a bird.

Matsura's shadow stands; it reaches for something, and he pours. "Drink, Feliciano. In honor of your prize. For days we have tried to track this guerrilla and you fool him with a few kind words."

I am struggling with my ties. They will not loosen. My breath comes quickly. I strain and twist, but the rope will not unravel. I try to quiet my anger.

"I will kill him," I curse. "Roman, there is a knife in my right boot."

Roman nods. He can barely move. He is lying on his back, on a slab of metal. The metal appears to be large pieces of a truck or airplane. His wrists are tied tightly and the ropes are staked to the ground. I put my foot near his hands, and he strains with his fingers.

"Tell me, how can we reward you?" Matsura voice booms. "Anything."

"I am humbled by your words, Commander," Feliciano answers. "But it is I who must serve you. As I have told you, I just returned from the Villamor Hotel, where I have selected ten beautiful Filipinas. They are on their way as we speak. That was how I ran into that fool Domingo."

Roman is unable to reach my knife, yet he continues to try. My ties are unbreakable. I wrestle with them furiously. One of the guards has returned. He notices our movement and walks toward us. He approaches and we stop moving.

"Water, please," Roman moans to him.

"Silence," the guard spits. He stands and watches us for some time, his hand on his rifle. I do not move. He walks around us and checks our ties. He is satisfied and resumes his patrol around the encampment.

Again the voices come from the tent. "I want only *dalagas*. The young girls are the best," Koiso tells Feliciano.

"The younger the better," Feliciano agrees, and they laugh loudly.

I think of Isabelle, and my body hurts with anger. "I will tear out his eyes," I tell Roman. We work furiously at our bindings. Their rejoicing urges me on. I am like a madman; my wrists burn as I saw my hands against the rope.

Two shots pierce the sound of their laughter, and immediately I scramble to sit up. I look at the other two captives lying beside us. The children are unharmed.

The three guards in the center wake and look around the area in confusion. Feliciano emerges from the tent behind them and fires six shots into the body of soldiers. Two guards fall, one fires back and races quickly into the darkness of trees. The guards walking the perimeter rush through the brushes, calling out to their comrades. Feliciano runs to us and slices my ties and Roman's. He hands me a Japanese Arisaka .25-caliber bolt-action rifle, with bayonet attached, and Roman a pistol reminiscent of a German Luger. The rifle weighs about ten pounds with the bayonet, but there is no time to detach the blade.

"Untie the others," Feliciano orders. "I will protect you."

As he says this, shots come flying past us in the dark. We duck and I crouch low and fire back as Roman unties the others. He unties the boys first. Alejandro looks around weakly. He can barely stand. My heart leaps as I approach my son. I hug him to me, and my soul feels healed. Taba is delirious with fear. He trembles visibly. But that is not what bothers me; what troubles me is that when I pick him up, he shoves my face away. "No, Papa. You are a killer. Grandfather said you murder people. I am frightened of you."

His words wound me more than any bullet. Lorna's parents have turned him against me. In my absence they have filled his head with terrible images. He fights feebly, his small hands pushing against my arms.

"Stop it." I shake him. "It is me, Papa."

"No!" Taba cries, in hysterics now.

Roman guides Alejandro by the arm. "Can you walk?"

"Jando . . ." I call him by his nickname and push the hair from his eyes. They seem to fade before me. He does not respond. "Give him water."

Roman hurries to one of the bodies and returns with a cantina. "It is sake, drink."

Alejandro takes the container with shaking hands and swallows slowly.

"You must go. Now," Feliciano orders. "Take the children. I will follow."

I reach out a hand to thank him.

"Go!" he shouts.

I try again to pick up my son, even though he protests. We struggle until Roman reaches out and stops me. He pleads with his eyes for me to understand, then bends down to gather my son. "Take Alejandro instead."

I nod and crouch down to place Alejandro on my back.

"The others?" I ask Roman.

He shakes his head. "They are too weak."

I glance back at Feliciano, crouching silently with his rifle aimed toward the darkness. The three remaining guards have positioned themselves behind a tree.

We move at a steady pace. Roman is beaten badly, yet we push ourselves, resting against rocks and trees. My head spins from hunger, and my chest tightens with pain. I feel my bones brittle and raw against my skin. We hike for hours in silence. I stop once to tend to Alejandro when his hands fall away from my neck. His eyes are flat and lifeless, frightening me. He responds slowly to my questions with a limp nod.

"Be strong, Alejandro," I say. "We are almost home."

We reach Bulacan at dawn, and the sounds of battle greets us in the distance with a series of mortar explosions that rumble the earth like thunder. When we enter the house, Alejandro is in bad shape. Aling Louisa and Isabelle run to meet us as we descend into the cellar. They take his listless form from my arms as they ask frantically for water. Louisa orders Roderick to give his brother the rest of his bowl of soup. Roderick does so immediately.

Isabelle reaches out a hand to help steady me as I descend. I nod to tell her that I am all right. She looks up expectantly and tries to hide the disappointment in her eyes when Roman steps down with Taba. She waits still.

"What of Feliciano?" she finally asks.

"He is coming," I tell her over my shoulder. "He was held back by soldiers."

"You left him?"

I have not the strength to fight with her. "Yes."

She bows her head and helps her mother, Aling Louisa, care for Alejandro.

"Help Roman," I instruct. "He was badly beaten." She hurries to Roman with apology in her eyes.

Lorna is speaking to me, but I do not hear a word. My body aches with exhaustion. I reach out for my son, but he sobs into his mother's chest.

"Shh, Taba. It is me, Daddy. I am here to protect you. I would never harm you."

"No," Taba says, and pushes me away with a feeble hand.

I look away to hide my embarrassment. Lorna sees this and touches my arm gently. She rushes to make things right.

"He has not seen you for some time, Domingo. It will take a while for him to become comfortable again. You are gone so often. *Na ninibago*," my wife says. He is getting reacquainted.

I nod and hug her to me. My poor Lorna. So easy for us to ignore our dwindling marriage. There has been no passion for so long now. Instead we have had a desperate agreement not to speak of it. We look down at our baby, and I brush the hair away from her face. Alma, created during a night of loneliness. Such a sad baby, she never speaks. How will Lorna feel when I tell her what she must already know? That I cannot stay. Will she feel relief? The urge to tell her now, to end the play we enact every time for each other's benefit, rises to my throat, but my body warns me that I have not the energy to do that now. I want to be present when we speak of it. I owe her that much.

I hate the thought of the smug expressions her family will have when she runs back to them. I wish to protect her always. I know they will be happy to have their daughter back, to marry her off to a more appropriate candidate. And I know, no matter how painful, that she will be better loved, happier. My children will be better cared for. This marriage has taken a toll on her. She has been ostracized from friends and family. I am not the person she had hoped I would be. And at times I see that her mind has been slowly poisoned by her parents. At times I see judgment in her eyes. During arguments their words have flown through her lips.

I thought we could bridge our social differences with care for each other, but it has not been enough. Still, I feel so protective toward her. The thought of letting go of this family pains me beyond words. I have failed again. I can no longer stand this pulling of my heart in every direction. One would think it would be an easy task with the passion Nina and I share. But they are separate things. Related, yes, but still separate. The pain of losing Lorna after all we have been through will still be tremendous. I value what little time we have left together. I touch her cheek with the backs of my knuckles. She smiles at me tenderly. There are unshed tears in her eyes. I know she can feel something gaining momentum, some oppressive wind hovering over us. Strange revelation, that the war is what keeps us together. I let Lorna strip me of my shirt. I can manage only a grunt or nod in answer to her questions. I close my eyes and my mind drifts to Nina. I pray that she is safe.

AN HOUR PASSES, maybe two; how long have I slept? I wake to see terror on Mang Selso's face. "Someone is walking upstairs," he whispers.

I reach for my rifle as the heavy clumping of feet moves above our heads. We sit tensely; the sound is just at the cellar door now. I stand.

"Roman," I whisper, remembering his pistol.

"I am ready," comes his answer.

The cellar door is thrown open and something slides down the ladder with a loud landing, followed by moaning.

"Where is the lantern?" Aling Louisa hisses.

A match is struck and the room fills with a golden glow. Feliciano lies in a crumpled heap on the ground. He is bleeding from the shoulder. His skin is an ash tone, he has lost much blood. Isabelle lets out a shout, and his aunt, Aling Ana, hurries to help him. They assist him to a corner and lay him down. Isabelle rushes to make a pillow for his head from her sweater. She tears an extra shirt to make bandages. Feliciano reaches out as she does this and takes her hand. Isabelle begins to cry. She throws her arms around him and sobs.

Mang Selso protests, "Put him upstairs in the house. The Japanese may follow him here. He will give them our names. We cannot have a sympathizer with us."

"This man has proven his worth ten times over you," I tell him.

Mang Selso is in a frenzy of fear. "The both of you should not be here. You must take Feliciano and go."

"Enough, Selso," Aling Louisa tells him calmly. "This is my house. Domingo and Feliciano will stay. They risked their lives to save my son. Everyone is welcome here. If you do not wish to be in their presence, then you should leave."

"Yes, they have earned their place," Aling Ana says. The others nod in agreement and step forward to help Feliciano with offerings of water or clean rags.

"Louisa . . ." Mang Selso tries a quieter tactic. "Louisa, I had to remain to protect the children, and who would care for my father?"

At his words, Tay Fredrico, the old Spaniard, chuckles. "My son, the coward." He shakes his head at Mang Selso.

Mang Selso's attention snaps to his father; he is instantly hurt by the stinging words.

"You came from my second wife. She was not very brave, bless her soul. If you had come from Divina, my first wife, what fierceness you would have had running through your veins. If my first son had lived, he would have been more like me. But he died prematurely, along with his mother. I wait now, only to join her in heaven."

Mang Selso's eyes are red. "How you weep over your lost son. He has become a hero in your mind. Always you give him praise, but none to me, the only son who looks after you."

"And why should I give you praise? Because you look after your aging father? All children should do so. You wish me to give you praise for wanting to turn out one of our own?" The old Spaniard points at me. "This man is the only one who fights for our cause, yet you would throw him out to save yourself."

A loud thumping above us interrupts their words. The latch is pulled open and Japanese soldiers peer down, bayonet first. "No one move, we throw grenade in. Show yourselves!"

We stand and hurry to the opening with our hands raised above our heads. There are many of them; I can hear their boots stomping above us. The soldiers come down the ladder, and I have the urge to pull the ladder down and make them fall. The first soldier jumps down the last few steps and his boots kick dirt into our food. He looks at us with no expression on his face, no soul in his eyes. He sees the radios and walks quickly up to the bigger one. "American sympathizers!" he announces to the rest of his men.

"No, no!" Aling Louisa shouts, grabbing his arm in panic. The soldier puts a bayonet to her throat, and Roderick embraces her. Isabelle begins to scream. My eyes fix on the gentle figure of Aling Louisa while Isabelle grabs fists full of her hair to keep from screaming.

"No!" I shout. I run forward to protect her, but a rifle is brought down on my head and I struggle to rise from my knees.

"It is mine." Roman steps forward. "I am a journalist for the *Manila Herald*," he explains, and pulls from his pocket an ID card stating that he is a journalist. He holds it as if it is some talisman that will save us all, but it is only a piece of paper.

"Everyone, on knees," the soldier says.

My terror is great now that the danger includes my loved ones. I want to weep at my carelessness. There is a reason I warn my men not to visit their homes, to not endanger their families. And now, now I have brought the danger to mine. I grow dizzy at the sight of the bayonets so close to Aling Louisa, to Lorna and the children.

Roman moves forward. "Do not hurt them. It is my radio."

I do not dare look at Feliciano, but they recognize him immediately.

"Feliciano Bautista—" A soldier points. "You have been playing both sides."

"No," Isabelle moans. The soldier puts a bayonet to his chest, and Feliciano says nothing. He stares at the soldier with anger. Another soldier stops the man from running the blade through. They speak in short sentences, and then Feliciano is pulled forward and shoved toward the ladder. Two soldiers escort him. We are herded outside.

"Domingo Matapang." The young Japanese commander eyes me with derision. "The fearless guerrilla leader." He walks quietly; his rubber shoes are split in the cloven design. His English is exceptional. "The rat that has been causing so much trouble. We shall have a special ceremony for you." He smiles to his comrades, and they grin.

I remain silent. The others blink under the glare of the gray sky. The clouds press overhead, filtering through a blinding white. They press hands over their brows like awnings to shade them from the intensity. I feel naked in the face of the weapons that surround us. Always I have fought far from the location of my family. Now, here I feel as if my bare feet sit tenuously beneath a suspended heel. I would lay my body down for any one of them, even Selso, but there is not enough of me to bargain with.

Alejandro leans with lifeless eyes on his mother's waist, while his right arm hangs tethered around his brother, Roderick, who supports him on the other side. I can see the desperation in Roderick's face. I can almost hear his thoughts. *Think of a plan,* his expression says. He looks to me, but I shake my head slightly. *Do nothing rash,* I say with my eyes. Roderick bows his head. Yet I continue his thinking. *What can be done? Is there any way? Could I escape and*

return with help? Would they punish them if I left? I cannot leave my son again.
Aling Louisa embraces her children to her. Isabelle stands beside her mother. Her body shakes visibly, while her gaze is fixed on Feliciano with great concern. She sees him held captive between two soldiers, their hands gripping him tightly under his arms. They have pried him with questions and bloodied his face, yet he wisely stares at the floor, refusing to acknowledge anyone for the soldiers' benefit.

Feliciano has proven himself a braver man than me. I could never admit my mistakes publicly. Yet here is this boy, without any guidance, willing to change sides, willing to weep for his errors, willing to love someone though she may hate him for eternity. My wife, Lorna, rocks our baby in her arms while our son, Taba, clings to her skirts. Does she think of her family, safe in the country? Does she regret waiting stubbornly for me so near to the city? I pity her. Her matted hair, her raised chin. So far from the life she could have had.

The soldier brings my thoughts back to the present. "No words from the one who has been delivering these?" He pulls a fistful of paper from his pockets and throws them at my face. The propaganda I have been circulating.

"Do you recognize these?" The commander picks one from the ground and reads it. The paper is dark with blood. "MacArthur's time will come. Be prepared."

I stare at him blankly.

"You shall take back your words." He shoves the paper in my mouth. I taste the dirt from the ground and the blood from the paper. He continues until I am choking.

"Ah, finally a sound from the great Domingo, the Filipino hero. But I see you are injured." He points to the wound on my shoulder and hammers it with the butt of his rifle. I drop to my knees with a muttered curse.

The Japanese looks at me with a tight smile. "Yes, we will have a grand reception for the hero." He swings his split-toed shoes back and into my stomach, furiously, until he is foaming at the mouth. My breath becomes lodged in my throat. Then he spits and walks away.

"Harboring a guerrilla is a crime!" he shouts, and pulls Aling Louisa down by her hair.

I cannot find my breath. I stay on hands and knees until I can get up slowly, but I do not dare to look at Lorna or our son. Few know that I have a family. Lorna knows not to embrace me. They separate us, the men from the women. The children to the front, so that no one dares to run. Yukino is dragged by her hair. Her daughter, Mica, is pulled from Isabelle, who cries out as her friend is taken away. The Japanese commander slaps Yukino and screams out in Japanese at Mica. Mica tries her best to answer, but she is more fluent in Tagalog than her natural language of Japanese. The commander repeats his question, and Mica begins to shake. Tears roll down her heart-shaped face.

"Disgusting. A Japanese who does not recognize her own language. How could you let this happen to your own daughter?" he asks Yukino. "She is a disgrace to the emperor."

Yukino answers plainly. "She was born here. I saw no reason to teach her Japanese when she would be surrounded daily by Filipinos. I thought it best that she learn Tagalog first, and be able to communicate with her classmates. We planned to live our lives here. It was a practical decision."

"It was a stupid decision. You wish to be Filipino? Then you will be treated as one."

A gray-haired soldier walks up to the commander. He talks in a low voice, and the commander stares at him incredulously, then slowly begins to laugh.

"My uncle, a lower-ranked officer, dares to challenge me. He asks that I show you some kindness. You see what this damned island has done to us? It has made him soft. Very well, Uncle, take care of your new toys." The commander gestures with a dismissing wave to Yukino and Mica. The uncle walks to Yukino. He helps her to stand, and then he helps Mica. The commander watches from his post at the front and shakes his head with disgust and amusement. To me he says, "Get in line, guerrilla. To the front. You have the place of honor." He laughs and the others join him.

As we wait, two of the soldiers light torches and Aling Louisa's house is set on fire. She screams, and the women hold her back. Isabelle and the children try to pull away. Something breaks within me when they do this. Uncontrollable rage fills me, and I break free and lunge to stop them. I manage to pull one of the torches from the entrance. I am hit again and again as I try to pull the torches from spreading fire.

"Carlito!" Aling Louisa cries for her absent husband. "Please. Do not burn our house. He will think us dead! Domingo! Make them stop."

"Please . . ." Aling Ana pushes a bayonet away, and it is brought back with pressure on her belly. But still I hear her plead, "Please, spare the house. It is all we have."

Roman tries to tackle a soldier, and he is rewarded with a blow to his nose. Still he fights. It is as if the house is our last hope, the last proof of our existence. I refuse to be pulled away. It is only with more kicks and the use of the rifle like a hammer against my shoulder that I relinquish my fight to stop the fire. Mang Pedro and the others step forward timidly, and bayonets are pressed against them to force them away. New torches are lit and thrown on the house. There is no hope now. We have become homeless. The others weep silently. This house that has kept us all from the enemy takes quickly to the flames. The windows shatter and the flames reach the interior. The wooden beams creak as they fall from the rooftops. I imagine the entire house crumbling into the cellar. The sound of the fire is like a strong wind blowing hot against our faces. Roderick and Alejandro stare mechanically at the house. What happens to people who have no homes? I ask myself. *They die,* the wind seems to whisper.

Finally, we are forced back into the line by the commander and ordered to march. Our eyes cling sadly to the burning structure that once protected us. We head southeast, back to Manila. The hunger pains are constant and painful. We pick up other Filipinos along the way. It is the same drill: the people are ushered out and bullied, and their houses are set on fire. The faces of the people are identical, blank, hopeless. It is a strange sight, children who do not utter one word. It is as if a great spell has been cast and the souls of our people have been sucked away. I want to shake the children and urge them forward. *Run, find your voices again. Do whatever it takes, but do not give up.* I search in vain with every step for a way to flee, but every plan ends with, *They would punish the others.* I must wait, bide my time. There will be an opportunity. I need only keep my eyes open.

Back to Manila. A caravan of walking skeletons. After an hour some of the women begin to fall. The men keep walking. When someone does not get up, the soldiers prod them with the points of their blades. Those without kin are not helped by the others. Those who fall are stabbed. They do not cry out, and no one speaks. It has become dog eat dog.

The sun bludgeons us with its heat, and the dust from the road infiltrates the eyes, the mouth, the nose. Tay Fredrico, the old Spaniard, begins to sway before me. He is nearly seventy-five years old. His legs bow out, but he catches himself. By force of will he walks a few meters. I keep my eyes on his frail form. The soldiers watch him closely. When he stops and brings a hand to his chest, I take his arm and place it around my neck. His added weight takes the breath from me. The soldiers watch, unsure if they will allow this. They take drinks from their cantinas. Roman moves to help us, but I warn him away with my eyes. We walk on through the night, when we reach the outer section of Manila. It is dawn when we cross one of the few remaining bridges over the Pasig River.

We have entered hell. The smell of decaying bodies in the tropical heat suffocates us. The others weep at the sight. Our city is unrecognizable. The

Amerikanos have set up the heavy artillery. They crouch among the decapitated trees and the rubble of ancient Spanish churches. There are snipers in every tower. The concussion of the explosions threatens to bleed the ears and bring us to our knees. We are paralyzed by the sound. Another shrill whistle, and Mang Selso shoves his wife aside so that he can take cover. We dive forward. A loud explosion encompasses the area, and the ground shakes and shudders in contractions. Hard pieces of rock and earth are thrown about, scratching our faces and arms, landing on our heads. The rattle of rifle fire brings us to attention.

"Up, stand up!" the Japanese soldiers scream, kicking the people.

No sooner do we stand than tier upon tier of the Amerikano bombers and the older P-40 fighters strafe the ground. The *thud, thud* of the bullets as they cut through the Japanese and stray civilians causes the people to scream and flee. They are chased down by the soldiers and brought back.

Several Japanese Zeros rise over Manila Bay, and a dogfight ensues. The planes dive and swoop like metal birds. The Zeros are superior planes to the Amerikano P-40s. They are light and fast climbers. They dance the P-40s into confusion. The Zeros turn easily, appearing at the Amerikanos' tails with guns fixed. The P-40s are good only for climbing to higher altitudes, choosing their shots, and then hurrying out. But the Zeros are distracted. They rush to protect their machine-gun emplacements and their antiaircraft guns as the Amerikanos climb away from them. A Zero is hit and the pilot dives without a parachute. His plane unravels behind him in a trail of smoke. The people look around for cover, thinking that the plane is heading for them. It always appears this way. But the plane falls farther out and explodes into shards of metal.

Then come the newer P-38 fighters, escorting Amerikano B-24 liberation bombers with the Western stars on their sides and their bellies ripe; they let drop five hundred pounds with each bomb, and the Japanese evacuate their pillboxes, the low-roofed emplacements they have created to house their anti-tank guns. A Zero pilot retaliates by sacrificing his own life as he heads for the Amerikano howitzers lined across the way. The explosions are horrendous. Our beautiful city has fallen.

"Go, Joe!" Roderick shouts, cheering on the Amerikanos. Alejandro tries to quiet his brother, but it is too late. The Japanese commander's face twists, and he backhands Roderick. The boy falls to the ground, and before they can kick him, Aling Louisa grabs her son and spanks him harshly. The commander is satisfied for the moment.

It is as I have predicted. The Japanese admiral Iwabuchi has disobeyed the Japanese commander Yamashita's declaration of an open city. It is no surprise.

They ignored it when MacArthur announced an open city three years ago. They will follow their suicide resistance against the Amerikanos. Downtown Manila is smoldering. Three-fourths of the factories have been devastated; the entire business district is destroyed. Iwabuchi would rather demolish the buildings than let them fall to the enemy. The problem is that they consider all Filipinos enemies now along with the Amerikanos.

What remains of the long narrow streets is perfect for rifle fire. Amerikano soldiers take advantage of this and set up tripod machine guns to welcome the enemy. The most dreadful is the sight of babies on the roadside, green and stiff, clumped together like hardened *pili* nuts. Their tiny bodies have been ravaged by the animals. The city floor is pockmarked from the battle, and the remaining trees wear bullet-riddled leaves.

More booms, like an ongoing earthquake, take the balance from our legs, and we crouch with our arms over our heads. The women and men scream, echoing similar voices in the distance. Then eerily it quiets, with only the smell of the smoke and the sounds of the unceasing rifle fire. We get up slowly and look around. Mang Selso, the coward, is the only one left crouching beside a tree. His wife will not look at him.

Aling Louisa approaches. "Selso, get up. It has passed," she says to him, coaxing, the way she would to one of her children.

"Women to one side," a soldier orders.

I step forward and offer Selso my hand.

He takes it, blinking up at me, bewildered, and stammers, "It w-was so loud. So loud."

We hurry down Taft Avenue, and the post office with its Roman columns is a stone skeleton. We veer right onto Padre Burgos, and there is the legislative building, crippled and leaning precariously to its left. Intramuros is to our right; the walled city is a house of fallen cards, leveled to the ground, smooth like a chess board. We turn left as we pass the palatial Manila Hotel, with General MacArthur's arched penthouse windows, still standing for now. The red-and-white poolside umbrellas lie on their sides. I wonder what the Mac will think when he sees that the Hapons have taken possession of his rooms and his family library. We pass through the old *luneta* onto Dewey Boulevard. *Karatellas* and horses are toppled to their sides in a scattered mess of wheels and hooves.

Bodies lie on the streets, throats slashed, limbs missing, decapitated, though some are alive and crying out in a delirium. A corpse lies facedown, his hands tied behind his back. I watch Aling Louisa, her eyes searching in horror for her husband, Mang Carlito. My heart twists in pain for her and for our people.

"Alejandro, Roderick, do not look. Look straight." Aling Louisa puts a hand in front of their eyes.

A soldier pushes her away. "Women not walk with men." He urges Alejandro over to us, and Alejandro stumbles, his eyes in shock. There is too much to see and hear. The sight of the crumbled villas, the sounds of the tanks as they crush the ground, with the high whine of metal churning against metal and sniper fire, sporadic and deadly amid the thick cloud of smoke, consumes us all at once.

We are ushered with many shouts toward the Ermita district, to the Villamar Hotel, which to my amazement is still standing. At the sight of the hotel, Isabelle's face contorts. Aling Louisa embraces her. "Be strong, Isabelle. We will survive this." Isabelle nods, but Aling Louisa is not satisfied. "Tell me."

"We will survive this," Isabelle says, and I see a resolve form in her face.

We run pass the steps of the General Hospital and are hurried through the rubble into a nearby warehouse. Inside, the stench of sweat, feces, and dysentery assaults us. Hundreds of Filipinos are milling about with hungry looks on their faces. Old men and women lie on the concrete floor without mats or blankets. Their feeble bones press against the ground. The mosquitoes feast on the soft wrinkles of their skin, but they are too weak to fan the creatures away. I think of the malaria and dengue diseases the insects carry.

We find a spot in the corner and try to collapse to the ground, but the people do not make room; we sit with a leg shoved against theirs until they slowly give space.

"They have brought us here to die," Aling Ana declares.

I am surprised at the number of Japanese soldiers. "There are only fifteen, maybe twenty at best. There are over a hundred of us. We could overtake them," I tell Roman.

He is skeptical. "I am game, but the others . . . I do not know."

Mang Pedro looks to the soldiers. "Now is not the time. I do not need my visions to tell you that."

Mang Selso shakes his head sadly. "Do you see how much I weigh? I can barely lift my little finger. What will we use for weapons? How will we block their bullets, by putting the women before us? Some of us wish to live."

"I will take my family and whoever wishes to come."

Lorna carries our baby in her arms. She looks at me sadly. "*Pagod na ako,*" she says. "I am tired, Domingo. I will not put the children in more danger. Where will we run? To your caves? If they find us, they will chop our heads. My family stays here."

"I will follow you, Domingo." Alejandro stands, swaying. It is the first he has spoken since his rescue. I am unsure if he is delirious. I motion for him to sit down.

I want to pull my hair in frustration at their surrender. I cannot believe what they are saying. "I tell you all, if you cannot overcome your fear of these *demonios*, we are defeated."

"We are already defeated," Mang Selso answers, his eyes downcast.

Aling Louisa looks at me. "Domingo, we are too weak."

My heart sinks at her words. Am I the only one willing to fight? I see for the first time their faces as a whole, their exhausted look of surrender. So tired, they are willing to die here or, worse, pretend they will not. My son lies asleep, his head against his mother. I saved him from one prison only to bring him to a larger one. I should have hid him in a cave. I should have stolen them all away from that cellar. We stayed there too long. There were so many hideaways I could have taken them to. If only I could have believed for one second they would follow. But instead it has taken this for us to leave the house as a group. We will die here. I must find a way out.

The room has a series of chalkboards. On one of the boards, there are the words *MacArthur is coming*. I am surprised to find no one has erased it until I see the mark of several bullet holes against the wall and a large splattering of dried blood.

The commander who accompanied us goes up to a small Japanese man walking the perimeter of the room and holding a notepad. The commander points to our group, then specifically to me. They drag Feliciano out of the main room as Isabelle sobs hysterically.

"Separate them," the man with the notepad instructs.

The soldier bows and points a finger to me and the rest of the men. He indicates we are supposed to sit with the other men across the room.

I can feel Lorna watching, willing me to look at her as I walk across the room.

The commander is called away by another officer. The matter seems urgent, for he glances at us, barks a few orders at his soldiers, and then runs off to follow the other officer.

A man beside me snickers. "Not enough, their time has come. They do not have enough men to watch over us and to fight the Amerikanos. The Joes are giving them hell."

Someone comes to sit beside me. It is Lorna, and I look at her as if she's gone mad. "What are you doing? Go back. Have you lost your senses?"

"Yes," she says with great desperation. "I do not care whether I live or die.

I know you search for an opportunity to escape. You must choose now. Choose this family that needs you or that jungle life that you treasure so much."

"Lorna, please go back to your side," Mang Selso says softly. "You put us in danger." This gives Lorna pause, for Mang Selso is never one to ask. It is more common for him to complain or give orders.

"Domingo, I am your wife. Look at your children. You have not even acknowledged your son."

"This is not the time," I tell her.

"When, then? If we survive this? When will I see you? In hell?"

"Stop it," I tell her.

"I will not have you go back to those people." She grabs my arm, and I pry her fingers from me. "Let them lead themselves. Your family needs you, yet your love is with them. Which is more important, Domingo? We are the obligation."

"You embarrass us. Go back to your side," I tell her.

"I embarrass you? Damn you. You took me from a good life, and I followed you into this inferno, and you decide I am no longer the prize."

"Lorna."

"I tell you this, Domingo Matapang. Leave this family and you will not come back. Do you understand?"

"I understand," I answer.

She returns to the women and crumples to tears. Aling Louisa holds her as she cries. Isabelle eyes me with quiet accusation.

Tay Fredrico, Mang Selso's father, frowns. "A bad match. She is not for you," the old Spaniard announces.

Mang Pedro looks at me. "Domingo, she is right."

"There are other things to consider," I tell him.

"Domingo," Mang Pedro repeats, "do not forget what it is you fight for."

I look at him sadly. "How can I forget? I am the only one fighting."

He is not easily daunted. "When there is no more family, what else is there? Heed my words. Leave this obsession to be a guerrilla. It will only end in death. It is vanity that calls to you. Do you truly believe you can lead a hundred men to go against the Japanese, when the Amerikanos with all their power could not defend us three years ago? Lay this stubbornness to rest. It will only bring you death. Your place is here, with your wife and children. What else is there?"

What else? I ask myself. I feel his words deeply. I am torn between wanting to stay and needing to go. Or is it the opposite? I look at my son with his head cradled in his mother's lap, while our daughter slumbers in her arms.

Yes, what else? I think of Nina Vargas. Nina with her pistol hanging from her hip. I think of my men eager to fight, waiting for directions, yet here, it seems as if the people would rather lie down and die. They have lost their will to fight, so I must do it for them. How I wish I could protect them all. Don't they know that their refusal to fight means that more will die?

Alejandro reaches out for his brother and places his arm around Roderick's shoulder. Roman studies the people around us.

"Domingo, do you hear what I am saying to you?" Mang Pedro insists.

"I hear your words. You remind me of how much I value this family. I would rather die than lose them. But I have other obligations. There is more at stake here than just my simple life and those that I love. More will die if I remain. But perhaps there may be a way to save us all."

My words have softened the faces of the others. Isabelle leans under the crook of her mother's arms, her other hand entwined with that of Mica, who also sits embraced by Mrs. Yoshi.

"Yes, we must be thankful that we are all together. And we must believe that there is a reason we are still alive," Aling Louisa says. "Family is important above all else." The others agree with her. I am torn. I feel like a criminal for having others to worry about, others who are not my family but have become just as close to me.

We wait another hour in silence as more people are brought in. Our bodies grow used to the shaking and rumbling outside. At times it feels as if the battle grows cold, but then a loud explosion reminds us that we are in the midst of it all.

Mang Pedro chooses this moment to say again what he feels deeply.

"Domingo, your family needs you. Let me explain why I feel strongly that you must stay with them. I had a family once too that loved me. But I made a mistake. I was lured away by other things. When I realized they were what mattered, it was already too late."

~ the twilight people

WHEN I WAS A YOUNG MAN, our family was not considered the lowest rung on the ladder. We were the dirt, below the lowest step. But within our village my family was well respected because of my special gifts. I was born under a red harvest moon, with the birthing sack still covering me. If the sack is buried immediately under a chosen place, revealed to the mother in her dreams, the infant will inherit certain gifts. I had the gift of sight, of seeing those beings that others cannot. I could see the twilight people.

We lived in the Visayans, in a village in northwest Samar. The houses were all the same, made of palm leaves and bamboo. All were raised on six-foot stilts to allow the ocean to rush under without washing away the houses. They were known as *bahay kubos*, "straw houses." I called them feather houses, because they were so fragile that they threatened constantly to blow away with the wind.

In between each dwelling, coconut trees sprouted, inhabited by lime green parrots, chattering mynah birds, and the red-hornbilled bee eaters. The large branches cast shadows on my face at noon. Our farthest neighbors were a few feet away; the nearest ones, an arm's length. The houses were so flimsy that during the tempestuous monsoons, our father ran around with palm leaves, patching the holes carved in by the strong gales. The winds were so forceful that the purple salamanders crawling upside down on the ceiling lost their footing and fell kamikaze onto our beds at night.

Every evening, during high tide, the water came through our floorboards and floated our slippers away. I woke shivering and barefoot in the mornings, searching for my thong *tsinelas*. I found them at the end of our short hallway, holding congregation with the other slippers.

My LIFE WAS seeking every conceivable type of employment. The most perilous was collecting bird's eggs in limestone caves where *salangana* bird's nests were perched sixty feet high, above crystal clear waters and coral reefs, with nothing but crevices to cling to. The eggs were a delicacy, and the saliva from the young was considered a cure for certain illnesses. *Salanganas* are the chief ingredient in bird's nest soup and were considered an aphrodisiac by our Chinese residents. The work paid handsomely. My father and I were very talented at finding such caves, but I tried my best to keep him from this; he was growing too old for such climbing. I worked as many jobs as I could to help my parents put rice on the table for my sister, Addie, and me.

Adeline, my sister, was only a year younger than me, twenty-four. She had developed a rare type of cataract in her left eye. We did not have the money to take her to a real doctor, so my father allowed the people at the nearby clinic to operate on her for free, to further their studies. They told him that they could take the nerve from her good eye and attach it to the bad in order to regenerate it. The result was that she became completely blind.

But let me tell you about my visions. I could see the spirits and other beings, just as I see you before me now. I could see the old man who used to live across from our house. He had been dead for weeks, but I saw him follow the same ritual each morning, as if he were still alive. He opened his door, walked to the end of the path, and looked out into the gray ocean, with his fishing spear over his shoulder. He still did this after his death, but I was the only one who could see him.

I could walk into a house and see the anger that hovered in the air from a fight, in the form of a sneering woman with a pale face. I was gifted, the old people said. But I thought otherwise. I did not want to see these things. It was troublesome to sit in a room full of people and not shout when a spirit came to stand in front of me or ran its fingers through my hair. A neighbor once took me to a gambling establishment in hopes that my talent extended to reading cards, but it did not.

There is more. In the forest behind our house I could see little people, no taller than my ankles. They never said a word, but they watched me with their eyes. I walked through the forest and whispered, "Excuse me, pardon me," so as not to disturb them. They were called *duendes,* elves. It was in that same forest that I became friends with Diagos, a powerful creature known as a *tikbalang.* But of him, I shall save for last.

The forest was not as it is now, sheared in some places to allow for telephone poles. Back then it was a magical place; even the texture of the air was different, like inhaling nectar, and when someone called your name, you could not be sure it was someone with two arms and two legs. No, you could not be certain at all.

I WAS TWENTY-FIVE, already an old man. Most of my schoolmates had married at eighteen. People asked what I was waiting for. I told them that I was waiting for the right time. But truthfully, I could not bring myself to be so selfish. Who would watch over my parents and Addie? They could not survive without my contributions.

Because of my gift of sight, our house was always busy. People came to our house for all spiritual questions. It was no different the morning of Todos los Santos, All Souls' Day.

I opened one eye to see my mother standing over me with our neighbor Mang Cristobal as I lay on my *baníg* shivering. The floor mat sucked in the cold from the outside, and it was difficult to stay warm.

"*Anák, anák . . .*" She still called me "child." "Are you awake now?"

"What is it, Ma?" I asked, pulling my blanket out from under Mang Cristobal's slipper, where his big toe with its yellow nail gawked at me.

"It is Aling Sally. She is having trouble breathing."

"Then she should go to the clinic." I threw an arm over my eyes in irritation.

"No, Ped, it is Abner, he is torturing her. You must ask him to leave."

Abner was Aling Sally's son-in-law, whom she had nagged constantly until his death a week before in a boating accident. His little *bangkâ* turned over in rough waters, and he was pinned beneath and drowned.

"How does she know it is Abner?" I asked, getting up. There would be no sleep for me. My mind was already awake, and my mother did not have the heart to send people away.

"The house smells like his cigarettes," Mang Cristobal explained in a whisper.

I sighed and put on my shirt. Abner had always told me he would pester the old woman if he died first. She had never forgiven him when his wife, her daughter, had died in childbirth.

WHEN WE ARRIVED at their house, there was a large gathering of neighbors.

Mang Cristobal sniffed the air. "Not yet, not yet. Soon you will smell the smoke. Wait, just wait." He held up his hand, motioning for me to be still.

I did not need to wait. I could smell the smoke the minute I entered. The moment the door opened it rolled out like fog, but I was the only one who could see it. I followed the scent to Aling Sally's room, where she lay on the bed, gasping for breath.

It took all my strength not to laugh, for there was Abner's spirit smoking a large cigar, but that was not all. He was sitting cross-legged on top of Aling Sally's chest.

"Is he here? Do you see him?" Mang Cristobal held out a shaking crucifix before him.

"Leave us," I said. The spirits did not talk with too many people in the room. It disturbed their energy. It did not take much to encourage Mang Cristobal. He and my mother hurried out.

"Pedro, help me. I feel he is strangling me," Aling Sally pleaded.

"No, he is not strangling you," I assured her. "Abner, what are you doing?" His spirit sighed and gave me a smirk. "I am going to take her with me."

"Ay, he is here," Aling Sally began to moan. "I can smell his cigarettes now."

That was how it was when a spirit spoke; their presence gave out a familiar scent.

"Shut up, old hag." Abner took a deep breath and blew into her face.

Aling Sally coughed hysterically.

"*Hoy*, Abner." I shook my head.

Aling Sally's eyes grew large. "What is he saying? Does he wish to kill me?"

"No, he would not wish that."

"Yes, I wish that." Abner nodded. "Truly I wish to kill her."

"That will only get you a ticket to the wrong side, my friend." I tried to hide my laughter. I knew Abner too well. He was a good man, and the guilt of his wife's death had weighed heavily on him when he was alive, for he had loved her very much. Aling Sally's accusations had only added to the pain.

"I knew they would send for you, Ped. My God, you should have seen the fish I had before I drowned. *Dios ko*, it was tremendous," Abner said, and whistled.

I smiled at him.

"Why are you smiling?" Aling Sally gasped. "He has possessed you."

"Shut up. Smoke some more, witch, choke some more." Abner blew another cloud at her.

"Ab," I said, "come now. This is really too much."

"You see what I had to live with? I cannot believe that my sweet Carmella came from that." He looked down at his mother-in-law with great disgust. He was quiet; he looked a little embarrassed. "What do you do now, Ped? Remember how many times I begged to come along with you? And now here I am, the spirit you wish to chase out."

"I remember, my friend. There is nothing to this, really. I simply ask that you leave this dwelling place."

"And then? There are no prayers?"

"None," I told him. "But your soul has heard the request. It will know what to do."

"My God, I feel it, Ped. This is a frightful thing. I feel I am being sucked out of the room. Where do I go now?"

"Go with God," I told him. "There will be guides. Rest now. You are riding on a current." He sighed, and I felt his presence leave the room.

WHEN I OPENED the door, my mother and Mang Cristobal looked ready to flee.

"Well?" she asked.

"It is done. He will trouble her no more."

My mother lifted her chin proudly. "You see? What did I tell you about my son?"

Mang Cristobal peered into the room and was reassured by his wife. "I feel like walking now," Aling Sally announced.

We left with a sack of rice, our payment.

AFTER ALING SALLY'S, I fetched my lantern and went straight to the caves, where I risked my neck for a fifty-foot nest buried deep in a crevice. Afterward I went to the market to sell my find.

Our neighbor, Pidring Bonifacio, hurried to my stand, leading Addie by the hand. "Pedro, when will you be done here? Do not forget tonight is Todos los Santos. Have you forgotten our plans? People are already at the cemetery."

"Eight more to sell and we can go."

"But Addie has been waiting all day," Pidring complained. He liked to use my sister as leverage.

"Not that long, *kuya*." She smiled in my direction. I would do anything to make her smile. It pained me to think of her sitting by herself at home, in the dark. She was never more than two steps away from me.

Pidring lived in the house beside ours. He was my best friend, as good as a brother.

"All day, ha?" I studied Addie. Her face was rosy from running with Pidring. I had had a good day. I had sold twice my usual and still had eight eggs to sell.

"How much for four? I give you one peso." A customer waved several coins under my nose.

I looked at Addie, bent over and adjusting the broken strap on her sandal. She had tied it into a knot. "Four pesos and you can have all eight," I announced.

The man felt the uneven stubbles on his chin. They sprouted unbecomingly, like weak trees planted on bad soil. My offer was more than generous.

"Three," the man bargained. He could sense my anxiousness to leave.

I snorted and looked at Pidring.

"Let him have it, Pedro. I will give you the other peso," Pidring said in frustration.

"Done." I scowled and spread out a newspaper to wrap the eggs in. Addie clapped her hands in excitement.

We watched as the man left. "Where is the other peso?" I asked Pidring knowingly.

He shrugged sheepishly. "Pedro, you know better than to listen to me. Where would I get an extra peso?"

I nudged him in the head and took my sister's hand. We hurried to catch a *kalesa* ride to San Isidro.

We arrived in San Isidro just as the sun was setting. The sky around the sun was a halo of purple and pink, lavender and blue. Perfect clouds freckled the horizon like a stream of pebbles. Once we reached the hillside overlooking the cemetery, Pidring and I exclaimed at the sight below our feet. The graveyard was full of the living.

"There are candles twinkling on every gravestone, like fallen stars," I told Addie. "Blankets are laid out on top of each mound, with food, and people sitting and chatting to one another."

"And the women? What are they wearing?" she asked breathlessly.

"Yellow dresses, Maria Clara dresses, some with black lace on their heads, some white. Mostly everyone has a banana leaf for a hat, and they are wearing cowhide for shoes."

"You beast." Addie hit me playfully.

"They are not as pretty as my sister." I rubbed her back. I did not have the heart to tell her the fine clothing everyone wore. The people of that town were very well-to-do. The three of us were used cigarette stubs in a box of fine cigars.

"Tell me the truth." Addie pulled my arm. "Pidring," she insisted.

"Nothing very special about them, Addie," he answered. "What is lovely is the entryway, shall I tell you?" He threw his arm around her.

"Yes, yes." She elbowed us playfully.

"There are two very big stone angels at the entrance. There are many families. The men are dressed in *barongs*. How can they stand the long sleeves in this infernal heat? Some are wearing Western hats with a wide band of ribbon and a single feather attached. Almost every marker is blanketed with food, as if in a picnic. People are strolling about, visiting with neighbors, talking about the dead."

She frowned. "I am not deaf."

"The stones are different sizes. Some are oblong, others are short and square. There are wreaths, sweetcakes on the blankets. Small glasses of wine are left out for the dead."

"Do they not bother the spirits with such a display?" Addie asked as we walked down into the graveyard.

"The spirits know to stay away when there are too many people," *unless it is their dwelling place or they are stuck and cursed,* I added sheepishly in my own mind.

"Do not encourage her, Ped. It will give her nightmares again," Pidring said.

He was the only one in the village who did not believe any of my much talked of gifts. If it brings you an extra meal on the table, he would say with a shrug. Lost souls, he called the people who asked for my help. I could be ordinary with him, and I was thankful for it.

I looked around. It was difficult to relax. My skin was tingling and being pulled in every direction. There were spirits seated in between each family. They studied me as I walked by. A man floated beside his young widow. He tipped his hat as they passed. Others were not as nice. "Leave us. This is our home," they hissed.

To the right a woman sat with a basket of sweet rolls that kept tipping over when there was no wind. She trembled as the spirit of her jealous sister continued to interrupt her prayers.

"Stop that," I said below my breath. "Can you not see she is trying to apologize?" The specter crossed her arms and pouted at me.

Pidring tapped me on the shoulder and nodded to a group of young women sitting in front of the steps of a large mausoleum. I felt my legs grow hot. Their dresses fit their breasts to perfection. The shorter lengths exposed their tender ankles.

"How wonderfully indecent," Pidring said, grinning.

I shook my head, embarrassed by his loudness.

"What, what is it?" Addie asked with a knowing smile.

"Pidring wishes to make fools of us."

"It will be perfect, Ped," Pidring insisted. "If we could get them to walk down the road . . ." He laughed and clapped his hands.

We had set up a prank the night before, as we did each year on All Souls' Day. I had been hesitant to play one this year, because Addie had asked to come along. Sometimes our pranks got us into fistfights, sometimes not, but there was always a certain amount of running involved each time. The family he was pointing to were the Villanuevas, the wealthiest in San Isidro. The father owned many acres of land. He had four daughters and no sons. I glanced at the gravesite. There was no sign of the father, only three of the girls and the grandfather.

I made a face. "Not that family. Pick another, Pidring. Do you wish to see us thrown in jail? The father is great friends with the constabulary. Those girls are—" I turned and saw the fourth sister standing behind Pidring with her arms crossed.

"Socorra." I nodded in greeting. She had a doll's face. She was small; with high heels she barely reached Addie's height. Her hair was pulled up into a simple knot, emphasizing her brown eyes. The hair on the corners of her brow were baby fine. She brushed away a few loose tendrils with a gloved hand, then pulled off the gloves in irritation and smoothed back her hair.

"Finish your sentence. Those girls are what?" she demanded.

Socorra's voice startled Addie, who squeezed my hand and began to shuffle her foot one on top of the other, back and forth. I was speechless. I was mesmerized by her first-class clothing, the richness of her blue traveling suit, the matching Western hat with a small veil and pin. I was a roach crawling near her fineness.

"That is a lovely fragrance you are wearing," Addie murmured. I closed my eyes and inhaled. She was strawberries and almonds.

She ignored Addie's compliment and looked us up and down with contempt. I am ashamed to say I was impressed by her airs. She fascinated me. She reeked of authority.

"Let me finish your sentence for you. Those girls are beautiful, above us, educated. Shall I continue?" Socorra asked, lifting her chin at me.

"Yes, all of the above, lovely lady." I laughed nervously.

She rolled her eyes in disgust and walked past us.

I stood rooted to the spot. I studied her every movement, her back straight as a ballerina's, the way she stopped and turned her head to survey the others.

"Who is that you were speaking to?" Socorra's grandfather demanded. "Your father would be angry to see you speak with strangers. Our servants are better dressed than they."

I heard Addie's intake of breath. "Who is he speaking of? Does he mean us, Pedro?" she asked, her voice caught between anger and tears.

"That old swayback had better watch his mouth. It is a good thing he is an old man," Pidring said.

I was too angry to move. I was going to speak to the man, and throw manners to the wayside, when to my surprise Socorra bristled at her grandfather's orders.

"Those are friends of mine, *Lolo*. Why must you and Father constantly order me about?" She spun on her high heels and motioned to us with her hand. "Hey, come sit with us. What are you waiting for?"

Pidring and I looked behind us. We could not believe she was calling to us.

Addie tugged at my hand. "Pedro, I do not like these people. She is only trying to anger her grandfather. She may try to embarrass us."

My eyes swallowed the lush blankets, the coconut drinks, slices of mango, guava, pandesal, and cheese. The sight of a plate of palabok made me wet my lips. I could almost taste the thick clear noodles with egg, green onions, and shredded orange-colored spices. Their clothes, the smell of their perfume, the cream-colored gloves her sisters wore, held me spellbound. I pulled Addie forward, and Pidring followed.

The Villanuevas looked up at us, Socorra with one brow raised in amusement. She pulled out a long cigarette stem, placed a cigarette at its end, and lighted it with the snap of a slim gold lighter. "Well? Sit," she ordered impatiently.

I positioned myself across from her, then helped Addie to a seated position. There was no place for Pidring, except a small patch of blanket next to the old man. Pidring expected the grandfather to make room, but the man simply glared at him.

"This is my sister, Addie," I announced.

"Hello," Addie mumbled, holding out her hand. For a long moment no one moved, then Socorra took the hand and shook it limply.

"I thought you knew these people, ha?" the grandfather grumbled.

"There is plenty of room here on my side, ladies," I said to the sisters, patting an empty space to be courteous.

They laughed to one another and shook their heads.

Socorra studied me. "What are you doing here?"

"*Ay, tamà na ha. Ikáw ang nag imbita, imbita,*" the grandfather said with disgust. Oh, stop it. You are the one who invited them.

"You should just say yes now, *Lolo.*" Socorra smiled. "Ask Papa to buy me the car and I will tell these people to go. I always win in the end."

"Okay, darling, you win." The grandfather chuckled. "Now tell these people to go. I am sure they have other friends to visit."

I felt my heart drop. Pidring got up and dusted his pants. He reached out a hand to Addie.

"Yes, you are dismissed," Socorra said sweetly, and her sisters patted her as though it were such a good joke.

"Thank you, folks," I said, getting up, which only caused them to laugh more.

"See, *kuya,*" Addie whispered, grabbing my hand, "I told you what kind of people they are."

My eyes were locked on Socorra. I coveted her wealth, the power she exuded. I wanted that for myself. I saw how the other families looked their way, how the other girls mimicked Socorra and her sisters. I would never stand a chance with a girl like her. Socorra continued to smoke her cigarette, already dismissing us from her thoughts. The image of that fine cigarette burned in my chest as we walked away.

"You know the Villanuevas?" a young woman with braided hair asked from a nearby headstone.

"They are good friends of ours." Pidring puffed up his chest.

She gave a crooked smile as she looked over toward the Villanueva blankets, particularly at Socorra. "That family is like hollow fruit. Very sweet looking on the outside, but on the inside, the ants and worms have eaten through the good portion. There is much hate and jealousy among the sisters."

I looked to check the accuracy of her statement, and to my surprise, the sisters were each facing in a different direction.

"That one in particular"—the girl gestured with her chin to Socorra—"is the worst."

"I did not like them," Addie announced, feeling more comfortable with our new friends.

A PALE MOON was rising and gray clouds floated thinly before it. The white trumpet lilies had begun to close, but their fragrance drifted all around us.

"It is past twilight time," Pidring announced. "We should be home. You know what the old people say."

It was his tone that caught everyone's attention. Several people had come to share our blanket space, including a young man with a cane and a bad temper who knew the answer to everything.

"That is foolish talk," the bad-tempered Augustino snorted.

Pidring pursed his lips. "Do you know why the *asuwángs* favor this area and not the city?"

"Because witches like to eat beautiful young women?" Augustino smirked, leaning on his cane. "So that when you tell the story the women will grab for your hand?"

"Because of the lack of telephone lines." Pidring clenched his teeth and pointed out toward the space between the trees. "The witches can fly at night and flap their wings unhindered." He shrugged. "But if you do not believe, what is the use in continuing this?"

I took Addie's hand. "We must go. I think this way is the safest." I pointed to a route Pidring and I had prepared the prior day. "Thank you, everyone, for the company."

"Wait!" the girls shouted in unison. "We shall walk out with you. Let us finish packing our things."

We waited beside them, and I began to speak to Pidring in a loud manner.

"We will be fine. There is no need for concern. The *asuwángs* hunt for the pregnant women first, you know. They fly over the houses very late at night. If you are awake, you can hear them flap their wings. They land on the houses and dig for a crack in the ceilings. If there are none, they make a hole with their long fingernails right above the pregnant woman's bed. Then slowly they trickle a string of saliva down to the woman's mouth, and from then on, the woman becomes paralyzed and the baby is eaten in that way."

"What a horrid way to die," one of the girls exclaimed, snapping the blankets in the air to throw off the crumbs.

"What about when the *asuwángs* crawl beneath the houses?" Pidring shook his head.

"What happens then?" Augustino taunted.

"Oh, it is horrible," I said. "When the roofs of the houses are guarded with holy objects such as crucifixes and statues of saints blessed in holy water, then the *asuwángs* search for a way to get below the house. And if your house is raised on stilts, well then, all the easier."

"What do you mean?" asked the girl with braids.

"Well, have you ever heard the wild boars that root beneath the houses sometimes? Those are not wild boars. They are vampire-witches in their animal form. They root below the houses looking for a hole to pull the pregnant mother through."

The women screamed and giggled in fear. We now had a tight circle, and Pidring and I were in heaven.

"How do you kill such a thing?" the girl whispered.

"That is easy," Augustino interrupted before Pidring could continue. Really, the urge to box his ear and steal his cane was incredible. Pidring and I waited for his explanation.

Augustino's expression was smug. "All that is needed is garlic and holy water."

"And?" Pidring asked.

"One need only throw either at the creatures," Augustino finished, looking off to the dark. A cold wind was threading its way through the warmth, and we pulled our coats closer to our bodies.

Pidring choked, "That is the most ridiculous explanation I have ever heard."

I laughed. "Be kind, Pidring. He has not seen the things we have."

"Well, genius, for that is your name, is it not?" Pidring asked Augustino. "Are you ready to hear how to truly kill these creatures?"

Augustino shrugged. "What is your explanation?"

Addie surprised us by speaking. Her voice was soft, and it pierced the darkness with the strangest pitch. I shivered as I held her hand. "These *asuwángs* are normal humans by day. They have the power to walk among us, and to mark who will be their victims after twilight time. The time when the moon begins to rise and the goodness of the sun begins to fade.

"When night approaches, they begin to howl and scream as wings sprout from their backs. Their hands grow into claws, and their vampire fangs come out. They detach themselves from the waist down, leaving their human legs standing behind. They can be killed in this demon form if someone were to find their lower half and place holy water or garlic on it. When daylight comes they cannot attach to their human form, and they burn."

The families were packing their belongings to leave. The graveyard had grown very dark. The wind howled high in the trees. Soon a pack of dogs echoed the cry throughout the village. We laughed bravely, walking as one body toward the back of the cemetery. Our eyes shifted steadily to the rustling of a tree or the squawking of a bird.

"Pidring, is this the way?" I asked. The majestic mango tree I had remembered as a guidepost was obscured by the clouds floating rapidly before the moon.

"Pedro, do not joke," Addie whispered.

Then came the sound of footsteps behind us, light, rustling the leaves, as if they floated, barely grazing the ground.

"Who is there? Would you like to join us?" Addie's voice broke as we stopped to listen.

"Join us or we will leave you behind," Augustino shouted, brandishing his cane.

No one showed themselves, and we turned to move ahead.

"Can I join you?" a woman's voice asked.

Everyone shouted.

"It is only me, Socorra." Her childlike voice sounded strange in the dark. She stepped closer, her face pale and smiling.

I put my hand to my chest. "Of course," I said. "Pidring, will you hold Addie's hand?"

"I can watch myself." Addie wrenched her hand from my grasp. "She is probably here to anger her grandfather again and extort more money from him," Addie muttered.

Socorra's face burned red at how close to the mark Addie's words hit, but for some strange reason, her being caught in her manipulation of the grumpy old man did not bother me. He probably deserves it, I thought.

We neared a solitary house at the edge of the woods.

"I thought that house was abandoned," Augustino breathed, his voice raw.

Socorra reached for my hand, and I jumped at the warmth of it. I peered at her. She was so tiny that I felt the urge to protect her; from what, I did not know.

"The basement door is open," Pidring whispered, breaking away from our group.

"Pidring, wait!" I shouted, but too late. Pidring disappeared into the dilapidated house. The front door had long ago blown away. It was a large, imposing house, beautiful surely in its day. There was a melancholy look to how the thick vines had overgrown the house, enveloping it. A snake consuming its prey. There was a faint light at the topmost room.

"Let us go," Addie urged. "Call Pidring and let us go."

"Yes." Augustino hid behind practicality. "What if there are thieves in that house? They may hurt your friend."

"I shall get him." I stepped forward, but before I could move, we heard the distinct sound of an infant crying. Pidring shot out of the basement, holding a small white bundle.

"There are hundreds of babies in there." He held the writhing form in his arms. "We must get help."

The women were crying now and wringing their hands. Augustino was at the head of our group, his feet pointed opposite the house.

"We must go in," I urged.

Within seconds the basement door burst open. "There it is!" Pidring shouted. A large winged creature shot forward, with long matted hair and a ragged, bloody gown. That was the last nut to tip the basket. The women took off running, shrieks rented the sanctity of the evening, and Augustino was truly a sight. Never had I seen a man make such good use of a cane.

We watched them go. Pidring and I were in tears, and laughter shook our bodies so badly, I lost my balance several times and fell forward. I looked up at the wigged and winged sewing bust. Its white gown swayed eerily in the wind. At my suggestion we had dressed and strung the creature on fishing lines the previous evening.

"We had better get that sewing torso down before my mother notices it missing. Or she will turn into something more frightening," Pidring snickered. He reached on tiptoes with one hand to grab the swaying gown.

"I feel bad," Addie said. "I liked those girls. Pidring, what is it you have in your arms that is making that ungodly noise?"

Pidring pulled the end of the small blanket. A white cat jumped to the ground, hissing, then leaped into the dark. "The damned thing has torn half my arm. Ahh, but it was worth it."

"Perfection." I clapped hands with Pidring.

"You had better go in and blow out that candle before we burn the house," Pidring instructed.

I turned toward the house, and suddenly my hands went cold. I could see the ghost of the previous owner hovering angrily near the window at our intrusion. I had seen him yesterday as well, when we first entered the house, but I had swallowed my hesitation and walked right through him. He had a right to be in that house. Of course, Addie immediately noticed something was bothering me.

"What is it, *kuya?* Do you see somthing?"

"Huh? Oh no, it is nothing. Let me blow out the light before—" I had not even finished my sentence when the light of the candle went out.

"Oh, better yet. It has burnt itself out," Pidring said.

Addie gasped. "It shut itself out?"

I swallowed hard. Some spirits were very strong and could be violent. Those were the ones I needed to consult my mentor, Diagos, about, but his forest was a long way from this place. I wondered if his powers reached this far. Probably he would be disappointed with my pranks. He did not like the spirits to be bothered.

"Let us be on our way," I urged.

"Ay, I have forgotten my coat, Ped." Pidring chuckled. "One moment," he called over his shoulder, already running back into the house.

I looked up at the window. I was the only one who could see the energy, like fire licking at the window frame.

"Wait, Pidring. I will come with you. Addie, stay here," I instructed.

When I reached the top of the steps, Pidring was frozen with his back to me. "Ped . . ." His voice was strained. "I cannot move."

There was a single chair in the room, and it teetered left to right, then tumbled. I could feel the bad energy trying to suffocate us.

"Speak to me," I announced to the room.

"I cannot," Pidring choked. His eyes were large, near tears. He was trying to hold on to his disbelief and not give in to the terror that threatened any minute to swallow him.

The table shook and slammed from side to side.

"This is my house!" The spirit appeared, engulfed in red. He was standing before Pidring with his hands tight around Pidring's neck.

"We meant no harm."

"What will you do? Ask me to leave my own house? No one living claims these walls. It was mine before I passed." The spirit's appearance had changed. It did not have the older face it had shown in the window; it was younger, consumed in fire. I had seen its kind before, the ones destined to damnation but choosing to hide and disobey their guides. His presence filled the room with the smell of dead flowers.

The chair lifted and flew toward me. I stood in place, and it lost its momentum. The apparition frowned at me. "Who are you, favored one?"

I stepped forward and placed my hand on Pidring's shoulder. Immediately the spirit let go as if he had been scalded.

"Let us pass," I ordered. It dared not touch Pidring as long as I held him.

The spirit howled with the wind. It berated us with profanity, and as we hurried out, it slammed the door behind us. Once outside, Pidring began to shake terribly.

"Are you hurt?" I asked. I could see his struggle. He was trying to stay composed.

"Do not speak of it." Pidring glanced at me.

"But perhaps if you talked . . ."

Pidring held up a hand and shook his head.

THE NEXT EVENING, as I lay on my mat, my thoughts of Socorra were interrupted by my father. "Son, are you tired?"

I smiled at the question. "What is it, Pa?"

"Ah, are you awake? I am sorry to trouble you, but Aling Penelope has invited us to dinner at her home this evening. There is something she would like you to observe, and after, Mang Damasaw has requested us to pay a visit since we will be in that part of town."

I sighed. "I was to go to a cockfight with Pidring tonight. Where does she live?"

"Just over the rise. We are not above a dinner invitation, are we, son?" my father joked.

"No, sir. When shall we leave?" I asked.

"Ah, well . . ." My father scratched his head in embarrassment, and I could see that he was already washed, with his hat in his hands.

"She is already expecting us?" I asked.

My father nodded.

~

ALING PENNY STARED at me for a long moment when she opened the door, and I could see that her eyes were watery. She held her hand to her chest. "Please come in, come in. Thank you for honoring my home, Mang Salvatore," she said to my father.

My father removed his hat. He inhaled deeply and closed his eyes.

"Do you sense something, Ped?" he asked. "This room, this room," he muttered. He sometimes sensed things, but there was nothing in the room.

"Maybe, Pa," I told him.

Dinner was served, and the servants placed two baskets of chicken and rice before us, and I sensed nothing. The chicken was piled too high, and a thigh tumbled to the table. I noticed with a start that the chicken floated silently back to its place, yet I could still not see anything.

I looked around in alarm. Aling Penelope was trading pleasantries with my father. There was a servant in the room, but his eyes were focused on Aling Penelope. He was very familiar with her. He brushed the hair from her face while she talked. He unclasped the napkin around her neck. I noticed that my father frowned at the man's familiarity.

"Please, could I have more water?" I said to the servant.

Aling Penelope looked at me strangely, then called out and another servant walked in and poured water into my glass.

I looked at the first servant in confusion; he had completely ignored my request. I studied him from head to foot, and it was then that I saw his feet did not touch the ground. When I looked up again, he smiled kindly at me.

I stood and excused myself, and the spirit followed me into the *salas*.

He stood with his hands behind his back. "You have come to ask me to leave?"

"Yes." I nodded. "How is it that I did not see you?"

"You saw me, but she has accepted my presence for a long time now, so there is no tension."

"If you stay too long, you will miss your opportunity." I shrugged. "It may already be too late."

"I cannot leave knowing she will not be taken care of," the spirit said.

"What is your name?"

"Pacifico," he answered.

"You were a good servant to her."

"A good husband," he corrected, and bowed.

It was then that I saw his energy was not the usual cloud that veiled the spirit; instead he wore it as the uniform of a devoted husband, and in a way, what he had been to her in his lifetime, his love, had made him a servant. He adored her. It touched me.

"Still, Pacifico, I must ask that you leave."

He bowed but willed himself to stay. His devotion was amazing.

"What does he say?" Aling Penelope stepped into the room, and her smile was beautiful, the smile of someone in love.

"He worries there will be no one to care for you."

She stifled a sob and placed a trembling hand to her lips. "How stupid I have been. Is this wrong, to let him stay? Truly it does not bother me; he is always welcome. . . ." Her voice trailed off hopefully.

"His place in line will be compromised. They are waiting for him elsewhere."

She nodded and studied the room. She took a deep breath. She did not know he embraced her from behind. "Husband, you may go now. I can care for myself."

As soon as she said those words, a breeze took him away.

IT WAS DARK as we departed. Our thin clothes were no match for the rain that had come in torrents. "Damn this rain. Someday I shall have enough money to ride us around in a grand car."

"Be glad that you have your health. Do not always be so concerned with money," my father said.

"I may still make my appointment with Pidring," I announced.

"One last place, *anák*. I promised a friend," my father insisted.

We arrived at Mang Damasaw's home at ten in the evening. It was a simple house, similar to ours but made of wood. He was younger than I expected, twenty years old. He looked much older from lack of sleep. The moment he opened the door I gasped as several spirits ran past me.

"Sir . . ." He took my father's hand and placed the back of it to his brow as a sign of respect. "You honor us. Thank you for coming. Please enter." He ushered us in, and I could not believe the sight. There was not one free inch of space. At least fifty spirits were crowded into the house.

They reached out to me as I walked by. I brushed away their hands. An old man stepped out. He pointed down the hallway. "This woman is a nuisance. I was resting until she called. I have already served one woman. I do not even know this one." He stood with his hands on his hips, and I walked through him. He cried out in annoyance. "Boy, I am speaking to you. Boy!"

"Be silent," I told him. He glared at me, speechless.

"Have you come to set us free?" a nun asked. Her robes swirled about her in a rose-colored cloud. "Did Father Paolo send you?"

A woman stood against the wall with a young boy. "We were walking on the roadside. A jitney car lost control. But I think we are in the wrong place."

"Please, move aside."

"You heard him. Move aside." An older woman banging a frying pan with a wooden spoon called out to me. "The bastard was cheating me. I was haunting him. He was almost ready to jump from the cliff until this stupid woman called." She also pointed down the hall toward the dining room. "They should not let just any fool use those boards."

Mang Damasaw watched me curiously. "Alicia," he called to his wife, who was sitting at the dinner table. The table was cleared, and on it was a candle lit with a picture of a young girl of no more than six or seven years old. The mother had a spirit board laid out.

"You have been using this?" I asked her.

She nodded silently. "It does not work."

I looked at her in astonishment. I looked to Damasaw.

"I have told her to stop this nonsense. I have not been able to sleep from worry over her. Please tell her it is complete foolishness. An old woman told her it would call our daughter's spirit back. She died several weeks ago. She fell from a tree."

I was thinking of a way to explain to them when the spirits all crowded around me.

"What idiots. Tell them!" shouted the woman with the frying pan.

"Yes, tell them." Two farmers prodded me with rakes.

"Quiet, I cannot concentrate. Leave me. You are free to go."

Mang Damasaw and my father looked at me in shock, then left the room quietly.

"Thank goodness," the spirits echoed. They lined up and walked through the door one by one.

I sat across from Aling Alicia. "This is a very dangerous thing you do. What is it you wish to accomplish?" It angered me. "Your child is in danger of losing her way from your selfishness."

"I want to speak to my baby."

From the corner of my eye a young girl stepped out. Her energy was sickly, fading.

"What do you wish to say to her?"

"That I am sorry I was not there to catch her."

"Come . . ." I urged the child forward.

"Mama is sad. I cannot leave," she said in a small voice.

The moment she spoke, the woman began to shake. "She is here. A mother knows these things. I smell her powder."

"She has always been here. You need to set her free. I have seen this before. When the spirits are tied to the living, they are in jeopardy of losing their guides and being trapped in limbo. Is that how you wish to comfort her?"

"No," the woman sobbed.

The child sat on Alicia's lap and laid her head against her chest. "I am sorry, Mama," the child whispered. "Please let go."

"My darling," Alicia sobbed at hearing her daughter's voice. "It is I who am sorry." She covered her mouth as the little girl slowly let go.

The child took my hand and looked up at me.

"Go now. Catch your train before it leaves."

"Son . . ." My father stood holding out a cup of coffee to me. I had fallen asleep at our kitchen table.

I took the cup, trying to make sense of the time by the fading light.

"I would not trouble you, I know you are very tired, but Claro Cardizon came to visit while you slept."

"That old gambler? He knows I cannot read cards for him. It does not work that way. He comes every time he has a bad streak. He is just *malas*, and I cannot change that. Each time I tell him the same thing. I can only see spirits, not which way his luck will turn. He will just have to wait it out."

My father chuckled. "Yes, even I know that, but he thinks his bad luck is because of a new player. He believes the man to have bad magic. Will you do me this favor, son?"

"Of course, Papa."

"*Ay salamat*, son," he thanked me. "You know I would not ask."

"I know, Pa." I clapped him on the back and reached for my coat.

"So was Addie upset at not being included in our little outing?" Pidring asked before we walked into the card game.

"Well . . ." I shrugged. "She knows there will only be men here gambling tonight, except for Mrs. Cardizon, but she is the hostess."

"Tell me again who this man is supposed to be," Pidring said.

"Old Mang Claro thinks one of his players uses black magic to win."

"He is *malas* again?" Pidring shook his head. "Why can he not just accept the bad streak? Why create these fantastic stories?"

I smiled. "Let us make the best of it. Maybe we can play a hand."

When we entered the house, I found the threshold to be resistant to me.

"What is it, Ped? Another ghost?" Pidring joked, his face paling.

"Maybe, maybe," I said.

"Pedro . . ." Mang Claro came and shook my hand. I felt fear and desperation pass between us. As I studied Mang Claro, my heart became excited.

"Pedro is here," he called out to the room.

"And Pidring," I said.

"Eh?" Mang Claro asked.

"Pidring has accompanied me."

"He has brought a friend," Mang Claro announced.

I grinned at Pidring.

MANG CLARO TOOK us aside and whispered, "He is playing with the children. I do not care about the bad luck, that will pass. Just make him leave."

I clasped his hand. The old man was shaking.

"Here they are." Mang Claro ushered us into the room and introduced us to the players. He did not have to tell me which one was the man, for when I walked into the room the man's energy revealed itself to me in a green fog around him. I had never seen anything like it; it was so strong.

I stared immediately at the man, and Mang Claro secretly made the sign of the cross. "This is Mang Fausto Tarluc."

The man was my father's age. He wore a dark suit, and he had a bald head, dented in small places like a bruised bayabas fruit.

"Fausto, this is our neighbor Pedro."

The man stopped playing with the children. He had been showing them how to tie an unbreakable knot.

"I know that trick." Pidring rocked back on his heels.

"Oh?" Mang Fausto asked. "Shall I try it on you? Give me your hands."

"No, no." Pidring shook his head, oblivious to the danger. "Show my friend. Ped, have you seen this one yet? He will tie a loose knot, but you will be unable to break it."

I knew the technique as well; it was an old magician's trick.

"Oh, you try?" Fausto asked.

"All right." I held my wrists together, and I saw that he whispered something before he started to tie the knot. So I said a simple prayer.

The rope would not tie, and the other players in the room laughed.

Fausto tried again, and still nothing. He stopped suddenly and looked deeply at me. "Where are you from?"

"I grew up here," I told him.

He closed his eyes, not long enough for anyone to notice, but longer than a blink. I felt a coldness pass through me.

"What a joker you are." He smiled strangely. "I was only playing with the children, but you think to embarrass me."

"Watch what you say," Pidring ordered.

I stepped between them. "You are right, I am a joker. It was wrong of me. Let me get you a drink, friend." He bowed curtly and we stepped away from the others. "What do you want with this family?" I asked.

"I like this view, I like this house, the location."

He was bold. I did not think he would speak so plainly. "I must ask you to leave," I said.

His body convulsed at my request, a quick intake of breath that unsteadied him.

"You should not have interfered." He glared at me. "Mang Claro," he called.

"Ha?" old Mang Claro asked timidly from the hallway.

"I must go now, but you should have thought of this boy's family before you called him here."

Mang Claro was speechless, and I clenched my fists. "Do not even try it."

Fausto laughed. "Ah, but it is you who has invited me to this dance."

I WAS NOT concerned; many spirits had threatened me with retribution, and it had come to nothing. It was only later, when Father had not caught any fish in over a week, not even the smallest *dilis,* and Addie was having the most horrible nightmares, that I knew Fausto's threat was now being acted out upon my family. I woke one night to go to Addie's room and there was this large wasp the size of a cantaloupe, transparent and hovering over her. I told it to leave, and it flew past me. The following night it was back again.

It went like this for many evenings, until I decided it was time to speak to Diagos. I hated to trouble him, but I was concerned for Addie. I waited until it was twilight time and then I went to the forest.

I checked behind me every now and then as I started into the jungle, for I knew Diagos would not show if anyone followed. The big-eyed monkeys were creeping out of their morning hiding places, their curly tails unwinding and hanging down like vines. They peered at me, gripping the branches with their long, froglike fingers. They made me smile whenever I saw them. Their eyes were tremendous in size, so they always appeared as if they had just heard the most shocking news. I was careful where I stepped, threading my bare feet in between the celery pine and the magical four-inch walking leaves that floated down from the trees and walked away.

More important, I made way for the little *duendes.* Tiny elves they were, the size of a cup, some with wings on their wrists and ankles, some behind their ears. They stared silently at me as I walked. They were small, but they were fearless, and God help you if you hurt any one of their flock. The females wore iridescent robes of green and gold and had colorful hair that blended with their long, birdlike tails. The males were covered from the waist down with fur.

As I told you, I saw things that no normal person ever did. I saw these little people often, and they became no more strange to me than walking next to Pidring or Addie. I walked deep into the forest to where the grass grew taller than me and the tall coconut trees grew in thick clumps. Soon I heard the familiar sound of horse hooves and I knew that my friend was near.

Then, as always happened when he was near, a certain tension filled the air. As if the texture of it were enhanced somehow. The birds and the crickets sang a different tune, magnified, yet at the same time, they listened.

"Why have you waited this long?" a voice said behind me.

I turned and bowed before the creature. His name is Diagos; he is one of four of his kind, and after them no more were created. He is immortal, and he is known as a *tikbalang.* He is larger than any horse you could ever imagine. He is the exact form of a horse except for his eyes, which are positioned in front and blue, with the white like ours. He is larger even than the ones known abroad as Clydesdales, twice as big. When he sits, he sits on his haunches, with his back vertical, in much the way a human does. His hind legs are tucked inward and reach the middle of his torso, in the way a human pulls in his legs. His forelegs fold so that they touch like elbows to knees. That is the only way I can explain it. I asked him once if he had magical powers and if others could see him.

"I am Diagos. Only the humble and the purest can see me. My powers are that of a watcher. My brothers and I cannot interfere, until the hour when He calls upon us. Then there is much that will be poured out upon this earth. So it is written."

He always spoke in riddles.

"Why have you waited so long?" he asked again.

"I did not wish to bother you."

"You were vain. You thought you were strong enough to match this man." I bowed my head.

"It is true, as you see; he could not trouble your sleep, but the others are not blessed as you."

"Addie cannot sleep, and Papa cannot catch even a stone from the river."

He sighed, and the entire jungle seemed to breathe with him. The sound resounded to the tops of the trees and below the earth.

"Leave him to me."

"I thought you could not interfere."

"I cannot use my powers. But my presence will mean other things to him."

"Who is he?" I asked.

"Human like you, but one who has promised much to his master in order to gain what he believes is power. He will later find it to be a weight that will drag him down. Woe to he who does not meet what he hath given oath to. That is all you need know. Ask what else you please."

"Aling Frances's daughter is sick."

"Pick the red flowers with the blue eternal flame, crush them, and they will ease her stomach."

"And the Riveros's boy?"

"It is his time."

"Can nothing be done? He is their only child."

"It is his time."

I was quiet. It was news I hated to bring. "He is all they have."

"They will have even less, and then it will be the wife's time. That is all that is recorded for them in this life."

I nodded.

"There is something else," Diagos said.

"Nothing, a girl."

"She is not for you."

"They live so well. To see my father in such clothes. Their food."

"It is temporary, fleeting."

"I would trade my gift for what they have."

"Misery and gold?" Diagos watched me.

THAT NIGHT A storm came and Addie tried in vain to stay awake, though I told her she would sleep well from then on. When she fell asleep, I heard a strong flapping in the wind, like the wings of a giant beast, and then the sound of a hundred horses thundering around the area. Our neighbors screamed and shut their windows. I peered outside, and there was Diagos positioned in front of our door, though only I could see him.

Then, from far away, I saw Fausto approach. He rode on a green fog in the shape of a large serpent. When I looked again, Diagos was gone and I was angry. He had fled in fear. The serpent came and enveloped our house. It was difficult to breathe. Addie was struggling for breath, trapped in a nightmare I could not shake her from. I shouted for him to stop, but Fausto continued to my parents' room. I will lose them, I thought.

"Yes," Fausto sneered. "They are weak, they cannot refuse me."

I ran to Addie and held her hand, but nothing changed. "Diagos!" I shouted. No one answered. "God help me," I cried.

And as Fausto's laughter filled the house, a voice like thunder roared, "Fausto Tarluc, come forth from this house."

Fausto hurried to the front. "Who dares challenge me?"

"The Four Horses, of He who sits on high," answered the voice.

I ran outside and my heart swelled. Diagos stood to the left of our house, his blue eyes pale, like the morning sky. He wore across his chest a gold band. On it, engraved in flame, were words I could not read.

Fausto covered his eyes immediately and looked away, ready to flee.

But Diagos was not alone. To the right was another creature such as he, with hair a dark copper, the color of fire. To the rear were two more, one with hair like a cloud and the other gray like the wind. They were his brothers, and they spoke as one. "Who dares bother one of His favored?"

Fausto trembled. He was blinded by their presence. He could not look upon them. He tried to flee, but he could not move past their four corners. "What do you want from me?"

"The time of the great battle approaches. He may show mercy on you yet. We watch for now. How shall your name be recorded?"

"Leave me in peace," he begged, writhing like a serpent on the ground. "I shall bother this family no more."

"Go, then, and await your trial," Diagos declared.

From then I knew that I was in touch with a great power, and I bowed low before the Four.

WEEKS PASSED, AND Pidring retold the story of our graveyard prank again and again to our friends.

"I wish I could have been there. What a treat it would have been to see those rich biddies running and tripping over themselves," our friend Danilo remarked. "But the part about the rich girl holding on to Pedro all night. That I would have to see to believe."

I laughed. "So would I." I waved to one of the children swimming in the filth. Our sewers had overflowed from the rain again, and the high tide had not helped. The sewer water was the same level as the top steps to our house and threatened at any moment to come in uninvited.

Children brought out rowboats and rowed between the houses. It did not matter that their mothers came out to scold them. Within seconds of a spanking, they would be swimming in the fetid water again.

"My God, our entire village is a toilet." Pidring fanned the air.

"I have to go to the market." I stood and waved the young Ocampos boy in a rowboat over to our steps.

The boy rowed quickly, bumping the bamboo stilts and shaking our house. "Be careful, be careful," I called out. "I will give you a peso to take me over to the higher ground. If you get me wet, I will not even pay you a thank-you. Can you do it?" I asked.

"Yes, yes, get in." The boy gestured with his thin arms.

"I don't know." I pretended to think. "It looks tricky. Maybe I should call one of the older boys."

"No, I can do it. Here, step in. I will not fail you."

The boy got me to shore without one drop of filth entering the boat.

"Call me when you are ready to cross back." He waved and went back to the business of playing chicken with the other children in their makeshift rafts, trying to tip one another into the filth. I winced as the brown water splattered the porch. Pidring and Danilo began to shout.

"Just in time." I shook my head.

I turned in the direction of the market, with Danilo's question about Socorra Villanueva still on my mind. Her image had haunted me night and day.

"So this is where you live."

I turned and felt a sickening in my stomach. Socorra stood before me, her fine leather sandals sprinkled with sand. She was wearing a long rose-colored summer dress. It was short-sleeved, with a square neckline and arched sleeves. The stiff silk fell straight, where two small slits showcased her ankles on opposite sides. She was accompanied by her father. The man stood with his arms folded, surveying the area. He wore a white linen suit with a wide-brimmed hat. His wealth impressed me more than Diagos's brethren.

She had to shake his arm before she could gain his attention. "Father, this is Pedro, the man I told you about. His family is very respected in this village. His word has much power here."

I waved off her words in embarrassment.

"This place is a rat's nest," he said, rubbing his chin with manicured fingers. He wore a wide ring, a flat ruby set in pale gold, in the shape of a pear. Along the band were fine etchings of other fruits. I shuffled my feet in anger, yet I was too embarrassed to reply. Obviously, what he said was true. Before I could let the anger grow, he paid me a compliment.

"You look like a smart young man. I deal only with intelligent people. You may need a little polish, but I see that you could become a shrewd businessman. How would you like to better the conditions of your community and make a large amount of money at the same time?"

I opened my mouth to speak, but again he interrupted.

"Socorra mentioned the unfortunate incident with your sister's eyes. If you had had better resources, that would not have happened." He frowned, dismissing the accident with a certainty emphasized in a simple shake of his head. "Come, let us discuss this at length."

I nodded and went along without having said a word to him. He urged us forward, placing his hand on my shoulder. I flinched, thinking of how soiled my clothes were from trolling that morning.

AT THE BAKERY, her father ordered coffee and cakes for us. I could not afford to have a cup and asked only for water.

"You do not drink coffee?" he asked.

"Oh, no." I waved my hand. "I have had my morning cup already."

"Nonsense. Miss"—he raised his hand, and immediately a young woman was by our side—"bring us another cup of coffee here, and also, do you have *braso de Mercedes?*" The girl nodded. *"Leche plan?"* Again the girl nodded. "Bring us both."

The girl was gone within seconds. Never had I seen such speedy service given at that establishment. Never had I been treated with such admiration. The man ordered everyone about, and it fascinated me. Socorra did not need to speak; her clothes, her manner, demanded authority. I could see the shop owners, their eyes calculating the money we would spend at their stores. I caught many glances that day, and I felt my chest expand at the jealous looks I received.

"Your village respects you greatly," her father said.

"They know my father. It is he they admire."

"Do not be modest. It gets you nowhere. Modesty is for virgins and old maids."

"Yes, sir," I said.

"Now, here is what we shall do. I am willing to invest a large amount of money to build decent houses, at a low cost, allowing your people to purchase them. I will build bigger houses on the hillside above that the upper class will be willing to buy, since the area will be cleansed of all these straw debacles."

"And what am I to do, sir?"

"You shall be my right hand. You shall oversee all my projects, and I will pay you handsomely. The people trust you. You are to assure them that they will be paid for the land they sell, and with the money they can buy the smaller houses I build, at a low cost. I will make my profit from the bigger homes."

I thought of the nice homes we could all have. It would be a step up for our community. All the while Socorra sat close.

"How long do you plan to stay silent?" Her voice held the authority of a man on business. I immediately snapped to attention, and she smiled sweetly.

Her father leaned back in his chair. "Are you ready to better yourself?"

"I am ready." I shook his hand.

THE FOREST WAS taut with Diagos's anger. He dug at the ground with his giant hooves.

"You cannot have both. Riches and purity do not match. Humility hates pride." He paced in a circle. "You have been warned."

"What are you telling me? That I have become proud?" I demanded.

"Your sight will be lost. It is not too late. You are humble still, pure. Let go of this fascination with earthly riches. You have so much more than they."

"I can see ghosts." I shrugged. "What good did my visions do me when Addie's eyes were blinded?"

"There exist earthly circumstances in which I cannot intervene. Only her one eye was damaged. It was when she was taken to the clinic that the other was harmed."

"And yet you did not warn us that would happen."

"There are situations with which I am not allowed to interfere."

"You are jealous. You do not have these opportunities, so you wish to take them from me."

"You know not what you say."

"Must I forever be a servant as you are?" I shouted.

He raised himself on his hind legs, and the earth shook when he landed his gigantic forelegs beside me. "You fool," he snorted. "You were given the keys, but you choose to throw them away. It will happen like lightning."

His tail lashed out like a whip. The forest resounded like a clap of thunder, cutting a huge tree in half. I watched him go. I did not know that would be the last time I saw him with my eyes.

OF COURSE, IT was easy to convince the people to sell their land, they held so much respect for me and my family. I led them all to sign away what little they had, and they trusted me. When the smaller houses were built, they were at a lower cost, but not low enough for the people to afford.

I became wealthy, but my father lost his face in the village. No one spoke to him, and he wasted away until he had a fatal stroke. Mama could not live with the shame, and she followed Father. I went to their gravesite to beg their forgiveness, but I had lost my gift of sight. I could no longer see the spirits. It all happened in the time it takes for lightning to strike.

ADDIE DID NOT grow sick immediately. It was much later, when Socorra's father cut down the trees. Addie grew delirious, and three bumps appeared on her throat the size of apples.

"What is it, Pedro?" Pidring asked. "What is wrong with her?"

"I have angered the creatures in the forest. I have cut down their trees. The *mangkukulam* told me so."

"What? This is nonsense, take her to the doctor. What is this bump on her neck? She may have broken a bone."

"She has a fever; I have sent for the *mangkukulam*."

"The *mangkukulam*? Addie does not need a witch doctor, Pedro."

"I have failed them. All of our friends and neighbors. They will not accept my money. The least I can do is allow the village witch doctor to cure Addie. Then I can pay them a large amount and my conscience will be at peace."

"This is ridiculous, I will take her myself." Pidring shoved me aside.

"Leave her!" I shouted. I was half-crazed. "Leave her here. The *mangkukulam* will be here soon."

Pidring begged me, "Ped, your sister is sick. You can afford to take her to a hospital. The *mangkukulam* does not have a cure. She is armed only with incense and her anger at your family. Take Addie to a real doctor."

"I will give the *mangkukulam* money. I will begin to repay the people," I insisted.

When the witch doctor came, I was happy. I had the maids prepare a feast. "I have faith in you," I told the woman. She smiled tightly at me in return.

The woman burned incense, she said prayers. "You have angered the people of the forest. A member of their family was hurt when you cut down their homes. They want to take Addie in repayment. I will try to appease them."

I was guilty. I let the woman burn smoke over my sister, even as Addie called out to me. I stood by the window and looked toward the houses Socorra's father had built. Addie's fever grew worse; the lumps on her neck would not disappear. The *mangkukulam* finished her chanting, and she let me pay her a large sum. I have made a little progress, I told myself.

In the morning Addie's lumps were gone and I shouted for joy. I hugged my sister, but her body was cold as the wind.

"You have killed her with your guilt!" Pidring screamed.

I WENT TO the forest one last time. It was sheared of its beautiful palms; the life-giving streams had run dry. The birds were gone. I felt Diagos's presence immediately, though I could not see him.

"You risk your life coming here. The *duendes* wish you dead. You have ruined our home, you have killed many *duendes*. It is only I who protects you. You have fallen. Yet you come still to ask."

"You let them kill her," I accused, my eyes searching the area. His voice was everywhere.

"I let them take vengeance. At any time you could have taken her to a doctor."

I fell to my knees at his words.

"You were humbled by your sister's sickness and yet still too proud to come to me, to ask for help. You are no longer pure."

"Give me back my sight, let me help the people once again, let me serve them my entire life."

He laughed scornfully. "You carried your visions as a burden, but it was a gift. You still think of it as such. You think He above would reward you after what you have done? You have ruined lives with your obsession. It became your curse. When have you known a gift to be given twice? Once the package is open, is it still a gift?"

"How can I repay them? I have my entire life."

"Yes, you must live your entire life."

I could feel he was about to leave. "Diagos, forgive me," I cried out.

There was a long silence. "I have not the power to forgive or damn. I am

Diagos, and only the purest and the most humble can see me. I am only a watcher, and in your own way, so shall you be."

~ MANG PEDRO STUDIES ME, to see if his story has had an effect. "My visions come now only in blurred, incoherent dreams and images. A sore reminder of what I once had. So I ask you again, Domingo. When there is no family, what else is there to fight for? I was blinded with obsession, for something that could never fill me. I lost everything that mattered. Not the visions, I could do without those, but my family, my sister, the village where I grew up, and the love of my people. Heed my words. Leave this obsession to be a guerrilla. It will end only in death. It is vanity that calls to you. Do you truly believe you can lead a hundred men to go against the Japanese, when the Amerikanos, with all their power, could not defend us three years ago? Lay this stubbornness to rest. It will bring you only death. Your place is here, with your wife and children. What else is there?"

Yes, what else? I think of Nina Vargas. Nina with her pistol hanging from her hip. Nina with more worth than ten good men.

"Yes, Mang Ped. I value my family. I have heard your words. They are thoughts that I have inspected daily. I would lay down my life for them."

"Well then?" Mang Ped asks.

"But mine is not the only family to consider. There are many others that may die if none of us were to fight. You see how many volunteer to go up against the enemy now? Me alone in this room of hundreds. If no one fights, then I will have the satisfaction of saving only my family above the thousands more. I could not live with that. If I lead my men, if we assist the Amerikanos in our own way, then many more may be saved. You yourself saw how being selfish served you. Only your family became rich, the others in your village lost everything."

Mang Pedro is silent at my words. Perhaps it is I who have taught him something. I am torn between leaving and staying. Mang Pedro's story reminds me of all that I have to lose. I wonder what Mang Carlito would do if he were here, since he values his family so much. I pray that he is still alive. He is a very resourceful man. If anyone could find a way to survive, it would be he. I pray that he is safe, and if he is not, that he is dead. I could not stand the thought of his torture. I have never forgotten how he welcomed me into his home. He is the closest thing to a father I have known. Even with his polio leg, he carries much dignity in his walk. I think about how he shared his home and his food with me even when it was sparse. I am in awe of his love for his family. He would work himself to death just to feed them.

I am still thinking of him when I see a figure limping our way. It takes a moment before I get to my feet and realize that he is one of the new prisoners being led into the building. Aling Louisa and the others watch me as I stand. They follow my eyes, and then I hear their gasps and exclamations.

"*Tay!*" Isabelle sobs, and runs forward.

"*Ay, salamat,*" Aling Louisa cries. Oh, thank you. She puts a hand to her chest and rushes forward. The two of them are ushered back against the wall to the women's side by the soldiers. Alejandro and Roderick run to embrace their father's legs and help him to walk to our side. He places his hands lovingly on their dark heads.

"Mang Carlito . . ." The words escape my lips, and I rush to help him the rest of the way.

"Where were you?" Aling Louisa cries, pacing with her back to the wall. "I saw your face in every body that lay by the roadside. Carlito," she sobs into her hands. "*Salamat sa Dios.*" Thank God.

His eyes search the figures of the women until they come to rest with loving surprise on his daughter.

"Isabelle, you are safe. *Salamat sa Dios,*" he whispers over and over again. Thank God. Isabelle beams at her father. She brushes the hair from her brow, and we wait for him to tell us where he has been.

"You have been returned to us." Mang Pedro nods. "My eyes rejoice."

"Mang Carlito, what happened to you that day?" Roman asks.

Mang Carlito shakes his head and looks at the ground. It takes a moment before he finds his voice. "I did not know if I would ever see all of you again. At times it looked very bad for me. Roman, Ped, I am glad the two of you returned home safely. As for me, I shall tell you how I almost died."

~ carlito's journey

WHEN WE LEFT the cellar that last morning, Roman, Pedro, and myself, I was certain it would be the last time that I saw all of you alive. We tried to keep up appearances, but the moment we opened the door to the outside and let in the glare, our faces dropped. I held on to the door and nodded for them to go first.

My heart was heavy. I felt this knowing deep in my arms and chest as I shut the door behind me. I let my eyes look back at our house, and I thought of all of you inside. I longed to rush back and embrace you. I wanted to inhale the familiar scent of my wife's hair one more time; the area below her ears and that certain place near her lips. It made me want to weep. I let my fingers linger on the doorknob before letting go. Looking at our house from the outside was like looking at a great coffin that would soon be lowered to the ground.

I TOLD MYSELF, *Shake this feeling. You should be ashamed. Was it not you who told Alejandro not to worry about his hands? And now look. Shall you be a liar to your eldest son? Move ahead. Walk, feet; look forward, eyes. Your only thought must be to find food.*

We walked in silence, the three of us. I think we were afraid to look up and see the hopelessness reflected in one another's eyes. We walked past the rotting corpses like bewildered souls let into hell. I could hear the devil laughing in the hot wind that howled in our faces. There on the corner near the old swing that I built for Alejandro and Roderick lay our neighbor Aling Panchang, with Jopie and baby Imelda cradled in her stiff arms. Their flesh was decomposing, melding with one another's. I could still hear her hoarse voice, the way she used to call hello to our house and enter without knocking. I pictured little Jopie with his favorite blanket trailing on the ground and the way he used to shadow Alejandro and Rod. *What will keep that from happening to my family? Why do I fool myself into thinking we will be lucky? These people prayed the same prayers. Why should we be any different? Stop this thinking.*

"Which way, Mang Carlito?" Roman asked. I could see the dread in his eyes.

"South, Roman, to the warehouse I spoke of and to Manila, where the battle is being fought."

As we approached Manila, we stopped and faced one another. The ground was shaking. In the distance were smoke, flashes of light, and the exploding thunder of the big guns. We braced ourselves, each waiting for the other to speak.

Roman was first. "I know a man who works for the Japanese. He is an old friend of my grandfather's. They have taken his shop, but he tries to give whatever food he believes they will not miss."

"I shall try the Red Cross," Pedro said. "Perhaps they can spare something. If they still stand."

"I will try the warehouse," I told them. I pulled a small advertisement from my pocket. The Japanese had distributed it weeks ago. I was not even sure if the warehouse was still standing. It said, "Workers needed. Men and boys to carry supplies. Sack of rice in exchange for a day's work."

We looked at one another. Roman attempted to hold out a hand to shake.

"I shall see you tonight," I told him. He pressed his lips together and tried to smile. I stood and watched him walk southeast. Pedro was already walking away.

I went directly for the city. I soon found that the majority of the bridges over the Pasig River had already been destroyed. I braced myself again. *Stay strong.* I walked toward the sounds of machine-gun fire and antitank machines. People were passing by me, escaping north, their clothing wet from makeshift rafts they had used to cross the river. They carried their children on their backs and in their arms. The babies all looked frail and were barely breathing.

"Friend," a man called out to me, "where are you going? Can you not hear the fighting?" He was an old man, though possibly he could have been my age. You know what the hunger has done to our appearance. His clothing was soaked from his crossing. I wondered if he had swum across. In his hand he carried a cane. His right leg had recently been amputated, and his trouser leg was folded over and pinned behind him.

"I am in search of food," I explained.

He frowned at me. "What will you feed when your stomach has been blown away? Can you not see my leg?"

"Good luck, friend," I told him.

"*Stupido!*" he cried out. "Come back."

People bumped shoulders with me. No one else spoke. Some glanced my way, but if they had any more warnings for me, they did not voice them. I thought how different from the festive attitudes we kept three years ago. I would not have been able to move five steps without a fond greeting from a stranger, but now . . . I shook my head and kept walking. I found an old raft someone had discarded. I found a tree branch and a broken oar beside it. That was all the encouragement I needed. I entered hell on the waters of the Pasig River.

Three hundred yards away, the west end of the river was engulfed with smoke and the sounds of machine guns and the automatic cannons. The Japanese were busy fending off the Amerikano assault boats. Explosions ripped through their formations, and the boats scattered. I focused my eyes and began to paddle. The waters were choppy from the explosions, and my wooden plank bobbed up and down. I lay on my belly and clung to the edges, rowing with one arm.

As I was crossing, I looked a hundred yards east of the river and there were

Japanese engineers waving to me. They carried rifles, so I did not protest. As I paddled closer to them, I saw there were Filipinos in the water, chest deep. They were lifting heavy pieces of equipment as the Japanese yelled out instructions. It was then I saw that one of the bridges was ripped apart and in the middle of the teetering bridge was scattered supplies and equipment that was falling into the river.

"Work for food!" a Japanese soldier shouted to me.

I looked back toward the west end of the river, where the fighting was occurring.

"Work for food!" the soldier shouted again. Four mean-looking soldiers glared down at me from the shore.

I nodded and lowered myself into the river. I was surprised to find the water was very low at that point, where farther up it was deep. The sun was blazing and reflecting off the water so that it was difficult to see. The soldier pointed me to a spot, and I fell into place. The equipment was very heavy, and a few times the weight caused my elbows to bow out and the metal containers to hit me in the face. We worked furiously for almost an hour. At first it was hard to concentrate. I was dizzy from hunger. Shells were flying, and I feared that the battle on the other end would soon come our way. But by some miracle the Japanese kept the Amerikanos at bay.

When we were done we were ushered ashore, and some of the men collapsed onto the land and did not get back up.

"Hurry. We go. Food in building," a soldier instructed.

He was pointing to an old warehouse. The building was made of sheet iron with a red cross painted on the roof. It had once been a Red Cross office. I wondered where the volunteers had gone. We walked as fast as we could. I could feel the soldiers staring at my polio leg. They whispered among themselves. It made me pick up my pace. There was a long line to enter. They were only letting groups of twenty in at one time. Finally they counted twenty of us, and the soldier knocked on the door. When the door opened the twenty of us were let in and then the door was shut again. Inside we stood in another line. The door was shut and locked behind me. I looked at the soldier for an explanation, but he held his rifle and looked straight ahead. The building was hot, but at least it took the sun out of my eyes and I was thankful. While we waited in line a soldier came by and gave each of us a small cup of rice and a package of salt. I swallowed mine whole. I craned to see if they were distributing water, but they were not. Suddenly from the front of the line one of the Filipinos broke away and ran toward the door, but a soldier wrestled him to the ground and dragged him back.

Our line became worried. We looked at one another and craned our necks to see what was happening. Four soldiers walked to either side of us and escorted us forward. Up ahead I saw that two soldiers stood at the center. With bland faces, they watched us approach. I squinted my eyes to see what was happening. When I neared the center, a strong odor caused me to stumble. It smelled like a slaughterhouse. I soon realized that the two soldiers stood guard over a large circle, and then I saw to my horror that it was a pit, the kind one would roast a pig over. It was twelve meters long and four meters wide. As I moved closer, a violent shaking took hold of me. I saw that it was deep with heads and decapitated corpses. I held my stomach to keep from vomiting. A few of the men tried to run to the door, but they were bayoneted immediately.

So this is your time, I said to myself. *You knew you could not be this lucky for this long.* And for some reason I thought, Better I die than any in my family. *Die like a man. Do not let them see your fear.* I repeated this to myself even though my legs were trembling. We were ushered forward one by one. I watched as a man was led forward, and when he refused to kneel, a soldier took his sword still in its scabbard and hit the man in the head so that he knelt and almost fell into the pit. Another soldier held on to the swaying man's hands and leaned away as the soldier spat on the blade of his sword and raised it in a great arc. He brought the sword down with such force that the man's head rolled across the room and blood spurted from the body. The Filipino had not cried out, nor had he tried to run in fear. I felt my chest swell and my eyes water. He had refused to cry out. *If nothing else, we will die with our courage.*

I looked at the other Filipinos beside me. They were quiet, their faces ash colored. My chest constricted at the thought of such an undignified ending. *We are to be slaughtered like pigs.* I wanted to weep.

As the next man was brought forward, I told myself again, *Be strong.* I stood with my legs quaking when I felt someone staring at me intently. I looked to my side, and an older soldier was staring from my polio leg to my face. He repeated this a few times, and I became uneasy.

The soldier called out to me, "You, come forward."

I took a shaky breath and walked to him. I tried my best not to let my foot drag. *Perhaps he will let me go because of my leg. Maybe he has decided I will not be a threat to them. How can I help the Amerikanos with this leg?* I changed my stride and walked as I normally do. He put his hand on the back of my neck and led me away from the line. I felt a relief wash over me, but at the same time my heart was pounding, screaming to be let out of my chest. He led me out a back door and into an enclosed yard. The fence was woven at the top with barbed wire, and I watched him, waiting for him to pull his gun. He shut the door behind him and kept looking over his shoulder.

"Undress," he ordered.

"What?"

"Take pants off. Now."

I knew the Japanese were fond of taking the wristwatches of the Amerikanos, even their shoes. My pants were tattered and wet from the river, but we were the same size; maybe he would use them later.

As I began to undo my trousers he walked behind me, and I noticed that he was unbuckling his own pants. That was when I realized what he intended to do. I cannot explain what happened next. I was weary from working, I was dizzy from hunger, but I felt all the indignity at that moment overflow. They have raped our women, they have butchered babies, and now this bastard wished to rape me? He selected me with the injured leg. He thought to take the weakest from the group. What he did not know was that this leg has taught me to fight early on in life. I became a madman. I lunged at him with all the anger and terror and shame of the last few days. I broke his nose with one punch. He dropped his bayonet and I picked it up. I became like a rabid dog. I stabbed him in the face. The feel of the blade as it tore into his skin gave me immense plea-sure. I took both his eyes out. I ripped him open from his neck to his waist. I spoke no words. There was only the sound of my heavy breathing and the grunts that came from my belly. All the while my mind was screaming, *Run, run!*

He tried to raise a hand to protect himself, and it only angered me more.

I yanked the scabbard from his waist and pulled out his sword. I raised it high as I had seen the other soldiers do, and I split open his skull. Blood splat-tered hot and salty against my face. But that was not enough. I raised it again and chopped his head. And still I could not stop. I cut off both his arms. I sep-arated the hands from the arms. I chopped at his severed head, raising the sword again and again until his face could no longer be recognized. When I was through I was drenched with his blood. I staggered over to the barbed wire, and by the grace of the Almighty I managed to climb the fence and escape.

I lost my mind. I walked for days. I could not cool the rage that burned in me. It was only by some miracle that I saw all of you led into this place. And then a soldier found my hiding place and brought me here. I thought the Lord had deserted me, but He was with me all the time. You have survived, all of you, and I thank God a thousand times. Do not fear. He has brought us together for a reason. He will see us through. Perhaps Domingo will save us yet.

~ **WHEN MANG CARLITO FINISHES HIS STORY,** he is weeping. He looks at his son.

"Alejandro, did you watch over your mama?" he asks with a weak smile.

"Yes, Papa," he answers.

"I see that you have become head of the household once again."

"Carlito," Aling Louisa weeps, and smiles. "If only they would let me clean your wounds. How badly are you hurt?"

Mang Carlito raises his hand. "I am fine. Only a flesh wound."

"You have been returned to us." Aling Louisa whispers.

"It is a sign. There is still hope for us." Aling Ana smiles.

"You are like a mouse that survives again and again, old friend." Mang Selso claps him on the back. Everyone is rejuvenated by the sight of him.

"You see how everyone is strengthened by his return?" Mang Pedro asks me. "You see what family does for one another? I had a family once that loved me. But I was lured away by other things." He turns to me and says with great conviction, "Do not make the same mistake."

"I hear your words, Mang Ped, but I have a duty, a responsibility, to fight."

Tay Fredrico, the old Spaniard, interrupts our discussion. "But if one does not fight, then what becomes of our families? Will there be any left?" His Castilian accent still comes through, though he has not spoken the language in many years.

We watch Tay Fredrico carefully. Nearly seventy-five years old and still strong in his opinions. This last year of the occupation has taken his strength, but not his spirit. The sounds of warfare seem to have awakened something in him.

"Domingo, I asked you a question. Show some respect to your elders," he barks.

"If there is no one left to fight, there will be no families." This answer comes easily to my lips, for it is what I truly believe.

"*Bueno*, good. We see eye to eye, eh?" He leans back and gives his son, Mang Selso, a disparaging eye, then winks at me conspiratorially. "Let me tell you about the family I had, and the second family I found. And all of you, tell me which one was the more important."

~ portrait of an aristocrat

WHEN I WAS A YOUNG MAN of eighteen, I was fast creating a name for myself as an artist of Michelangelo's caliber. I had a great future ahead of me, but I was told by a fortune-teller that I had only one more year to live. There was a curse on our family, on the Jacinto-Basa name.

It began long ago, in the sixteenth century, when the Philippinas was still ruled by village chieftains. My ancestors descended from their Spanish galleons and took the land from the tribal chiefs. The tribes were not united, so there was no solidarity with which to fight off our superior Spanish hordes. The tribes raged against our Spanish conquistadores. In the battle, eight of the chieftains' sons were killed, ending their legacy. We claimed the land and divided it into *encomiendas,* districts, and these districts were distributed among the Jacinto-Basas. The chieftains bowed in prayer on their stolen land, lacerating themselves and swearing vengeance on us as their blood poured onto the earth. Eight of our leading families were then cursed. The curse was this: In each generation one male would not live past his nineteenth birthday. After a total of eight died throughout the years to replace their eight sons, the curse would be lifted.

My mother forbade us to speak of it, as if by not speaking a word, she would fool the curse somehow. My brother, cousins, and I joked about it often. No one knew for sure who would be the eighth to die. We were after all a big clan, and several of us, including myself, were to turn nineteen the following year. "This may well be your last night. Live hard," we used to say. That was our motto. It would enrage my mother to hear such talk.

There were many of us cousins, both Jacintos and Basas. The families were either Peninsulares, Spanish of pure blood born in Spain; Insulares, pure blood born on the island; or mestizos, not even pure blood, but mixed with that of the islanders. My brother, Oscar, and I were the lowest rung, the mixed blood. But even so, our status was much higher than that of the natives. We were the open sky above their dark heads.

My great-great-uncle had died one summer in Marinduque from a cholera epidemic the day before his nineteenth birthday. His father before him had died from a poisonous snake. Our father had died when he was eighteen, and he had been the youngest boy. Our grandfather had died from a landslide. Before that, a distant ancestor had drowned in a boating accident, one from turberculosis, another was shot in a hunting expedition, all before turning nineteen. The curse also seemed to favor the youngest. So being the youngest of all the Jacinto-Basas, it seemed my manifest destiny to be the next and final candidate to complete the curse.

My brother, Oscar, would joke, "What do I care? I am the eldest. Maybe it will get cousin Edgar and we will all be happy." We would laugh. Edgar was very feminine, and it pained my brother when Edgar accompanied us on our outings. You must understand, ours was a very manly group. We could be wetting our pants from fear, but we would never show it. I for one liked Edgar. He would rather go to the grave than spill a secret, and whenever he promised something, it could always be counted on, like rain on a suffocating day. I think secretly Oscar was quite fond of him as well.

WHAT WAS THE Philippinas like in 1870? You would not believe it if I told you. You must remember this was nearly thirty years before the execution of reformist Dr. José Rizal became the match to light the voice of oppression against Spanish rule. Manila in particular was so new, like a baby flower just sprouting from the dirt, but with a promise of great beauty. Spain had opened Manila to world trade and foreign investment. Everywhere one looked, great churches were being designed and baptized with Spanish names, Santa Isabela, Santa Teresa, San Pedro. Houses were being built on hillsides, with great verandas that circled the entire villa. And in Manila Bay, where the white flowers grow, you could see ships of every possible nation represented. Dutch ships, barges carrying spices from India, from Thailand, from France. Great ships arrived from Spain each month, carrying more of our people. We Spaniards owned all the land.

At the square, our women paraded in elaborate dresses. They wore the most delicate lace to cover their silken hair. The señoritas were exotic flowers adorning an already outlandish island.

Our ancestor was said to have arrived in 1521 with the Portuguese explorer Ferdinand Magellan serving under the Spanish royalty. This ancestor was whispered to be a bastard, a descendant of Philip II, the king of Spain, for whom our beautiful islands are named. Our grandmother was rumored to have been a *lavandera*, a Filipina woman who cleaned clothes. Our uncles had admitted to this on numerous occasions when they had partaken of too much wine.

To look at us, you could not tell. We looked pure Spanish. Oscar, in fact, had blue eyes. I myself have only the hazel, as you can see. Brown when I am near the earth, green when I am in a garden or forest. We were very handsome, and we were favored among the ladies of both classes, of both nationalities.

Although Oscar liked to dabble with any beautiful woman, he courted the Filipinas only in secret. He did not like to be frowned upon by his peers or turned away by the lovely Spanish flowers, who turned up their noses at the delicate Filipinas. "Why lie with the filth of the savages?" was the common saying then.

I loved only the Spanish women. I thought that nothing could compare to them. The way they looked down at you, with their straight noses, and enticed you with their dark round eyes kept me awake at night. I painted many images of them to canvas, just from memory. I thought of those arms that could wrap around your neck like clinging vines, their skin the color of cream, ah, and those bodies . . . ay, María.

I was very different then. I felt I owned the world. If Oscar and I were at the market, even if we had money to pay, and quite often money was literally falling out of our pockets, we would grab up a mangó or *suhà,* the giant orange, and take it without paying. The merchants knew our family controlled most of their trades, and they could say nothing.

We would peel the fruits with our teeth and spit it back at them. Even as the merchants were scrambling to clean away the mess, I would kick it away. We were wild boys. What would you expect? No father, with only rich, arrogant uncles to mimic.

We lived in a large house with an upstairs and a downstairs, with more than a hundred or more hectares of land. We were of the Ilustrado class, descendants of the educated upper class. We had completed our studies in Spain. Oscar studied law, so he could "always fool the officials with their own game," he used to joke.

I was creating a name for myself as a great artist. I had studied with the famous Spanish artist Joaquín Sorolla in Valencia. Probably only the old people know that. You know the grand mural in Santa Teresa church? The three panels of the Virgin as she beholds the Ascension of her Son into heaven, where the doves are flying around her like a halo and the angels with their great wings are bowing down before Him, the Messiah? I painted that one.

The one of large yellow orchids on the cupola of the library in Santo Tomas, that was me at sixteen. Tsk, tsk, that was a romantic one. I was very romantic as a boy. If you look closely at the corner flower, the name on the bumblebee is "Ana Lisa," a Spanish girl I was in love with for a week. I was also commissioned to do many portraits for private families. I painted many of those, but the ones that sold for high prices were the ones I was later persecuted for.

They called me a child genius at the time. In Madrid they said I had great promise. I was their answer to Italy's Raphael. My teacher wanted me to stay longer, but even then I had the Philippines running in my mind. The hot days and nights, the tropical flowers, and our lovely señoritas dark from the island sun.

I have seen a few of my paintings since then, in the homes of people who do not know that I painted them. Imagine, people turning up their noses at me and saying, "But what does a peasant like you know about art? Look, look at this . . . ah, but only a master could have painted such a design, no? Study the balance of this piece. Look how he captures the light; look at how the eyes of the woman in the painting seduce you." You can imagine how I laughed inside, when I agreed, "Yes, you are right, only the very best master." Yes, I remember now, I walked on stars then.

Painting was in my blood, the deep colors of olive, green, blue, yellow, and rust, all flowing through my veins. You cannot imagine the gaudy sunsets that our islands displayed, unmarred by the smoke and mechanical instruments of today. I can still smell the yellow paint, and with the yellow paint, the yellow flowers I had conjured in my mind. It pervaded the room, so sweet. So sweet, that time was.

I STILL REMEMBER the morning of Oscar's nineteenth birthday. We woke very early, with the golden rose of the sun just breaking the sky and the cool mountain air still lingering at the base. I loved those mornings, waking up and inhaling from my window the sweet smell of a certain kind of flower we called *bella maria*, which climbed outside our house. It had the scent of jasmine, rose, and orange rinds. That is the only way I can think to describe it. Think of the fresh scent of an orange when you first peel it, add to it the fragrance of the rose, then you will be close. It was colored like a flame, deep yellow and red. My mother loved this flower, so it clung to our house, perpetually scaling to touch the heavens. That morning our house was still asleep, for our family loved to rest. First they slept, and then they rested in their beds, curling and stretching their toes beneath the silken Indian sheets.

I was awake before Oscar. I remember becoming instantly alert and padding barefoot to his room. "Oscar, psst," I whispered. There was really no need to whisper; I could have shouted to the rafters and no one would have stopped me. The men in our family were allowed to shout and throw tantrums whenever we wished. Oscar was such a heavy sleeper that I kept chunks of garlic in a tin beside my bed, which I used in place of smelling salts. I took out a clove, hammered it loudly with the heel of one of my best shoes, and shoved it into his nose until he woke up shouting and we wrestled to the ground.

Oscar was a good fighter; he managed to flip me over and land on top of me before he even opened his bleary eyes.

"Oscar, the cliffs, remember?"

"¿Qué? Oh, the cliffs! Sí. Bien. Vamanos. What are you waiting for, imbecile? Get dressed."

I rolled my eyes and immediately put on my short pants and shirt. When I looked over at him, I realized what he had meant by telling me to get dressed. He had fallen asleep in his clothes, still wearing his sandals from the night before. I remember I had left him at a card game with a woman five years his senior draped over him.

"What hour did you come home?" I asked.

He merely smiled. "If you're not old enough to stay awake, baby, then you're not old enough to ask."

I hated when he called me that; it was short for baby brother, but it was incredibly embarrassing in front of the women.

We took two of our uncle Hector's new Arabian stallions; they were loco, not broken in yet, but not as crazy as Oscar and me. We laughed as the horses threw us a couple of times and kicked out at tree stumps. We flew through the woods, dodging the trees as the horses sped left, right, left, right. They were magnificent. We were so stupid.

"Come on, Eighth, I dare you!" Oscar shouted. That was what we called the curse. It became a being we were fighting against, no longer an idea, but an actual force of energy.

We hired sea gypsies to take us across the turquoise freshwater lakes in their battered boats and colorful masts, to Busuanga Island. Barracudas cruised alongside and bared their fangs at us as we maneuvered past the fissured limestone rocks. We arrived in Busuanga in the evening and the next morning when we visited the chalk cliffs on Coron Island, we looked up in shock. They were tall, fifty meters, eighty in some places. There were little crevices, thin and narrow, where you could barely stick your fingers in. Oscar began to shout and take off his shoes and shirt.

"Come on, little brother, I will show you how this is done." Oscar loved to be the one to say he had initiated me into this or that habit. So of course I liked to beat him, to say I had done it first.

Within seconds I had stripped down to my trousers. He had gotten a head start of about two feet when I reached up and grabbed his ankle and pulled him down and then scrambled up without looking back at him.

As I scrambled up the cliff, he shouted, "I am coming, Fredrico, damn you, you had better hurry!"

It was very dangerous, this thing we were doing. The rocks were not smooth, like the ones in the ocean, curved from the passage of time and water. These were like pointed sickles. You had to spread your legs on either side of you, like this, and you had to spread your arms so that you were anchored in more than just one area. You had to curl your toes like this, tightly, as if they were trying to write with a pencil. The cliff in some areas jutted forward, so at times you were hanging with your back parallel to the ground.

It was going smoothly, our little adventure, when I got to an area where the cliff jutted forward. I could have moved to the right, but then Oscar would have passed me. I shoved my fear down my throat and reached for the protrusion.

"Fredrico, no!" Oscar shouted as I lost my footing. We were hanging twenty feet in the air and I with my back even with the ground. I gripped as hard as I could and my other foot scrambled to stay put, but the cliff began to crumble and soon I was hanging only by my hands, and then by only one hand. I could have died. And do you know what Oscar did? He let go of one of his hands and put it beneath my back until I regained my footing. I was breathing hard, the tears stinging my eyes.

Then I heard it, the awful crumbling, the breaking off of a portion of the cliff. And when I turned to look, Oscar went sliding down the face of the cliff. He hit his leg on the way down and landed with his arm twisted behind his back.

That was how my brother started his nineteenth year. We arrived home two days later with Oscar roaring drunk from the doctor, his broken arm in a sling, and the party for his birthday had just begun. "The Eighth tried to grab me. But I spat in his face," Oscar boasted. My uncles clapped him on the back and roared that he was now a man.

"My boy, have you visited the church today?" asked Friar De Guzman.

"I have said enough prayers to satisfy our Maker," Oscar replied. "Say one for me when you go home tonight, Padre."

The friar sniffed. "I am to accompany your group. I have been invited."

Oscar looked at the friar curiously, but our *tito* Jorge grabbed my brother by the arm and paraded him around to all the lovely señoritas, saying, "This is my nephew."

"*Que guapo*," said the young señoritas behind their black-lacquered fans. How handsome. Zoila Rodriguez was there.

Zoila was tall and statuesque, with a graceful neck, much like a swan. Her hair was the color of honey, and her eyes were like sherry. But she was not a sweet girl. In fact, she was spoiled like a rotten papaya. She bruised easily if her wishes were not followed, and she would never let you forget it.

In the middle of the evening I noticed that Oscar was having trouble with his woman. She was becoming sour, stomping her feet and looking away from him. Zoila also was watching us from across the room. Friar De Guzman walked over to them. I did not like his familiarity with Zoila.

The men were uneasy, like a group of carabaos in a field of lionesses. Oscar stood beside me and put away a small glass of whiskey. He was glassy-eyed, and he smelled of alcohol. My brother could drink even a Russian to his grave and afterward run faster and fight better than any man I knew. Except for the smell, you could not tell how many bottles Oscar had enjoyed. Alcohol affected him differently; it enhanced his coordination, it made him stronger.

"What is happening with the women? Why are they staring at us like that?" I asked.

"They forget their place. Guadalupe believes she has influence over me. I only let her entertain the idea. They know where we are going tonight."

I leaned back and looked up at Oscar. "Where are we going?"

Oscar grinned. "Didn't Tito Jorge tell you? We take a trip to the other side of the island."

"Where do you mean?" I frowned, knowing the other side of town was infested with Filipinos. "Why not go to one of the dance halls on our side? Surely we have better, cleaner ones."

"It is not the dance halls that we care about, Fredrico." Oscar laughed. "Just when I think you are catching up to me, I realize that you are still just a boy."

You can imagine how his taunt irritated me. He was watching my face. He threw back his head and laughed, then bent close.

"It is not the dance halls we are interested in, but the dancing girls." He grinned. "Tito Salvatore knows a place. All virgins."

I made a face. "That is what they all say. Why are you interested in such women? Our women are ten times lovelier than any in the world."

"But what about our *other* women? Do we not have their blood running through our veins as well, brother?"

"That is just a rumor."

Oscar studied my frown. "Oh yes, and your skin turns a deep brown in the summer for no reason. Of course, you can stay here with the women if you like." He clapped a hand on my shoulder. "We shall tell you all about it in the morning. You've had too much excitement for the day, Fredrico."

I pushed his hand away. "Lead the way, imbecile."

Oscar put his good arm around me and announced to the room, "My brother has spoken. We go."

I was unsure about the whole affair. It was true we had Filipino blood running through our veins, but we had been brought up as mestizos; we looked down upon the natives. They were unintelligent and unsophisticated. I hated the way they squatted in the streets begging for food, or the way they ate with their hands, like savages. I could not imagine Oscar wanting to lie down with one of these women. But I was always curious and always game for anything.

"Look at these streets." I gestured wildly with my hands from the window of our *kalesa.* "They are riddled with squirrel holes. What could *Tito* be thinking bringing us all here?" We had ridden with a caravan of men, at least forty of us from the party and some we had picked up along the way. We were going through a very poverty-stricken part of town, and the villagers sat out on their stoops, watching us curiously. I shifted uneasily in my seat. I entertained thoughts of dingy chairs supporting my weight and my clean suit soaking in the dirt. I thought of roaches walking over my fine Italian shoes.

Young boys dirty and dark from the sun ran up to our carriage with their hands outstretched, begging for money. Little girls with their unkempt hair plastered to their faces stood in the streets barefoot, twisting their skirts.

"Fredrico—" My brother elbowed me. "Stop frowning, you shall frighten the children."

"Well, how long do we plan on staying?"

"We have not even arrived yet! Heavenly Father, you are starting to sound like Mama."

Our retinue continued down the crippled street, and thankfully the houses began to look more respectable. As we approached a satisfactorily large house, I was surprised to find we had left my brother's party to arrive at another. Music was coming through the large double doors; they were thrown open, with two servants sitting on the steps. Two stocky Filipinos stood as we alighted, and they looked at us with cold eyes.

"Look at them. They do not want us touching even their whores." I shook my head, stepped down, and began to roll up my sleeves. "I would have preferred not to fight tonight."

Oscar lifted his chin at them and glanced at me. "Whores? What are you speaking of, baby? This is a birthday party. There are no whores here. Not publicly. These are all young women from well-to-do Filipino families."

"*Madre de Dios.* You will get us killed tonight, brother."

My uncle Flavio led the way as the rest of our uncles looked at the Filipinos and made a good joke about them. Friar De Guzman stayed close behind my uncles. We walked into a grand hall and people stared. I heard whispers of "The Spaniards have arrived," and all the guests turned to look. The women were nervous, while the men gazed at us with stone faces. A group of ten men came to stand before us, their arms crossed.

"Get out of my way. You block my view," Uncle Jorge ordered.

"*Tito*," I said.

A woman came and invited us to sit. I remained standing, expecting a fight to break out at any moment. Oscar strode right up to the birthday girl and asked for a dance. She blushingly went out onto the floor with him. I stayed stuck to the wall.

I watched the women as they ran around trying to make things right. The air filled with tension with each gesture they made. Their men watched us through slits, their mouths tight. The birthday girl's mother offered us drinks and sweets as the rest of our group told jokes and took bets on whether they would bed her daughter by nightfall. Friar De Guzman disappeared behind a table of tubâ. He filled a glass for himself and then boldly took out a flask from his robe and proceeded to fill the tin, heedless of the deadly looks the Filipinos directed his way.

"We shall get shot," I muttered, cursing. It was ludicrous, all this way when we had our own women waiting for us at home. Does a dog in heat go searching in the next yard when he has a willing mate nearby? "To hell with this," I said, and went outside to smoke a cigar.

A boy of nine or ten stepped out, looking about as if I were the one he was searching for. I blew smoke and looked down at him from the corner of my eye. I do not think he expected to find me so quickly, for suddenly he seemed shy and stayed flat against the house. I chuckled, for he reminded me of myself just minutes earlier.

"Come out for a smoke, too, eh, *joven?*"

He shook his head, looking down at his shoes. I recognized him as the birthday girl's younger brother. "You are a Spaniard," he stated.

"You have not seen one before?" I joked.

"Your hair is brown. Mine is black." He pointed to his head.

"Yes, that is so." I nodded, tapping the ashes from my cigar.

"But your eyes are brown like mine. Not so different." He made a lopsided inspection of me from shoes to head. He put his shoes next to mine. They were the same type of design, what is called "wing-tipped" these days. Where the design at the tip is shaped in two arches, like wings.

"Same shoes," he said boldly now. He went to stand in front of me with his arms crossed. "Not so different, what makes you so different?"

I stopped smoking and looked at the boy with appreciation. I shrugged. "Different blood, from different countries. Our ancestors are from different countries," I said, satisfied with my answer.

The boy sniffed. "You were born in the Philippines?"

"Well, yes, but—"

"Then that makes you Filipino." He watched me carefully.

I pursed my lips, then could not help but grin. "You could say that."

"I did."

He stopped once more to study me, looking even more unimpressed, before he went back inside. I remained, feeling properly dressed down, so that I laughed out loud.

NOTHING MORE HAPPENED that night. Of course, Oscar bedded the birthday girl in the back of our *kalesa*. The carriage still smelled of sex when we entered, and I angrily lit another cigar to burn out the sweet stench. My uncles and all the other men had had their share of the women as well.

Of course, the next day was a different story. Zoila plied me with so many questions that I had to beg her to stop. She made my head spin with how quickly she fired the questions at me.

"Did you enjoy the party?" and before I could answer, "Did your brother sleep with any of the women?" and then before I could lie and reassure her that he had not, "It is not my place to ask. What of you? Did you find anyone you fancied? Prettier than me? No, of course not, that is a silly question. No one is prettier than me."

I wanted to put the whole incident behind me. The thought of Oscar bedding down with one of the natives was revolting. The excursion set my teeth on edge, like tasting a bad persimmon, with the chalky taste indelible on your tongue.

MY PORTRAITS WERE becoming well-known. I was to have a showing at the end of the following month. One of the *hacendados* had commissioned me to paint a mural along the side of his barn. He wanted it to be a portrait of our homeland, of Spain. He desired it to face east, where the sun first rises, so that the blessings of God would begin with him. I had decided to do one of Magellan's ships, with an image of the *hacendado* descending, in the costume of an aide to Magellan. I knew the man's ego, and I knew this would please him. I would paint the bright yellow bananas, the green jungle and palm trees, the monkeys, and the rich land. The *hacendado* was greatly pleased with the idea I proposed. In fact, he suggested I include his wife in the dress of the queen herself.

I told him it might not be a wise move, that the image might offend the others. So he agreed that his wife be one of the ladies-in-waiting. In truth, I did not like the woman and would have painted her as one of the sows if I'd thought it would escape his notice.

I ran out of supplies that day, and since I had not had the forethought to order them, I made a trip across town. There was a small shop in the middle of one of the markets in what is now the San Andres district. It meant that I would have to cross through the Filipino markets, but anything concerning my art was always a matter of life and death. If I had an image burning in my head, I would go crazy until I could begin.

Once, I had gotten up in the middle of the night and had painted a whole sunset using only egg yolk, flower, olives, and red and blue berries.

That morning I dressed more simply. I feared being hounded by the villagers for money. But as I dressed, I became angry at the thought of making concessions for them, so I tore off my cotton clothes and put on my best suit, a sombrero with a wide brim, and polished shoes. I ordered Manuel to fit our best *kalesa* and dress it with two of our Arabians. I left the house whistling. Little did I know that that morning would change my life.

OF COURSE, ALL the peasants stopped and stared as our *kalesa* drove through the streets. Again, the young children chased after us with their hands outstretched for money. I shooed them away with my hat.

"You want a carriage like this? It takes hard work. You cannot expect to make any money chasing carriages all day. Find some work," I said with disgust. Soon I noticed we were slowing down. I stuck out my head. "Manuel, what is keeping you?"

Manuel shrugged, looking back at me. "A woman has dropped her package and the people are stopping to help her."

I was overheating in the carriage and came out to inspect the delay. A woman was indeed picking up her belongings, dozens of mangoes, papayas, guavas, plums, and small packages on the ground. It would take hours before we could pass. I walked up to the crowd. I did not know if the woman spoke Spanish or not, but I did not think twice.

"You are keeping me from my appointment," I told her, tapping my foot. Her helpers dispersed at the sight of me.

"Sorry, sir, I paid good money for these," she said in broken Spanish. "*Uno momento, por favor,*" she begged, holding up one finger.

I walked away and looked at the men on the streets watching me with derision. "What are you staring at?" I shouted.

They shook their heads and laughed among themselves. If there was one thing I could not abide, it was to be ridiculed. The Jacinto-Basa name was not one to be scoffed at. We had come from two families of generals, doctors, admirals, heroes. I walked to the woman and pulled her by the arm.

"*Basta!* Enough, you have made me late."

"Please, sir . . ." She scrambled, trying to chase a few guavas. "I am almost done."

"Manuel!" I shouted.

"Señor?"

"Help this woman pick up her baggage and let us be on our way."

"Thank you, señor." She smiled.

I waited ten seconds, then shouted, "Manuel!"

"Yes, señor?"

"Let us be on our way."

The woman looked around frantically "Señor, please," she begged, "only a few minutes more."

I led her by her elbow and pulled her aside. "You see this *kalesa?*" I pointed. She nodded. "I am getting on. If you do not move aside, you will be crushed along with your belongings. I shall give you two seconds."

I counted out loud, "One, two," and ordered Manuel to ride through, and he did. The woman cried out. She must have felt every plum as the carriage bounced over each one. She stood with her strong calves spread slightly apart, wringing her hands.

WE ARRIVED AT the supply store just in time. I managed to gather what I could, but I was annoyed at having to choose my items quickly.

We returned to a quiet house. I was told that Oscar had waited for over an hour for me before departing for a card game. I ordered the servants to leave me and settled myself in my workroom, a room with large windows overlooking Manila Bay. It was once our father's study. I loved the room, because it stayed cool from the shading of the large *narra* trees and the breeze from the bay. The light allowed me to catch the various subtleties of color, the sage green to the darkest olive, the stark white of the clouds, and the brilliance of a clamshell. I could catch every phase of the horizon, from the pristine blue of a morning sky to the violet and then the deep indigo of night.

I was painting flowers that day, the wildflowers against the cliffs my brother and I had scaled the week before. I was sitting back, contemplating where to set Oscar's image as he climbed, when the door opened. One of the servants walked in and stood behind me. "Lovely picture."

"Mmm," I said, annoyed at being spoken to first. Another new servant in need of manners.

"You are quite talented," the woman said.

"I did not ask your opinion. Fetch me some wine." I was not particularly thirsty but wanted to remind her of her place.

The door slammed, and I heard the servant walk down the hall heavily; it set my teeth on edge. When she returned she let the door shut even louder.

"Watch how you enter a room. You walk as though you have rocks in your shoes. Where is my drink?"

"Here," she said. And before I could turn to reach for the drink, the red of the wine was flung across my canvas.

I shouted a curse.

A young woman stood with her feet set apart and her hands on her hips. Her skin was a smooth brown, her dress simple, a tan sleeveless thing. She had the figure of a dancer.

My eyes moved upward appreciatively, and I found her slender neck to be even more pleasing. I watched, transfixed, as the little pulse on her neck beat a fast tempo. The set of her wonderful chin was tight, and her almond eyes flashed hatred. Her hair was pulled back in a knot made by her own hair.

"You must learn some manners." I laughed, my anger turning into interest.

"The same can be said of you, señor," she said, the last part with obvious disdain.

"Who are you?" I folded my arms with a pleased smile.

"Not your servant, *Señor Estupido*. Today you were at the market?"

"Yes." I raised my brow, inspecting her features and realizing she was Filipina. I'd been so struck by her fierce beauty, I had not realized it.

"You drove over a woman's bag of foods?"

"Is this an inquisition?" I asked. "I was late. I would not have been able to purchase my supplies if the woman had kept me any longer, and in fact I was not in time to accompany my family on a social gathering."

"Ah, I see. You were headed somewhere important. Well, why did you not say? And these are the supplies, señor?" Again she said the title with scoff, as she inspected my paints.

"Yes," I said as if I were addressing a child.

"A pity your trip was a waste," she said, and spilled my entire table of paints to the floor.

I roared and reached to grab her. I managed an arm. She swung around and laid the palm of her hand strongly against my ear. I heard a ringing in the room for some time after.

"That was my *inay* you ridiculed, and you wasted a week's worth of our food."

"*Inay?* What is that word?"

"You are the educated class, are you not?" she asked with a smirk.

"I do not speak your language."

"So you deny your Filipino blood?"

"What are you speaking of?"

"Are you not Fredrico Jacinto-Basa?"

"The same."

"Then you also have Filipino blood coursing through those pathetic veins of yours, or do you dupe yourself into believing otherwise?"

I was speechless. It was no secret that our grandmother was Filipina, but I did not know the entire province knew.

"It is harder to tell with your brother and his blue eyes. But you, though you look full-blooded Spanish, at a certain angle I see the face of my people. I have seen you before in that high carriage you ride. The word *inay* means 'mother,' you idiot. You would do well to ask yours who your ancestors are."

"*Basta,* enough!" I roared. "What makes you take such liberties at calling me such things?"

"What makes you take such liberties with other people's dignity? Do you think my mother was proud to have a Spaniard run over her food? Do you think it was with gratitude that she thought of those few seconds you gave her to pick up just one more apple? What gives you the right to take one's pride away? What if that were your *inay?*"

I laughed. "No one would dare do such a thing. It is out of the question."

"You bastard," she spat. Then she turned and walked out of the room.

"Wait," I called, rushing after her, but she walked quickly past an amazed servant and out the front door. I tripped over a small bronze statue of a donkey my mother had recently purchased. When I swung open the door, Zoila was standing there tapping her heels, looking over her shoulder at the Filipina's departing figure.

"Who was that, Fredrico?" Her eyes were thin slits.

"I do not know," I said with exasperation. "And you will not talk to me in that tone."

She looked taken aback. "I merely asked."

"Do not ask!" I shouted. I took a deep breath, then said more quietly, "Come, let us find where Oscar has gone."

We found Oscar at a restaurant called El Loro Azul, named for the bright blue parrot of the owner's. There was a small floor for dancing and three men playing flamenco guitars while a fourth sang. Oscar was with our cousins, and as always there was a bevy of young women nearby.

"*Hola, Fredrico.*" He waved. "Here is my brother now," Oscar announced to the room.

As we crossed the floor, I noticed a young woman with the same build as the nameless Filipina who had visited me. It was not she, but that was how it went the rest of the evening. I noticed anyone who had her hair, her style of dress.

I took Oscar aside; I wanted to ask him his thoughts in this matter. I found myself watching the Filipino servants as they passed. An older Filipino came to clean our table. I watched him closely, glancing down at the color of my skin, then back to his. He must have felt my scrutiny. He became anxious and spilled a glass of sangria onto my pants.

"Damn you!" I shouted.

"Sorry, señor. My apologies, sir." The man tried to clean the mess. He smiled, trying to elicit a smile from me.

Oscar clapped a hand on my shoulder. "Leave us," he told the servant. "Brother, what is it? You are as nervous as a mare in a room full of stallions."

"Do you ever think of us as one of them?" I gestured with my cigarette to the servants moving from table to table.

"As a servant?" Oscar scoffed.

I frowned. "No, as a Filipino."

"Ah." Oscar nodded. "I see. No, Mama never recognizes that part of her, so why should I?"

"Is she still alive? Our grandmother?"

"If she is, Mama will not say. You should know that. The woman did not want her."

"Grandfather forced her. Isn't that the story? She was a Filipina servant, and Grandfather had an eye for her. She became pregnant and left Mama on the doorstep."

"Who cares what the story is. I heard Tita Anabella say that the woman was indeed Filipina, but that she seduced Grandfather. She found herself with child, then abandoned Mama as an infant, and that is that."

"I met a Filipina woman today."

"Ahh." Oscar smiled knowingly. "She was very beautiful?"

"Yes, but that is beside the point."

"Of course. What is the point?"

"Well, she was very proud for a peasant."

"Peasants cannot have pride?"

"That is not what I am saying."

"What are you saying, Fredrico? You are starting to make my head hurt."

"She ruined my painting."

"*Madre de Dios,* Fredrico, so paint another one. You are becoming too obsessed with your work."

"Of course, that is your answer to everything. Everything is replaceable. People are replaceable." I put my hand through my hair.

Oscar looked at me. "Fredrico," he said, "you are starting to unnerve me. You have had too much to drink. Have Manuel take you home."

"I can take myself home. You are right. I am tired. I should not have come."

"Yes, everything will be better after sleep. *Buenas noches,* baby," he said in that familiar way he used to smile and frown at the same time, as if I were some amusing puzzle.

HE WAS WRONG. My sleep was restless. I dreamt that I woke in the jungle and that my skin was a dark brown. I was one of the natives, and I wore deerhide trousers and carried a spear. I followed a trail to my house, and when my brother opened the door he did not recognize me.

It was past noon when I woke. Oscar was having coffee in the *sala.* His legs were crossed, and he was reading the paper. "You look like you've been in a cockfight without spurs," he said.

"Shut up." I sank into the sofa. "This is all your fault. You have poisoned my mind with these dark-skinned women."

"That is the problem, Fredrico. What you need to do is poison your body with them instead." Oscar lowered his paper and grinned. "I will find a woman just like the one you cannot stop thinking of, and after you bed her, phh." He waved his hand in the air, shooing away the image. "She will be out of your mind for good."

"Save your remedies. I will not taint myself with those women. You know I prefer our señoritas."

"That is not what Zoila thought after you left her last night. I had to take her home. You left without saying good-bye."

I shut my eyes at his words. "She was angry?"

Oscar laughed. "You are being too kind to yourself. She was furious."

"She will flog me with that vicious tongue. Why did you not remind me?"

"How was I to know you would leave so soon after I suggested it? When have you been known to follow any suggestions I make? Are you coming to the fiesta tonight? If you are, may I suggest you dress appropriately? Take a shower, shave that forest of a face. You smell like a horse's ass."

"I will meet you after I work on Señor Cardoza's mural."

"You will not be late?"

"No."

"I have your word?"

"In the name of heaven, Oscar, you begin to sound like Zoila."

He grinned, folded up the newspaper, and hit me over the head with it. "Then I shall see you this evening. You are certain you do not wish to come to the dog races?"

"Here." I handed him a few pesos. "Bet on the red."

I DID NOT tell Oscar that I wanted to go to the market. I waited until he left before I dressed and called Manuel to ready the *kalesa*. Maybe I did not even tell myself.

We crossed back to San Andres, and I stood up in my seat and asked Manuel to pull to the side. I recognized the woman I had injured the prior day. I quickly got out of the *kalesa* before Manuel could bring it to a stop. She did not notice me approach. She had two baskets of fruit, the very same kind that I had damaged.

"Señora . . ." I walked beside her. "Señora, let me help you." I took one of the bags from her.

She squinted at me as if trying to recognize an old friend. A smile teetered on her lips. "Oh, no." She grabbed frantically for the package when she realized who I was.

I shook my head. "Señora, I merely want to ask a question. The young woman who paid me a visit, she is your daughter?"

"I am sorry, sir. I begged her not to go. She did much damage?" she asked in broken Spanish.

"What is her name?"

The lady stopped and wrung her hands. "How much to fix the damage?"

"The damage is not an issue. I merely ask her name."

"Please, señor." She looked near tears. "She is a good girl, headstrong at times, but that is my fault."

"I do not wish to hurt her. I am curious."

The woman sighed and looked down the street. A group of Filipinos were walking our way. They exchanged words, and the woman looked at me. The men made a fence around us, and they ushered the woman away. I stepped aside to follow her, but they would not let me pass. I could see Manuel waiting in the *kalesa* for me to give the signal for him to step down. Manuel was a giant of a man, and there would be many with broken bones if he stepped down. I shook my head at him and turned to the Filipinos.

"What is this about?" I demanded.

"You tell us, Spaniard," said the spokesman of the group. He was a slender man, my age, perhaps a few years older. He had the tight muscles of the cliff climbers.

"Step aside, I have business with the woman."

"The woman is my mother. Your business is with me," the man said.

I looked at him squarely. "You do not want trouble from me. Do you know the bad luck that will follow if you start?"

"Worse than sharing our home with Spaniards?" the man said, smirking.

"It is a good thing that you smile, *cabrón*." I stepped back and lifted my fists.

There were footsteps behind the men, and I saw that the woman had returned with her daughter.

"Virgil, let me pass." The girl shoved her brother aside.

The sight of her eased my temper.

"You were looking for me?" she asked, hands on hips as in the day before.

She made me smile, though I tried my best to hide it. "I came to apologize." The words were out of my mouth before I could stop them.

She laughed. "That is ridiculous. What is it you want? I warn you, these people will not let you hurt me if you have come to repay me for what I did."

"I came to ask if you would let me paint you. As a kind of apology." Again the words were out of my mouth without thinking. I had not intended to say them. I felt like an outsider listening to someone else speak. I was curious to hear what would come next.

"And why would you do such a thing?"

"I would like to. Your *inay* would like a portrait of you, would she not?"

"Of course, we could display it in our *sala* whenever our guests arrive for tea and biscuits," she said with magnificent derision.

My face fell. I reached into my pockets and pulled out a few pesos. "Here, then, let me repay your mother for mutilating her food."

She looked at my money as if I held out carabao dung. It was a wonder she did not spit on my hand. "Surely you do not think you can assuage what my mother experienced yesterday with your spare change?"

Again I misunderstood her and took out more money, feeling like a fool, with a crowd now starting to form around us.

She ignored my outstretched hand. "What is it you want, señor?"

"Fredrico, call me Fredrico, please."

"What is it you want, señor?"

I looked from her to a little beggar boy pulling at my shirt. I gave him the money and he took off running, with five other children chasing after him.

"I want to make amends. We started out very badly."

She looked at me and laughed. "Go home, Señor Basa, this is no place for you."

I could not move. I could hear myself saying, "Is there any way?"

Her mother stepped close. I had already forgotten her presence. "A portrait, you say? You can do this? Make a grand picture of my daughter?"

"*Inay,*" the girl protested. She spoke in a flurry of Tagalog, pleading and arguing with her mother.

The mother looked at me hopefully, then back to the daughter. "He has offered. I did not ask him to come here. Oh, but it would be so lovely, would it not, Divina?"

"SEÑOR, SEÑOR FREDRICO . . ." I could hear Manuel's voice in the fog of my dreams.

"I shall have your head for waking me this early, Manuel." I looked around the room. My silk sheets were crumpled at the bottom of the bed. I looked toward the window. "It is still dark, you imbecile, what is the meaning of this?"

"You asked me to wake you, señor. To paint the Filipina, remember?"

I looked at my bare feet. The urge to pull the sheets over my head was overwhelming.

"*¿Quieres café?*" he asked.

"No coffee. Quickly," I told him, looking at the clock. I could picture the girl smirking at my tardiness, and that image was like a dousing of ice water.

~

I ARRIVED AT the flimsy excuse for a house at thirty past six. Manuel looked at me dubiously as I stepped down. "Have Luisa prepare a meal for me at noontime."

"*Sí, señor.*" He watched me walk up the three steps and waited until I waved him off. I had with me my easel folded under my arm and the rest of my paints and brushes in a leather bag. The mother opened the door and curtsied at the sight of me. She was visibly nervous.

"*Buenos días,*" I said with difficulty. Good morning. It was hard for me to address the woman; I would never have greeted our servants in the morning, but I thought it best to be on civil terms.

"*Buenos días, señor.* Divina is not here," she blurted, then wrung her hands furiously. "She wait, then she become tired. She is stone-headed," she said in broken Spanish.

"Stubborn, you mean?" I asked sarcastically. I was furious. I had told Manuel to go, and I was impossibly stuck until noon.

"Please, señor, do not be angry with she."

"Her," I corrected.

"Pardon?"

"Never mind. *Nada.*" I paced irately.

A little boy and girl were peeking out from behind the mother's skirts. She shooed them, and they skipped away, shouting, "*Nada! Nada!*"

"I came all this way to paint her. I should have the two of you thrown in prison. This is incredibly disrespectful."

"*No, señor, por favor,*" she begged. Please.

"This is a setback, you understand?"

"*Sí, sí, señor.*" She agreed with anything I said. "Will you sit, please?" She opened the door and pointed to a stiff-looking wooden chair. One of the legs was bent at an angle, and I was not certain it would hold my weight. I could picture the girl laughing at me as she worked in the fields. She would expect me to turn around and leave.

"Yes, I shall sit. Have you no better accommodations?" I frowned at the chair.

"*¿Qué?*" She squinted at me.

"*La mejor silla.* A better chair?"

"*Eh, anó? Ah, ¿qué?*" she said in a mix of Tagalog and Spanish.

"*Nada.*" I put down my belongings and gave her my best scowl.

I seated myself and was surprised at the sturdiness of the chair. I took off my coat and watched a roach scurry across the table. I put the coat back on. We looked at each other. I must have looked as odd as a peacock in a henhouse with my fine suit and hat. I decided to go about my business and opened my leather bag and began to bring out my brushes. I laid them out according to size, and when I bent down to bring out my paints, I saw that the mother was still standing there.

"Yes?" I looked up at her.

"Señor, I cook morning food." She pointed to the stove. "*Desayuno.*"

"You want me to move?" I asked in disbelief.

"*Sí*, move, here. Outside here." She pointed to the back.

I let out a big sigh, gathered my things, and followed her to the back of the house, which was only a few feet away. I saw two rooms as I passed. One had two mats folded on the floor. The other was smaller, with four mats folded up against the wall. There were no cabinets for clothes. The clothes were separated neatly in four piles against the wall. I was surprised to find that the back of the house was not so much a garden as a glorious field of wildflowers. She disappeared into the house and returned with the crooked chair.

"What is her name, your daughter?" I asked.

"Maricel." She curtsied.

"Maricel, very good." I waved her off and set up the easel.

"And you, señor?" She waited.

"You may call me Señor Fredrico Jacinto-Basa." I inclined my head.

"Ah. *Sí.*" She looked confused and hurried out of the room, then came back and curtsied once again.

The children came out and watched from the corner of the house. They threw little stones until I got up and told the mother what they were doing. The stones stopped coming, and the little boy later appeared rubbing his backside humbly.

An hour before noon I heard voices and could understand a little of the Tagalog. An older man peered outside the door. "Señor." He bowed.

I inclined my head and continued painting the sketch of wildflowers I had started. The man went back inside and said, "It is true he is out there."

Next came the sound of stomping feet. The door flew open and the young woman appeared. Her perfect olive complexion was red. Pieces of her hair were stuck to her face from sweat. She wore a simple man's shirt folded at the sleeves, worn trousers also folded at the ends, and sandals. The rest of her hair was twisted and pinned up loosely.

I stood. "Señorita Maricel," I said.

"This is ridiculous," she said in perfect Spanish. "There is much work to be done. I do not have the time to sit for a silly portrait. You have made your point. Your apology for the other day is accepted. Now please go."

"My God, your arrogance matches my own."

"Do not flatter yourself. This kind of attitude is forged from strength; yours is simply from good looks."

"So you admit to it, then? My appeal." It was difficult not to tease her.

"Who denies it? It simply does not impress me."

"Why do you grow angry, then?"

"This is not anger, it is boredom."

"Fantastic." I grinned.

"Go." She pointed.

I raised my voice to match hers. "I did not come all this way, wait all this time, to be treated in such a way. You are truly a peasant."

I could see I had her, for she started to push up both her sleeves as if she were ready for a fight.

Her mother had been watching from the window and came running out. "*Anák*, please, I would like this painting of you very much."

The young woman clenched her fists and stalked inside the house. She came back with a second chair, sat down, and folded her arms, glaring at me.

"Your hair, it needs to be taken down."

She chewed her lip but did not move to take it down.

So it went with us. I would ask something, and she would do the opposite.

AT NOON MANUEL came with my food. A crowd had gathered to watch my preliminary sketches of the young woman. They stared at the lavish display of food. I felt awkward and put the food aside, pretending I was not hungry. But then my stomach growled and I grew angry at my concern for them. I was midway through my fare when I noticed the crowd laughing. The two children were imitating my motions with wide, expansive gestures. In their hands were sticks they had broken off to the size of a fork and spoon.

The family squatted on a blanket and ate with their hands from a bowl. The bowl contained a small portion of rice and a few strips of meat and onions. The young woman sat with her legs crossed and her back straight. She was eating a banana, and a young man was sitting next to her. I watched her face then. Very soft, her expression was, as she talked to her kinsman. It angered me.

After the meal, her brother Virgil came to stand near the perimeter of trees with several of his friends. I concentrated on my art, but I could not help but hear their snide comments, most of which I did not understand. The few that I did decipher were infuriating. They questioned my masculinity, jeering that painting was an excuse for men who were not physically agile. I sat through it all, gritting my teeth and telling myself to concentrate. More than once I locked eyes with the brother.

Next, her father came to stand beside me, and as he viewed the sketches the crowd held its breath. They strained their necks and whispered to one another. The father nodded, put his chin in his hands, and looked worthy enough to be one of the caretakers at the galleries.

"This is very good." He nodded at me. "The flowers—" He pointed. "They have no color. Her face is not finish," he stated imperially.

"Yes, this is so." I turned my back on him and shook my head; what an ego the man had.

The crowd began to talk furiously. Nothing annoyed me more than their giggles and their laughter. I glared at them to show I needed silence.

"I will sit for one more hour, then we must stop." The young woman sat back down.

I took out my silver *reloj* and studied it. It was only three o'clock. "We will stop in two hours," I stated.

"You will stop in two hours. I will be gone in one." She raised a brow in challenge.

"You are talking crazy." I began to mix the paints.

"Does the crowd embarrass you? Did I not tell you this was a stupid idea?"

"What are they saying?" I asked.

She looked at me in disbelief. "You know nothing of your language?"

"There you go again. I am a Spaniard; I speak my language. Your language I do not know. Never mind. I care not what they are saying."

"That is a good thing. For they are making fun of your dress, and your pretty manners," she said, and gave me her first real smile. I felt as if someone had pierced me with a dagger.

AT EXACTLY AN hour she stood to go.

"Is it finished yet?" She straightened her dress, untied her dark hair, smoothed it out, then swept it up into a coil again. The image was intoxicating.

"Finished? I have not yet begun. This is merely the groundwork. You understand, the framework of what is to come."

"Well, how long will this take?"

"I do not appreciate your tone, señorita. These things cannot be rushed. Possibly two weeks, possibly a month."

"A month?" she shouted, then went into the house to further argue with her mother.

I was near to breaking the brush I held in my hand.

"Fredrico." A voice boomed through the house, and I recognized my brother Oscar's voice.

"*Hola, Oscar,*" I called to him as I packed, and the crowd began to disperse. I watched her brother Virgil's face darken as Oscar approached.

Oscar returned Virgil's gaze, grinning condescendingly at the Filipino.

"Brother." I stood. "Come see what progress I have made."

Oscar would not move; his eyes remained locked with the Filipino's. Finally I walked in between the two of them and willed Oscar to look at me. "I intend to finish this portrait," I said firmly.

Oscar glanced at me, and immediately his tone changed. "Manuel said you had come here. But I had to witness it myself. Whom did you wager a bet with? Was it Edgar? How much did he wager you to come here? Why was I not in on this? Am I not your favorite brother?"

"You are my only brother." I shut the case and clapped him on the back.

"Well?"

"Well?" I looked at him.

The girl came out with her furious face once again. "Come back at seven tomorrow. If you are late again, I will not return until you are gone. Is this understood, señor?" She glanced at Oscar, who was grinning like a fool.

"*Sí,*" I said, wanting to wring her neck at her tone.

She turned on her heels and slammed the back door, leaving Oscar and me to walk around to the front.

Oscar was smiling the entire way. "Thank God, I thought you had gone mad. I see now, younger one. I see now. She is exquisite."

"It is not as you think." I brushed his hand off my back in irritation.

"Oh, I think it is." He laughed.

ZOILA BURST INTO the dining room that evening. "Is it true?" she demanded.

"Zoila, sit down," I commanded.

Oscar leaned back in his chair and folded his arms in amusement.

Zoila continued her tirade. "Is it true that you sat in the dirt house of a peasant girl all day just to paint her, and in front of an entire village?"

I must admit it sounded ridiculous even to my own ears.

"Yes, it is true." I shrugged without apology. "This is something you do not know about artists, Zoila." I pointed a gilded fork at her. "Any artist who is worth his paint must experience different things; they must endure hardships."

"My God, you are good." Oscar raised his glass in toast.

"Shut up," I told him.

"I demand you stop this. It is an embarrassment that my beau be seen in such places." Zoila looked to Oscar for help, but he continued to pour himself another glass of wine. He couldn't have been happier had he been at a bullfight and the matador just walked out onto the plaza to fight two bulls.

"I intend to stop when I have completed the portrait. Now have a seat." I gestured to one of the five empty seats. Manuel rushed to pull out a chair for her.

Zoila looked pleased. "Where is Consuelo? I would like one of her famous empanadas, and not that wine." She frowned at Oscar as he was about to pour a glass for her.

Oscar put down the bottle and opened his palms placatingly, like a priest. "*Querida,* you have not even tasted this."

"If it is already opened, it is already spoiled. I want a fresh one." She liked to demand things in our house, and we entertained her in that way.

I WOKE UP on the floor and very late in the day. When I lectured Manuel on forgetting to wake me, he claimed that he had been trying for the better part of an hour amid my kicking out and throwing things at his person. Only when Oscar had walked in, returning from a long night, did he manage to obtain some help. Oscar came into my room, put both his hands to the side of my person, and shoved me onto the floor. He then walked out of the room, leaving a horrified Manuel to explain himself when I woke up shouting.

Of course, the young woman was gone when I arrived at her home. And true to her word, she did not return that evening. I left the house furious, threatening to throw the entire family into prison under suspicion of crimes against the aristocracy. The mother begged me to return the following morning and assured me her daughter would be there. I was so angry that I could not sleep the entire night, and when dawn broke I was the one who woke Manuel and arrived at the ramshackle little lean-to and waited on the doorstep as the young woman opened the door to let in the fresh air. After glaring at me determinedly for a long moment, she let me pass into her house. She made me wait another hour in the garden, while I watched an old beggar man picking berries from a nearby tree. I got the idea to practice and warm my fingers by sketching him before the family woke and ran him off the property.

I had to admit to myself that for a Filipino, there was a certain dignity about him. He greeted me with a single inclination of his head, as if reaching over the fence to their papaya tree were nothing out of the ordinary. Nothing spectacular when he crept up and drank from the dog's water trough. When he peeked into the bedroom of the house, I stood and he backed away and resumed his picking of berries with the air of a man studying a velvet satchel of loose jewels. He held each berry up to the rising sun and turned it in certain ways to the light. I do not know why he did that; it was not as if he threw away any that he deemed inedible. He ate each one that he picked.

As with the previous day, there was much stomping of the feet and a small argument ensued before the young woman came out to sit for me. I sat up watching with pity as the old beggar man backed away from the berries, but to my surprise, she took out a small cake from her skirt pocket. "Mang Thomas," she called.

I watched as the beggar approached and thanked her as a beloved neighbor would and not a thief. When he left I said to her, "Maricel, you have just rewarded a thief. He has been picking your berries since I arrived."

"My name is Divina; why do you insist on calling me by my mother's name? And those berries my mother planted just for him," *estupido,* she added with her eyes.

I shut my mouth and began to sketch her. "He bears my father's name," I said, trying to find a common ground where we were not each at each other's jugulars.

"You insist on drawing this portrait for my mother when we have no place for it."

"Why do you insist on her not having the portrait? You do not wish for her to have something beautiful?"

"Beauty is for the Spaniards to sit and watch and sip their wine while they expound on the sunset. Others such as us need that time to harvest the rice, to chop the trees, to plant the sugar cane, while there is still yet sunlight, and then to pay the taxes imposed on our trade."

"You are beautiful. Do you think perhaps your God wasted His time in creating you?"

She eyed me. "Is there a separate God, then, for the Spaniards?"

"Of course not," I said.

"Then why do your people act as if they have a different God to answer to?"

"Again you speak nonsense. We treat the peasants as peasants. Show me a Filipino who is an aristocrat and I shall treat him as such."

At that moment her brother Virgil walked in, grimacing and holding his back with one hand. His face was badly bruised, and his lips and teeth were bloody. "Forget this talk, sister. He will never acknowledge their treatment of our people, much less that he has Filipino blood running through his veins."

"Virgil." Divina ran to him.

"Who has done this to you?" I demanded.

He brushed Divina aside and regarded me with a wry smile. "Go on painting with your eyes closed, Spaniard. You do not wish to know."

Oscar was waiting for me when I returned that evening. "Have you bedded the Filipina yet?"

"Don't be crude," I said. "You know my great love for our Spanish women."

"Then if you have no intentions of bedding the girl, why do you keep returning to that house?" He anticipated my answer. "I know"—he waved his cigar in the air—"you owe a debt. To a peasant, Fredrico. Pay them and be done with it."

"Her brother was badly beaten by the constable this evening."

"And did he play the innocent? Incredible, what do these people expect if they do not work hard, a pat on the back?"

"From the calluses on his hands, he appears to be a good worker."

"Fredrico," Oscar said with deep gravity, "leave them to the constable."

Divina's eyes were red the next morning as she let me in. There was a certain stillness to the house. "Come in." She opened the door with a sweeping gesture. I merely raised a brow at her.

"Good morning, señorita." I inclined my head and headed for the back room.

"I am afraid that I will have to cancel our sitting this morning."

Another trick of hers. I turned on my heels and pursed my lips. "If you would only let me finish the portrait, we will both be out of each other's skin."

She clenched her fists. "I must hurry to the jailhouse. Your constable has taken my youngest brother and my father to be questioned. Pepe is only seven years old." Her voice cracked.

"What?" I asked in astonishment. I knew the inquisitions could be brutal, even fatal. A peasant, especially a non-Spaniard, had about as much say as a chicken after the cook has decided it is to be the evening meal.

"They came early this morning, so sure that my father had stolen from one of your friars. A man of God lying. My father is no thief. He would rather cut off his hand."

"When did they take him?"

"This morning, were you not listening?" Her voice was a mixture of sarcasm and fear.

I grabbed her shoulders and shook her. "This is not the time to be spiteful. I need to know."

"An hour ago," she stuttered.

"Come with me." I grabbed her hand and called out to Manuel, "Take us to Fort Santiago."

WHEN WE ARRIVED it was as I feared. Both father and son were badly beaten in the area of their hands. The father was sweating profusely, and his hands shook. He was about to confess to stealing the friar's coins simply to stop them from punishing the boy. I recognized Friar De Guzman immediately. He stood straight, his hands folded before him, with his brown robe moving in the breeze.

I knew De Guzman liked to "borrow" from the donations he collected. I had seen him many times at cockfights and drinking in the corners of the taverns late at night. I also knew there was a big collection that had been accumulating from the parishioners. It was to go to the purchase of a second stained-glass window. It was not difficult to guess where the money had gone.

The constable stood immediately when we strode in. "Señor Basa." He nodded. He had a wide grin for me. My family came from a long line of generals and dignitaries on the Basa side and a great deal of money from the Jacinto side. We had given quite a bit of money to the rebuilding of that particular garrison.

"What is the meaning of this?" I demanded. "This man and the boy are my servants. What are the charges? Speak carefully or there will be hell to pay."

"Señor, the friar insists that his money was stolen from his pockets and that the man and his son were the only ones present."

"When did this happen?"

"Yesterday afternoon, señor." The friar stepped forward. His eyes surveyed my polished shoes, my silk trousers and matching vest.

"Yesterday!" I shouted. "And you only thought to report this transgression this morning? These people were with me yesterday, Padre. Can you explain how your money came to be in their hands? Or will you accuse me, too?"

Friar De Guzman became immediately flustered. He took out his wooden rosary beads and began to feel each sphere. I was not sure of their innocence until that moment when the friar could not find his tongue. His eyes opened wide, emphasizing the dark rings under his bulging eyes. He struggled over his next words. "Perhaps I am mistaken. It was growing dark, you see."

"Yes, I suspect it would be dark in the taverns. I have seen you praying there on several occasions. Possibly you lost your coins in your ale, Padre." It was a statement, not a question. I noticed then that the toad stole glances at Divina, hungry ones that even I could feel. Divina rubbed her arms, moving away from his leering look, and edged closer to me. I stepped in front of his vision.

His attention snapped back to me. "Possibly, Señor Basa. As I said, it was growing dark." He looked away with effort and stared at the ground, but not before he touched Divina's breasts with his eyes.

I addressed the constable. "Captain, how do you expect my servants to do my work now that you have injured their hands?"

"Señor Basa, this is a terrible mistake." The constable's mustache twitched. He pulled out his own purse. "Here, señor, please take this. I feel terrible. Will that cover the cost for their time until their hands heal?"

I looked at the friar. "That and the promise that I will never come here on such a fool's errand again."

"Done, Señor Basa. Again my apologies." The constable bowed.

Friar De Guzman bowed his head. "Our apologies, señor. There is no need to fear, Divina, your father and brother are safe, you see? I shall say a prayer to ask for the swift recovery of their hands." The friar reached out quickly and brushed her hand, speaking in a whispery, sniveling voice.

He made to reach for her again, but I moved his hand away. "Say a prayer for your own soul."

I ushered the boy and his father to our *kalesa*. I could feel the friar's eyes boring into the back of my head as we left. Probably praying for a torturous death for me. Of course, I thought with amusement, his prayer had to stand in line behind the Jacinto-Basa curse.

The noon sky had softened to a powder blue, and the ocean was silver. The colors melded until they were one with the horizon. Divina watched me quietly on the ride back. Her father had thanked me once with deep gravity and then collapsed in exhaustion to sleep. His head bounced with every jolt of the carriage. The boy, too, had fallen asleep under his father's arm. "The padre does not like to be challenged. This will be bad for you, Señor Basa?" she asked.

"Such concern from my best enemy?" I joked.

"I never said you were my enemy." She looked away to the emerald-colored leaves of the banana trees that bowed and lifted as we passed. "Your countrymen, they will trouble you after this?" There was such dignity and solemnity in her almond eyes. The sun filtered through the trees and danced shadows on her golden skin, her full lips.

"So we are friends now?" I asked.

"I never said friends." She looked away, but I could see the traces of a smile begin at the corners of her lips.

WHEN WE ARRIVED at her house, her brother Virgil rushed to open the door. Her mother came out and fell to her knees, hugging my ankles. Virgil moved past his mother in irritation, his eyes counting first his father, then their younger brother, and then Divina. I watched as relief flooded his face. I braced myself for another confrontation with him, but to my surprise, he seemed almost apologetic. "*Gracias. . . .*" He nodded to me. Thank you.

"*De nada.*" I inclined my head. It is nothing.

"This was Padre De Guzman's doing? The joy it would give me to burn down his precious church." His eyes were dark with revenge. I had seen that look too many times on my own brother to mistake it.

"Do not let your anger misguide you, my friend."

"It is time you go home, amigo." He looked straight at me and then beyond, to the cloudless sky and the birds circling in the distance.

"I still have much work to do. I will decide when it is time to leave."

We locked eyes once again, then Virgil seemed to sigh and he walked out onto the road.

"Virgil," his mother called out. She clutched her skirts, the green veins of her hands bloated from the effort, watching as he walked down the road, worry etched in the deep grooves of her tanned brow.

DIVINA SAT VERY still for me that afternoon, and every now and then I caught her watching my face. When we took a siesta, I kept my hands limber by sketching the image of the priest with his deceitful eyes. I mimicked the desperation and fear I had witnessed in her father's face. The image haunted me, for I had never seen such a look. It was one born of hate and dwindling pride, of protectiveness toward the younger boy, and of pleading. I became so obsessed with the drawing that I did not notice when her mother stepped out into the garden. I had been so preoccupied, I was surprised to find the position of the sun was now in descent. The horizon was brilliant. It was as if someone had borrowed the soft pink of the flowers that lined the roadside and brushed it with romantic strokes across the pale blue.

She arrived with fried bananas made just for me. I took them. *"Gracias."* I nodded.

"Salamat," Divina said, watching me.

"¿Qué?" I asked. What?

"In our language you say *'salamat'* to thank someone."

"Salamat," I said to the mother, who smiled and covered her mouth. I heard as she hurried into the house to recount what I had said.

Divina studied me, and I followed the soft lines of her shoulders, the straight, delicate posture of her back. "Have you changed the sketch, señor?" She gestured to her portrait, which I had set aside on the chair.

"Just a few sketches," I mumbled, placing a cover over the image I had drawn of her father and the friar. "I was working on an idea, a concept."

She did not let me finish my explanation. She reached out and pulled the cover away. I watched as her eyes narrowed in fascination. "You see the padre as I do," she said in wonder.

"I was distracted by this morning's events." I stood, tipping the chair backward, and pulled the cover down again. I began to pack my brushes.

WHEN I STOOD to leave, I passed the father's room and watched as the man stared helplessly at his hands. Beside him, the boy lay asleep on a mat, his hair matted in perspiration, grinding his teeth as he dreamed.

I knocked softly against the wall. "Señor," I said, my voice gruff.

"Sí." The father stood, bowing to me. I fumbled in my pockets and took out the purse the captain had given me. I had intended to donate it to another church with a more trustworthy priest, but instead I held it out to the father. "Take this."

"Salamat," the father said. Then, realizing he had spoken Tagalog instead of Spanish. *"Gracias."*

I nodded, moving past him to leave. As I reached the door, a Filipino of my age entered. He regarded me with level eyes, and we nodded to each other. I noticed the flowers in his hand and glanced in time to see Divina coming down the hallway in a fresh cotton dress. I could feel my hands tingle and an angry heat take over my face. I swung the door open harshly and heard her call out to me.

"Señor Fredrico . . ." Her delicate sandals skipped on the floor. She stopped, breathless, as I stood in the doorway.

"You should have worn this dress for the portrait. Why did you not tell me you had such clothes?"

"I wanted to thank you again. What you did was . . ." She searched my face for the right words, and I was caught in those eyes. I wanted to remain there in her sights. "What you did was honorable."

I inclined my head. "I must go."

"Of course," she said, and took a step back.

Her mother was standing in the hallway, and she heard our exchange. "Señora," I called her over.

"Yes, Señor Basa?"

"Tell Manuel when he arrives that I wish to start on foot. I wish to stretch my legs. I have been sitting too long today. I will stick to the main road; have him come find me."

ON MY WALK I remembered the younger boy's hands, both broken. I thought of the father and the expression of worry he wore, even after I had given him the money. I had never known that desperation.

You are overwrought; these things occur, I told myself. It was as I was reasoning this that I came upon Divina's older brother and his friends on the roadside. They carried sticks for burning. And I remembered his comment regarding the church.

Virgil was speaking to one of the loudmouths who had pestered me with his taunts the first day I was at their home.

The loudmouth laughed with amazement. "We have been blessed. Look, the bastard approaches. Come, let us show him how it feels to have his hands broken so he can no longer paint." The man gestured the group forward. He walked with a fake confidence and with maliciousness in his eyes.

I placed my belongings on the ground, never taking my eyes from the approaching band.

Virgil spoke. "Roland, stop. He is under my protection."

"I do not need your protection," I spat, counting the number of men and watching that no one walked behind me without my notice. There were eight of them. I would go down fighting, and I would not forget a face.

Virgil locked eyes with the loudmouthed Roland. "He stopped the friar from hurting my family."

A loud murmur went through the group.

"Why did you not mention this earlier?" Roland asked with accusation.

"Since when do I answer to you?" Virgil answered with equal venom. "I am the leader of this group."

"Enough of this rambling, are we to fight or not? " I demanded.

Virgil chuckled at my audacity. "Go home. Consider us even in our debts."

"Virgil, I know you are angry at the friar." I looked at their sticks. "But you must not do this."

"This is none of your concern. You see only what happened today. That this friar insulted my father, that he hurt his hands and those of my brother. You see nothing of the other injustices. The chiseling down of our souls. The taking of our land, of our women. How do you think it feels to be a beggar in your own country? Where once we were powerful chieftains and generous hosts. Do you think it is a good thing for my brother to see his father helpless to stop his beating, or the roving eye that the friar has for his sister? Each meeting he looks at Divina more boldly than the last. There is nothing to keep him from taking her."

"But that is one man, Virgil. One friar. I have fixed the situation. He dares not lift a hand against any I have named my servants."

Virgil shook his head in disbelief. "An enemy of one friar is an enemy of the whole. You do not know the power they have. They have poisoned the spiritual mind of the Filipinos with their teachings. My people fear to raise a hand against them. They fear that God Himself will strike them down, that He is on the side of the friars."

"The Filipinos were in need of guidance. They needed religion."

"We had our own religions."

"Paganism, praying to false idols."

"Who is to say the God we prayed to is not one and the same? Go home, Spaniard. You do not wish to know what I am telling you. We are enslaved to you."

"I see no chains."

"Ha, for three hundred years you have chained us spiritually with your religion. Your friars pound it into our minds. But think of this, Spaniard. Why do they teach us so much of the Bible, and nothing of the Spanish language? It is because they wish to cripple us spiritually but keep us ignorant of the laws. Because changes are made within the law."

"Virgil, burning the church will not endear the Spanish government to hearing your pleas. Violence will only bring violence back to your family. Is this what you wish?"

"There is no other way," he said. His eyes were deeply sad, and I felt his grief.

"There are many ways, but do not confuse what you hope to accomplish with your personal anger. It will only muddy things." I held out my hands placatingly. The air had grown cold, and I could see their fire was waning.

Roland could feel it, too, and he cut our conversation short. "Virgil, enough. So he did your family a favor. He knows nothing of our cause. Too long we have had no voice. Tonight we speak out."

I was at the end of my patience with this man. But I knew that to dismiss him would be to dismiss myself. I pleaded once again with Virgil. "Your cause is one thing. You can find a voice, you can write to Spain if you feel there are injustices being done. But this, these plans of burning down a house of God is a personal vendetta. I will say it again. Do not mix the two."

"And if we write to this government, we shall be heard?" Virgil asked.

"It is worth a try."

Virgil contemplated the sun as it descended. His eyes roamed to the tree-tops, where the golden rays were fading. Behind us, the moon was full and rising. He was strongly built, with wide shoulders and muscled calves. He wore cotton pants drawn by a string that stopped just above his ankles. The color had long ago faded into a vague gray. His shirt was nothing more than a gentleman's undershirt, a size too large, the neckline pouting outward in the back.

"Let us think on this matter."

"But Virgil, we are here. We are ready." Roland put a frustrated hand through his hair, then crossed them and tucked them under his armpits. "You let a Spaniard interfere with our plans."

"The church will still be there to burn in the morning," Virgil replied. "I will hear more of what Señor Basa has to say."

The group dispersed, their allegiance to Virgil evident. Roland threw the stick aside, but not before he fixed me with a tremendous scowl. I was not one to take such a look, but I did. I decided that this was more important.

We did not speak immediately. It was as if we both knew we teetered on the brink of credibility in each other's eyes. The sky began to rumble, and a light shower overtook us. We walked in the rain in silence, with only the gentle tapping as it touched the palm leaves in descent. Virgil's neck was gnarled from two large scars that crisscrossed and traveled down into the back of his shirt. His hands were marked with scratches and cuts. The texture of his skin would someday be like hardened leather, so brown was it from toiling in the sun. I saw nothing of Divina in him, except perhaps in the wiseness of his eyes.

"I will have the friar transferred. He will bother your family no more."

Virgil laughed, then pinched his eyes shut with his fingers. "They will only replace him with another. I would rather keep him; at least I can anticipate his evil. To gain a new friar would be to throw ourselves in the dark."

"What is it that you want, Virgil?"

"I want our land back. Why must we toil every day on our land, only to have the Spaniards reap the profits? I want respect for our people. I want to smear the condescending looks from the faces of the Spaniards who collect our money and eye our women. We want to be left alone to govern ourselves. We have no voice. I wish us to be heard. There are reforms that need to be made."

"You ask a lot for a servant," I said.

"You risk your life by calling me that."

"I have saved your hides. This burning of the church would have been blamed on your family, and your father would be in chains by morning. I know one thing. If you let your personal hate interfere, you will bury your cause."

We parted each with a new understanding of the other. I felt assured he would not risk the lives of his family.

As I expected, word of my antics had reached Oscar. He was smoking a cigar, his back leaning against the opening that divided the dining room to a large balcony. He accosted me the minute I walked through the door.

"Fredrico, this is really too much. You cannot make a habit of protecting this girl's family. If the man stole the money—"

"He did not steal the money, Oscar. The friar lies."

He studied me. "Be careful, baby, this girl is starting to affect your thinking."

I woke with an image so compelling that I rushed to my easel. It was a very domestic scene, villagers gathering corn and chopping wood. Nothing out of the ordinary, except for the Spaniard I sketched at the top of the rise, a priest by his side. The Spaniard stood with his arms folded arrogantly; he was taking payment for the people's land. Land that was theirs before the Spanish had arrived. Nothing worth noting, as I said, except that when I sketched the Spaniard's face, I realized that I had drawn my own.

There was a pounding on the front door and I shouted for someone to answer it. When the pounding continued I remembered that the house was empty except for me. I got up slowly, my eyes still fixed on my sketch. I threw my brush aside in irritation.

"It is prayer time, everyone is at church!" I shouted as I opened the door. It was the constable and three other men.

"Señor Basa, my apologies."

I looked to their rifles. "What is it you need?"

The constable cleared his throat. He crooked his finger and loosened his collar. "Señor, I know this is a grave mistake, but I must take you to Fort Santiago."

"Fort Santiago?" I barked. "What has happened now? If Friar De Guzman has bothered that family, I swear—"

"Señor, I must take you in under suspicion of arson."

I stared at the constable with utter astonishment and fury.

"Señor, Friar De Guzman's church was burned last night. Several of our people saw you walking with Virgil Zamora, the subversive, the upstart. Furthermore"—he took a deep breath—"it was rumored your group carried sticks. Señor, it is simply a formality until the matter is cleared. There is no need to put you in chains."

I laughed threateningly. "The four of you could not manage that. I will come. I will know who is behind these accusations."

At the fort the constable asked me to step into one of the cells, again for formality's sake. I had never been in a prison cell, and the thought was intriguing to me; but once I stepped inside and the key was turned, the matter grew serious. The constable backed away and almost stumbled onto the floor. He backed out into the dark, cavernous hall. I could hear his footsteps resound against the walls. The cell was cold and the passageway lit by lanterns. The sound of water trickling gave the room a colder feel. I remained standing. There was a simple cot, the sheets yellowed and no doubt infested with lice. I could not help but chuckle at the situation. My uncles would tell this story again and again. I shook my head.

"The situation is amusing to Señor Basa?" a voice asked from the darkness.

"Show your face," I ordered.

"Perhaps the burning of God's house is also funny?" The man stepped into the light, and I could see his well-polished shoes beneath his dark robes.

"Ah, Friar De Guzman. You have me on another fool's errand."

"They hang people for lesser crimes, Señor Basa. Of course, a formal trial must be held, but that is a trivial matter. Several people saw you burn down this church."

"Who are these cowards? Let them show their faces to me."

There was movement behind the friar and two other men stepped forward, both in the robes of their organization.

"I am Señor Rodriguez, and this is Señor Ricardo. We were walking home after prayer last evening and we did see you light the fire."

At their words, I remembered Virgil's warning: "An enemy of one friar is an enemy of the whole." I knew a moment of fear. "Where is my brother? He will straighten this matter out. Do you know who my family is? You risk your churches by fooling with me."

"Again he threatens the churches," De Guzman said.

The others nodded. "We have heard the threat with our own ears."

Friar De Guzman inclined his head. "The trial is set for this afternoon, Señor Basa, whether your family arrives or not."

When they had gone, I paced the cell. I laughed, I thought of how I would repay the friar. Later I watched as the sun began its descent in a glorious veil of muted rose and orange through a small window. I closed my eyes and imagined the way the dirt outside would turn a warm clay color and how the pace of the day would begin to slow on the islands. People would breathe in the scent of the *sampaguitas* and purple lilacs. They would smile softer in greeting to one another. They would sit on their steps and drink wine, or the thick sago, with the sweet sugared balls I could almost taste.

When there was still no word from my family, I began to grip the metal bars in irritation. "Has there been any word from my brother?" I shouted. "Constable, I demand to hold the trial until my family is notified. Constable!" I roared.

I could hear footsteps. I imagined they were above me, cleaning the gun barrels for my execution.

WHEN THE DOORS finally opened, the sun was already past the horizon and the gentle night had begun to temper the heat of the day. I craned my neck to watch who it was that approached. Though my confidence had diminished, I still felt that the matter would be resolved and I would be set free. The only show of my nerves was the shaking of my hands, which I shamefully could not control. Momentarily I shoved them into the pockets of my trousers. "I am ready to have all your heads." I shook the bars of my cell, then walked to the corner and forced myself to remain still. When I caught the first glimpse of Friar De Guzman's robes, and those of his cohorts Ricardo and Rodriguez, I had trouble catching my breath.

The friar surveyed me with a pious smile. I locked eyes with him. "Has news reached my family?" I asked.

"News has reached your family." He smiled.

I searched the shadows behind him but could see no one.

"I am afraid they have declined to come," he announced with pleasure.

"What?" I shouted, causing the friar to step away from my cell, but not before I was able to stick my hands between the bars and clutch at the neck of his robe.

If not for the sound of sudden laughing and the grinning faces of my three uncles, my cousin Edgar, and my brother revealing themselves from the shadows, I swear to you, I would have strangled the man.

"Let go of the friar, Fredrico," Oscar said softly.

My uncles continued to chuckle, folding their arms before them as they shook their heads. My uncle Juan Benito stepped forward and pried my hands loose from the friar's hood. "See what happens to you when you do not attend church, youngest?"

"Unlock the cell," Oscar ordered.

As soon as I stepped out, the three friars stepped back with their hands out before them.

"Come, Fredrico." Oscar clapped me on the back. "It was our idea to joke with you."

"This is true." Friar De Guzman nodded, his eyes nervously watching my every movement.

"What took you this long?" I shoved Oscar's hand away.

This, of course, brought more laughter from my uncles, who immediately clapped me on the back, locking my neck with their arms in play. "We just now arrived, as soon as we heard. We were half a village away. You know they fear our family name. These priests would instantly have been executed had anything happened to you. Have you no faith in your uncle?" Juan Benito asked.

"Well, has the matter been cleared?" I demanded.

Oscar could see my foul temper and stopped my uncles from further joking. "Yes, of course. Your name has been cleared; they are hunting several Filipinos. They still think possibly the brother of the girl you have been visiting. Several people have come forward to say you were not present."

"Where were these people earlier?" I walked upstairs, and the procession of robes and chuckling relatives followed me.

"It was a terrible mistake, Señor Basa, our apologies, but I was overwrought at the damage to my church. Surely the señor understands?" De Guzman asked, holding out his hand. But I could see in his eyes the challenge.

I ignored the outstretched hand. "You will catch the hell you preach if I am ever placed in this position again, Padre. Is that understood?"

De Guzman bowed his head.

"You see, Fredrico?" Oscar asked as the carriage bumped and swayed. "De Guzman is showing you that he too has power. You can be assured you were never accused. He wanted to show you the extent of his hand within the community. He is not without force. He has the whole Catholic organization behind him. You would do well to follow my advice and not cross paths with him. He wants this girl; let him have her. Finish your portrait and move on to the next face. Besides, you have been neglecting Zoila."

"And the brother?" I asked.

"Whether he caused the fire is not the issue. It is just a matter of time before he commits a crime. De Guzman will do all in his power to take any obstacles out of his path. You have already seen how he has humbled the father and the youngest boy."

"And this sits well with your conscience?" I asked.

Oscar sighed. "These people are beneath us, Fredrico. They are not our business. Why do you court trouble? Our life is easy, why make it hard? We have so much before us. Turn your head, bury it in another beautiful woman. We can go to Spain again, Italy. Wherever you like. It was my mistake in taking you whoring in the gutters. Let me make it up to you."

"Listen to yourself," I sneered. "Do you know how it felt to be trapped in that damned cell with lies piled against your person? They could have decided to kill me at any moment. These people, Divina's people, experience this daily."

"They would not have killed you."

"I thought better of you, brother. I never realized how you prefer to sit on your throne and act the rich lord."

Oscar's temper flared. "Do not judge me. I give excuses to no one. I am a Jacinto-Basa."

DIVINA AND HER mother greeted me at the door. "Señor Basa . . ." Divina grabbed my arm. The contact was jolting. "Señor, we have just heard this morning of what happened to you. Are you hurt?" She searched my face.

"Where is Virgil?" I asked, walking past her.

"He is in the back. Señor Fredrico . . ." Divina hurried to catch up with my pace. "He has done nothing. I promise you. He explained how you . . ." Her voice trailed behind me.

I walked to the back of the house and flung open the door. Virgil was kneeling to help the younger brother tie his shoes. He stood when I approached.

"You bastard!" I shouted, and immediately we were rolling on the ground. "I warned you to leave the church standing. I could have been killed." I grabbed his shirt and shook him. Divina fell down trying to pry us apart.

"Listen to what I have to say." He struggled and shoved me back. "They did it without me. They burned the church at Roland's instigation." I hit him twice in the face and we wrestled some more before his words soaked in.

"And you let him live? This man is a danger to you. Why do you risk your life by coming home? You should be in hiding until the matter is cleared."

"It will never be cleared. De Guzman has his loins set on Divina. I cannot leave my family. I must help my father work the fields. I will sleep in the forest until the matter is resolved. This is how we live, under the constant threat of the friars. Like ants walking beneath a suspended heel."

"What are your plans?"

"Not of your concern," he answered, his jaw set. His youngest brother called out to him and jumped into his arms. He hugged the boy and placed him back within the fenced enclosure, then disappeared into the blanket of trees.

"Is it true? You finish the portrait today?" Divina asked softly.

"After today, señorita." I inclined my head. I had stayed awake the entire night, letting Oscar's words penetrate my mind. He and Virgil were both correct; I was bringing too much attention to their family, and I needed to return to my own life. I had a mural to finish and Zoila to think of.

Divina bowed her head.

"This saddens you, of course, since you are so enamored of me," I teased.

We finished our last sitting with a day that could have been taken from paradise. The jade of the leaves behind her house were brilliant, the caress of the warm breeze soft and scented with the dozen mango trees. I could not hold her gaze for long, it went straight to my soul. At the close of the day I presented her mother with the finished portrait, and within minutes she had invited the entire neighborhood to appreciate my work.

I rode home in confusion, unable to get the vision of Divina out of my mind. I had been away from Zoila too long, I told myself. Zoila would clear my worries and remind me of where I truly belonged.

When I arrived home, I found Zoila and Oscar in an embrace.

"Fredrico." Oscar pushed her aside.

"Pardon me," I said, not moving, my head spinning.

Oscar was in a panic. "I have been meaning to speak with you on this matter. But you are always gone before I open my eyes in the mornings." He brushed a hand through his hair and looked over at Zoila, who had started to cry.

She ran to me with her fists clenched. "You have brought us to this, you."

Oscar rushed to her and pulled her away. "Stop it. We are the ones who have wronged him."

I could not think; I pointed to my belongings. "I need to gather my supplies. I came only to get my brush. I forgot this one, you see." I pointed, not knowing what to say. I was sick to my stomach. I did not want to let the thought in. I did not want to believe that my brother had betrayed me. Later, I said to myself. I shall think about that later.

Oscar stumbled after me; he watched as I went about picking through my brushes as if nothing had happened. "Fredrico, say something. You know I would do anything for you."

"Would you?" I raised a brow at him. "So this was your plan all along. Lead me to find other women so you could take mine." I do not know why I said those things. I think I was more frightened by the fact that I had no feelings for Zoila at all. "My own brother," I said with disgust. Even now it hurts me to think I said those things to him. I meant to stab him as if with a dagger with each word.

"Fredrico, please," Zoila sobbed, throwing her arms around me. "I have been so lonely."

I removed her arms. "It is too late, Divina," I said, staring at her with solemnity. The room went silent with her sharp intake of breath. I felt the hard sting of her hand against my face.

"How dare you call me that peasant's name? You play games with us. With yourself. You are obsessed with her. It is utterly disgusting." She dusted off her clothes as if I had touched her with dirt.

Oscar watched me. "Fredrico, what is happening to you?"

THAT WAS A desolate time. I locked myself in my gallery for five days. I painted with so much passion, I could barely stand it. I would wake each morning with a new scene to paint burning in my hands. I painted until my canvas turned pink from the glow of the evening sunset and long after that. I painted three or four portraits a day. It was never necessary for me to sketch. The images came out complete. I painted five portraits of Divina. They still hang today in the Plaza de Luna, near Malacañang Palace. The one of the beautiful Filipina with the proud eyes.

EVEN THOUGH I burned to speak to Divina, I refrained. I was in agreement with Virgil and Oscar. It was better to leave her alone than to challenge the friar's interest in her. I did not know how long I could stand to be away, but I was trying. She visited my dreams. A week had passed when word reached me that her brother Virgil had been arrested for the burning of the church. I was saddened by the news. They will kill him, I thought. You can imagine my surprise when news again reached me one morning that he had been released and that Divina was now serving Friar De Guzman's household.

"The little fool." I raked my hands through my hair. "She wishes to sacrifice herself to that pig. Come, let us go to her house, I will straighten her thoughts," I ordered Manuel, but he only looked at me steadily.

"Señor, your brother instructed that I not take you to the señorita's house. He made me promise, señor."

"Take me or I will have you banished." I threw down my paints.

Manuel was unaffected. "Your brother has assured me that I will not be dismissed."

I laughed in vexation. "I will take the horses myself."

I toppled the large desk from India. The statues from Thailand, the portraits from Italy, fell to the floor. I went crazy and scared away my mother and the servants. I turned to see Oscar standing at my door.

"Fredrico," he said.

"Do not start with me. I am on the verge of using your blood to crimson the red of this gown I am painting."

"Fredrico, do not interfere with her life. If she does not give herself to De Guzman, he will plague her family. You know this. These things happen. You must turn your face away. She gives herself to De Guzman to placate him. To stop him from harming her family. There is honor to this."

"Leave me!" I roared. I saw the truth to his words, but I did not need to be in his presence. I had renounced my ties with him and Zoila.

Oscar was hurt; I could see it in his demeanor. His shoulders fell, the lines of his mouth went slack. "What has happened between us, brother? Let us fix this breach."

"There is no cure for it." I stomped about the room, organizing my brushes only to throw them against the wall.

"No cure," Oscar murmured. The next time I looked up, he was gone. I wanted to run after him, but there were deep ravines between us now, steep cliffs, impassable mountains. I listened to the echo of his receding footsteps, and his sigh resounded like the lapping of the ocean against the rocks.

~

THE DAY OF my gallery showing arrived, and I was excited. The household was in an uproar as everyone busied themselves with dressing. They were very proud of me. When we arrived at the grand plaza, there were many guests, many patrons of my work. My mother walked proudly. She had ordered a special gown made. It was a pale green to match her eyes, with a matching silk shawl. There were toasts made to my success. I had created twelve pieces initially, but they had doubled to twenty-four.

De Guzman approached and offered his hand, palm down, expecting me to take it and place it against my lips. He relished my blatant refusal. He gloated at my silence.

As the unveiling began, there was a great stir as one piece after the other was unsheathed. There was the one of the gondolas from our visit to Italy, and the one of the market in France teeming with people, then the transition to the Philippines and the lush jungles; there were several portraits of the wives and children of the local *hacendados,* and one of a young Insulare inspecting his father's land. People were congratulating me and bidding for the portraits with the viewing only halfway through.

Manuel ran back to tell me, "Fredrico, already there is a war between Don Alfonso and Señor Trinidad for the one of the bullfight in Madrid."

"Very good." I smiled.

Slowly I began to notice peculiar looks come my way. Oscar rushed to my side. "Fredrico, are you crazy?" he asked. "These pictures of the Filipinos are offensive. The ones of the *hacendados* whipping them, the one of the friar himself leering at the young Filipina, then there is the one of the old Filipino beggar man. Already several people have walked out. What are you trying to accomplish? You had better say your apologies."

I looked around in surprise. People were indeed aghast. In fact, a great tenseness had befallen the room. De Guzman was in attendance, he who had been the inspiration for the portrait of Divina and the leering friar. He looked at me with such intensity, I almost laughed. Even our closest friends looked away in embarrassment and made their excuses and left. My mother left, weeping, and only my uncles stayed, shaking their heads.

"I have only drawn the truth. Can I not become inspired?" I had suspected something of a sensation, but not the dangerous and castigating looks I was receiving.

"Fredrico, what has this woman done to your head?" Oscar hissed. "You have made our family a scandal, a laughingstock. You could be killed for this."

"Ahh, but I have never felt so alive, brother."

"You must shake this. I will tell them you have been under a great strain. Look, they leave as we speak."

"Let them go, idiots. They do not know true art. All they wish to see is lies."

"I blame myself. I should never have taken you to those places to mix with those people. Knowing how easily impressionable you are. That Filipina whore has taken your reasoning."

I turned to Oscar and hit him full in the face. He got up with a shout and tackled me. We were rolling on the ground until Manuel and Tito Salvatore pulled us apart. They ushered Oscar out and left me without a backward look. I was alone.

I went to the table of food and made myself a plate. I grabbed a bottle of wine and sat. The door opened and I shouted, "Leave me. No one is welcome. The showing is finished." When I heard no footsteps of retreat, I looked up to see Divina. She was wearing a Filipina dress of dark turquoise with a beaded bodice. I stood, my heart pounding.

"Is it true, you painted my people?" she asked.

"This is true," I said.

"Will you show me?" she asked.

I walked up to her and held out my arm.

"Wait." She walked to the front door and opened it. A Filipino stepped humbly forward.

"Come," I said. "Come see your people." I gestured to the walls.

The man took off his straw hat and held it to his chest. He was clothed in the material we used for the sacks of rice, a rough canvas material. The ends of his trousers were frayed, as were the sleeves of his shirt. As he stepped forward I saw that many Filipinos were lined up behind him. I went to the door and greeted them all as they entered. After that day, Divina and I were inseparable.

Soon the entire Spanish community knew of our union, and my family became ostracized, my mother snubbed. Friar De Guzman had Divina's brother arrested once again. I used the last of my powers to set him free. They labeled me as a traitor. Several of the Jacinto-Basa homes were set on fire. My gallery was burned. I continued to paint feverishly, using the sides of churches and the underbellies of bridges as my canvases. I painted in the dark, and the themes were all the same: the persecution of the Filipinos by the Spaniards.

I became a criminal to Spain. It seemed I was living up to the threat of the Jacinto-Basa curse. We went to live in the mountains to escape the wrath of the friars. In the early mornings I woke before the roosters and painted on the church walls, on the homes of the wealthy, and by daybreak I was safe in the trees. I painted a grand mural along the entire side of St. Catherine's, of the great warrior Lapu Lapu spitting in Magellan's face.

I learned I had become something of a legend, an outlaw, and that young Filipinos were imitating my art around the islands.

It was a month before my nineteenth birthday when Virgil came to visit us. He was thin and ragged. There was continued discord within his group.

"Fredrico, your art has strengthened our people. You give voice to our suffering."

"I am honored, brother."

"You can do so much more. We need someone with your passion to lead us. Spain is not interested in the injustices being commited. We are the ones who must make the changes."

"Virgil, you put too much on my abilities. I am merely an artist who enjoys pulling the friars' robes."

He was disappointed. Divina tried to console him. The next day he was back again.

"Fredrico, I am not the only one who values your power. Come . . ." Virgil gestured, and a group of fifty Spanish farmers entered with their hats in their hands. "Look outside." He brought me to the windows. Outside were more farmers, Filipinos and Spanish. "They wish to follow you."

"Tell them to go home. I shall only get them killed."

"Then they wish to die with you," Virgil replied.

I wrote endless letters to Spain; I painted many murals. My followers enjoyed re-creating my art on all the islands so that it seemed I was everywhere. What did it do? It incited the wrath of the friars even more. I was labeled a revolutionary, an enemy to Spain. I could not walk out in daylight without bodyguards watching me and Divina's family. But I could not stop. It was a feeling that fed my soul.

Ours was not even a group—thirty, maybe sixty people. What we accomplished may not sound like much to you, but it was big then, what we did. We put a voice to the suffering, and that, to me, was worth dying for.

It was not even a thumbnail to what Rizal later did, but if you must, compare the two. I would like to consider myself the small thorn that pricked at the conscience of the Filipino people, reminding them that the abuses were cause to be angry.

~

I COULD NOT stop. When Oscar sent a message to me, pleading for me to take care and that my nineteenth birthday was approaching, I laughed. I sent back a message to him: "The curse cannot find me here." Later, when Virgil was caught and executed, I became consumed. I painted his execution with a saintly halo upon Virgil's head and Friar De Guzman as the devil, with a tail and cloven hooves. After that, I completed one of the queen having deaf ears, ignoring the pleas of the people as she bathed in her luxury.

The day a price was put on my head by the Spaniards was the day Divina announced to me that we were with child. I grew a beard, I became thin, but there was passion bursting from my chest that I had never felt before. My previous life became but a memory; my present, all-consuming.

What we called home was ever-changing. We lived out of underground caves, caves hidden on the sides of mountains, with nothing but a forty-foot drop below. We were on the run in the evenings, in the rain, in a storm. Food came to us in the form of stale bread, fish, monkey meat. I worried for the condition of our child. But Divina never complained. "For Virgil," she would assure me. I pulled strength from those eyes of hers. They haunt me still.

I WAS DEEMED an upstart, a subvert, a traitor to my country. My portraits were painted in the dead of night and raised in the light of God's sun. Accompanied by a few men and the bag of paints tied to my back, I would leave Divina guarded in the safety of our group and return in the morning, exhausted and impassioned. There was a high price on all of my portraits; people paid for any of the originals I had previously painted. Rich Filipinos and Spaniards as well purchased them. The latter, I am sure, was done in perverseness, in anticipation of my execution.

THE REST I will tell you quickly, lest I die from the pain. Divina and I were separated, for she was big with our child and I thought it best to keep her in hiding. She was ambushed. The men I sent to protect her were shot, only one escaped. He told me the men were ruthless. They held him down, though he fought. They shouted curses at the Filipinos. They claimed Divina was my downfall, calling her a witch. She had clouded my thinking. They took my beloved and dragged her to a cliff, thinking to frighten her. They promised to bargain with her. They offered her her life for my whereabouts. She surprised them by refusing and fought them with all her might, though she was big with our child. The bandits were beyond reason. They asked her again to give my location to spare the life of our child, but she spat in their faces and with a curse they threw her over. She fell hundreds of feet and died with our unborn child.

I searched for her body myself, without care for my safety. I found her at the bottom and thought I would go mad with grief. I carried her to a grave I had dug. I buried my heart with her that day. I went against my own preaching and burned down many of their churches. From then on, I cared not for myself. I lived only for the people, to be their voice of anger.

THE DAY OF my birthday, Oscar requested to meet with me. I conceded. He arrived at my hideout with Manuel, my uncles, and many cousins. They waited outside the cave to give us privacy. It had been a long time since we had talked.

"Fredrico, this is madness. I can still plead for your safety. You can live in Italy or America, India or China, wherever you wish."

"Do not throw your life away," I said.

"Is that how you see it?" he asked.

"It is different now, brother."

We were not talking long. My eyes had not even grown accustomed to his face when Manuel rushed in.

"There is a firing squad at the base of your camp."

"Come, Fredrico." Oscar brought forth a gun.

"Oscar, I am no longer the same brother you once knew."

"That is your infatuation speaking."

"These are people, they have families, they smile, laugh, just like us. Who decided that we should lord over them?"

Oscar grabbed me. "Brother, let us go. We shall fight side by side as before."

"No, I cannot." My words brought tears. I had never seen my brother cry.

"Fredrico, please," he said. He implored me with his eyes. I could see him searching mine, as if he could find some ghost of the brother he once knew. Then slowly I could see the realization hit him. His face smoothed away. He let go of the pleading. He nodded. "*Vaya con Dios,* baby," he said. Go with God.

He went back out, and I heard my uncles say, "Well?"

"He does not wish to come," Oscar announced.

I heard Manuel say, "Perhaps all your *madre* has done to avoid this curse on your family is for naught. The curse will take him after all."

"Shut your mouth!" Oscar shouted. "The curse shall not find him. I will not allow it. I will take his place. I swear it."

My hideout was atop a great cliff overlooking a narrow entryway for any army. We were heavily fortressed, and though we were cornered, the chances were still great that we would escape.

As my group prepared to fight, the exchange of rifle fire could be heard. My brother and uncles had joined our fight. They fought like Jacinto-Basas, with the honor of generals and doctors, and artists and saints, flowing through their purple veins.

I lost them all. My brother, Oscar, my uncles and cousins, and my beautiful Divina. How my heart still aches for her. I can still hear her call my name, pick up the scent of her fragrance, smile at the thought of her laughter, even after all these years. I can still feel the gentle kicking of our child from those times I placed my hand on her belly. She was the only woman for me.

And Oscar. It was easy for me to turn my back on him, be angry with him, knowing he would always be around. I never expected he would be the one to die. I thought certainly it would be me. I will feel that loss eternally. I wish that I could have told him many things. Sometimes I feel as if he is still in a room with me. Particularly when there is laughter.

The curse took them, but it gave me something as well. My eyes were opened for good. I saw so clearly how no people should rule over another. This is something worth fighting for. Divina and her brother believed the same. And with such beliefs there can be no compromise. My deepest regret is that I could not protect them from danger. I would have given my life for either one of them. If I could have hidden Divina away, even if it meant not seeing her for many months. But these are scenes I have enacted again and again in my head. And they are gone. I will see them again someday. I believe this. God will see to it. My soul will find theirs.

⌒ **WHEN TAY FREDRICO FINISHES HIS STORY,** it is daylight. We have stayed awake through the night. I see the old Spaniard in a different light. His love for this woman was thick in his voice. His affection for her brought her to life. I could feel her spirit nearby. He conjured her presence just at the mention of her name, Divina. At times I was almost ashamed to gaze at his face. It seemed too private a matter to be told.

His passion for our people matches my own. My respect for him has grown twofold. He is the only one who truly understands my plight. He alone knows the conflict and the pain of being unselfish. To have a conscience can be a horrible thing. God blessed him with the gift of leading his people. To have to choose to use that gift or care only for yourself, your family, is a terrible choice. My biggest fear has been the thought of regret. I am encouraged by his unwavering belief that he did the right thing. There is no regret that he made the wrong choice, only regret for those he has lost. He has brought a new resolve to me. I see clearly now what I must do. The men now behold him with gentle faces. The women dab at their eyes.

Mang Selso is the only one unmoved by his father's story. He seems hurt by it.

"So you are proud that you left your family behind? That you deserted the very brother who would have died for you? This is what you teach this man?" Mang Selso asks.

Tay Fredrico is incredulous. "My son, have you heard nothing that I have said? Each of us has a responsibility to the whole, the greater good. In order for all to continue. Danger or not, curse or not. That is what this man fights for. You are instructing him to stay, and be selfish, to think only of his family, of himself. I say bravo to you, Domingo. Continue to fight for all of us, you must.

"Take my example. What was the use in trying to fit myself into an old life? I would have been miserable. Had I married Zoila, she would have been miserable. We would have lived a lie. Do not try to force yourself back into this old life. It is like trying to fit into a pair of old trousers once you have grown taller. It no longer suits you. It never will again. It is best to admit this, lest you force the fit and look ridiculous. Better for the pants, better for you, better for all who would see you wear them.

"But I warn you . . ." Tay Fredrico holds up his finger. His hair is thin and very white against the dark skin. "This you must remember. Choose quickly, and do not look back. If you decide to stay, then leave the jungle life behind you. If you decide to go, do not return to this place. Remember this, stick to your decision. It will be very bad for all concerned if you try to keep both lives. Do not be greedy. I was greedy. I chose a life with Divina and left my brother. But after Divina died I was lonely and I let the old life back in. I agreed to a visit from Oscar. If I had kept my back turned to him, if I had stayed firm that we were no longer connected, perhaps my brother would still be alive today. Remember the woman at Sodom and Gomorrah whose husband told her not to look back, as the angel of God had instructed? And what did she do? She looked back one last time, and turned to a pillar of salt.

"When you start to say to yourself, Just one look back, just one glance, the danger will have begun for you. When you begin to think of returning to your old life, flee, flee to the opposite direction. Or it will be very bad for all concerned. For then you will be divided, and then you will be of no use to anyone."

"Yes, yes." Mang Pedro points his crooked finger at me. The joints are swollen from arthritis. "On this we are in agreement. You must choose one or the other and not look back. Decide, and do not waver in your decision. Choose to stay with your family or to lead your troops." He studies me for a moment with sadness. "But it cannot work. Not that life that you choose. Yes, I know which one you choose. I see it in your hands, the way they tap restlessly as we wait. They long to reach the door and turn the handle to the outside, and in your eyes, ever shifting, searching, longing for danger. Much murder and darkness in that life. Better to stay on the side of God, to live with the family He married you to."

Tay Fredrico dismisses him with a wave of his hand. "Pah," he says. "God sanctions any life that is true in nature, in here." The old Spaniard beats his chest twice with the palm of his hand, as if swearing allegiance. "God would not have a man live a lie." He shakes his head and smiles wistfully. "Ah, to accompany you. *Pero estoy cansado.* I am tired. And as for my son, Selso . . ." He holds out a hand to Mang Selso. "I must stay with him. I have not been a good father. I learn still, even at this age. I must value what I have. He is a good man."

Mang Selso is stunned by his father's words. He expected anger, I think, not understanding.

A Japanese soldier approaches, the one who helped Yukino and her daughter. He motions for me to stand.

"Sir . . ." Mang Carlito stands on shaking legs to address the soldier. "Is there nothing that can be done? Perhaps we could pay you. At home, I have some money. Not much, but we could repay you. Please, he has fought like you, like a soldier."

"Mang Carlito, do not bring trouble upon yourself. You have been through enough," I say. Then in Tagalog I say to him, "Have faith in me."

He nods with concern at my words and sits down. "I shall watch over the others," he says. "Do not worry for us. Domingo, do what you must do."

"Thank you, Mang Carlito. I feel better knowing you are here with them."

"Mang Ped, I will keep my family close to my heart. I shall not forget the lesson you must live with every day. But there are many more to think of."

"*Vaya con Dios,*" Tay Fredrico tells me. Go with God. "It is not an easy decision."

"Thank you, Tay Fredrico. I value your words. It is not an easy thing to do, risking your family for a cause." I clasp his hand. "I am inspired by your story. Do not give up hope. I may find a way out for us yet."

He frowns. "No. Stay to one course, my son. Do not let yourself be divided." He holds my hand strongly, then lets go.

"I will return," I assure him. He shakes his head with concern, but I am urged ahead by the Japanese soldier before he can speak further.

"Domingo," Lorna moans from across the room. I must not bring further attention to them. The others watch silently, in terror. Lorna will not stop calling my name.

"Think of your children," Aling Louisa chides her.

Lorna is beyond reason. She is screaming for me, and her crying causes the children to cry. I look straight ahead. The room is mesmerized by her outburst.

"Domingo!" She falls on the ground, shouting my name. "No!" She struggles as the women try to keep her still. "Let me go. *No!*"

The Japanese turns his head to study her. My heart thunders in my chest. "Your family?" he asks.

"A whore that will not let me be." I study my wife and children one last time, then force my eyes away from them and look into the crowd. Yet their images are imprinted in my mind. My son with his head against Lorna's lap, our baby in her arms. She has been nothing but the truest wife. I feel as if I have grown a forked soul. It hurts me deeply to make her look the fool, even though I know it will save her life. She has been good to me, and I disappoint her again and again. I keep my eyes averted, and when I see a familiar face in the crowd, I look away quickly.

"It is the same in every country." The soldier studies Lorna, then chuckles and leads me out of the room. Our footsteps volley down a darkly lit hallway. The rancid smells stir as we walk. We go through a door and into another corridor, and then into a room. We are in the latrine. The walls are covered in feces. He lights a cigarette, and I wish for him to keep the match lit to burn the smell. He lights another and offers one to me. His bayonet is fixed and he holds it firmly.

I take the cigarette. "Is this to be my last, then?"

He nods. "The general shall wish to question you, and then afterward it will be time."

I inhale the smoke and study him. "Your English is very good."

"Yes, very good," he agrees. He studies me. "You do not wish to give the location of your group to save your life? I would set ten people of your choosing free."

My breath catches, but I shake my head.

He nods. "They will torture you."

"I am prepared," I say.

"That is good."

"The Amerikanos have come as we foretold." I watch his countenance.

"Yes, it was only a matter of time."

"Who do you suppose will win?"

"Who do you suppose?" He cants his head.

"The Amerikanos."

"Of course." He chuckles, takes a smoke, and studies me again. He says without arrogance, "They are no match for us. You do not know the training we have had since we were children. Bushido. You know this?"

I shrug and shake my head. "A little."

"The way of the warrior. Our code. To die for our emperor is the greatest of honors. It is our will, and no other nation possesses such a will, it is indomitable. The Americans do not have such a code."

"I have seen your will. A hundred men walking into a hailstorm of bullets."

"One life is not worth but a feather in the wind to the glory of the emperor. It is for him we fight. He is descended from above." The soldier points upward. "You are surprised at our beliefs? I thought you believed the same. To die with honor. Are you not the fearless leader whose name I have heard carried throughout the barrios and towns? The very same who risks death day and night?"

I shake my head. "I am not one to run when there is a fight, but neither will I sacrifice my life if I can live another day. I am not this legend they speak of."

"Yes, stories grow big, when there is a need. And your people are in great need."

We smoke in silence. The planes fly low overhead, rattling the windows. We wait, our eyes to the ceiling. A bomb explodes nearby, but the soldier does not flinch.

"You have a request before your execution?"

"You would grant this?"

"No, but I would be interested in what a worthy opponent would ask."

"I wish to know what will happen to the others."

He studies the end of his cigarette. I watch the burning end flare and fade, like the fate of my people.

"We have orders from our superior, General Sato, the leader of this post, to use as little ammunition as necessary. In three days, before he returns to this warehouse."

"In three days and not sooner?"

"Not sooner. We keep them as a safety, to bargain with if needed. If the Americans cannot be bargained with, then your brothers and sisters shall join you in heaven."

"You believe this?" I ask.

"No, but I understand it brings comfort to say this."

Another soldier peers into the room; he glances from me to his comrade smoking beside me. He says something curtly in Japanese, then disappears. My escort nods, drops his cigarette, and crushes it beneath his boot. He motions for me to get rid of my cigarette. "It is time," he tells me.

I inhale deeply and then throw the cigarette into a clogged urinal. The door opens again and the soldier turns casually. He is surprised to see the face of a young boy, too astonished to react as Bartoy shoves a knife into his arm and causes him to drop the bayonet.

I grab the rifle instantly and look at the Japanese as he holds his arm, bewildered.

"Finish me," he says. "Or let me do it myself. I am a disgrace to my family."

"I will do it," Bartoy offers. He walks behind the man and jabs the knife in his throat. He pulls it out again and plunges it behind the collarbone and into the heart. The Japanese falls to the ground, clutching his throat. His stare searches the ceiling, then grows still.

I look at Bartoy sharply. He enjoys the killing. It is plain in his eyes, the anticipation. He was never like this. When we found him, after his parents had been executed, he was still tender. The business with his parents, being forced to watch, it has done something to his soul.

Bartoy does not flinch. He takes the knife from the Hapon, cleans it, and then pockets it. "This way—" He motions to me.

We leave the room. There are no guards in the hallway.

"The other guard?"

Bartoy jerks his chin ahead. Nina is standing at the end of the hall. "She has taken care of the guard. We walked right in. They guard this place thinly," he says with disgust. I hear his voice but cannot shake my gaze from Nina. The sight of her holds me transfixed as always.

Nina frowns. "The soldiers are too busy with the Amerikanos. If the others would rise up to fight, we could take them together."

"They will not rise up." I spit to the side.

She looks at me with surprise. "We will leave them, then?" she asks.

At the end of the hall I see a figure, a second Bartoy, but the eyes different. I squint and realize it is Alejandro. He has come in search of me. He looks at me without accusation, waiting for me to call him. I want to grab his arm and tell him to come with us. That he must help me convince the others or they will die. Bartoy stops, too, and stares at Alejandro with fascination, as if catching his own reflection in a store window. I break my gaze from Alejandro and look to Bartoy and Nina.

"Let us go," I order. Three simple words; why, then, do I feel as if I have just signed their deaths? I stare one last time at the hallway leading back to my family. I burn their images into my mind. *I will find a way to return,* I promise.

We stoop low and run through the streets and alleys we know so well, avoiding the rubble and sniper fire. We stop behind an abandoned building.

"There is much grumbling about your absence. There is talk that you put your family before the group," Nina tells me. "Have you changed your mind?" she asks, and I see the fear in her eyes.

"I leave my family here, for them." *For you.* My heart sings to be next to Nina again. I cannot stop watching her. I reach my hand out for trivial things, to support the small of her back, to tell her to walk before me. Small pleasures that feed my soul.

WE HEAD NORTHWEST at a furious pace. At noon we cross the Pasig by a raft covered in palm leaves, by nightfall we arrive at our new encampment, in the lowlands of the Zambales Mountains, in the foothills of Florida Blanca.

"Why do we stop?" Nina asks.

"Meet me here in two hours," I tell them. She checks her watch and nods. Bartoy takes a step as if to follow me.

"Go with Nina," I order.

They turn to go, and I reach for Nina's wrist and let my index and thumb feel the texture of her skin beneath. I raise her hand and bring my lips to the underside, where her pulse beats strong and steady. "I forget myself. Thank you, for coming to my aid."

Bartoy grins at our display. My heart tugs at how he always rallies to smile. Nina stares into my eyes with such intensity, I shudder. She is never satisfied with the surface, she always reaches deeper, wanting to touch my soul.

"Go now," I say.

I am alone again. They have armed me with an old Browning and a .45-caliber pistol. I take a drink from my cantina and proceed straight up the mountainside, using the thick vines for climbing. The tall sawgrass claws at my clothes and lashes my arms. The grass hides deep gullies that cause me to stumble and curse myself. I am an infant learning to walk.

After an hour I can go no farther. The wounds have stolen my energy. I see eyes staring at me from the thick groupings of trees. There are clouds of malarious mosquitoes everywhere, from the recent rains.

"Who the hell are you?" An Amerikano steps forward.

"Domingo Matapang to see Lieutenant Holden."

He laughs. "Just like that? Just let you in to see the lieutenant? Stupid son-ofabitch, check him."

Another Amerikano steps forward with his rifle poised and aimed at my head. Five soldiers close in. Three Filipinos and two Amerikanos. I raise the rifle over my head and place it on the ground.

"You can do better than that, sweetheart," the Amerikano voice says.

I raise my arms and turn fully around.

"What's this?" The American comes closer and takes the pistol from my waist and hits me with the butt of the gun. I shove him, ready to fight.

A Filipino steps forward. "Sarge, I know this man. The lieutenant is expecting him."

The sergeant takes aim, then drops his arm. "You'd better be right, Mercado."

The sergeant and I lock eyes. Mercado greets me with a nod. His name is Angel Mercado, a childhood friend from my old *barkada*, one I stole many things with. Angel pats me down for more weapons, and then an Amerikano soldier orders him aside and checks me. The Amerikano is not gentle with my injuries.

Mercado nods. "I will vouch for him, Sergeant. This is the man I spoke of to the lieutenant."

"It is, or you're both dead." The sergeant spits, still watching me. "Don't let him pull no tricks, Angel."

"He's clean, sir," the Amerikano soldier announces.

The sergeant studies my eyes for a moment longer. "You pull any stunts, sweetheart, and that's the end of you. Got it?"

I give him the same stare. Mercado rushes to the cave to tell Holden.

"Take your shoes off," the sergeant orders.

"You first."

"Listen . . ." The sergeant puts the point of the rifle to my ear.

Mercado comes back, breathing heavily. "The lieutenant will see you now."

LIEUTENANT HOLDEN'S NAME is legendary. When MacArthur divided Luzon into four parts via radio for his guerrillas, Holden was given the western district. He has chosen to live near the foothills rather than in the mountains. The mountains are safer, away from the Japanese. The foothills are closer to the food source. My men have encountered his many times.

The lieutenant is thin and much taller than I had expected. His hair is black and his skin almost as dark as mine, a fisherman's brown. If it were not for the gray eyes, if he were seated, at first glance he could be mistaken for a Filipino.

He wears a rifle slung vertically across his slight frame, a straw hat, and two crisscrossing bands of ammunition. His trousers have been cut off at the knees, and he wears leather sandals.

He has malaria; I can see it in the pallor of his face and the shaking of his hands. He nods at me. "Mr. Matapang . . ." He pronounces my name in perfect Tagalog. He places his pistol on the table facing me.

I return the greeting.

"You've thought on why I invited you to this meeting?"

"Yes," I answer. "You have been joining many of the Filipino forces to yours." Several times Holden has extended an invitation to our group. As far back as June he contacted us.

"What are your thoughts on this matter?" he asks.

"What are your conditions to the joining of our forces?" I counter.

"What is the total number of your troops?"

"One hundred and fifty strong. But you know this," I say.

"Yes," he answers. "My group is forty squadrons strong. We hold the low-lands of these Zambales Mountains, Tarlac, Pampanga, and Bulacan. I have connections east of here extending to the Sierra Madres and Tayabas. We are well supplied, and as you may have already heard, we recently received another drop-off of munitions and food. A fifty-ton sub drop at Baler Bay. We have received these regularly now from Australia. I don't tell you this to impress you, only to convince you that you would do well to join us. I am sure you have heard the general's broadcasts regarding his wishes for us to have faith and stay strong and fight. Well, now his promises have come true. MacArthur has returned. The fighting has begun. Manila is in chaos. My agents there tell me the Japanese numbers are dwindling along with their resolve."

At the mention of Manila, my family again flashes before me. I fight the temptation to ask him to send a runner to watch them. A selfish request, one that would be frowned upon. I force the image from my mind. *Do not divide your thinking.* I study my rope-soled sandals and try to keep the astonishment from my face. I had thought their number was closer to twenty squadrons, but forty . . .

"Can you trust your men?" Holden asks.

"If I am present, yes. Under a different command . . ." I shrug.

"I will fit and arm only your most trusted men. The others I do not want. I need men who cannot be bought off."

"My woman, Nina Vargas, is the best intelligence woman you will meet. Half of the Japanese high officers are in love with her. She is mistress to General Yomma's aide. They trust her implicitly. We have a young boy, Bartolomeo.

He can walk through the jungles unheard, like a snake. He knows how to set a land mine and can lead a group of men through any path. I have a man named Inocencio Ramirez. He is the best sniper you will ever see." I tell him all of this, and my heart grows big at my words.

"I have heard of your shooter Inocencio. My Filipino troops speak highly of his skills. But again, can he follow orders without your presence?"

My shoulders sag. Mine is a motley group. Some would take orders only from me. "I will not desert the others. They have been loyal to me."

The lieutenant studies his pistol for a long moment. "You must trust your men either completely or not at all. If there's any doubt . . ." He leaves the thought hanging in the air.

"I trust them. Under my command, I trust them."

"I won't make any false promises. When the situation gets hot, I can't promise that your men will be under your command. I will plug them where I see fit."

I study the ground for a moment. I let the excitement subside and the truth set in. "Then there can be no joining of our forces. My men stay by me."

Holden scowls. "Are you certain? You would benefit by joining us. We would outfit your men. The Damdamíns, the Dangáls, the Kawans, all have joined us. We could use your strength."

"We will fight in our own way." Even as I say this, I envy the glint of new weapons hanging from their belts. The new-shaped helmets the soldiers wear.

He watches as I peruse his men, then he sighs and begins to cough. A flask is handed toward him, but he waves the hand away and gestures to me.

The soldier gives me the flask. I take the drink and raise it in gratitude. I feel the cooling liquid burn down my throat. He takes several cigarettes from his pockets, black-papered Filipino cigarettes. I see that he has grown accustomed to our stronger tobacco. He hands them to the guard to give to me. I put one behind each ear, and as I put one in my mouth, a hand is at the ready to light it.

"What are your plans?" I inhale the smoke. It is sweet to my senses. I feel the tobacco hit my blood immediately.

"I have orders to remain in the mountains for further intelligence, and to meet the enemy when they come. Our forces in Manila may push them west, to us."

I stare at him. "There will be no escape for you."

"I am prepared."

"They will fight to the death," I tell him.

"I will be here." He echoes my own sentiments. I feel a kinship of understanding. He does not care for the sadness he sees in my face. "There is another matter I wish to discuss with you." He hesitates. I watch the deep rise and fall of his chest.

"Speak," I encourage him.

"There is a sympathizer within your group." His eyes lock with mine.

"I have already taken care of the matter."

He looks surprised for a moment, and then he responds, "No, I am not talking about the one called Miguel. Though you did well to terminate him."

Now it is my turn to be surprised.

"You only killed the symptom. Listen to what I'm telling you." He coughs and his eyes water.

I brace myself and swallow. "Say it quickly."

"The man you call Palaka, he's the cancer."

"He is no sympathizer," I argue. But already I feel the ground unstable beneath my legs. Palaka, my most trusted friend. I try to hide my pain.

"Think what you want, the Japs have bought him off."

"What proof do you have?" I ask, but already I know. It is what my instincts have told me but my mind has always rejected.

"I don't expect you to take my word for it. My men have seen him walking freely in Fort Santiago, and as you know, that place is crawling with Kempeitai. But you have been warned. I only stopped my men from executing him until I spoke with you. I did not want to start a war between us. If we see him again, he's a dead man."

He lets the information soak into my head. "I understand," I tell him.

"Do you want us to handle him?"

"No, I will take care of it."

"You are certain you will not join?"

"I am certain."

He nods and holds out his hand. His guards become immediately alert. But the lieutenant has already made up his mind. He extends his hand with honor and no uncertainties. I grasp it, and for a moment the taste, the opportunities, of joining their group is sweet to my mind. In my hand is a paper, one that I was to bargain him with for ammunition. On the paper is information from my own intelligence teams regarding further Japanese hideouts and plans we have intercepted. I give it to him.

He looks surprised but places the paper slowly in his pocket. "Mercado," he calls out.

Mercado comes and salutes with his left hand. "Sir."

"It is as I suspected. Lieutenant Domingo Matapang wishes to concentrate on his own operations," Holden tells him. Then to me he nods. "Lieutenant, good luck."

"*Mabuhay, Lieutenant,*" I tell him. Long life. I watch as he disappears into the recesses of the cave. His guards immediately block the entrance.

I am escorted outside, and then I am told that the lieutenant wishes several men, six in all, to accompany me to the bottom of the hill. I nod in agreement. They carry with them a large crate. I know better than to ask its destination. I cannot help but wonder. At the bottom of the hill, Nina and Bartoy wait with their guns cocked. When they see the soldiers they take aim, and I shout out for them to cease.

The Amerikanos study the boy, Nina, and then me dubiously. Four of the soldiers place the crate on the ground. One of the Amerikanos comes to salute me. "A present, sir, from the lieutenant to your group. We cannot carry it further. I suggest you send some of your men to retrieve it. I would not leave it unguarded, however."

I nod. "Please send the lieutenant my gratitude." We wait until they are gone.

Nina and I stare at the crate in fascination. "Perhaps it is ammunition, do you think, Domingo?"

"Say nothing of this to the group, do you two understand?" I order them.

"Yes, of course," Nina answers with a frown.

"Bartoy," I say. Even though I know that he would rather die than give away any information, I feel the need to be reassured.

"Sir, I will say we found it."

"That is exactly what we will say."

"Shall we guard it while Bartoy calls the others?" Nina asks.

"We shall carry it," I tell her.

"But it took four of them."

"We cannot leave this," I tell her.

Without a word Nina and Bartoy take the one end and I take the other.

BY THE THIRD circle of guards, the rumor has already reached our inner circle that I come bearing a gift. The others rush to take the weight from us.

"What is it, sir?" Inocencio asks anxiously. He circles the crate like a child at a birthday party. Palaka gets up slowly.

"The Amerikanos were unloading boxes," I tell them. "We borrowed one."

At the same time, Bartoy announces, "We found it," with a wide grin, then looks to me with consternation. He can see in Palaka's eyes that it would have been better had he not spoken.

"You found it, did you?" Palaka asks. He watches Bartoy until the boy turns red and mumbles something, before finding a corner to sit by himself.

"Have you checked it, sir? Shall we open it, sir?" Inocencio voices what is on everyone's lips.

"I did not carry it this far just to stare at it," I tell him. It is hard not to smile at their excitement.

A metal bar is produced and many hands go to work in the opening. More heads peer into the cave. "Palaka," I say.

Palaka gets up immediately. "Who is watching the second circle?" he barks.

The men disperse quickly. The crate is labeled "U.S. Army." When the crate is opened, the straw stuffing is pulled from it and it is even more than I expected. A chorus of awe fills the cave.

"What is it?" Inocencio breathes. "What type of gun, sir?"

"A bazooka," I tell them.

"A bazooka." Inocencio repeats the word several times.

Nina is glowing at the sight of the massive piece of metal.

"Can we try it, sir?" Inocencio asks.

Palaka slaps his thigh in excitement. "See what the Amerikanos have? I tell you we must join them. We could each have one of these to our names," he insists. "We must try this, Domingo. We must find out where this Lieutenant Holden hides."

I watch him with new eyes. I entertain him while my family suffers, waiting. I study the gift from Holden. I could liberate my entire family and the other prisoners from that warehouse in Manila with this weapon. *Shake this thought. Stay focused.*

"Yes, when do we join with the Amerikanos?" someone asks.

"Were we not to meet with them soon?" asks another.

"The Amerikanos would outfit us with their new uniforms." The talk continues. "And boots," another adds. "Even a tank, perhaps."

"No one would give you a tank," Palaka jeers. "You cannot even drive a carabao."

There is excited laughter at Palaka's joke, and at the sight of the weapon.

"Will we meet with the Amerikanos' boss?" Inocencio asks.

"When the time is right," I tell him. I think of my family and repeat the same thing to myself. *When the time is right. Remember what the old Spaniard said. Do not divide yourself. And do not look back. But what of Mang Pedro's warning? About family? My family is here now. Yes, but they are also in Manila. Both men were right. Both ideals important, but the crux is to choose one over the other with a cold heart. You have chosen. Do not look back.*

"The time is right, today," Palaka urges. "The Amerikanos need us."

"Not today." I stare at the eager faces. The ringed eyes reflect the exhaustion and the crippling boredom of days spent waiting and hiding. This game of being a ghost begins to wear on one's soul.

"Can we try it, sir?" Bartoy asks, and everyone waits for my response. The entire cave has stopped breathing.

"We shall see," I tell them. "Let us take care of business first." The others sigh in disappointment; they walk away, their eyes filled with the sight of the machine.

"Palaka, what is first?" I ask.

He searches my face, detecting a difference in my tone. "Is everything all right, Dom?" he asks.

"Yes," I tell him.

He nods. "The others refuse to sleep with Bartolomeo. I myself have trouble with it. The boy is crazed. He is a liability."

"Bartoy? What nonsense is this?"

He shrugs. "The boy has taken to the killing. They think he is possessed. He smiles in his sleep. It is a strange sight."

"He can sleep in my quarters. Tell me something of importance."

"Senator Bulosan is here from the Philippine constabulary. He has some information that may interest you. The Japanese have been shipping out more of their officers."

I nod at the name of our agent who works beneath the noses of the Japanese.

"Also, one of our own, Tomas Fulgencio, wishes to speak to you. They have taken his family hostage."

"He knows the rules, remind him. No personal vendettas. They are in God's hands now. How did it happen?"

"The Japanese sent a Filipino to each house, asking for donations for the guerrilla forces. When his parents donated, they took them."

"He knows the rules," I repeat.

"Still, he wishes to speak with you, sir. To plead his case."

"Send him in. Is that all?"

Palaka sighs. "The meeting with the Paghamons."

The Paghamons are a dangerous group of Filipino guerrillas, anti-Amerikano, Communist in their beliefs, extreme and deadly in their practices. We have fought with them many times. They are great enemies with the Amerikano guerrillas. Some of the guerrilla groups do not want the Amerikano support. They fear that the Amerikanos will only use us to defeat the Japanese and then turn and want to take control of our islands again.

The reasons for the various Filipino groups fighting among themselves have become petty and disruptive to the true problem at hand. Some fight for personal vanity, to be known only as the strongest guerrilla force. Others fight for political positioning once the war is over. They envision themselves as heroes and therefore candidates for government positions. In the meantime they wish to have no rivals for those positions. The Paghamons are known troublemakers. Yet I will listen to anyone who offers peace among our guerrilla groups. There has been enough killing already. I try at every opportunity to convince them of the simplest matter: that we can be stronger together.

"What else?" I ask.

"There is another paper guerrilla."

I roll my eyes. Paper guerrillas are nothing better than bandits using the guerrilla name to oppress and rob our own people. They are tiresome and a great liability. We deal with them quickly.

"Have him taken care of." Even after all this time, it is difficult for me to give the word *kill* when I order an execution. The physical act is so much easier. Palaka barks an order and a runner is sent out to order the murder.

"Send in Tomas."

Tomas is in tears the moment he begins. This is the boy who refused a bottle of whiskey before we pulled out a bullet from his neck. He did not scream when the hot knife cut into his flesh or when the needle pierced his skin again and again. When half his foot was blown off by a mortar, he wrapped the stump in cloth and never said a word. He walked this way, carrying an injured comrade, until we were well into the Zambales Mountains.

"Tomas, I grieve at the news of your family, but you know the rules. No personal interests or vendettas. Our mission is to gather intelligence, to harass the enemy, support MacArthur's forces in our own way, by incapacitating the Imperial Army whenever possible. We cannot make exceptions."

"I understand, sir. That is why I am asking that you let me go. I shall rescue my parents. They were taken to Manila."

"I cannot let you go, with all that you know. This is what they wish. We would be in grave danger if you were caught."

"I would never speak a word."

"It is different when the knife is put to your loved ones. The tongue cannot be controlled."

"They will kill my family," he sobs.

For a moment the thought of my family in Manila flashes before me. I see the exhaustion in Alejandro's eyes, the panic and desperation of my wife, Lorna, but I shove it back down my throat and focus on the man before me.

"Yes, they would kill you, too, but first they would torture you for information leading to our group. Many more families would be at risk." Tomas is one of my most able men. He cannot swallow the information. "Do you hear what I am saying?" I ask.

"Yes, sir. I understand, sir." His voice cracks. He salutes and turns to leave.

I call to one of the guards.

"Sir?" A guard peers in.

"See that he does not leave your sight or the camp."

The rest of the night follows in the same way. The agents come in and put their findings on the table. We discuss the Amerikanos, who are already infiltrating the jungles and being led closer to the city to join their units. There is talk of a delivery truck that could prove to be a good source of food and sake, of all things. I listen with half an ear. The image of Alejandro in the warehouse appears. I remember his face as he watched us leave, the desire to come, and the understanding when he could not. I hallucinate. *Concentrate. Your duty is here with your troops.*

"The truck makes the same route each evening. It will be a good source of morale for the men to attack the supplies," Palaka urges me.

"I will think on the matter."

Night envelops us, breathtakingly beautiful. My heart constricts. I remember many such nights when we could roam freely on our own island. Those days seem so long ago. My thoughts stray to my children. Will they even know that Manila?

"The men are dispirited. They need a distraction," Palaka tells me.

I look at him, one brow raised. He can sense a difference in the air between us, but he has not yet guessed its origin. "There will be enough to do with this meeting of the Paghamons. We must not spread ourselves too thinly." This ceases his talk.

"Nina, bring me some wine," I order.

"For me also," Palaka adds.

"You have hands," she scoffs at him.

Palaka stands beside Nina. He says softly, "I have grown used to you serving me when Domingo was away."

I pull out my pistol and study the handle, but my ears are vigilant.

Nina chuckles. "That was because you were in command, nothing more. You thought there was more?" she asks without pity.

THEY HAVE CLEARED the cave without my request. The remaining men excuse themselves to get ready for the evening. A light rain patters in the distance. I stand outside and let the rain fall like tears down my face and study the land below. Down there my people are dying. I shut my eyes and retreat into the cave. There is a small cove within, a small indentation along the rock formation, big enough to fit two bodies lying side by side comfortably. It curves deep into the wall like the place on a woman where the collarbones dip and meet. This is where I sleep when I need my peace. "Hello, old friend," I say to my mat and large velvet blanket. The blanket is a frivolous gift Palaka once stole from my father's home.

Long ago, before the dog disappeared, I would find him here curled up on top of the blanket. I would feign anger as the mongrel stretched leisurely, then slunk off to the corner until I called him back to me. I remember the mat would be warm from his old, brittle body. Each time I left I made sure they gave him free rein of my quarters. At times I think he will appear in the middle of the night as he used to and curl up at my feet. I still look for him every now and then. I still catch his figure out of the corners of my eyes when I first walk into the cave. Whether it is his ghost or my memory I do not know. I did not realize I could miss an animal so much. Never had I seen a dog so unafraid of explosions. Palaka liked to joke that it was not bravery but deafness that caused the dog to carry himself so, but he always came at my low whistle.

"What are you smiling at?" Nina asks, approaching on bare feet.

"I was remembering Pogi. How he would humor me by acting the obedient dog."

"Remember when he ate Palaka's prized catch? Before he could even brag to anyone of the fish he caught." She covers her mouth with mirth and comes to sit facing me with her knees tucked close to her chest and her slender arms hugging them.

"Yes, and I told him he'd better not hurt the dog because the dog was his only witness to the fish he'd reportedly caught. That beast ate it whole, bones and all. He was truly a scavenger."

"Yes, just like us." Nina nods.

I watch her thoughtfully. The things she says at times, though she does not realize it, endear her more to me. Lorna would never call herself a scavenger, not even in jest. But then Lorna does not know how to joke so well. She comes from a long line of frowners.

"And now what do you smile at?" she asks.

"Why have you not worn that dress I brought back for you a month ago?"

"The red one?" she asks, her pale gold eyes round with surprise.

"I have brought you others?" I laugh.

"No, just the one. But I have no use for it at the present time. I thought to wear the dress after the war. Remember, you promised to take me dancing and then for a carriage ride and a stroll near the *luneta* during Pasco. How fun that will be with all the lights and the paper stars lit up. The war will be over by then."

"Christmastime is still a long way, *mahal.* It is only February. I would like to see you in this dress before then. Think of it as practice."

"Now?" she asks with a giggle.

I nod. "Please."

She opens her mouth as if to protest, then laughs and shouts over her shoulder as she gets up, "Stay where you are."

SHE RETURNS WITH the smell of the flowered soap I have procured from the Manila Hotel filling the air. Her hair is damp and left down, not pulled from her face, as is her usual style. She carries a lantern in one hand. The dress is Spanish style, which is why I stole it in the first place. It reminded me of her. It is sleeveless, with a low neckline, ruffled at the edge, tied in the middle of the chest, allowing for a teardrop outline of skin, and belted at the waist. She has pulled down the ruffles to reveal her shoulders. The color is deep crimson and enhances the fairness of her skin. Her ankles seduce me as she turns on tiptoes. The smile leaves my face and I am, as always, in awe of her beauty. How could I have ever thought another could take her place?

"Come sit beside me and let us pretend for a while we are somewhere else."

"Tell me again about the farm we shall have," she says happily.

I trace a finger down her neck to her shoulder, and she shudders. "We will find one that is close to Boracay beach. In the daytime we shall work our land side by side, with the sun coppering our faces."

"And in the evenings?" Her voice grows deeper.

"In the evenings we'll walk the white sand beaches of Boracay and build small fires to toast our feet."

"Yes, and what else?" she asks.

I stop my dreaming at her tone and meet her eyes. I lean up on my elbows and reach behind her neck to pull her close. She sighs and I inhale the sweetness of her and bring my lips to the middle of her neck. I touch my tongue to her skin, and she moans..Her tapered fingers come up behind me to caress my face and entwine themselves in my hair. She grips my hair and pulls my head back to trace her tongue upward to my lips, where I capture her mouth. She pushes me back down with one hand and straddles my waist. I look up as she reaches again into my eyes. It takes the breath from me. I'm shameless, unable to take my eyes away, unable to let the breath out. She brings her slender fingers to the ties at her neckline and pulls down slowly. The red dress falls over her shoulders to her waist. I pull her down to embrace her and take the tip of her breast in my mouth. I want to cry at the perfection of her.

"Never leave me," I whisper. Always our coming together is desperate, fed on borrowed time. I blow out the candle and our hands swim in the dark over the ocean of our bodies.

LATER, WHEN WE lie in the dark, she asks again, "And what else with the farm? What kinds of animals?" Before I can answer she says, "The first one shall be a dog. If Pogi does not find his way back," she says, looking at me quickly. "If he does not return, I shall get a puppy for you. Would you like that?"

"I need no gifts with you by my side."

She smiles. "We could save all our earnings from the fruit trees and go to Spain. I would like to visit her someday. To see where my other blood comes from."

"Yes, but what if Spain does things to your mind? What if you also become interested in the men of your other blood? What if you decide to become a true Spaniard and marry only a Spanish man?"

"What? Domingo, surely you joke. I would abandon this skin for you. I am a hundred percent Filipino inside. How can you even say?"

I arrange the hair from her face. "I only joked, *mahal*. Your mixed blood is beautiful. It is part of you, and so I am biased to it."

"Truly?"

"Yes, even with the many men who will certainly come to admire your beauty." I pause, mulling over my statement. "Wait. I've decided we cannot go. I just remembered something."

"What?" she gasps.

"I am jealous, after all."

"No! You have already promised." She laughs.

The sound of footsteps alerts me, and I throw a blanket over Nina. "What is it?" I ask the dark. Nina pulls the red gown back on beneath our blanket and stands to put on my coat.

The footsteps hesitate. "I can come back." It is Bartoy's voice, near the entrance.

"No, come in, Bartoy. Is everything okay?" I ask.

He comes forward timidly. My eyes adjust to see his outline. "I cannot sleep. The woman and man today. Remember, Nina? The ones lying newly dead at the mouth of the river. They reminded me of my mother and father. I am afraid to sleep."

"Then come here," Nina says. "Talk to us. We cannot rest, either." She lights the lantern once again.

"Are you sure?" he asks.

"Of course, " I answer. "After all, this is how it will be on our farm. The three of us under the same roof. Or have you changed your mind?" I joke.

"Oh no. I think of it every day." Bartoy comes to sit at our feet. I throw him an extra blanket. " I am sorry, Bartolomeo. I have not had the time to sit and talk to you as is our usual practice."

"I know you are busy. I would not have bothered you. But I was frightened."

"There is no need to apologize. Every man needs company," I say.

"About the farm . . ." Bartoy blushes.

I look at him curiously.

"The other day. I boasted to Inocencio that you had invited me."

"Yes?" I raise a brow in amusement, and Nina stifles a smile.

"He seemed so sad. Do you think there would be a place for him in this farm of ours? Even perhaps in the barn?"

"Of course," I tell him. "You should invite Ino. Perhaps he would like to join us."

"Wonderful." Bartoy lets out a breath of relief. "For I accidentally promised him there was a free space."

We laugh and talk more of the farm. We have added coconut trees at Bartoy's insistence. We talk until the boy falls asleep, and then Nina and I ready ourselves for the night's excursion and do not wake him for another few hours, until it is time to go. The moment our clothes are on and I step outside, the urgency of the night fills me once again. I think with guilt about my family in Manila. What kind of man am I to rest while their lives are in danger?

WE WAIT FOR the clouds to veil the moon. The conditions are good. The rain has thickened, and it is an even better omen. The men are anxious to start. They whisper continuously back and forth. Bartoy in particular is excited. He walks beside me, his eyes shifting as I have taught him, his rifle leading the way.

If not for the whispering, we would walk like ghosts. This is not true for the noisy Japanese patrols, who have grown weary of confrontations and hope to warn us in their own way.

Near me are Tomas and Palaka. I watch each for different reasons. I cannot let Tomas out of my sight. He would go to rescue his parents. He is a sore reminder of my own thoughts. I inhale the fragrance of the jungle. The forest in the rain is unlike anything I have known. There is the scent of the many mango trees, the citrus of the fallen guavas, their pink flesh exposed as the tiny flies attack the fruit. There is the mustiness of the trapped air, the wet earth mixed with the tart scent of berries, the endless orange petals that line the roadside, and scurrying creatures. Even the many streams and dozens of gushing waterfalls carry a scent. Perhaps it is the damp moss on the large rocks, the ginger plants that dot the roadside, or the salt from the ocean that rises into the clouds and then showers down into the canopy of trees.

All around us the oversize leaves battle for attention. They push among one another, rising to find the sun. For every tree, there is moss growing on the trunks and lianas climbing upward and around their base. For every tree there are vines as thick as a man's thigh hanging down. We leave the vines undisturbed, stepping around them. We try not to disturb the plants and shrubs as much as possible, but it is difficult, for they fill every open space. The giant leaves bend in the rain, but they are shaped like a spade at the tip to relieve them of the heavy downpours.

We creep through palm and bamboo trees, avoiding the exposed roots of the mangroves and the giant buttresses of the banyan trees that grow outward to support the top-heaviness of their branches.

My mind wanders. The men love going on these missions. With my men it would not take much to free Lorna and the babies from the Japanese. The men would enjoy the opportunity. *No, this is insanity. You have made a choice.*

Palaka hurries to my side. "Tomas is gone."

"What?" I ask, looking around, already knowing the answer. I despair. I never would have let my thoughts stray like this. I never would have taken my eyes from him before. My thinking has become clouded.

"He has fled. I blinked and he was gone. From the very start he was looking for an opportunity to escape and avenge his parents. One of the runners has confirmed they were executed. I told you we should have shot him. He is without reason. He will compromise our location."

"Send someone to find him. Only one person. We cannot split the group now."

"What if he cannot be stopped?" Palaka asks.

I sigh. "Then have him executed. He risks all our lives."

Palaka watches me closely. "Also, the runner has returned. He mentioned the situation with the warehouse in Manila has grown bad."

"He said this?" I ask with concern. "Where is he?"

"What are these plans with the warehouse?" Palaka asks. "Again I do not know. Have you also replaced me without my knowledge?"

"Let us not fight," I tell him. "Where is the runner?"

"Sir." A recruit hurries forward and salutes.

I pull him aside under Palaka's scowl. Palaka leaves the circle angrily.

"What is the news?" I ask the runner.

"I did as you told me, sir. I watched the area. I came as close to the warehouse as possible. I listened. That was how I injured my shoulder. All over Manila the orders are to execute the civilians. The Japanese admiral Iwabuchi has gone mad."

I nod, I hear myself thank him. My head is spinning fast. I see my family lined against a fence for execution. *Do not go back there, not even in your mind. You knew this could happen.*

"What is it?" Nina asks.

"It is nothing. We proceed to the meeting with the Paghamons as planned."

She hesitates, watching me. "There is another matter I must speak to you of." Her voice is thick, strained.

"Later." My mind cannot take any more information.

"Now," she answers.

"Speak, then. We have little time." I lead her from the group.

"Domingo, you cannot return to Manila to save them. The Japanese will be hunting for you. You cannot risk your life. You are the leader of this group. We will die without you."

"I do not need you to remind me."

She grabs my arm. Her eyes are pleading. "Domingo. I would never ask you to choose between her and me. I only tell you the truth. Our group will die if you leave. But if you go, I will go with you. I cannot stay apart from you any longer. I will help to save your family. Me, and the boy, and Inocencio. If it will be just the four of us, then so be it."

I brush the worry from her face with the backs of my knuckles. I graze them against her cheek. "I have not decided to go back, Nina," I lie. *Go to Lorna* or stay with Nina? To rescue your family or lead your troops? Ay, now, now it has begun. What the old men told you. They have not lived this many years without learning. But one thing is certain, I have already chosen Nina. Long ago I chose her. When this is over, we will live like a family. Bartoy, Nina, even Inocencio, for he is like a child, and me. We will find a simple farm. There, you have admitted your dreams. It is not such a bad thing. Not a bad thing at all. But you cannot leave the others to die. Can you live with their deaths?

She watches the thoughts fly across my face. "Domingo?" she whispers.

"Whatever I decide, you will be there with me."

A smile of relief crosses her face. "Then I wait only for your directions. My heart is at peace."

I pull her close to me and kiss her brow. "I do not deserve you. But I shall never let you go."

"Promise me? I want to always be by your side. Even if it means to be in the shadows," she says. Her hands grip mine almost painfully.

"We will be together until we die," I promise. She kisses my palm and then steps away and sighs. A smile spreads over her lovely face.

When we return to the group, Palaka continues to move ahead. He does not look at us. "I have forgotten to ask about Lorna. How are your wife and son?"

So now the fangs begin to show. "Let us focus on our meeting with the Paghamons," I say. "If we can form a peace, this meeting will be worth the trip."

The name *Paghamon* means "challenger." The Pags occupy these Zambales Mountains with us. Their group is also strong in the Sierra Madres. Their goals are to use others, lie to all other guerrillas, Amerikanos and Filipinos. They defend no one and no thing but their personal interests of empire building. They have political aspirations for after the war.

The Pags live southeast of our present encampment, and after tonight we will be southeast of them, in a different location. It is necessary to change every few days.

The stars in the heavens are brilliant, with opal-colored clouds as big as lakes covering portions of the night sky. Inocencio is humming a melody. It reminds me of women and balconies and the moon and music. I forget the name. Palaka will not stop his glances at Nina; they begin to claw at my neck.

"Nina, stay here with the others. I do not want you close to Kulaw. He has an eye for you. If something were to happen to us, they would take you."

"Let me come with you," she protests. "I will stay out of his sight."

"No, you are to remain here. If something happens, we will meet back at the base." She pouts, but I shake my head and move on. My conscience pricks at me. I did not have time to consider the base camp. We should have moved on. It is not safe now that Tomas's family has been captured. I have grown lax from my confusion. I would never have left out such an important detail. I will move the camp as soon as we return.

Macario keeps checking his gun, as if the bullets will somehow disappear.

"Maco, do you wish to lose the contents?" I scowl at him.

"Sorry, boss," he answers, and then promptly begins to replace and draw his pistol. Replace and draw quickly, as in the movies. I shake my head and walk ahead of him. I feel bad. Macario is a good and loyal soldier. He has a good head for strategy, and often I have consulted him secretly over Palaka. He loves our men as much as I. I will smooth things with him later. Bartoy is unusually quiet. He turns to me instinctively.

I look to the wound he earned a few weeks ago. "The wound on your brow begins to heal," I tell him. "It will leave a nice scar. You will be able to tell good stories to the ladies."

He shrugs in embarrassment. Within minutes I know we are in Pag territory. The hooting of owls begins, their signal. Bartoy looks to me.

"It means nothing. Only that we approach."

When the Pags come out to meet us, Bartoy blinks at the sight of them. They are fierce looking with their tribal paint and their teeth red from chewing betel nuts. I have brought fifteen of my best men into the inner circle. The others are farther out to guard the circumference. Macario shakes his head as we follow the Paghamon soldiers through the maze of ferns and trees. "This is bad, boss. Why did we not meet in a neutral place?"

"You represent us well with your questions, Maco. Why not just shout out your fears for the entire forest?"

Macario shuts his mouth and skulks back to his position. He would not have liked my answer. His question is a valid one. But I grow weary of hiding and of running. Still, I have taken precautions; I have placed two rings of our finest men at intervals surrounding the forest. If we are hurt, not one Paghamon will leave alive. As we walk deeper into the thickness of trees, groups of Negritos join us. They are our smaller counterparts, shorter and strong fighters.

The wind has started to blow high in the trees, and the sound is deafening. Yet it is a warm wind, and here, closer to the earth, it is not so bad.

We come to a set of bamboo houses with thatched roofs. We are ushered to the longest one. Three windows are propped open by sticks. Cigar smoke filters through, and I smell the fine quality. I motion for our men to remain at various posts as the rest of us enter. The house is twenty feet by fifteen, and there is a long table running the length of the room: a block of wood, set atop three wooden sawhorses. Even with the windows thrown open, the room is filled with smoke. Some of the Pags are seated, but most are standing, lining the walls. I do not like this. At the head of the table is Orlando Kulaw, the leader of the Paghamons. He has dubbed himself Napoleon, in regards to the Frenchman. He does not stand when we enter. "Matapang, you have resurrected?" His group laughs at the question.

"It would take more than a stray Japanese bullet to kill me," I answer.

"So, you have come to break bread?" Orlando continues with his biblical references.

"Is this to be our last supper, then?" I ask.

"Yes. Who is to play your Judas, Palaka?" He laughs, looking to Palaka. "Then you must be seated on this side of Domingo, and remember to dip your bread after he does. That will complete the prophecy."

"*Puta ang iná mo*," Palaka growls. Your mother is a whore.

"*Hoy, hoy,* I was only joking," Orlando Kulaw says, grinning. He watches Palaka, pleased that he has struck a nerve. "Inocencio, have you decided yet to leave this unworthy group and join us?" he asks.

Inocencio says nothing, but he smiles good-naturedly.

Everyone is armed to the teeth. Those seated have guns on the table. This was to be a good-faith meeting. It is a testament to how bad Kulaw is with his promises. In the corner of the room is an open pack of dynamite.

A soldier steps forward with a tray of glasses and whiskey, a very short cigarette protruding from the corner of his mouth. Kulaw slides a glass to the empty seat beside him. "Matapang, sit so that your men follow suit," he orders.

I look at Ino and then to Palaka, who both remain standing at opposite corners of the room. I pull the chair and serve myself a cup, then my eyes and Kulaw's lock. I wait for him to drink first.

"They will not drink?" he asks, glancing at Palaka and Inocencio.

"There is still much work this evening," I answer. "What is the first order of discussion?"

Kulaw studies my men standing. He fingers the top of his glass, tracing the rim with his finger. "Ino, how are you with your gun stripping? Can you beat me yet?"

Inocencio looks questioningly at me. I remain silent.

"I can beat you now, sir," he answers.

A great whooping shout goes through the room, and more Paghamons crowd the doorway. Palaka looks at me.

"There is much to discuss," I remind Kulaw.

He nods and again begins to slowly trace the rim of his glass. "Okay, later, Ino, ha? After this you must show me."

"Yes, sir," Ino answers.

"What is it again you wish to discuss?" Kulaw asks me.

"You were the one who invited me," I answer.

He chuckles to himself. "Oh yes, those subjects. Tell me again."

I take a cigarette from behind my ear and light it. "We are to discuss a peace between our groups. I believe we are in agreement. This fighting between our guerrillas must stop. We must band together against the enemy. And then there is the issue of your desire to absorb my group. As I have told you before, that is not possible. I lead my own. Then there is the talk of kidnapping the senators who sympathize with the enemy. All my efforts go to keeping the Japanese from backing into our mountains, now that the Amerikanos have begun the invasion. If you wish to leave now and play war with the politicians, that is up to you. They will get their rewards soon enough. My group will remain."

"I command more than four thousand men, we could swallow your one hundred," Kulaw responds.

I see now there will be no discussion of peace. I lean back and scoff at him. "If you count your villagers. I count only my soldiers, who are armed. You could not absorb us, it would be impossible."

The corner of Kulaw's mouth twitches. His men look around unsurely. One beside me swallows. The lump of his throat moves up and down continuously, and his hand strays from the table. "You wish to die?" I turn and ask him.

Kulaw laughs. "Relax, you frighten our guests." He motions to another soldier, and the soldier rushes forward with a rifle. Kulaw holds the rifle pointed upward, and he gestures to Ino. "Ino, before you go, ha? We will have a little competition."

Kulaw sets the rifle on its butt against his thigh and chair, between the two of us. "For later," he tells me. "I heard of your debacle with the Japanese convoy the other week. How could you not know there would be more troops to protect a munitions drop-off? What did you expect they were transporting, food?"

I smile. "You were there, and you did nothing to aid us?"

"I would not commit my men to such a mistake." He waves his hand. The ashes of his cigarette float in the air between us.

"No, of course not, especially after the incident with the Philippine constabulary. You lost many men then," I tell him. "I had almost forgotten that. I told you there was only so much you could ask the police to do under the noses of their Japanese masters." I laugh. "They have families. They need to live with these bastards. That was a bad one," I say, still chuckling. "How many men did you lose? You would have been able to boast four thousand and five before that day, eh? Now only four thousand. It is a pity."

Kulaw's eyes are on fire. The room grows instantly hot. I feel my body protest at how far I push this man in his own territory, but I cannot stop my tongue.

Macario peeks in. "Sir?" he asks. We planned this earlier, in case things were growing hostile. If I answer, "I did not call you," he is to signal the others to be prepared.

"I did not call you," I tell him. Palaka frowns at the impropriety of Macario's actions.

Kulaw looks at me. "I have seen that one in the towns. You grow lax in your selection."

"Is there anything else?" I ask.

"Yes, why have you not told the others of your meeting with the Amerikano Holden?"

There it is. Thrown on the table like a glove in challenge.

Palaka's expression gives away any lies I would make. Inocencio's face is riddled with confusion.

I look at Kulaw. "That is none of your affair."

He looks at Palaka. "You did not know of this?"

Palaka swallows hard. "Of course I knew."

"Ah, so you knew. And that he refused the invitation to join without consulting you, his right hand? You knew this as well?"

"Yes, it was at my urging that we not join," Palaka answers.

"All right, then, all right," Kulaw announces, bored with the response. "Then there will be no joining of forces with us or with the Amerikanos. As it should be. It is as it should be." He looks to Inocencio one more time. "Ino, are you ready for the challenge?"

I will Ino to look at me, but he is already grinning at Kulaw. "Yes."

"Come, then, let us lay our guns on the table."

The others begin to stand, and I motion to Palaka.

Ino faces Kulaw, and someone shouts, "Begin!"

In a flash they are stripping their rifles, and I grip my pistol at my hip. I see instantly that we are in trouble, for not only is Inocencio incredibly fast in stripping his, but Kulaw is purposely slower. There are flashes of hands clicking and snapping metal back, and for a moment I get lost in the competition. There is horrendous shouting in the room. Then Inocencio raises both his hands, and his deadly weapon is now only a mass of pieces. He is smiling brightly.

"Ah, you have won now?" Kulaw asks Ino. "But who is without a gun?"

The laughter subsides in the room; it grows smaller until it is hovering just among the three of us.

"This is a bad game you play," I tell Kulaw.

He shrugs. "If you will not join us, then you will die."

Inocencio's face falls. "Boss," he says to me. "Boss, I thought . . . When you said nothing, I did not realize."

I look at Kulaw. "You would do this now, in the hour before the fighting? When our people need us most? You would risk our victory for a simple rivalry? They will be short this many guides—" I motion my hand between my chest and his.

"Victory? What victory? To have another country rule us yet again?"

Before I can answer him, Macario looks in.

"Get out!" Palaka shouts.

"Boss, Japanese patrols on all sides of the mountain."

One of Kulaw's men runs in, breathless. "It is true, they are only a kilometer away."

I look at Palaka.

"Tomas," he answers. "They have made him talk."

I shove Inocencio aside; he is not half as fast in putting his rifle back together. I slam the parts together.

"This is not over," Kulaw tells me.

"Get out of my way." I finish the rifle and push him away.

Outside, Bartoy and the others look toward me anxiously. "There is only one way, a single track, very narrow." I point. "We must beat them to it."

Some of Kulaw's men follow. They have left Kulaw behind in his madness, shouting orders for his men to stay and face the enemy. Kulaw's rifle goes off on his own men as they try to desert him.

We sprint through the mountains, up, then farther up, with our chests near bursting from the run. At a break in the top, we can see the Japanese swarm into Kulaw's camp, and a battle ensues. We do not stop to watch. The rain has continued nonstop and the mud slides beneath our feet, and with it, my men. We cross a running creek with large boulders that part the water. The men slip and lose their footing on the moss; their weapons plunge into tight crevices. Kulaw's men slide on their behinds and come to a stop several feet below. They sit from exhaustion.

"Get up!" I shout down to them. "Get up, it is not over. If they beat us to that trail, then it will be over." Palaka watches me with unhidden anger. I give him the same. "Say it," I tell him.

"What is this about the warehouse in Manila?"

"I go to help my family. I will take no one but myself. It is not your concern."

"You, who has told us time and again not to let personal interests affect our promise to fight."

"It has not affected the fighting. I have come to the meeting, but now the meeting is finished. There is nothing more to do but stay in the hills and wait for the enemy. I will return as soon as I can. The others know what to do."

"You are divided now." He echoes the warnings of the old Spaniard. It sends a chill through my body. "You have betrayed us. The choice with the Amerikanos was not yours to make. It was ours. You met without our knowledge." He glances at Bartoy; the boy looks away and continues to climb up the steep of squat coffee bushes, grabbing on to the exposed knees of mangrove trees. "And you, you knew of this?" Bartoy does not answer him. "You, Domingo's pet." He grabs for Bartoy, and the boy glares back.

"Let him alone," I say.

The others stop to stare at me with many questions in their eyes.

"Keep moving," I tell them. To Palaka I say, "Yes, I met with the Amerikanos. They only wished to take a select few. So I told them all or none. You were one of the ones they would not take."

"You lie!" he shouts.

I wipe the rain from my face. "Do not talk to me of lies," I spit. "Where did you get that pistol, that German Mauser? I know you brownnose with the Japanese. For your own profit."

Palaka looks down at his belt in surprise. He has no words of denial, and my heart closes with finality.

"It does not matter," I tell him. "You must leave our group come morning. You know what I do to traitors, but I will give you a chance. Do not go to the Amerikano Holden, he knows about you. They will shoot you on sight. You have been warned," I tell him.

"You—" Palaka throws down his rifle and shoves me against a clump of large rocks. The men shout for us to stop.

I grab for his throat and throw him sideways, away from me. We are heaving now, still walking upward. I brace myself, waiting for his next attack, glancing down to the Japanese still climbing the mountains. Palaka's eyes begin to well.

"So I met with the Japanese. So I told them lies, maybe I told them where to find the Amerikanos. So what? They gave me this. They gave me food, cigars. They look after my family. It is more than I get here."

"And who here gets anything? Are we not under the same circumstances?"

"Yes, we are." He gestures in a circle to include all but me. "But you, you have everything. You are a legend in the villages," he spits. "I am sick of hearing of your noble name. Are any of us mentioned? We, who have made the plans with you, died beside you, who have killed at your orders. Do we not count? What makes you so special?"

"I have never asked for recognition."

"You have a wife and children, a second family with the Karangalans. Yet you must have Nina, too. And this boy—" He points accusingly at Bartoy's retreating back. "I was the one who brought him into the fold. He looked up to me, but you stole him."

Palaka begins to cry. At first I think it is the rain. The group has come to a full stop now. He is crying so hard, he holds his belly and leans against the sides of the cliff. He lifts his head and, in the same motion, his pistol toward me. Before I can respond, Palaka crumples against the rocks and grass. It is a clean stab through the throat, and instantly he begins to gasp for breath, and then the blade appears again, near his heart.

I look, and there is Bartoy, with a foot against Palaka as he pulls the knife from Palaka's back. Blood spurts from his wounds. I back away, confused at the sight of my old friend, my new enemy. Bartoy's mouth turns up in pride, and I see a little of the madness. The others step away from the boy with superstition in their eyes.

"Hurry," I tell the others. "Throw him over, or they will know we are ahead of them." I grab Palaka's legs, and he tries to grab at my hands. I bite down hard and force myself not to look at him. He falls silently over the cliff.

We reach the top of the rise just as the Japanese arrive where Palaka fell. We crouch down as an officer orders his troops to set up a post. They mean to block any entrance to the trail, but we have already passed.

WHEN WE REACH our base camp, I inform the men of my decision to help my family. They look at me with confusion and disappointment.

"You will kill us with this decision," Macario says.

"Why, boss? Have we angered you?" Inocencio shifts uneasily.

Several of the men are angry. "We should kill you for deserting us."

"There will be no such talk," Macario orders. The veins on his neck protrude from his anger. "Domingo has risked his lives many times for us."

"My conscience will not let me rest. I must return."

I turn the command over to Macario. No one balks at my selection.

"Macario, this camp is no longer safe because of Tomas. You must move—"

"I am in command now," he says, looking off into the distance. I stifle the urge to insist they move this minute, but I have given over my right. I turn to bid the men farewell, but they will not look at me. They place their hands on their hips and look off to the distance. They speak quietly to one another, and I study their faces. I feel ashamed, but it is like trying to stop a waterfall with your outstretched hand. There is nothing to be done. I tell myself they are better without me, for I am divided.

Nina waits with her rifle slung across her back.

"I am sorry, Nina. I cannot live with the thought of leaving them to die in that warehouse. I must try to save them. They are innocents. They are what we fight for. You must stay. It is safer here for you. I have compromised the group. My thinking is unclear. But I promise, whether it is God's will or not, I will come back to you. I have chosen you, and we will raise Bartoy as our son."

"I am coming." Bartoy steps forward. He holds a pack of dynamite, the very one I saw at Kulaw's hideout.

"Me too, boss." Inocencio steps out of the trees.

"I have already told you I will come regardless," Nina tells me. "I sent a runner to tell the Amerikano Holden that if he can spare any help in our direction in our rescue of this warehouse and its civilians, he must do so."

I nod and look away quickly. I have divided the group. "Then let us go to finish this one last thing."

AFTER ONE HOUR the sound of rifle fire opens up above us at our base camp. I stop and look stunned toward our camp. Two large explosions rock the ground even at our distance. We do not have that type of artillery. Inocencio and Bartoy gasp in alarm. Nina looks at me and takes a deep breath. Tears fill my eyes. I think of Macario and my men. I see their faces, and I picture them fighting with no hope of living through it.

"Our camp has been raided! The Japanese have found us. What has Tomas done?" Nina asks.

I stop to stare at the dark plumes of smoke. "The same thing I have done. We have let our concern for our families rule our thinking. I have led them all to the slaughter."

She reaches out a hand and places it on my shoulder. "Then we must go to Manila to save those who still live," she says.

WE RUSH ALL night without break and reach Manila at dawn. There is chaos, fighting everywhere. The four of us take cover on a hillside overlooking the warehouse. The ground shakes at various intervals, and bombers fly overhead, wave after wave. The sound of battle is deafening. I stay low, and soon our runner, Gregorio, comes out. The warehouse is not heavily fortified on the outside, but I see that there are many jeeps. Their commander has arrived. I send a prayer that all are still safe.

"What is the situation?"

Gregorio shakes his head sadly. "Sir, they have taken the men out in groups and shot them in the fields, there—" He points. "I could not tell at this distance if they were any of your people."

"We will set free those who are left. Their general has arrived?"

"Yes, did you see the jeeps?"

I nod. "Are there many of them?"

"No, I have counted ten. There were more, but they have driven away to battle the Amerikanos."

"Only ten? We can take care of ten."

"They have machine guns, sir."

"We have dynamite," Inocencio tells him.

"Wonderful, but how to use it without hurting the others?" Gregorio asks.

"We set off two here, and here—" I point to one end of the warehouse. "I have been inside, as have Nina and Bartoy. That is nothing more than a courtyard. It will kill but a few. Then all should come out there—" I point to the east end.

"There are Japanese snipers everywhere. They are like flies. I cannot keep track of them. There was one there on that rooftop earlier, and one below, there, do you see him now? But the one on top, I have not heard from him for the rest of the afternoon. I do not know if he is dead, or if he only waits. How will we lay the dynamite?"

"I will lay it myself," I tell him.

"I can help," Bartoy volunteers.

I look at him for a long moment. I cannot let my worry get in the way. Once you begin to worry, you are finished. "Good," I tell him.

"We will lay it, then hurry back here. Simple enough?" I ask Bartoy.

"Very simple," he answers as if he thought up the plan himself.

"Inocencio, watch that sniper. He may give us trouble."

"He will be a dead man, sir," Ino says.

"Is everyone ready? They may come out shooting."

"We will be ready." Nina nods, checking her sights and setting her chin. I feel a pain and pride in my heart just to look at her. We are the same, she and I. And when this is over, the four of us, me, the boy, Nina, and Inocencio, we will find a farm or a business together. We will remember the danger over a glass of beer and talk of it for many years after. When all this is over, Lorna can take our children and return to her family, and they will take her in and raise our son and daughter in wealth, and it will be as if I never existed. All will be taken care of.

Bartoy and I descend carefully, and I check the rooftops for Japanese snipers. We run unharmed to the building. We get as close as we can, when suddenly three dogs begin to bark and a Japanese soldier walks out from the west end of the building. He takes aim and I shoot him. From the other end, the doors open and soldiers rush out. "Light it now," I tell Bartoy.

The boy lights the dynamite and throws it in the direction of the soldiers. I take the other and do the same. It is the wrong end, but there is no time to think. We rush to the hillside for cover, and Inocencio, Nina, and Gregorio fire down at them to cover us. There is a great explosion, and I stumble as I run. We make it to the middle of the hill when Bartoy begins to slow. I see that his ankle is injured. I grab his arm and we hurry up the hillside.

We hide for cover, and Nina lets out a cry. "It is not his ankle that bleeds, the wound is in his hip." The boy pales, and I see that he is in a bad way. The ground soaks immediately.

"It is bad. The bleeding will not stop." Nina curses and turns to fire on the Japanese soldiers as they hide behind their jeeps.

I grasp Bartoy's hand and tell him that I am here. He tries to smile; his breathing is labored. "It is not bad. Just press here," I tell him. His eyes fade quickly and I am thankful. "Papa," he whispers, "is it bad?"

I cannot answer. The blood on his teeth puts me in a daze. My throat will not swallow at the sight of him. I do not see the young executioner that the others fear. I see only a boy without a father. I tell him, "I am here. Papa is here, son. Go to sleep."

"Papa, can I join you now? Why did you leave me?"

I feel it hard in my chest, yet there is no time to feel. I had pictured him on the farm, back in school, as a grown man, later with a young wife. *Stop this, think only of the battle now.* I try, but my hand will not let go of his smaller one.

"Bartoy, think of the farm. What was it you wanted? Coconut trees?"

"Yes." He tries valiantly to smile. "I will plant the first one." He lets out a ragged breath, and then his eyes stare blankly.

My mouth falls open. "Bartoy, tell me again what kind of trees. Bartolomeo," I say sternly. He usually snaps to attention when I use that tone. I grab him by the shirt. "I have not spent enough time with you. I should have found the time to talk. Even if it meant just walking beside you. You must have been so lonely all those times." I sob. "He is just a boy!" I shout.

"Domingo," Nina calls out.

I look at her without seeing.

"Help me!" she shouts, and I turn to join in the shooting.

I stumble up to help her. There is still Nina; with Nina there is still much to live for. We shall name our firstborn Bartolomeo. And it will be just as though he never left. Too bad about the boy, he was a good boy. I would have liked to see him leading a carabao on the farm. I would have liked to take him fishing. He will join his family now. *Do not be stupid. You felt strongly for this boy. Allow yourself to feel a little of the sadness, you can only bury so much.* Now is not the time, I think, shaking myself.

We have killed six Japanese that I have counted. But there are more than the number Gregorio gave.

"I counted only ten," Gregorio repeats.

I cannot keep myself from turning to Bartoy's body. There is movement to my left, and I see a Japanese soldier crouched in the high grass, like a wildcat waiting to pounce. We raise our guns at the same time. A shot comes from Nina's gun and the man falls.

A soldier runs up to our hill with a grenade. He shouts something, then Inocencio takes him down. The explosive shatters in the dirt. A shot comes from the left again; the man Nina has shot has returned fire on her. She is lying on the ground, breathing in short gasps.

"No!" I scream. I raise my rifle and finish the man. I run to Nina and take her hand. She struggles to focus. Her proud chin is dark with blood. I taste the salt on my lips from my tears. "Nina," I cry. Her eyes roll upward, and she struggles to keep them on me. I bite my lip and hold her gaze.

"Boss, boss," Inocencio calls out, "I need your help."

I have to let go of her hand. But she is not yet dead. I have to let go. *Let it go. Do it now.* There are four more Japanese climbing our hill. It is as if they want to die. The Amerikanos must be winning. I take one down. Gregorio has been shot in the arm and can barely raise his rifle. I cannot see through my tears. I cannot keep from crying.

Inocencio gives a curse, and I see two soldiers coming from his right and two more in front. He takes three down, the last shoots him through the arm, and then he is down. The soldier jumps on Ino with a knife, and I shoot him. I am paralyzed without Inocencio. The expert marksman down. It cannot be. Such a simple soul. If only we had stayed in the mountains. If only I had stayed here. I reach again for Nina's hand, and she looks at me quietly, calmly. Her face grimaces as she tries to move.

"This is to be our last fight together." She chokes horribly.

"Be still, Nina."

"Finish me, help the others. The warehouse," she begs.

"I will not leave you."

"Do not let our efforts be in vain. Please, Domingo." Her words are slurred.

I stare at her in horror. "Do not ask me to do that. I cannot!" I shout. "Get up. I will put you behind the tree. We will take you to a doctor. You must help me. Nina, we are to have a life together, remember? Do not leave me!" I try to pick her up. "I do not want to be without you. I will die!" I hear my voice like a child's. "Please stay."

She stares at me, her breathing just gasps of breath now. She cannot even answer. Only the small pressure of her fingers on my hand tells me she is still holding on. I feel for my pistol and put my fingers to my eyes. I cannot do it. But I know I must. I grit my teeth, and my hands shake horribly.

"Forgive me, Nina." I close my hand slowly around my pistol and put it to her head. She closes her beautiful eyes. I look to the heavens, pull the trigger, and scream. I sob into her chest for a long time, oblivious to the sound of Inocencio's cry for help. I don't know how long I stay that way. For a while I struggle not to bring the pistol to my own head. Then slowly I remember her plea. It is as if she is still near, watching over me. *Help the others.* I kiss her hand, then drop it without looking back and run to Inocencio. He lies on his back and tries to raise his head when I approach. His chest is soaked with blood. He sees my gun and nods. "Do it, sir."

I am numb now. I cannot feel. My head feels submerged in water. Sounds reach my ears distorted. How has it come to this? When I only intended to help the others. My hand reaches out and I touch his shoulder. He is still alive. My mind screams, *There may be hope for him yet! He is delirious. He thinks he is dying, but perhaps he is not. Maybe Nina was delirious. Maybe you could have saved her! Oh God, you killed her! Perhaps you can save him still. You've killed them all!*

"What have I done?" I shout.

Inocencio reaches out and touches my hand. "Sir, please. Not your fault. Do not want to bleed. Do not want . . . slow death."

"Yes, Ino," I choke, and bring the gun to his head. I close my eyes and fire. I hear my own ragged sobs. I have killed my people. I turn to Gregorio to see how he fares and perhaps to ask for forgiveness. He has witnessed the killings. He looks at my gun with terror, and in a panic he runs up the hillside, fearing for his life.

I have led these good people to the slaughter with my indecision. Is my coming too late? Will it be the same for those inside?

part 4

A L E J A N D R O
K A R A N G A L A N

⌐ THE BACK DOORS TO THE WAREHOUSE open with a kick from the Japanese boots. The double doors bang loudly against the wall. Everyone is silent. Something is happening outside the building. The soldiers have been running frantically in and out. Two soldiers appear, holding a body. We crane our necks to see whom they bring.

"Alejandro, make room," Mama tells me.

We watch as the Japanese bring out Feliciano. They hold him by the armpits, with his feet dragging on the floor. They have kept him in the back room for the entire night. It was hard to pretend that nothing was happening. We could hear his screams the entire time. There would be short moments of silence, as if he fell unconscious, and then the screaming again.

"Feliciano," Ate Isabelle cries out.

The soldiers twist their lips in disgust. "Now he will remember whose side he is on." The soldiers throw Feliciano our way, and Papa and Roman catch him before he falls. His head falls back and his eyes roll upward. His arms fall around him like a puppet's. They have taken off his shirt, and his chest is soaked with blood. Aling Ana is sobbing openly. Feliciano has dark bruises all along his face. His eyes cannot open from the swelling. He tries to lift his hands to his face, but I see that his fingers have been crushed. They bend in strange directions.

Isabelle searches his body frantically for his wounds. "They have carved their flag on his body!" she screams. "Animals!" she shouts to the soldiers. They watch my sister with disinterest. Mama tries to hold Isabelle back, but she twists and turns. I crane my neck to see. There are deep cuts on his chest, his belly, and his back. They have carved the Japanese rising sun on his body in three places.

"Stop it," Mama says. She shakes Isabelle. "Be thankful he is alive. We will survive this. The Amerikanos are winning."

A man seated next to us raises his gaze. His eyes are weak colored, not the brown I see beneath the film. He breathes deeply and shakes his head. To Mama he says, "The Amerikanos are winning, yes, but the Japanese refuse to let go. They are ready to die with us. They refuse to leave the Amerikanos anything."

The man shudders. "Outside, the Japanese are making a suicide stand. They believe it an honor to die." He points to the doors. "Outside they are executing the citizens. We will be next."

Aling Ana shakes her head. "What good would it do them to harm us? You have wrong information. Do not frighten the children."

The man looks at Aling Ana sadly. "Wipe the sleep from your eyes. They are killing us. I do not know why they keep us alive. I only know their intentions cannot be good." He breathes heavily and closes his eyes. I want to ask him a question, but Mama shakes her head at me.

The sounds of shelling rock the warehouse like an earthquake. The Japanese soldiers look at one another and talk quickly among themselves. Most of the Japanese have left for the fighting outside.

"He is right," Papa says. "The Amerikanos are winning. But they do not know we are inside; they are bombing our warehouse. We must escape this death trap."

"My God . . ." Mama clasps a hand to her chest. She and my sister hold hands, while Isabelle cradles Feliciano's head in her lap.

We look around the room to our only outlets. The three doors are guarded; two soldiers stand before each door. They watch us with stone faces, holding their bayonets before them, unmoved by the shells that rock closer and closer to our warehouse.

"Why have they locked us in?" Mama asks.

Roman stands and places his hands on his hips. "We must do something now. There are only two guards per door. Two against our two hundred. We can wrestle the guns from them."

"Ridiculous," Mang Selso sniffs, and crosses his arms. "That man does not know what he speaks of. They will not execute us. The Japanese need us to bargain with the Amerikanos."

"Enough," Tay Fredrico says to his son. "Selso, wake up. We must fight the soldiers. All of us, the women too. Roman is right, our only hope is to escape. Together we can fight them."

"I will not be the first to catch a blade in my belly." Mang Selso shakes his head.

Tay Fredrico addresses Roman and Mang Pedro. "I am an old man," he says. "I will be the first to go forward. This door. I select this one. I see the sunlight creeping through the bottom. I want to bathe myself in its color. If it is to be blood red and gold, then so be it."

"We must pray," Aling Ana announces. She takes her gold rosary beads from her pocket and kneels, while dust from the roof begins to crumble upon us with each shaking of the ground. The sound is awful to hear. I close my eyes tight against it all. Many of the women follow and kneel.

A priest who has been seated against the wall struggles to stand. "Yes, pray for absolution," he tells the women.

"There is no time for prayer." Mama stands. "Pray in your heads. We must attack these soldiers. God helps those who help themselves. Stand up, all of you."

The soldiers look toward our group. "Sit down," a soldier orders.

I raise myself on shaking legs, beside Roman, Papa, and Tay Fredrico. Ate Isabelle helps Feliciano stand, and Aling Ana looks up at us with bewilderment. She continues her prayers but struggles to stand on shaking legs. Her words tremble with each pounding of the outside guns.

At the other end of the room, women begin to scream. The soldiers are taking away the babies. A few of the men protest but are pushed away.

"Do not waste bullets," a soldier orders.

The soldiers march toward us with their eyes fixed on Ate Lorna and baby Alma.

"No." Mama reaches for the nearest soldier, but he shoves her to the ground. They close in on Ate Lorna. She stumbles to the middle of the floor, carrying baby Alma. The soldiers wrestle the baby away from her. The room erupts in shouts and angry faces. The other captives begin to stand. They come to her aid but cannot reach her as the soldiers slash out at anyone who approaches. Ate Lorna becomes a madwoman. She lunges at the soldiers and claws and kicks at their faces. The soldiers appear stunned at first, but then they regain their composure and begin to stab at her with bayonets. The blades are raised and brought down with such strength, a quick rhythm of silver and flesh that spins my head. I watch as Ate Lorna puts out her fingers. The bayonets slash through them. I gasp and wonder if that was truly what I saw. A soldier elbows his way through and aims for her head. Her head gushes blood like a fountain.

"Stop it, stop!" I shout, covering my ears. I hold my brother Roderick close to me.

"No, please!" Mrs. Yoshi and Mica cry out. Mrs. Yoshi tries to speak Japanese to the soldiers, but they will not hear her. They push her away, too. One of the soldiers grabs Mica by the hair and forces her to kneel at bayonet point. He spits at her with disgust, turns on his heels, and joins in the beating of Ate Lorna.

All of us are weak from lack of food. We have not been given water since we arrived, and our lungs are dry from the dust and smoke. The men gather their strength to protest, but they are pushed back with a kick of boots or a stab of the bayonet.

A soldier orders, "Let her bleed."

Taba comes running from his mat to scream for his mother. The soldiers plunge a blade to his belly.

"Stop it!" Roman struggles with a soldier. "Help me!" he shouts to the others.

"They have guns." Mang Selso cowers, pressing his back to the wall. "We could be killed." A few people mumble in agreement with Mang Selso.

"We *are* being killed." Papa stands. "Selso, we must fight. Some will die, yes, but at least some will survive."

Soon Isabelle runs to his aid. The women stand and rush to help, encircling the soldiers.

"The building is burning!" a man screams. "They wish to burn us all."

The flames come down the north side of the building, and the heat is tremendous. I hurry to my brother Roderick. People are running over one another, shoving and pushing. Tay Fredrico has fallen to the ground, and Papa and I rush to help him up as people kick and claw their way past us. A mortar shell shakes the ground, then another, coming closer to our building. People crowd to one side of the room. The western side of the building has collapsed, and people stumble away from the explosion. A woman gets up from the fallen wall. She walks a few steps, then turns, confused, and reveals her open backside to us. I can see through to her ribs and the bleeding flesh. She collapses, and still the shelling does not stop.

Two doors remain open, but the soldiers stand like stone statues.

"They are crazy," I say.

"This way." I point to a door where the flames have not yet grown so large.

"We must risk getting stabbed, or we all die," Tay Fredrico, the old Spaniard, shouts.

Roman, Papa, Mama, Aling Ana, Mrs. Yoshi, and Mica all rush to the soldiers. Only Isabelle stays behind, holding on to Feliciano. They step closer, and the soldiers yell for them to stop. Tay Fredrico charges one of the soldiers, and the man kicks him to the side. Mang Selso shouts at the sight of his father falling to the ground. The sight feeds his courage. He shouts for the other men to help him, and together the others run and throw shoes, cantinas, rosary beads, whatever they can find, at the soldiers. The soldiers slash and stab at the people, but it only makes us crazier. A few shots are fired, but we keep on coming. The women have joined in; they pull and kick at the soldiers. The men wrestle the bayonets from the soldiers and stab them with their own blades. The same happens at the other door.

"The doors are locked," Mang Selso shouts. "We must find something to break them open."

I see a bench toppled to its side. "*Itó!*" I shout. Here! Papa orders the men to carry the bench and run with it to the door. The room has filled with smoke, and our eyes are streaming with tears. Some of the people have fainted from the smoke.

"Again!" Papa roars to the men, and they rush the door a second time.

"The door will not open," Mama cries.

Then suddenly it bursts open, and outside is a Japanese soldier. "Out," he orders, and people rush by us like a million ants. They pour out from all sides, and we are swooped out with them. I make sure to hold Roderick's hand tightly. People are trampled. My arm feels as if it will be ripped from my body, but I do not let go of my brother. Out of the volcano and into the lava. The first out are caught in a crossfire. The bullets fly by us like giant mosquitoes. I shut my eyes and grow dizzy from the sound. I cannot think.

Someone shouts, "The Japanese are using us to distract the Amerikanos."

"Civilians!" an Amerikano voice shouts. Amerikano soldiers call out for us to rush forward. "Hurry, hurry."

Bullets are flying everywhere. People are falling. The building collapses behind us, and people are trapped inside the fire. Their screams are terrible. We are led away from the fighting.

"*Hayop!*" screams my sister, Isabelle. Beast! She hits the yellow-haired Amerikano with her fists. "You almost killed us with your explosions." The Amerikano soldier looks at her with surprise.

"Isabelle," Mama says harshly, grabbing her.

"Lucky for you this man over there insisted." The soldier gestures to a small hillside ahead. "We didn't know there were any of you left in there. We evacuated the internees in this building weeks ago. We didn't believe him till he ran down and got shot trying to open one of 'em doors. This is the last building, the last of the Japanese left fighting. The Americans have reclaimed the Philippines."

"It is Domingo!" Isabelle shouts. She leads Feliciano like a precious cargo, while Mica helps carry his weight on the other side. Mrs. Yoshi follows them, blinking her eyes against the glare of the sun. I smile to see Isabelle holding him. I have always sensed there was something between them. I blush when she looks at me. I turn my face from them as she kisses Feliciano's face and helps him to sit against a tree. She calls out to the soldiers for a doctor. "Morphine," someone shouts. There is so much to see. More bodies.

"Domingo is here?" Mama gasps. She is reluctant to leave Papa's side.

"Let us go to see Domingo," Papa tells her.

We walk slowly up the hillside. There is still scattered fighting below. The sounds of rifle fire pop like oil in a hot pan. There are several bodies lying bloody beside Domingo. He is cradling a woman's head. When he looks up, there are tears in his eyes. He sees Mama carrying his son, Taba, who is quickly losing conscious. His blood leaks through Mama's fingers.

"Domingo," Mama sobs. "Lorna. The soldiers. They took the baby."

Domingo looks up to us with confusion. It takes a moment before her words sink in, and then his face collapses. His mouth twists as he looks at Taba. He takes his son into his arms. He groans from deep in his belly like a dying animal. His tears flow freely. He envelops Taba and cries into his chest. This time Taba does not fight him.

"I have killed them all with my indecision." Domingo buries his head in Taba's hair and rocks back and forth. He looks at Tay Fredrico. "You were right, old man. The moment my thoughts turned back to this warehouse, I should have run the opposite way. I should have listened to your words. At least I would still have my men and Nina. I have led them all to their deaths. I could have saved them. I have lost everything."

I walk to Domingo and embrace him. "Domingo." He puts a hand on my shoulder, then holds me close. I avoid looking at Taba, but I see his small hand, bloody and lifeless, against Domingo's chest.

The others gather around to thank him, Papa, Roman, Tay Fredrico, Isabelle, Roderick, and Mama. All except Mang Selso, who nods from afar.

"You have saved us," Tay Fredrico announces.

"You saved yourselves," Domingo answers.

"This is true." Tay Fredrico nods. "Selso," he calls out. He waves his son to us.

Mang Selso comes forward with his head bowed.

"My son, Selso, was one of the first to fight," he tells Domingo. It is the first time I have seen Tay Fredrico put his arm around Mang Selso.

Domingo looks at Selso and nods. Mang Selso's eyes water at his father's words. "I could not let them hurt you, Papa. When I saw you fall . . ." His voice trails away.

"You did good, Selso," Mama tells him. "Without you we would not have made it. You see how strong we became when we stood together? Together we were strong." Everyone agrees with Mama. They clap Mang Selso on the back.

Mang Pedro looks sadly at Domingo. "I am sorry for your loss."

The others place hands on his shoulders and echo Mang Ped's words. Domingo refuses to let his friends or Taba be put together with the other bodies the Amerikanos are stacking to one side. He almost fights an Amerikano soldier who tells him the bodies must be moved away. Papa speaks to the soldiers and returns with a shovel. Together Papa, Mang Pedro, and Mang Selso help Domingo to bury his friends. When he is done we find wooden sticks and make a cross for each grave, and Mama prays beside each one. I was shocked to learn the boy was a guerrilla fighter, and I remember the woman from the other day. She was the one who came to rescue Domingo. Maybe if I had gone with them, as I so badly wanted to do, I would have died also.

After they are buried, Domingo still will not leave. He stumbles from exhaustion but insists on going back into the warehouse to retrieve the bodies of Ate Lorna and baby Alma. Only when Papa and Tay Fredrico take him aside to tell him that half the building is burned and that it is unsafe does he finally listen.

FOR A LONG time we stand in circles, unsure of what to do. I hear the words *stunned* and *shell-shocked* spoken by the Amerikanos to describe us as they offer water and medicine. Finally Aling Ana speaks. "Come," she says. "The Japanese are retreating. Let us go home."

"Home to where?" Mama says. "They have destroyed my home."

Aling Ana smiles sadly. "But not mine. You forget the Japanese officer that took my home. Though I hated him for doing so, it has turned out to be a blessing because my house has been one of the few they preserved. If it still stands, everyone is welcome. If not, we will visit my other houses in the province."

WE CROSS OVER the Pasig River on pontoon bridges, and once we arrive on the opposite side we rest and the Red Cross gives us food. Hours later we are separated according to residence, and army wagons and jeeps take the civilians in groups back to their nearby provinces. Along the way we hear scattered fighting, but mostly we see the Amerikanos ushering away remaining Japanese soldiers who have surrendered. We avoid looking at the ground or in ditches. We stare at one another instead. Feliciano lies with his head on my sister's lap. Mama and Papa have fallen asleep in each other's arms. Roderick and I sit beside one another and point to buildings that have fallen. Mang Selso, his wife, and Tay Fredrico sleep. We stop often to let people descend near their homes and pick up others. It feels like an endless journey.

We reach our hometown of Bulacan by nightfall. Mama cries when we drive past the burned remains of our house. I shut my eyes and look away. One more block and we say good night to Mrs. Yoshi and Mica. They hug us all tearfully, and we promise to visit one another in a day or two. Their house is still standing. They speak to Amerikano soldiers posted outside their block regarding claiming their house. Our driver assures us there will be no trouble for them. Our eyes follow them as they stand in front of their door and hug each other. It will be sad for them without Mr. Yoshi. I miss his laughter and his joking. He was the only one I loved bowing to. He used to call me Alejandro-chan. I feel my eyes fill at the memory of him. I am so sad for them. I am so thankful I have everyone still.

Another hour and we reach Aling Ana's house farther up the hill. There are many Amerikano soldiers and Filipino constabulary from our old neighborhood. Not the puppet ones who were led by the Japanese, but the good ones, the ones who became guerrilla fighters. Like Mrs. Yoshi, they vouch for Aling Ana, and she is allowed entrance back into her home. I let out a deep sigh when I hear this, and we all descend from the wagon. Domingo is the last to follow. We were not sure if he would even come. He would not leave the graves of his friends until Papa told him gently that his friends would not have wanted him to starve and be without a roof over his head. Most of the houses have been abandoned, and Aling Ana's area appears unharmed. Hers was the wealthy area, and most of the houses were commandeered during the war by the Japanese officers. They are all in good shape. Aling Ana gains new energy when we enter her home. She leads us each to a room.

I WAKE IN the morning from a nightmare, and Roderick taps my shoulder.

"You were crying, *kuya*," he says. "We are safe now, remember? We're at Aling Ana's house. Time to eat. You should see all the food they had in the basement. So much rice and canned tomatoes, peaches, chocolate, canned everything. Papa is already awake and drinking beer to celebrate!"

I smile broadly and for the first time in months, and I am surprised how good it feels to do this. I walk downstairs and it is like a dream. My family is sitting down eating! Isabelle and Feliciano talk quietly at the corner of the table. Tay Fredrico sits on a sofa with Mang Selso and his wife. Aling Ana is frying sardines and rice. A feast!

I go to Mama and Papa and hug them each. A plate is set before me and my stomach roars, making everyone chuckle. The flavor of the fish explodes in my mouth, and I feel I will not be able to keep the food down.

"Slowly." Papa nods to me.

LATER IN THE afternoon, while most of the house is napping, Domingo comes inside and our eyes meet. He has been working in Aling Ana's large field behind her house for hours. He has been tending to her empty barn and would not come in to eat. Papa told us to leave him alone. Isabelle brought him some food, but I do not know if he ate any of it. He looks away when he sees me. I look away also, ashamed to see he has been crying. He sniffs and wipes his nose on his sleeve.

"Alejandro . . . ," he says, and his voice trails away.

I see him look aside at Feliciano and Isabelle talking in the other room while they hold hands. Feliciano's eyes have stopped their swelling and look black and blue but better. They have bandaged his wounds, and Papa says he will have permanent scars from their carving his skin but that he is otherwise— "miraculously," was the word Papa used—fine. Domingo watches them for a long time with a soft expression. I wonder if he remembers Ate Lorna when he looks at them.

LATER, WHEN I am riding the neighbor's carabao, Domingo looks at me strangely, almost as if he is frowning, and I feel frightened with nothing to say. I smile unsurely at first and then start to step down.

"No, do not get down, Alejandro. I'm sorry. For a moment, my eyes fooled me. I thought . . ."

"Were you remembering someone?" I ask. I do not say his son's name because Mama told us not to mention their names unless he wanted to first. But she said it was all right to tell him how sorry we were about his loss.

"Yes," he says, and his voice sounds hoarse. "Another brave boy like yourself. He spoke often about riding, living on a farm." Domingo swallows quietly and walks away.

I am confused, because I know Taba was afraid of riding.

DURING THE DAY, two or three groups of people stop by to say hello. And always there are shouts, embraces, and happy tears. My cousin Esteban returns with my aunt and our cousin Maria Elena. They stay for a while, exchanging many stories, and then leave, promising to return the next day. As they visit my heart feels as if it is slowly being pieced back together. In the evening we all sit down together for dinner. Mica and Mrs. Yoshi join us, and Aling Ana announces the good news. First she promises my sister, Isabelle, that if the schools are not opened soon, she will send Mica, Feliciano, and her abroad to study wherever they wish. The three of them jump for joy and embrace her with many kisses and thank-yous.

I am happy for my sister, but my heart turns. I hope they fix our schools soon. I have just found my big sister—I do not want to lose her again for a long time. Aling Ana's second announcement is that she wishes my family to live with her. She has six extra rooms and a smaller house down the street for Mang Selso and his family. She offers for Domingo to stay with us as well. Roderick and I are to share a room, and we all look to Papa, holding our breath.

"Thank you," Papa says, holding Mama's hands. "When we are on our feet again we will repay—"

"Repay no one," Aling Ana says. "You opened your home to me when you had no reason to. You are all welcome to stay with this old maid until I die. But I warn you. That will be a long time yet."

"Amen," Mama says. "*Salamat sa Dios.*" Thanks to God.

"At least for the next two years," Aling Ana says softly to Papa, knowing he has much pride.

"Thank you," he says again, and his eyes shine.

Domingo is the only one quiet at the other end. "I thank you for your offer, Aling Ana, but I cannot stay. There are too many ghosts here for me. I cannot look around without seeing their faces. All of them. My men, Lorna," he says. He struggles to finish his sentence. "Others, very dear to my heart," he says with much difficulty. His voice again breaks off almost into a sob, but then he finally tells us, "Nina Vargas was a good woman. She gave her life for all of you." He seems to want to say more, but he stops, unable to go further.

We are all quiet at his words, waiting. He excuses himself and leaves the table. We all look at one another. Isabelle says something softly, and it is Feliciano who follows after him. Papa stands, too. Roderick and I follow quietly. When we reach them, Feliciano has his hand on Domingo's shoulder and Domingo cries.

"I must go. I am thankful that all of you are safe. That you have accepted me like one of your own. But I cannot stay. This will not be the last you see of me. But I must retreat like a bear and find a cave to lick my wounds until I am strong again. In time I shall return."

"I do not understand," I tell Domingo. "Stay with us. Mama will take care of you." It pains me to think Domingo will leave. Who will care for him? I do not like to imagine him sad by himself. "But why do you need to leave, now that we have won? There is no need to hide anymore." I cannot take my hand from him. "I do not want you to leave us."

He places a hand on my head. "I do not hide, Alejandro. Remember this day. Remember how everyone fought together. Keep it in your heart, and never let anyone divide us again. As for me, I will try to build something from what remains. My soul needs time to heal. I go now to see where this new peace shall lead us. Please, tell the others good-bye."

"Here . . ." I take the dead man's watch from my wrist. "So you remember to come back and return to us as you promised, when the time is right."

He takes the watch and pulls me to him and embraces me, then Roderick.

"We love you, Domingo," Roderick says shyly.

Domingo chuckles at Roderick's words and kisses us both on the tops of our brows. "I have not heard those words in a long time. Thank you, Roddy." He shakes hands with Papa and Feliciano. He looks at us for a long time as if he is burning our image into his mind. Without a word he turns and walks away.

We watch him slowly climb the last steps up the hillside. He turns in the soft light of the morning and raises a hand and gives us a brave smile, though I know he is sad. "*Mabuhay!*" he shouts. *Long life!*

"I don't understand, Papa," I say.

"The war has spared our family, and God has blessed us with a home. But others still have many miles to go."

~ **PAPA SAYS THAT THE PHILIPPINES** is far, far behind the other countries. He says that we are like abused children who have never been allowed to grow. How can we care for ourselves when we have always been told what to do? How can we stand together when so much division has been created between us? He says I must pray that there will not be another war such as this, for we may not survive a next time. He tells me that we have been granted a second chance now that the Amerikanos have given us back our independence.

I have my own thoughts. I keep remembering Domingo's words. He said it is up to Roderick and me to build and to teach the other children that it is better to stand together than to let other nations divide us. My chest expands at the thought of how we survived. *We* fought beside our Amerikano brothers to take back our independence. It was not just given to us. I will remember how we Filipinos stood together and put our differences aside. I shall remember how strong we were. It is up to me now to keep our pride intact. We faced the enemy without weapons. We did not let them defeat us. I am proud to be a Filipino. I shall lift my fist forever in honor of my country. *Mabuhay,* my Philippines! Long life!

—*Alejandro Karangalan*